Embracing
Zak

Jodee Kulp

With Marcia Chambers, Antonia Rathbun Lindsey,
Patricia Kasper, Deb Evensen,
Justen Overlander, Joel Sheagren, and Carl Young

Better Endings New Beginnings

Minneapolis, Minnesota

EMBRACING ZAK
Copyright © 2024 Jodee Kulp

Published by:
Better Endings New Beginnings
Minneapolis, MN
www.betterendings.org

FIRST PRINTING—AUGUST 2024
Printed in United States of America

Books.by

Foreword

odee Kulp is a talented author who will take you to a small Midwestern town filled with characters she has brought to life so convincingly and with such depth that you will feel like you've known these people for years. In *Embracing Zak*, you will gain an understanding of various aspects of neurodiversity as you connect with intricately intertwined characters whose challenges and strengths shape the life of a vibrant community. By connecting with multiple neurodiverse characters, you will recognize that embracing our unique learning preferences and strengths is how we come to accept our humanity and find ways to contribute to the lives of others in our community. You will learn that Fetal Alcohol Spectrum Disorder (FASD) encompasses strengths as well as challenges. Our unique combination of strengths, learning preferences, and challenges is as individual as our fingerprint. As we embrace the characters in this story, we come to a fuller appreciation of the saying about tapestries being woven from the threads of many colors. A complete and rich life must include diverse ideas, perspectives, and gifts, creating a delicate and sometimes dramatically intricate pattern. I am honored to recommend *Embracing Zak*. The characters, the lessons each one has to offer, and how each person touches others in creating moments of life more significant than any of them individually will stick with you long after you read the last word and turn the final page. You will not want this story to end.

Patricia Kasper, MA, MTh
Patricia Kasper Training Services
Neurobehavioral Coach and Professional Development Trainer
Podcast Host: Living with FASD: Candid Conversations with Patti Kasper
Author: *Sip by Sip: Candid Conversations with People Diagnosed as Adults with Fetal Alcohol Spectrum Disorders (FASD)*

*Dedicated to the
lived-experience of
individuals worldwide
who have been
prenatally exposed to alcohol
and the people who love them.*

*Liz Kulp 1986-2024
Beloved Daughter*

Thank You

I want to give all Glory to Our Father, whose hand has been on this project as I penned it while my daughter struggled with organ failure to survive, and to everyone who contributed to bringing *Embracing Zak* to life. This book would not have been possible without the collective effort of many dedicated individuals. To my family, I owe an immeasurable debt of gratitude. Your unwavering support, patience, and love throughout this journey have been my anchor. Your belief in the importance of this project and your constant encouragement have been the driving force behind its completion.

I extend my heartfelt gratitude to *The FASD Meliorists*, our editing team, whose keen eyes and invaluable insights helped shape and refine the narrative. Antonia Rathbun Lindsey, Marcia Chambers, Deb Evensen, and Patricia Kasper, your expertise and commitment to excellence have been instrumental in crafting the final product.

I am profoundly grateful to *The Embraced Movement Project* conceived and inspired by Joel Sheagren whose initial planned documentary became much more. Thank you also to Carl Young. A special shout out to Justen Overlander who will be producing the upcoming feature film, *Embracing Zak*. You all shared your knowledge, experiences, and perspectives which enriched the story and added depth to our exploration of neurodiversity and FASD.

I am especially indebted to the 100 individuals with lived experience who graciously shared their stories during our *Embraced Movement* interviews. Your courage, honesty, and willingness to open up about your journeys have been the heart and soul of this book. Your voices have brought authenticity and power to the narrative, helping to foster understanding and empathy.

Finally, I want to acknowledge the broader *FASD community*, whose resilience and strength continue to inspire. Your experiences and insights were invaluable in shaping the characters and themes of *Embracing Zak*. Thank you all for being part of this journey and for helping to bring greater awareness and understanding to FASD and neurodiversity.

Introducing the Cast

JORDAN FAMILY

Zak Jordan is 18 years old and the son of *David and Carly Jordan.* David is Sheriff Ben's younger brother.

Sheriff Ben Jordan is David's younger brother, and his wife, *Kate,* lives in Riverdale, Minnesota. Kate is the Riverdale High School Science teacher.

RIVERDALE FAMILIES

Lindsay Larkin is a single mother of *Quint,* referred to as *Q,* age 17, and *Shay,* age 16. She is a wait staff member, along with her son, at Dee's Cafe, which Margie Jones owns.

Doc Johnson is the school principal at Riverdale High School, his wife, *Nicole,* is a stay-at-home mother, and his 16-year-old daughter, *Missy,* is a popular cheerleader.

RIVERDALE COMMUNITY

Mantha Dawson is a returning Afghanistan veteran living at O'Riley Garage.

John Mason is Riverdale High School's in-school suspension teacher.

Sam O'Riley, age 80, is a Vietnam veteran and owns O'Riley Garage, referred to as Rileys in the community. He has a pitbull named *Penny.*

Margie Jones owns Dee's Cafe and has lived in Riverdale for over twenty years. Her son *Quintel* (who also went by Q nickname as a teen) s an attorney in Alabama, and her daughter, *Tasha* is an unsolved homicide.

Trapper Palmquist leads the snowplow crew, his wife *Annie* runs Han's Hardware store, and his daughter *Kissy* a Navy pilot.

Peter Brakket owns the mercantile Homestead Provisions.

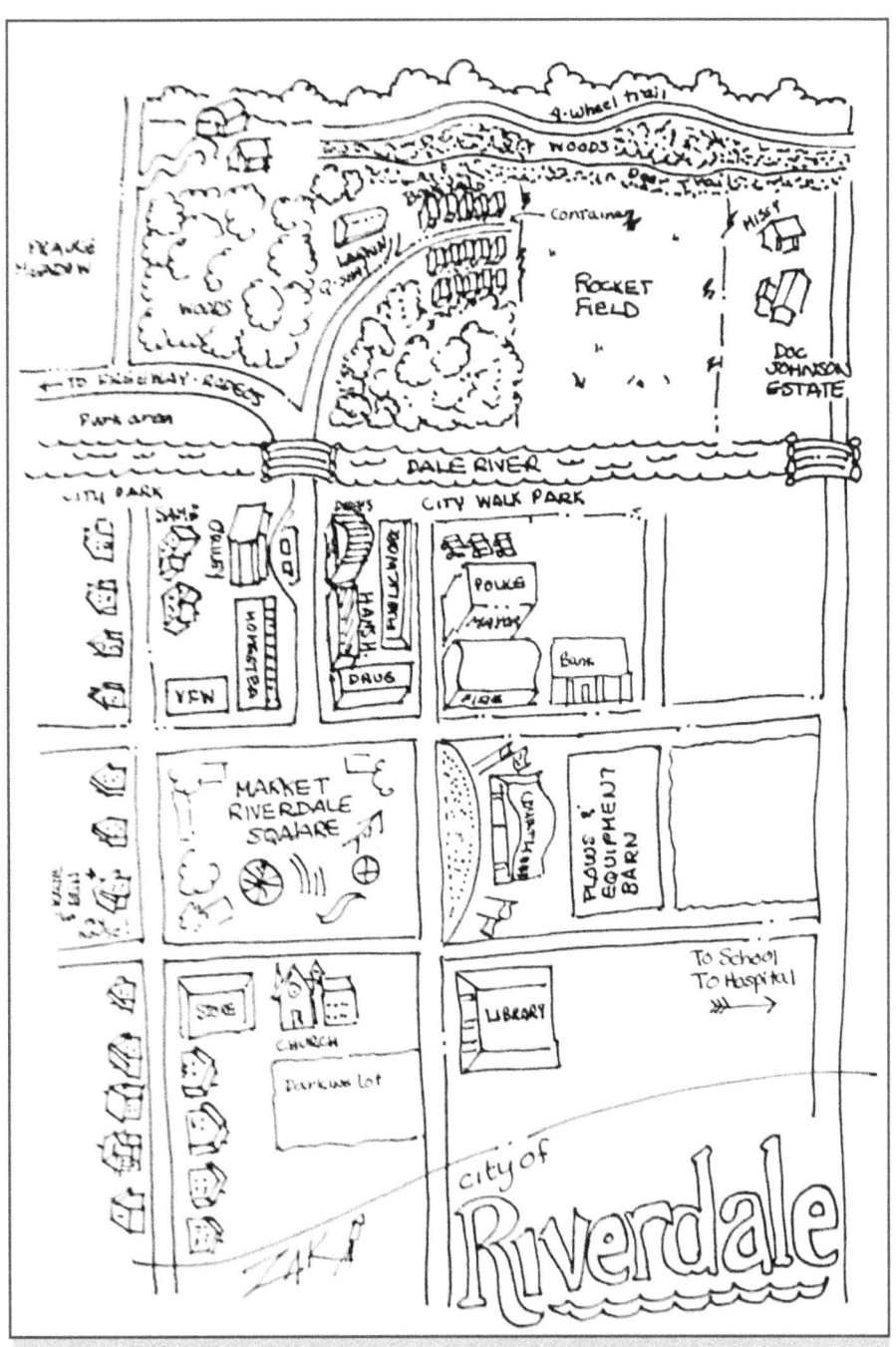

3

2

1

Blast
Off!

~1~
BETTER ENDINGS ?

This morning, like so many others, had a hectic start. Zak was elated because his teacher had asked him to bring his rocket to class the day before, turning astronomy into his new favorite subject. Zak had worked hard to prepare, placing his textbooks on his dresser next to his rocket and setting out a good pair of jeans with his new shoes. He woke filled with so much energy he stubbed his toe as he bounced over to quiet the alarm clock and found some socks. It hurt so badly he hopped on one foot, gripping his sore toe, screaming. And now he was running late.

"Zak, get a move on, or you'll miss the bus!" His mom pressured him to get going. Her pushing raised his anxiety. He had just put on his third pair of socks and none felt right. The sock seam irritated his toe. He haphazardly put on his unlaced shoes. He was now mad at his little toe and gave it more space with the wider part of the shoe.

"You're going to miss breakfast," Mom shouted. "You can't be late, and if I told you once, I've told you a thousand times, I am not driving you again!"

A loud CLUNK echoed from the upstairs bedroom. His rocket fell to the floor. Expletives flew down the stairs in a cacophony of echoing ballistics. Two textbook missiles flew out his door. The astronomy book crashed at the base of the staircase, where a thick math book soon crushed it. Grumbling, the older teen with bright red high tops slowly descended the stairs. His leaden steps dragged one stair at a time as he gathered both feet together before dropping to the next step. He gripped the railing with both hands. Finally, he slid down the banister, launching himself off the last ten feet and scattering his textbooks. His right foot planted an extra hard stomp on the math book.

His mother's arms crossed over her chest, and she rolled her eyes, settling into a glare as she witnessed the uproar. "Your shoes are on the wrong feet."

"THEY'RE THE ONLY FEET I HAVE! Leave me alone," he boomed. "You know I am 18 and can do whatever I want. I don't even have to go to school if I don't want to. You can't make me go." Zak ran back upstairs to switch his shoes and get his rocket, leaving the textbooks in shambles on the floor. He rode the railing down and jumped over the books.

Mom knew her safest choice was silence but offered, "Zak, here's peanut butter toast. Now scoot!" She extended his breakfast with one arm, making no eye contact, knowing it best not to add fuel to the fire.

Zak grabbed the toast as he pushed her. "You don't know nothing. I said leave me alone!" The door slammed.

A moment later, the door cracked open, and there was Zak's head, with a cat smirk. "I forgot. Bye, Mom." He licked peanut butter from his pointer finger and blew her a kiss.

Zak made the bus, holding his rocket carefully to avoid getting peanut butter on it. He struggled with balance as he tried to get to the far side of the bus.

"Look at that idiot with the painted paper towel tube," sneered one student.

"You think you can fly that piece of junk?" Said another, jabbing his buddy in the ribs and laughing.

"Yep, it might go up," snickered a girl. "Then crash!"

Zac clenched his teeth. Fire burned between his ribs. He would have punched their lights out if he had not been holding his rocket. Breathing deeply, he held the rocket with his forearm and pressed his thumb to each finger to calm down. He turned his face to the window to shut out the taunts of other students.

"What is wrong with me?" He asked the universe out loud and to no one. Zak curled his knees tight to his chest, his rocket cradled safely between his legs, waiting until everyone else was off the bus. Too many times, he had been tripped or tricked.

The bus driver leaned towards him. "Zak, you're safe to go." The big man's reassurance was kind.

Zak plodded into class just as the bell rang. The teacher, Ms. Hanson, quieted her students and explained the rings around Saturn.

Zak raised his hand. He wanted all the details. "Could you slow down and say that again?" He asked without being called upon. The teacher repeated the information. Zak was genuinely interested in knowing more.

Zak's hand shot up as he blurted, "Make this make sense to me; where did the rings come from?"

"Mr. Jordan, stop interrupting me. If you listened more than you talked, you might learn something. I need you to listen carefully. We already covered that yesterday."

"I'm just asking questions. Isn't that what I am supposed to do in school?" He slapped his forehead. "Duh!"

The teacher drew an exasperated breath. It was all it took for students to rotate in their seats and chorus: "Yeah, Zak, you gotta learn to listen more." And, "Yeah, Zak, We did that yesterday." Zak put his hands to his ears.

Five minutes later, Zak asked again for clarity. Exasperated, Ms. Hanson walked to Zak's desk, tapped her pencil loudly on the upper corner, and stated, "I asked you to listen better. If you cannot keep up, I can assign you extra reading. Would you like that?"

As she headed back to the front of the room, a student to Zak's right pushed his rocket. It thudded to the floor and snapped in two. Zak was dumbstruck.

Ms. Hanson, exasperated, spun back to Zak's desk. Face-to-face, she leaned over Zak. "You are acting like a child. You are disturbing my class on purpose."

Zak's urge to bolt was instantaneous; as he jumped up, his hand went to Ms. Hanson's shoulder to move her out of his face—an ultimate act of defiance in the eyes of any teacher. His haste and her startle collided: she lost her balance, falling backward into the other desk, hitting her elbow, and landing bum-first on the classroom floor.

Students gasped. Some stifled giggles. Others outright laughed. Zak fled only to be captured in the hall and forced to the ground, face down by school security. He fought like an alligator—snapping and clawing.

Things escalated quickly, and the police, not Zak's parents, were hailed to calm the chaos. The principal, Ms. Hanson, two police officers, and a few students attempted to sort the matter out in a conference room during the next hour.

Zak sat with his skin writhing. He needed a break. The accusations were a blur of noise to him. He picked at his skin, looked at his feet, and followed a fly walking on the window. The principal laid a paper before him. "Mr. Jordan, sign this, and you can return to school in five days."

Zak tapped five days on the table with his fingers: Friday, Saturday, Sunday, Monday... "So, I will be back Tuesday."

"Next Friday," said the principal.

"Well, aren't you a liar? Can't you count? Friday, Saturday, Sunday, Monday... I will be back Tuesday," Zak squinted.

"Friday, Saturday, and Sunday don't count," explained the principal.

"You are joking with me, right?" Zak snapped.

"No, Mr. Jordan, I am telling the truth." The principal had no mercy. "Sign this! Now! You've taken enough of my time today."

Zak scrawled a scribble in blue ink. He had not read the document, and no one had read it to him. It stated that he was at fault for the disturbance and further accused him of terroristic threats because he had shouted at the security guard who pinned him down. That conclusion alone could set a course for a lifetime of misunderstandings and negative consequences.

"I quit. I hate school! You are all assholes!" Zak ran out of school, slamming the door as he left. "I'm 18. I can do what I want!"

"That's it!" Said the principal. "He can find a new school. He will not be returning here. I'm calling his parents to let them know."

———

Carly held her sore shoulder where Zak had impulsively pushed her earlier that morning. The impact of his fingers stuck into her like a claw had left five red welts that were blooming into dark purple bruises. "David, I don't know what to do anymore. We've tried everything possible to help Zak, but nothing seems to work. I used to stand up to him, but David, I am scared of him now."

David sighed. "He's hanging out with a bad crowd, getting into trouble at school, and now this. The school principal called me at the office today, and the administration has agreed. They are not allowing him back. Today is his last school day."

Tears streamed down Carly's cheek. "I'm exhausted. I don't know what he's going to do next. I can't manage him. We've tried talking to him, grounding him, hiring tutors, providing extracurricular activities, behavior programs…" She wiped her cheek and put her elbows on the table, looking longingly at her husband. "What has happened to us? Are we this bad at parenting?"

"Carly, stop," David countered. "Three different therapists could not reach him. He caused trouble at three different schools. We tried. We both tried, and nothing seems to make a difference."

"We're grasping at straws here. Maybe we need to explore something else," Carly offered. "This is taking a toll on us and our marriage. I don't know how to help him!"

"He is eighteen, and we could let him test his wings," David shrugged. "Maybe rent him an apartment and make him get a job."

Carly looked up, horrified. "You and I both know he's not ready for that. He flies by the seat of his pants and would, land on his head and crumble. He'd be fired on day two!"

"Maybe that's it! REAL LIFE experience," David was exasperated.

"Then he would be in your courtroom. Which Zak do you want to give his independence? The eighteen-year-old or the eight-year-old?" Carly lamented quietly. "I never know which one I am going to face."

"Maybe we need something drastic. I will ask my brother, Ben, if he and Kate can help." David had to search for Ben's number to find it. It was not frequently called. He reached his hand across the table, touching his wife. "We're in this together."

Carly dropped her head into her arms. "You haven't talked to Ben in years. Not since that court case you won, and he lost."

"Is there a better choice?" David muttered.

———

Ten years ago, a large national chain built an empire at the cross-roads of the interstate and the county road. The expressway exit facility boasted twelve 24-hour gas pumps, hot pizza, groceries, and coffee. For truckers, they offered showers, private restrooms, bunks, and parking in the back. They also had a car wash. The vehicles that zoomed under the county bridge at 80 miles per hour frequented the national chain, while the local folk drove the county road, driving past it in allegiance to locally owned businesses. Locals did not waste their time at Rodeos for oil, gas, or air. They did use the car wash. The Rodeo manager seemed distant and unfamiliar, while the bright, neon-lit convenience store, offering milk, bread, hot dogs, and fast food, was draining the business of Riverdale's local shops.

Down the road and around the slight bend was O'Riley's garage. Its red neon sign had lost its **O**, and the gas price was never listed. Referred to now as 'Rileys, locals chatted as they waited for an available gas pump. The little garage hosted two twenty-four-hour pumps, a soda machine, and an old chest ice cream freezer. Sam also had a small stock of chips, gum, and candy bars inside. The children sat on his park bench, discussing things Sam found interesting and munching snacks. Riley's had been Sam O'Riley's empire for fifty years.

Riley's was more than a gasoline station. It was a neighborhood icon. Sam, now eighty years old, still futzed and puttered. He shared stories and wisdom as he listened to others' secrets, which he held in the vault of his heart. He detailed classic vehicles, changed oil and wiper blades, and fixed meters, radios, and tires. Though he had quit fixing local engines and transmissions except on classic vehicles of all types, he often repaired broken dreams and put air back into the tires of weary souls.

—

Mantha Dawson swallowed hard. The rain pelted her windshield as the single wiper valiantly cleared a small patch between spatters. She hoped O'Riley Garage remained viable. It was everything that the blight of a gas stop at the freeway exit ramp was not.

As a child, O'Riley's was where she and her high school friends Lindsay and Quintel, nicknamed Q, hung out with a little preschool tag-along named Kissy, who wandered over when bored while her parents tended the family business at Hans Hardware. Sam O'Riley had an aerobatic airplane. He built rockets and flew them with families and kids. He fixed local machines, large and small engines, and even broken appliances if you would haul them into his garage. He fixed speedometers, odometers, and tachometers that arrived in packages from all over the country in old boxes. He also had the quarter soda machine, the ice cream freezer, the dog washing car wash, and a secret closet containing a ham radio base station. Sam guided Mantha and her friends as teens by fixing broken-down cars after school if there was an empty bay. It was a refuge from a town that did not accept them. Riley's was a wonderland of invention, history, and adventure.

Once she received her second prosthesis, which proved workable, Mantha was determined to drive her old junker home alone. The wobbly jeep sputtered into Riley's garage. It had been six Afghanistan tours since Mantha returned home. Her mom and dad passed away during the COVID-19 pandemic while she was out of the country. Injured and convalescing, she was prevented from returning stateside for their celebration of life. And now here she was, returning home to her childhood town, missing parts, pieces, and parents.

Weathered by eight decades, Sam O'Riley limped out to greet her. He wiped his greasy hands on an old red rag and exclaimed, "Sammy, Sam, Sam, is that you? You finally come home?"

Mantha bit her lip; she had outgrown his childhood nickname of Sammy, Sam, Sam. She was thirty-nine and a retired captain with a purple heart. She did not know what to say but was glad her driver's side profile still held her youthful charm. She tilted her head up and half smiled.

"Whatcha come by for… a cup of coffee? Sounds like this vehicle of yours needs some help." Sam paused as his arms reached for a hug.

Martha bristled. "Don't touch me, Sam. No one touches me."

"Gotcha six, Captain, I understand," Sam backed off in a salute.

"You ain't gotta do that, Sam. I didn't mean anything by it. It's just that…" Mantha stammered.

"It's just that, what…," Sam paused, compassion in his query.

"I need your help," her eyes watered.

"Where are you staying?" Sam asked.

"No place. Our house was sold to pay bills. I got no one left."

"You got me. Deb died the same year your mom and dad passed. We're alone together." Sam's heart ached for his fellow veteran. He understood returning veterans' struggles and knew he had an opportunity to make a difference. He offered her the extra room in his family home. She declined. He offered her the space and bath in the back of the old garage and a job working with him starting Monday. She opened the jeep door. She said nothing but pondered his words.

"Are you hungry? We still have Dee's Cafe across the street. Margie makes the best comfort food on Friday nights this side of the Mississippi River," Sam coaxed.

Mantha stepped one boot out, swinging her right leg around. It dropped like a rock next to her left leg. Sam noticed the missing index and pinky fingers. The phantom pain in Sam's foot zinged upward to his heart. He knew more now than he wanted to know. Sam stood still, bracing himself if she needed support; he'd been there years ago. Too many years ago, he had worn that camouflage of bravery himself.

"Hey, I still make a good cup of coffee. Come on and meet my new dog, Penny," he beckoned. Somehow, dogs always broke the ice. "And hey, what do I call you?"

She stared into nothing. "Mantha. It's Mantha now, Sam." The woman kept her head turned to the right, looking at the dog.

"She's a young pitbull, Mantha. I picked her up off the road as a scrawny puppy. Sargent Reg the Fifth died. I'm too old to keep breeding shepherds. I know your story. You will like this dog, even if she's not a German Shepherd."

"Penny, go say hi," Sam commanded.

The tawny pitbull greeted Mantha with a perfect front sit. Mantha squatted carefully, and Penny put up her paw. The woman reciprocated with her injured hand. The dog ignored the healed injury and began licking her face. Mantha dipped her head to avoid the licks, exposing the long scar from forehead to chin. Sam left the two, getting comfortable with each other, his heart heavy knowing much was at stake. He fetched Penny her dog dinner.

"Mantha, I know you're hungry. Bet it's been a long time since you ate at Dee's, and Friday is still…" Sam began.

"Margie's chicken pot pies?" Mantha dropped a hint.

Sam winked. "Get up, Captain. Penny, guard the garage. I am taking one tough, beautiful woman out to dinner." Sam noted the same little girl's smile he had enjoyed when she was eight. "It's a date!"

"Offer accepted. At ease, Corporal." Mantha gave the order to relax and maintain comfort without compromising discipline.

Sam laughed. "Girl, you outrank and out-gun me. Get up; you got a new battle to fight, and I already have been there, done that, and got through it." He removed his hands behind his back and reached down to help Mantha. She declined.

~2~
THE CALL

Kate smiled as her best friend and husband of twenty years, Ben, entered the kitchen. Groceries were piled on the counter, ready to make a quick dinner. It was the early weeks after a new school year had started. Her students were adjusting well. They were curious, which made teaching science much more enjoyable. "How's spaghetti and salad, Ben?"

"Sounds great, sweetie," Ben held his customary ten-minute plank on the kitchen floor and hoped for a quiet night. Weekends often revved up after the bars closed at 1 a.m. As the county sheriff with a small team of deputies, late-night occurrences brought out the worst in people. Thankfully, Riverdale was a quiet village tucked away in a southeastern rural Minnesota community.

Ben's cell rang. "Hey, David, it's been long since we talked. What's going on?" Kate noted the call was from Ben's brother, who lived in the city. The two rarely spoke, and after what had happened, Ben had full right not to ever talk to his little brother. She shook the water off the Romaine lettuce.

"Sure, I understand. Of course, Kate and I can help you," Ben said as if this was a given. In a curious surprise, Kate looked over her shoulder as she put on a pot of water for the noodles.

"No, I know we have never raised a teenager. David, Kate's been a teacher for nearly twenty years with many challenging students. And you realize I am the sheriff. I handle every ragamuffin in town. I'm sure we can manage Zak." Ben said confidently. Kate set the spatula aside as the hamburger browned and reached for her homemade with love tomato sauce. She watched it glug out of the canning jar. Something about that kid Zak had always bugged her.

"Sounds like he just needs a smaller community and some structure. Get him out of the city. We can make sure he graduates and makes something of himself. Of course, I can. Kate will agree to it, so it's no problem. We have plenty of room here—no, it won't be a problem to help out." Kate wiped her hands on the dishrag and pointed toward Ben. They had wanted a child, but Zak—an 18-year-old dropout?!

Ben put his hand over the phone. "Honey, what do you think? Zak can move in here for six months and graduate high school. My brother needs help! Zak can sleep in my office upstairs. I know we can make this work." Ben turned back to the phone.

His first responder mode had kicked into full gear. Kate's eyebrows wrinkled, her eyes rolled, and she took a big breath. She bit her lip, trying to think of what to say next. "I am not..."

"Tonight..? Uh, got it… Meet me at the rest stop 35 between here and the cities. Get him ready to go. I will be there in two hours. We'll take care of that boy." Ben hung up as Kate put up her hand like a stop sign.

"See you soon," Ben had already sprung to action. He kissed Kate on the cheek and shot out to the garage. "Zak and I will eat when we come back. Just leave it out." He called as an afterthought. The door shut behind him.

Kate was stunned. Her jaw dropped, speechless. *What?! No conversation? What just happened here?*

———

The warm glow of early evening lights and a large orange neon open sign welcomed them. Dee's Cafe has been a cherished Friday night spot in the community for seventy years. The cafe retains its nostalgic charm with its timeless red checked tablecloths, black Formica tables, and revolving counter stools from the 1950s. The Naugahyde upholstery has stood the test of time. The meals are reasonably priced, locally sourced, and always freshly prepared. The walls are adorned with inspiring quotes and local news photographs, while the tables hold the untold stories known only to Margie and her staff. Surrounded by framed news clippings, the history of Riverdale is preserved.

Dee founded the cafe in 1952 and retired in Florida. Having no family left in Riverdale, she handed the Cafe to Margie, her chief cook. As Dee slowed down, Margie fed the wholesome and homemade food to the locals for twenty years. Margie was married to Sheriff Larry Kelly, who died years ago from a heart attack and being replaced by the present Sheriff, Ben Jordan. Margie's son was now a fancy lawyer in Alabama, whereas her daughter had passed on much younger. No other family was left in town except the townspeople she considered her family. She hoped to retire to Alabama to locate near her attorney son.

Margie followed in Dee's lead. She hired local women and high school students who could find no other jobs. She took care to train them well and provided steady work. Her latest hire, Q, was a teen who had care with flair! He needed money, something to do, and social skills. He avoided crowds, hated sporting events, and was available Friday and Saturday nights when other teens refused. He was a sweet kid named Quint, after her son, Quintel. Both shortened their name to Q. His mother, Lindsay, worked the weekday shift as she had done now for the past eighteen years. The community ostracized Lindsay as a pregnant teen. No one knew who Quint's father could be, and Margie did not care. She had lived that story herself.

"Good evening, Sir," nodded Q, overdressed in a white shirt, a thin black tie, belted black trousers, a white apron neatly tied, and shiny shoes, greeting the elderly gentleman. "And who is this lovely lady, Sir?"

"I'm Sam, Q, remember? I come here at least three times a week," Sam pointed at his face and raised his arm to wiggle three fingers.

"Yes, you are Sam, sir. And who is your lovely guest?" Q continued with script-like courtesy. "You are shaking three fingers to remind me you come thrice weekly. Sir, it is more often than three times per week," Q stated. "You did not answer me. Who is your guest?"

"I am Mantha," the woman offered.

"Nice to meet you, ma'am. Will you be dining with us this evening?" Q asked.

"Of course, we will be dining with you this evening, Q. Why would I come at dinner time if I did not want to eat here!" Sam said, huffing out the last few words.

"It is your prerogative to eat at Dee's Cafe. You may also want to come in and go out. Or you might want to say hello to Margie and go out. Or…" Q persisted. Sam saw Margie standing at the kitchen door, her hand over her mouth, her eyes twinkling, chuckling softly.

"Q, Mantha, and I would like a table," Sam interrupted, then sealed his lips between his teeth to avoid saying anymore. Margie was stifling laughter, watching it all play out in amusement.

"If you would like a table, do you have a preference? I have three tables left and two stools. Of course, you do not want the stools since you said a table. You may choose between the window table, the middle table, or the table by the kitchen. Which one do you prefer?" Q asked. He spoke softly and measuredly with carefully chosen words, conveying essential information without overwhelming his customers. That was his intent.

"The window," Sam gruffed in a low voice. "Keep an eye on things."

The young man picked up laminated menus, carefully walked them to the table, and methodically pulled out the chair for the lady and tipped his head. "This is your place, ma'am." He stood in a stately posture, handing a menu to Sam and Mantha. "Good evening, welcome to Dee's Cafe. My name is Q, and I'll be your waiter tonight. What can I assist you with? I will bring you water first, and then I will take your order." He took a slight bow and stood with a tiny head nod and smile. He did not wait for their answer, pivoted precisely on his toes, and went to fill two red plastic glasses of water.

Q returned, balancing the equally filled water glasses in each hand, positioned himself close to the table so as not to upset anything, and lowered each glass slowly to minimize accidental spillage. Then, he adjusted the spacing to be precisely the same distance from each table edge.

"I believe the glasses are now at perfect reach and have the right amount of ice." Q pulled two duplicate utensil packages from his apron. "Here is your silverware. The packages are organized with a knife, fork, and spoon. They are placed on each other so they do not roll over. I believe we have everything that you need. May I take your order now? The lady will properly go first?"

"Q, I would like the chicken pot pie," Mantha smiled, the widest smile she'd used in a long time.

"Thank you for choosing the chicken pot pie. That is an excellent choice. Do you have any dietary restrictions? Would you like any sides or drinks with that?" Q asked.

"I have no dietary restrictions, and I would like iced tea and no sugar," Mantha answered.

"Perfect, I've got your iced tea with no sugar, ma'am. It will have ice.

Our chicken pot pie is made with tender chicken locally sourced, a medley of vegetables from the farmers market, and a delicious creamy sauce. It is all enclosed in a flaky, golden crust made today by our chef, Margie. Is that alright with you?" Q asked.

Mantha changed her role from small-town cafe patron to refined dining clientele, "Yes, Q that will be perfect, and you are an exceptional waiter! I would like it served hot." She was entirely charmed by this eccentric young man.

"Yes, hot, of course, ma'am, Mantha, ma'am. We take great care in cooking our chicken pot pie to perfection. It will be well done and piping hot." Q offered a slight smile, nod, and brief eye contact. "And Sir, I mean Sam, sir, have you made your selection?"

Sam squared his shoulders. "Yes, Q, as a matter of fact, I have. I want the same things as my friend, Mantha."

"Yes, exceptional, Sam. You would like iced tea with ice, no sugar, and a perfectly cooked chicken pot pie. And would you like that hot like the lady, Sir?" Q asked.

"Yes, Q. I would like that hot like the lady. I want the chicken pot pie hot. I believe the lady is already hot enough?" Sam replied, smiling at Mantha.

Mantha laughed, receiving the flirtatious compliment from her 80-year-old compatriot with comfort.

"Would you like me to open the window to cool you off?' Q asked.

"No, I am comfortable, Q. You can get our dinners now," Mantha suggested, realizing the boy took things literally.

"Sir, she is comfortable, not hot. She does not need to cool off," Q inadvertently corrected Sam. Q was nothing if not precise. "I find it helpful to tell customers the estimated wait time for the chicken pot pie is twenty minutes. Would you like me to update you when preparation is closer to completion?" Q continued. "I will keep an eye on your order and provide an update as it progresses. Please don't hesitate to hail me if you need anything else or have any questions."

"That is perfect, Q. Thank you for letting us know. Can you bring out our ice teas?" Sam asked.

"It is my pleasure. I'll return with your iced tea with ice and no sugar shortly. Your order will be ready before you know it. Would you like me to get you a puzzle while you wait?" Q asked.

"We will be fine, Q, we can talk," Sam offered.

"Oh, yes, of course, conversations," Q noted quietly. He did an about-face and headed to Margie with the order in hand. Margie gave Sam a quick wink.

"There goes care with a flair," quipped Mantha.

—

Zak's father and mother were relieved Uncle Ben, and Aunt Kate had stepped up to steer their son toward graduation. David and Carly felt like failed parents. They worried their son was heading nowhere fast. What could be a better setting than a small-town rural high school living with an experienced teacher and the local sheriff? Carly's shoulder was still sore from where Zak had shoved her as he left the house for the bus. The teacher who had fallen during the altercation with Zak had visited an urgent care for elbow x-rays. Thankfully, nothing broke, though a large bruise was already forming.

"Zak, I just talked with your Uncle Ben. He and Aunt Kate have invited you to live with them and finish high school. You can have a fresh start beginning on Monday. We will leave in one hour. Pack your bags. Uncle Ben is meeting us halfway on the freeway," David delivered the ultimatum to his son.

Zak's room was a disaster. The word disaster hardly did justice to the heaps and piles of papers, candy wrappers, chip bags, trash, game pieces, unmatched socks, shoes, and dirty clothes strewn from one end of the room to the other. Zak kicked at a mountain of clothes and sat on his unmade bed. He felt overwhelmed. He hated change. *How could he leave his family, his room, and his friends? What friends? Most people he had as friends had abandoned him. What about the new guys at the mall who gave him little delivery jobs in trade for hanging out together?* He had just begun to feel competent in using their secret hand signals.

Zak convinced himself to see something good about this sudden turn of events. '*I always liked Uncle Ben and Aunt Kate, he thought. Uncle Ben was willing to shoot hoops outside and light fireworks in the backyard. On July 4th, he took him shooting at a gun range with a pistol. Maybe Uncle Ben's firework gear could fire up his rocket. Fireworks were cool!*' He quietly thought aloud, '*Going to Uncle Ben's is better than running away. Going to Uncle Ben's gets rid of the bullies at school. It is a do-over.*' Zak pulled his still-packed summer camp bag from under the bed and dumped it on his pillow, adding to the mess. He was surprised how many empty candy wrappers fell out. He rustled through the pile to find a lemon taffy. Chewing sour candy helped him focus.

He pulled a dirty black hoodie from under the dresser and a folded clean navy hoodie from a half-open drawer. He found four pairs of jeans in various levels of clean. He turned his t-shirts right side out to see the fronts. This took time, and he got frustrated after finding only two he liked. He filled the rest of the bag with three pairs of tennis shoes.

"Zak, we gotta go. NOW!" His father shouted from the bottom of the stairs.

Hurriedly, Zak hoisted his bag over his shoulder, grabbed the pieces of his rocket, and slammed his bedroom door.

———

Sam spoke quietly to Mantha. "You need to know how hard it was for me when I returned from Nam and Walter Reed. I….hated… everything and everybody—hated me most."

Mantha said nothing.

Sam went on. "…Had no future and no plans for a future. Had nothing to do but hate the neighbors and be pissed off at my reality."

Mantha said nothing.

"You can stay at the garage or in Deb's shed, or you can stay in the extra room at my place 'til you get settled."

Mantha said nothing.

Sam inhaled loudly and raised his voice. Patrons raised their heads from looking at dinners to listen in. "I need someone to help me at O'Riley's. You were a good mechanic as a teen. You need a job." Mantha gave a side smile, put her elbows on the table, hands to her chin, leaning in.

"I am thinking of retiring. If you want the garage business, it is yours for the taking. I'll still be around, but age eighty is too old to keep on keeping on the whole week. I'll keep my Ham Shack. The long closet is mine. We can share the dog."

Mantha lowered her forearms to the table, bent in, cocked her head, and set her jaw. Her eyes moved to the upper right, visualizing the potential and possibilities. Then, she darted back to her childhood memories of Quintel, the elder (whom young Q was named after), Lindsay, Kissy, and Sam. O'Riley's garage, the airport, and the gun range remained alive as her youthful Riverdale memories returned.

"You got a better offer, Mantha? What's your plan? We share the dog, and in the meantime, I buy the chicken pot pie."

Mantha offered no sound. The cafe went intensely silent. Then a tiny whispered "Thank you" passed over Mantha's quivering lips as she gazed gratefully at Sam. She lowered her eyes to the table, swallowing hard to restore composure.

———

Zak and his dad pulled off at Mile Marker 35 Rest Stop - Owatonna. Zak read the blue sign aloud. "Picnic shelter, snacks, beverages. Can I get a beverage?" He asked. "I gotta pee."

The parking area was empty except for a few snoozing semis in the truck lane. Uncle Ben had yet to arrive. Zak jumped out and raced to the facilities. Zak's father remained in the vehicle. A county sheriff's car soon pulled up while Zak was in the bathroom.

Zak finished his business, explored the restroom, looked under the stalls for feet, checked his hair, tried out all the faucets, turned on the hand blowers, wet his hair, put his head under the hair blower, and ran his fingers through the finished hairstyle. He was excited to appear his best for Uncle Ben. He stopped at the vending machine, spent all his money, and pocketed six candy bars and a soda.

———

The rest stop remained empty, with a dim light illuminating David's shiny car and Ben's squad car. The prairie flowers that once brightened and cheered the area had wilted and died during the first Minnesota frost. Two pairs of eyes locked as the world seemed to slow down momentarily. David stood tall and slender in his favorite red wool buffalo plaid shirt. The older brother, Ben, wore his holster with a sidearm, brown uniform, he was confident. The men faced off, seeing each other in a new context. Each man weighing their past to choose the present. As Ben took the first step forward, the family was family, and they embraced strongly.

The holiday ruse faded. The brothers' relationship had become estranged when Ben, five years David's elder, left for college in the big city. Some holidays still happened with all the niceties, but their inseparable closeness and youthful camaraderie were left behind. It faded with education, service, work, and marriages and shrunk further when Zak was born while Ben and Kate remained childless. The final blow splintered their relationship into shards when Ben arrested a perpetrator and David, an attorney, got the guy off Scott-free. David was a gladiator in the court system, and up until this phone request to take on Zak, no word had passed between them since that court battle. They could chew food against each other in silence on opposing sides of the holiday table, just as they'd lived on opposite ends of the legal system.

Ben noticed tears on David's face, and was surprised to feel liquid-pooling in his own eyes. The years of separation melted as they united for this present battle. Zak was in trouble, and Ben would turn him around.

"Where's Carly?" Ben stared at the car.

"She said it would be too hard to come, so she stayed home. I can't believe you are doing this for us, Ben! You have no idea what this means."

"Dad, you're crying. How come you are hugging a cop? It's Uncle Ben. Uncle Ben, what are you doing here?" Zak put up a peace sign and tapped his chest. The men parted, staring at him. Zak's gesture wasn't wasted on Sheriff Ben. "Did I do something wrong? Whoa. Whoa. Make this make sense. Uncle Ben, you come from a costume party? You ain't no sheriff. Where'd you get those handcuffs? They look real." Zak swaggered around Ben.

"They are real, Zak." Ben patted his cuffs.

"How did you get someone to give you a squad car? Man! That is the coolest, and that is the ultimate costume. Did you steal it?" Zak asked with excitement.

"It's the car I use for work." Ben eyed Zak's movements.

"What work? I thought you played basketball, or shot guns, or fireworks. Is that a real gun?" Zak impulsively reached to touch it.

Ben instinctively backed him off; "Hands up!" He bellowed.

Thinking Uncle Ben was playing, Zak rushed in for a hug and a tackle. This was going differently than planned. Sheriff Ben flipped him into a lock-hold.

"What the f----!" Zak screamed as Ben covered the teen's mouth.

Zak's dad, David, shook his head with an ironic laugh. "You've got a lot to learn about Zak, brother!" Ben removed the hand muzzle.

"Whoa, I get it. You're like Mission Impossible, or James Bond, or Superman. Like, I didn't know who you were until now. You're like that guy, that guy, that guy, Clark. Yeah! Clark Kent. Okay, okay, I can play this game," Zak coughed and breathed deeply, babbling nervously as he tried to get his bearings.

"No, Zak. I am not Superman or Clark Kent. I am your Uncle Ben and the Sheriff of Harris County; this is my work vehicle. Never touch my gun. Never." Ben unlocked the hold.

Zak rubbed his neck. "Wow, that's cool. A real Sheriff. Last time I got cuffed, I was shopping at the mall."

His father crossed his arms on his chest, expanded his lungs, puffed his cheeks, and stared at Zak.

"Ok, so I was running in the mall, and I got tackled," Zak blurted. "That police cuffed me!"

Uncle Ben placed his arms across his chest, eyeing his brother and then staring at Zak.

"Ok, so I was running in the mall, and I got tackled and cuffed…" Zak repeated.

"Because…" his father interjected.

"I don't know because. Oh yeah, because the kids I was with were stealing, and I was watching them steal, and then they shouted 'run,' so I ran." Zak breathed in deeply and then exhaled. "Yep, that's right. Now I remember!"

"And…" his father stomped on his thought.

"I didn't steal from stores; I only picked up things people leave behind that no one owns. You were really mad and had to come to get me, and you grounded me for a whole month on house arrest and made me do chores," Zak pouted. "You glued me to Mom; boy, she sure was not happy."

"We'll talk more, David. Call me. Give my regards to Carly." Uncle Ben turned to Zak. "Grab your stuff. I left Kate cooking supper; it will be cold by the time we return."

"What's supper?" Zak asked.

"Supper is spaghetti," Ben said.

"Supper is spaghetti?" Zak ran his fingers through his hair.

"Yes, and salad," Ben answered.

"I don't eat green things, including salad," Zak said.

"You do now," said Ben.

"Can we run the lights and sirens?" Zak asked.

"No, and unless you shut up, you'll ride in the cage," Ben shared.

"I want to ride behind the cage, never got to do that before," Zak said. "It's probably safer for me."

"Probably." His father exhaled heavily, thinking Ben had no idea what he was getting into.

Ben opened the back door. "Do you want me to push you in like a criminal, or do you want to get in like a man?"

"I'm a man. I'm 18 and can do what I want," Zak declared.

"Ok, then, be a man and sit down." Sheriff Ben closed the door. '*Is this a joke?*' "As far as I know, no man alive can do everything he wants. You got some learning to do, boy." Ben huffed and rolled his eyes. He knew at that moment he was in for a wild ride with this nephew. His word was his word—his brother, his brother. Ben, as always, would do his best. He would do what he could. After all, he was the sheriff.

-3-
DOZING

I t was a clear night until Sheriff Ben reached the thirty-min-ute turnoff to Riverdale by Rodeos. Then the drizzle started, and a roaring thunderstorm ensued. Flashes sparked. Thunder crashed. Rain pelted the windshield even with the wipers at full force. Water sprayed off the tires in the dips as it washed down hilltops.

Zak, finding comfort in his duffel bag, was quickly lulled to sleep within the first fifteen minutes of the two-hour trip. Sheriff Ben, grate-ful for the sudden silence after the non-stop chatter, was left to his own thoughts. The storm outside, in stark contrast to Zak's peaceful slumber, raged on. Lightning flashed, and thunder rumbled, but Zak remained undisturbed. It was only when the squad pulled up in the Jordan drive-way that Zak, in a sudden and unexpected motion, popped up like a jack-in-the-box, resuming the very sentence where he left off.

"Do you have gangs here?" Zak asked.

Uncle Ben had patiently listened to non-stop mall stories, bullies, and hated teachers. He heard about fights, knives, and beatings. The one time he tried to enter into a conversation, Zak politely said, "Please don't stomp on my words when I am talking. I can't think." *'Okay, then I will just listen and see what I learn,'* Ben never uttered another word. *'Sure glad I rescued him into a rural, small-town safe space. If he is telling the truth, I'm so happy I live in Riverdale.'*

—

Thankfully, Kate had used the time to chill. She ate dinner alone and settled into the den, grading papers. Hearing them enter, she announced, "Hi, Honey. Supper is on the stove, garlic bread's in the oven, and the sal-ad's in the fridge." She added, "I'll join you in a bit."

"Welcome home, Zak." Uncle Ben led the way. "I will show you to your room."

"But I'm hungry!" Zak turned toward the kitchen table.

Ben turned, put his arm on Zak's shoulder, and led him up the stairs, "Stuff gets put where it belongs before you eat." The room was Ben's home office and den. It contained a large desk, a bookcase filled with crime novels, and two sizable mounted rainbow trout on each side of a twelve-point buck on a dark-painted wall. The room was filled with a dresser, a twin bed, and a rolling swivel black leather chair. Zak promptly sat down and spun around, finishing with a red shoe foot plant on the surface of Ben's unmarred cherry desk. "You be careful with my stuff. Don't touch anything."

"Okay," Zak clapped, and the floor lamp lit. "Wow, cool room!" He clapped three times and lit the desk lamp. "Whoa, Uncle Ben, this is better than Alexa. What else does this room do without touching anything."

"Just the lights," growled Ben.

"How do I go to bed if I can't touch it?" Zak seemed sincere.

"Move your butt, boy. I'm hungry and need to show you the guest bath." Ben wanted to shout, *'Get your feet off my desk,'* but refrained.

Zak stood and gyrated his torso. Ben ignored the movement. "New towels once a week. You wash your stuff. I expect you to keep everything clean and tidy." Ben rustled Zak's hair.

Zak jumped back. "No! Not my hair! Now I have to fix it before dinner." He climbed and sat on the vanity to look closer at the mirror.

"No, you are eating supper, washing up, and then going to bed. Your hair is fine," Uncle Ben ordered. "Get down now. What kind of person sits on the bathroom vanity?"

"The better-to-see-better person." Zak looked at Uncle Ben like he had three eyes and laughed. "Are you serious? I'm 18 do what I want."

Ben stopped, squaring his eyes and shoulders. "My way or the highway, good buddy. There's a thunderstorm outside; if you decide to walk home from here, it will take you two full days. You choose Food. Bed. Hot shower head. Or…" He pointed to the front door. "Door to my house swings one way, and I am not afraid to kick your ass on the way out. You will not return."

Zak jumped off the counter and silently followed Uncle Ben to the kitchen. The older man proceeded to dish up his plate after he handed the second plate to Zak. Ben said nothing as he sat down at the head of the table to eat. Then, he quietly said grace and dug in.

Zak piled the noodles high and added a little sauce. "I love supper. He took all the bread and left the salad alone, rolling his eyes, lifting his lip, and sticking his tongue out. "I love supper." He repeated.

Kate rounded the corner and noticed Zak's dramatics. "We eat vegetables with every supper. We, meaning you, me, and Ben. Take salad."

Zak glared at her. Kate glared back with a teacher do-it-or-die look. He picked out one small piece of Romaine, a cucumber, and violently stabbed a cherry tomato.

"Thank you, Zak." Kate gave a sweet educator smile as Zak swung his leg over the back of the chair to sit down. "We say grace in this house."

"Grace," smirked Zak and stuffed his mouth with an entire piece of bread, chewing loudly with puffed cheeks.

Kate watched Zak while Ben ignored the fiasco. This was going to be interesting. It was October; her husband had promised seven more months and a graduation. She poured a cup of chamomile tea to watch the show unfold. She was not happy. She had tried to teach similar students; most had quit high school at age 16.

———

Q served Sam and Mantha attentively and interrupted their conversation for precisely five minutes with cooking status updates. Then he elegantly served them dinner with no spillage between the gravy and the crust, garnished with sprigs of fresh parsley. The plating was beautiful with a parsley pattern; even old Sam noted it with a surprised look.

"I added the parsley for color, beauty, and function as a palate cleanser," Q shared. "As you can see, the chef's special is a delightful dish incorporating various flavors. Our chef Margie takes great pride in the presentations I plate."

Mantha smiled genuinely. "I appreciate the attention to detail in taste and presentation. I admire when parsley is used creatively."

Q smiled back and glanced at her. "Creativity is something that our chef values highly. Speaking of which, I value it too. People often say I am funny because I think so clearly. I think that my logic and precision are what I can offer easily…whereas social interactions can be somewhat challenging for me. I take great pleasure in ensuring the plating of each dish, including the parsley garnish, is perfect. In the culinary world, they say, 'You eat first with your eyes before you taste each dish.' I keep this foremost in my mind for our customers."

"Thank you for sharing that, Q. Your dedication to your craft shines through. The fact that you pay such attention to detail is admirable. Your precise placement of the parsley has enhanced my overall dining experience, and I look forward to seeing what you come up with next time I dine here." Mantha shared kindly.

Sam looked stunned. This woman was a master at communication. He might have thought to add a "looks nice" to his thank you to Q and the conversation would have ended.

"Thank you for your compassionate words. It means a lot to me. I'll garnish your dishes with the utmost care and precision, ensuring each creative touch is placed elegantly. Is there any specific preference you have for the placement or design?" Q seemed to have made a friend.

"Oh, no need for anything specific. I trust your expertise. Surprise me, and I'm sure it will impress. Just knowing that you've taken the time to make it visually appealing will make the dining experience delightful, Q," Mantha stated. "Could you bring us fresh glasses of water?"

"Most certainly, I appreciate your trust. I'll make it a point to present your dish in a way that will leave you impressed and satisfied each time you dine at Dee's Cafe. I will be right back with your water. If you need anything else during your meal, please don't hesitate to let me know. Enjoy your evening!" Q pivoted on his radiantly shining shoes and pranced to the water machine.

Sam had already crushed the crust, set the parsley pattern aside, and stirred the pot pie into a big mess. Q's look of disapproval was apparent when he returned with the water.

"Q," Mantha said as she gingerly picked at the crust so nothing would collapse. "Sam has been working hard all day and is very hungry. Looks like he loves the chicken pot pie."

Q cocked his head quizzically and put his finger to his chin. "Hmmm, I suppose, yes, I guess he does."

———

"Zak, tell me about your friends at your old school." Kate sipped her tea and fished for small talk.

"Don't have friends at school," Zak chewed as he drove his cherry tomato around a spaghetti racetrack. He rearranged the track.

"What are your favorite subjects," Kate pressed.

"Like space, and rockets, and stars, and planets," Zak shared. "Astronomy and science experiments. Things that are real, not fake. See it. Do it. Prove it. Space exploration." Zak's face lit up when he noticed that Kate did not stomp on his thoughts and was listening. "I am going to build a reusable rocket. One that will significantly change space exploration. Launching payloads is astronomical, like wow, oh wow. It would cut down on space debris and keep the people working on the space station safer. The cost is reduced by reusing a rocket instead of building a new one for each launch. If the cost is reduced, more people can travel into space. More people like me would have space opportunities."

Kate smiled, having found a key to Zak's heart. "How can I help you with your project, Zak? Do you know what I do for a job?"

"No," said Zak.

"I am a high school science teacher," Kate said. "And in my 3rd-hour class, I teach astronomy. Would you like to see if I can get you into my class?"

"You're kidding me, right? I move to a Podunk town in a crap city into the house of Clark Kent and an astronomy teacher." Zak smacked both hands to his forehead. "Unbelievable. Unbelievable. Unbelievable! You're both joking with me, right? I am, like, dreamin'!"

Uncle Ben looked up. "Are you serious with this rocket stuff?"

"Yeah," said Zak.

"Well, I am the Sheriff, and Kate is the science teacher, and you will graduate and become somebody. I keep my promises," said Uncle Ben, carefully wiping his face on a cloth napkin. "And when a brother promises a brother something, that promise will not be broken. Kate and I will see this through for you until then."

Zak jumped up, whooping. He bumped the table and tipped his glass of milk into his salad and spaghetti racetrack. His tomato jumped off the plate and rolled onto the floor.

"And," commanded Uncle Ben. "Regardless of the mess you just made, you will finish eating all that supper at this house!"

"But," Zak countered, reaching for the tomato under his chair.

"No buts. Eat it." Uncle Ben had his gun. "And you will bus your dish and clean up your mess when finished."

Zak popped the tomato into his mouth. "Yes, Sir, Uncle Ben, Sir," he said as he chewed. Then he finished his food, slurped the spilled milk off his plate, and licked the remaining food off. He wiped his mouth on his sleeve. He threw the dish on the floor, shattering it. Then he got down on his knees to clean up the mess.

"Why the hell did you just do that?" Ben exploded.

"You told me to finish eating, bust the dish, and clean up the mess," Zak exclaimed desperately. "I am doing what you told me to do. I need a broom. Oh yeah, and no buts, but I am not sure which but…but butt or just but." He slapped his rump.

Ben placed his hand over his mouth to keep the words that came to mind from escaping his lips. Kate set down her tea, cocking her head and stifling laughter while looking at Ben. "Is that what you heard Uncle Ben say, Zak?" She asked incredulously.

"Yes," shrugged Zak blankly, as Ben mouthed over his head, 'something is wrong with this boy.'

Uncle Ben, with his sidearm and police belt still in place, fetched the broom and a dustpan, handed Zak the broom, and got on his knees with the dustpan to ensure all the shards were cleaned up.

—

Mantha bunked into the small room with a cot in the back of O'Riley's garage. "This will be fine, Sam. I've slept in much worse."

"I am sure you have, Mantha. I will see you in the morning with fresh coffee. Do you want to sleep with Penny tonight? That dog sure likes you," Sam offered.

Mantha smiled as the dog jumped up and lay on her pillow.

"Guess Penny decided," Mantha grinned.

"Sleep tight, don't let the bedbugs bite," Sam joked.

"Good night, Sam," Mantha chuckled. "Do I need to take out my permethrin bug poison?"

"No, Mantha, the garage is safe, except for some ants, spiders, and silverfish. Rest is taken care of with my Viet Vet Agent Orange glow."

"Night, Sam. Thank you." Mantha sunk into the memory foam of four mattresses piled on an old army cot.

—

Sheriff Ben was grateful for a quiet Friday night without any 911 calls. He would have slept better if his bedroom was not located under the den. It seemed every hour, the upstairs toilet flushed loudly, and hard-planted feet stomped overhead while Kate snored on his left side. The clock said 4:00 a.m. before there was silence. The upstairs ruckus stopped when Kate rolled on her belly, except for an eek-creek. He had no idea what it was from.

Ben tip-toed up the stairs to check on Zak. To his astonishment, his den looked like a tornado had struck! Everything in Zak's duffel was spread across the room. The bed was empty. Two pillows and a blanket lay wadded on the floor by his desk. Two enormous feet juggled his swivel desk chair, and two large red shoes lay yards away. He did not see any socks. Loud snores rumbled from under the desk. Candy bar wrappers were stuffed in the trout's mouth. A pop can hung on his trophy deer antler. "Well, I never," Uncle Ben shook his head as he returned to bed. He was too tired to engage with a sugar high, adrenaline and testosterone-filled Big Foot. He put his pillow over his head. What had he gotten Kate and himself into?

Kate woke up with Ben sleeping soundly next to her. She loved this man trained to make split decisions that mattered in life or death. He had been a beloved deputy under the old Sheriff named Larry, a local paramedic before that, and had served in the Gulf War. He wasn't a politician, and the local folk liked him. This split decision made no sense.

Ben was Sheriff Larry's endorsement when Larry married Margie Jones and retired. Besides being an excellent sheriff, Larry had been a great chef, and the two ran Dee's together for ten years before he passed away. As with the previous county administration, a known candidate was better than an unknown candidate. Ben's campaign began by declaring his candidacy, filling out the appropriate forms, setting up a few signs, and posting a flier in the VFW, laundromat, and local pubs. His real campaign took place every day of the year by having coffee at Dee's Cafe and talking to voters, being honorable and fair in challenging situations, chatting with the kids at local schools, attending funerals, and checking in on injured locals. Local folk appreciated one of their own being their sheriff. It just seemed right.

Kate had programmed the coffee in the evening and had an egg bake ready in the fridge. The smell of fresh coffee filled the kitchen. She missed early morning kitchen window sunrises that departed in Autumn to later daytime. In the quiet of the morning, with the sun still hiding from her window, she poured steaming brew into her favorite mug. Her soft flannel pajamas felt cozy as she sipped, feeling the warmth of the coffee flow down her throat and into her belly. She liked the solitude of the early morning before the day's hustle and bustle.

The trees rustled, dropping their leaves to feed compost piles. The woodpiles alongside neighboring homes rose higher. The fall air was crisp. She noted people already running along the sidewalk, a mother pushing a stroller, and a squirrel sitting on the post of her fence. Purple asters were in full bloom, the mallow greeted the sun, and lavender bushes spiked the last of their flowers. Leaves had turned from summer green to hues of reds, yellows, and oranges. Kate loved this contrast and enjoyed playing with the colors each season to highlight Earth's gifts.

She lit the hurricane lamp on the table instead of turning on the lights. Its softness gave a tender glow to the heirloom kitchen table, passed down now for three generations. A bookshelf behind her chair held her favorite cookbooks, self-development, and gardening catalogs. She grabbed the thick self-preservation book she studied each morning. Kate was glad she had pulled on her dark blue robe and mukluks. She drew her robe tighter around her neck, feeling the constancy and coziness of a long, loving relationship. Ben had given her the robe as a gift for her last birthday. It felt like wrapping up in his warmth.

In the silence of her day, Kate opened her journal to the long list of words. Ten words were currently circled. What would she choose next? The word GROW opened her heart, and she drew a circle around it. Taking the scarlet ribbon, she opened a new page spread for discovery. She loved the freshness of unpenned paper.

In the early months of journaling, she had rushed through learning. However, now she savored each moment. She no longer sought order or speeded completion when journaling but meandered through each of the eighteen empty areas as time and thought permitted her. What emerged revealed a direction to follow in the chapters of her life. She was a person of order, yet she had found herself hopping around and filling boxes randomly as she discovered new thoughts and answers. The completion of each page always surprised her and awakened a depth of knowing and love for herself, her friends, family, and neighbors.

Today, she began contemplating in the square called 'Silence,' the first open space in the upper left corner. She drew the word GROW in a black outline. Her jar of colored pencils, always handy for a science teacher, called to each letter in hues from yellow to orange. She took time as she colored to contemplate this word. For now, it was enough to meet–GROW. Kate pondered the second box, Awareness, and checked her smartphone to discover deeper meanings. Words in ancient languages were her hidden hobby, and she found English often used one word that was shallow compared to its origins. GROW, a little word, held many mysteries as cultures evolved from agricultural to modern digital societies. In Greek, 'auxesis' meant increase, as did Chinese, which included mature, evolved, and ripened meanings. Hebrew added accrue, raise, bring up. Arabic added gather, develop. She added a note to box number ten, titled 'Reveal the Hidden,' to increase development.

Kate started journaling early on the morning of January 1st. The word GROW was this day's gift. She would take whatever time necessary to understand and build deeper roots in this new word adventure. The path it took always amazed her. Some word studies took days. Some took weeks. She laughed at GROW. That word would take a lifetime.

Satisfied, she placed her journal and book back on the shelf and prayed for protection for Ben, wisdom for herself, and patience in understanding the new creature sleeping in Ben's den. She went to take a shower and grinned at her GROWth in this journey.

————

Ben dressed in his Saturday wool shirt and jeans. He laced up his old work boots for pre-winter yard work. Today, he would check the vehicles, add antifreeze, shut off the outdoor water to their home, roll up the hoses, and stack wood. If time permitted, he would bring in the first load of split logs for the wood stove. A glimmer sparked when he remembered Zak in his den. He had a helper! He ran up the stairs, stepping on every third step.

"Hey, buddy, wake up. We've got work to do," Ben ordered as he pulled away the chair with the large bare feet.

Zak popped up, hitting his head. "What the fuck!" Zak shouted.

"We don't use that kind of language. If you need to use expletives, you will say blank, or blankety, or blankity, blank, blank! You will not use the F, S, or any other letter swear words, or you will be dealing with me. You hear me?"

Zak rubbed his head, trying to remember where he was and what was happening. He rolled over, pulled the blanket over his head, and mumbled, "Blankity, blank, blank." Then, in a loud, determined tone, he shouted, "BLANK!" ending with a grand finale of snorts and snores.

Ben didn't know whether to laugh, be impressed that the swears were contained, or haul the kid out by the ankles, set him upright, and put him to work. '*What kind of person was he dealing with? Who was this kid?*'

He scratched his head, did an about-face, and decided to get a cup of coffee to set a strategy for today. '*His brother, a lawyer, and sister-in-law, an accountant, had been unable to handle him. Neither had been in the military or worked as paramedics or law enforcement. Regardless of how you looked at it, accounting was math, not science, and Kate was a great science teacher. He and Kate had taken on challenges in careers and life; somehow, they would get through this. It seemed like the suburb Zak had been part of exposed him to hooligans from the city's edges. It appeared Zak liked the drama and excitement. A small high school and town would be good for him.*'

Ben took out the egg bake, cut a piece, and set it into the microwave. He poured himself a cup of coffee, noticing Kate dressed in tapered jeans, cowboy boots, and a new sweater leaning at the kitchen door. "Hey, good buddy, can you pour me a hot cup?" Kate asked with a flirty smile.

Her beauty always took him aback; '*whoa!*' He loved that woman. "Anything you want, sweetie." Ben took her coffee cup and gently held her for a kiss. Kate melted into his arms. They had always wanted a child, but for some reason neither he nor Kate could have children. Ben and Kate had remained childless and had dreamed of a houseful of kids. So, they used their love of kids as they worked in the community without the responsibility of children or animals.

David and Carly decided one and done, with the intensity of Zak and their professional careers. Zak was a problematic infant and into everything toddler. The boy was a high-wired rascal, and that trajectory continued.

"I love you, Ben." Kate bit his earlobe and whispered.

"Forever," Ben's embrace lingered. "Let me get your coffee." They both sensed a conversation was due. Perhaps now was the time.

Kate sipped her coffee. She opened her mouth to talk and then gazed at her mug. "Sometimes though…you can make me SO mad!" Kate sighed.

Ben looked up to say something but drank his coffee instead.

Kate tried again, "Zak changes us."

Ben looked at his cup. The bird-pecking dance conversation continued until it became apparent to both of them they were unready to open up fully.

"Ben, what will we do about Zak?" Kate ventured. She gestured with her head that they go out to the patio outside to discuss their nephew.

"We're going to graduate him for David. He's going to learn to work a job and make something of himself," Ben answered. "Zak has already attended seven schools, and his last high school does not want him back."

"We're going to graduate Zak for Zak, not for David. What will he make of us if seven schools were confounded with him? And of Riverdale High School? Look, we didn't even discuss this. You just jumped in your car and set me up to get him schooled," Kate fretted.

"David said he tried everything he could think of. He wanted to give up and leave him to go live alone at eighteen without a diploma or any way to work. Family is family. Every kid deserves a chance. Kate, you're a teacher, and I've got experience handling tough people in hard situations. We can do this," Ben encouraged.

"Do this or want to do this?" Kate's tone and eyebrows challenged. "I think we need to get Zak up, but first, let's have a quiet time. Something tells me our mornings are going to change exponentially after breakfast." She stood up and took both coffee mugs inside to refill, leaving Ben to absorb her thoughts.

—4—
ESCALATION

en eyed Kate with his slight smile and a 'let's roll' look. Kate rolled her eyes inward, and Ben announced, "No time like the present."

"Sure," Kate sighed heavily. "No time like the present." She followed Ben up the stairs. She, too, was shocked at the mess. Clothes, pillows, trash, and smells assaulted her senses. In all the years she had owned her home, not even when they were moving furniture or adding fresh paint, had anything resembled this disaster. She held her breath. There was an odor coming from the corner where there was a haphazard pile of shoes.

Ben pulled out his phone with a smirk, gave it a couple swipes, and then—increased the volume while lowering the phone's speaker near the ear of the sleeping slob. BA DUM BA DA DUM BA DUM BA DA DUM — the trumpet fanfare pierced the silence. Zak knocked his head against the underside of the desk, and the chair scurried across the room.

Kate rolled her eyes as Ben nodded and winked proudly, noting the feet pulling in under the desk. He was about to pull them out when a tousle-haired teen poked his head between the columns.

Ben demanded, "Why are you sleeping under my desk?"

The head retreated into the darkness of his desk cave.

"Zak, the day has started. Get up now!" He pulled the extended feet.

"Stop! You're hurting me!" Zak shouted as Ben dropped his feet. He poked his head out from between the columns.

Ben confronted him again. "Why are you sleeping under my desk?"

"It's not your desk. You gave it to me last night. You said this was my room, and in my room, I can sleep wherever I want to. You said not to touch anything and didn't answer how I should get into bed without touching it! What time is it anyway? Dad and Mom let me sleep all day Saturday, so I don't bother them on their day off." Zak crawled out on his knees with dirty Spiderman boxer shorts and a too-big t-shirt.

"It's 9:00 am and time to get up!" Ben held his ground and kept himself from saying his thoughts by biting his tongue. He paused to calm himself. "Give me your pillows and blanket, Zak."

"Huh?"

"Please, give me your pillows and blanket," Ben repeated.

Zak stared at him, shook his head, and asked, "What did you say?" The prompt response and obedience Ben expected were nonexistent.

He was no longer cordial. "I said, give me your pillows and that damn blanket!" His voice rose and he bellowed. "Now!"

Zak crawled back under the desk to hide. "Well, that escalated quickly," Kate surmised from the doorway. "Let me see what I can do."

"He's 18 years old, for God's sake! He's a man. He can vote. He can join the military IF he graduates. And he can't get out from under a desk to wake up on a Saturday morning!" Ben snatched the blanket from the curled-up manboy. Two pillows hurled out after him, along with a raging bull. Ben jumped back, shaking the blanket at the lunging youth.

"Toro!" He shouted. "Toro, Toro!" Wrapping Zak in the blanket to hold him fast. The teen escalated. He began kicking and shrieking. Ben held him snugly until Zak gave up, confused and defeated.

Kate shot Ben a sideways glance; restraint was not allowed in their school system, and she was unsure what buttons and triggers were part of Zak's childhood experiences. She knew of families whose children had been removed into child protective services for things like the very response Ben had just had. *'But what else could he do?'* Kate looked around and promptly took action. She set the pillows back on the bed, then collected underwear, one dirty sock, and two printed T-shirts, calculating Zak's worldly goods as she continued. She found no toothbrush, toothpaste, shampoo, shaving tools, comb, or deodorant. It appeared the kid had arrived with no money, no skills, and no manners. *'Ben gave his word to David with a promise of seven months to graduation. Whew! What on earth was Ben thinking of taking on this kid? I need to think. Quickly—'* Kate picked up the garbage can and tried something. "Hey Zak, astronauts in deep space do not litter. Can you pick up all the debris and place it here?"

"When is trash day?"

"Every day is trash day in this house!" Boomed Ben. Kate glared at her husband, who was not helping the situation.

Zak wiggled out of Uncle Ben's clutches and stood facing his aunt. "Sure, Aunt Kate, I'll get it." He proceeded to pick up all the junk he had thrown and scattered, gingerly removing the can from the antler and the candy wrapper from the trout. "Guess the fish didn't like the candy."

"Trout," muttered Uncle Ben under his breath. Ben wrinkled his brow, grimacing. His wife was playing with this joker. *'I want to haul him up by the t-shirt and demand he clean up the mess he had made in my den.'* Ben thought. *'And my wife is playing an astronaut commander with a man behaving as a nine-year-old.'* Ben felt his blood pressure rise for the third time this morning. Not twenty-four hours had lapsed since picking up Zak at the meeting spot.

"From now on, Zak, this room is your space station. You will follow space station orders. You will sleep in that bed with the pillows and blankets provided." She pointed. "You will not sleep under the command central desk. The touch order has been removed; you may touch your bed or do whatever else you need. Just be careful. Everything has its place, so you must return it where you found it."

"Zak, as commander of this space station, you will keep everything clean. We need to check your supplies. Do you have socks?"

"I forgot them," Zak said.

"You are required to have five pairs of socks. I expect one dirty, one on you, and three ready for action. Do you understand?" Kate tapped each finger as she began the list.

"Yes, ma'am," said Zak with a salute.

'What the blankity, blank, blank. My science teacher wife gets a salute, and I get side-kicked in the shin by a bronco.' Ben grunted. "Pig."

Kate grabbed a notepad and paper from Ben's desk, ignoring her husband's grumbling. "Underwear?"

"I am wearing them," Zak answered.

"What are you wearing when they get dirty?" Kate questioned.

"They are already dirty, ma'am," Zak said.

"You're a regular pig," muttered Uncle Ben, shaking his head with dismay.

"No, sir. I'm a regular person," replied Zak.

Kate began her checklist. "That will be five new pairs of underwear and socks. Do you have hygiene equipment?"

"Huh?" Zak looked like Kate had hit him with a missile. "Toothbrush?" Kate asked.

"No."

"Toothpaste?" She asked. "No."

"Deodorant?" Kate continued writing. "Shaving gear?"

"Do you know how to shave?" Ben added. Kate glared. Ben held his tongue once more and observed the two of them together. He was frustrated but curious.

Zak was silent. Kate made her list and handed it to Ben. "Looks like today you will be going to the mercantile with Zak. He needs to get outfitted for his exploratory journey into Riverdale High School on Monday, and he has little here he can use."

Ben glared. "Hope you got money, Zak. Clothes are not free."

"I had ten dollars. I used it for the candy and soda," Zak mumbled.

"Guess you will need an after-school and weekend job. Meanwhile, I guess Kate and I have to spot you," Ben grunted.

"Spot where?" Zak asked. "I'm right here."

Ben ignored him.

"You got yourself into this, good buddy. I'm sure you will figure out a way to get yourself out," Kate handed Ben the long list and turned with the small pile of clothes toward the laundry room.

"Zak, you will learn to wash and care for your clothes like a man. I expect you to be an adult in my home," Uncle Ben lectured.

"I will help you with this one step at a time. Later, you and Uncle Grinch here can go to the store and fill in the gaps in your supplies,"

Aunt Kate nodded toward Ben and headed into the hallway.

Ben grunted again and offered a look of disapproval while Zak looked at his aunt in mild confusion. "Gaps? Yes, Ma'am, space commander, Ma'am," Zak furrowed his brows together, unsure what to do next.

"Get dressed in what's left, Zak. After breakfast, you and Uncle Grinch will go to town to gear up," Kate grinned.

Ben was not into Kate's space game or an 18-year-old playing like a kid. He was the sheriff, for God's sake, and not a cartoon! He fumed as he looked back at the tornado wreck of his den and man-child fumbling with his clothes as he and Kate walked out.

———

Before sunrise, Q rode his bike to Dee's Cafe, where he enjoyed camaraderie without the entanglement of relationships. Working for Margie gave him purpose. On Saturdays, tips were great. No one teased or bothered him as he moved about taking orders and pouring coffee. The aroma of the rich dark roast brew wafted outside as early risers arrived in force to enjoy a warm cup of Joe and catch up on the local news.

The moment between customer orders and service was perfect for Q's penchant for plating all the delicious items to his aesthetic taste. Freshly baked blueberry muffins, locally smoked thick bacon, and farm-fresh eggs emerged spaced and placed, plate upon plate. Dee's cozy diner invited hungry patrons to enjoy hearty and hefty meals. Chit-chat had gone around town, that Q was there with a flair. He liked that slogan. He carried another piece of apple pie plated with cheddar cheese and cinnamon ice cream served for breakfast!

———

Mantha woke to *[Click, crackle, static...]* Ham Radio?

Ham1-Sam: *(Sam, from the United States)* Good morning, fellow hams! This is KØKQR, Sam, checking in from Minnesota, USA.

Ham2-Mikhail: *(Mikhail, from Russia)* Good afternoon, Sam! This is RV0HAM, Mikhail, coming to you from the snowy land of Irkutsk, Russia. I've got my hot cup of tea. Weather is cooler, shifting to winter! Some leaves are left on trees. Winter tires on vehicles. Over.

Ham3-Akiko: *(Akiko, from Japan)* Konnichiwa, Sam and Mikhail! JS6H- AM, Akiko, is checking in from the Land of the Rising Sun. Good evening, vibrant red, orange, and yellow shades, especially in the surrounding mountains and parks. The weather's lovely in Numazu. Over.

Ham1-Sam: Great to hear you both! Mikhail, soon we will have cold. Akiko, your leaves sound beautiful. What's the latest in the ham radio world?

Ham2-Mikhail: Well, Sam, I've been experimenting with a home-brew Yagi antenna design for better DX contacts. Those Siberian distances require some firepower! And I'm fine-tuning my CW skills for fun.

Note to reader:

DX is when ham radio enthusiasts try to talk to people in faraway places, connecting with stations in distant countries or regions. Collecting unique cards called QSL cards is a way to prove that they've successfully communicated with these locations.

Ham3-Akiko: Akiko here. I've been participating in some QRP contests, trying to see how far I can reach with minimal power. The thrill of low-power transmissions is incredible. I've been learning about digital modes like FT8, which are getting popular.

Note to reader:

Ham QRP means using meager power in amateur radio. Instead of using the usual energy, ham operators challenge themselves using only 5 watts or less. They have to be skilled and use intelligent antennas to make faraway contacts.

FT8 is a unique way to send messages on amateur radio. It's a digital mode that's good at picking up weak signals. FT8 can still help people communicate over long distances despite lousy radio conditions.

Ham1-Sam: That's fascinating! I help newcomers to ham radio in my local club, teaching them about antennas and propagation. I've got my eyes on Field Day, the fourth weekend of June, for the US event. Setting up a temporary station in the great outdoors is always a blast.

Ham2-Mikhail: Field Day IS a blast! Ours is early June, Sam. Last year we made over 500 contacts. One day, you can join us here in Russia for a special Field Day in the snow. We provide hot tea!

Ham3-Akiko: Count me in for that snow Field Day, Mikhail! If you make it to Japan, Sam, we can be surrounded by our lovely trees. It's magical.

Ham1-Sam: That sounds amazing, folks. Have you picked up any interesting DX stations recently?

Ham2-Mikhail: I had contact with a station in Antarctica two weeks ago. It's always a thrill to reach those remote places.

Ham3-Akiko: I contacted a ham in Australia and chatted about our favorite radio equipment.

Ham1-Sam: I love the thrill of contacting someone far away. Let's hope for more exciting DX adventures in the future. K0KQR clear. We'll be QRT.

Ham2-Mikhail: Agreed, Sam! Keep those antennas pointed skyward; we'll catch you both on the bands soon. 73, everyone!

Ham3-Akiko: 73, indeed! Have a wonderful weekend, Sam and Mikhail. Akiko clear from Numazu. Sayonara!

Mantha rolled over. She was home. The **click, crackle, static** was a comforting sound. Russia and Japan said, "Best regards to you," or, "Goodbye and take care." A term Mantha had heard often as a friendly and time-honored way to conclude a radio conversation in the ham community. Mantha dozed back to sleep.

Note to reader:

"**73**" is a commonly recognized abbreviation used as a sign-off or farewell. It is a way for ham radio operators to convey their good wishes to each other at the end of a conversation.

The call sign was familiar. Mantha waited. Suddenly, loud popping sounds bolted her upright. Gunshots! She waited and counted. '*Seventeen'—the magazine had been full.'* She stabilized herself to move swiftly—unarmed—peering through the cracked door—life flashed to an earlier HAM conversation time two years prior.

DesertRose: *I appreciate your kind words. It's a different kind of battlefield here, surrounded by rugged mountains and an ever-changing landscape. We're adapting, strategizing, and doing our best to protect and support our fellow soldiers.*

VietW65: *"DesertRose, it's great to meet you. I've heard about your leadership in Afghanistan. How's the mission?"*

DesertRose: *It's been challenging, holding our ground. The terrain and weather are rugged. Our team is resilient. How about you? How was your experience during Vietnam?*

VietW65: *It was grueling. The thick jungles and unpredictable enemy made it incredibly difficult. But we managed to push through and achieve our objectives. I have the utmost respect for the battles you're fighting in Afghanistan….for the people of Afghanistan.*

DesertRose: *Thank you for your service.*

VietW65: *That kind of resilience is what defines true warriors. In the face of adversity, we must remain steadfast in our commitment to serving our country and fighting for justice. It sounds like you're leading your troops with inspiring strength.*

DesertRose: *Thank you. Leadership in such hostile environments demands understanding, compassion, and determination. It's not easy, but seeing* *the bravery and dedication of my team keeps me motivated. Together, we continue to make a difference.*

VietW65: *Absolutely. Our camaraderie and support for each other are vital in times like these. The bond forged through shared challenges is unbreakable. Please don't hesitate to ask if there's anything I can do to assist from afar.*

DesertRose: *That means a lot. The support of veterans like yourself is important to us. It's a privilege to serve alongside brave individuals who have faced their battles and become stronger. Your experiences and wisdom are invaluable.*

VietW65: *DesertRose, you're not alone in this fight. The legacy of warriors endures, and your leadership will inspire future generations. Stay safe, and know that you have my utmost respect and support. KØKQR is clear.*

DesertRose: *Thank you for your encouragement, VietW65. I'll carry your message on this journey. Stay strong, and may the bonds of warriors past and present guide us toward victory. 73 KØQTQ going QRT.*

Just then, her dog alerted. She saw the hidden trip wire, and two privates impulsively ran to save Fraun, her German Shepherd. Her world exploded. Mantha vigorously shook her head to clear her mind.

"Wisdom starts with seeds as small as a grain of sand." There he was, smiling. His radiant blue eyes twinkled, holding his old, beaten-up Stanley thermos of coffee and an empty cup. Sam winked. "Would you like a fresh cup? Join me on the bench, and we can watch the cars pass by."

Mantha smiled crookedly back. It had been two months since she had returned stateside from convalescing in Germany. She had recently left Walter Reed. It seemed Sam barged into her life no matter how hard she tried to shut down the world.

Had she dreamt the conversation with Sam last night? Did Sam really retire suddenly and give her complete ownership of O'Riley's garage? Was she really waking up in his Ham Shack? Was Sam VietW65? And his long closet? What was the Long Closet, and why did he choose not to share it? He offered her O'Rileys, its customers, tools, and unfinished projects. He'd said they could share Penny. He left her debt-free to start fresh. If it was not a dream—what then?

She needed coffee to shake the cobwebs from her head. *Did she dream of the explosions and gunshots?* Mantha envisioned owning something other than a detailing garage. *Hmm…she had no plans.*

"Come on, Penny, you need to go pee," coaxed Sam as Penny pushed the door open for Mantha. "That dog will open doors for you, Mantha. Come on out and sit with me."

"Just a moment, Sam, I have to get ready. I will be out in a bit." Captain Mantha Dawson began putting on her new right leg. Reflecting on the challenges she had already faced and the obstacles she had already overcome, she put the pieces of her prosthetic leg in place. She had lost her leg in combat due to an IED explosion and had been determined to return to full duty and deploy again. She'd changed her mind after her parents died, and she was unable to go home to their life celebrations. She was grateful for the support of her comrades but had missed her local community. She still wondered if coming home was something she could manage. She felt a budding sense of pride and accomplishment as she finished putting on her new leg. She knew she still had a long road ahead of her, but she was ready to face whatever challenges came her way. She had learned to adapt to her new circumstances and never to give up, no matter how difficult the situation. And now, if last night was true, Sam was offering her the opportunity of a lifetime, and even without any family left in the community, Riverdale was home.

She pulled a camo hoodie and her favorite pair of jeans from her duffle. She finally felt secure in putting on jeans. Each time, the challenge lessened. She sat on the edge of her bed, put her leg on the floor, and grabbed her jeans, holding them open. *Who would have thought something so simple could be this complicated?* With the waistband facing her prosthetic leg, she used her hands to control the leg, inserting it into the jeans and ensuring the leg was positioned correctly. Mantha pulled the jeans up and over smoothing away the wrinkles and bunching with her hands. She stood tall and adjusted the waistband, ensuring they fit comfortably and securely. The hoodie was easy, so she pulled it on over her t-shirt. No one needed to know if she stood just right, with her right hand in her pocket and left cheek to the public. *Who was she fooling?*

Mantha sat down to lace up her left shoe and looked at the right plastic foot. Thankfully, the sock was already on. She grabbed her right shoe and held it open, with the heel facing her prosthetic leg. She guided her shoe onto the foot, positioning it correctly with the heel snug on the back of her foot. She adjusted the laces, making sure they fit comfortably and were secure for safety.

She paused, struck by the irony of her situation; *who'd have thought this would be my life?* Then she slowly pushed herself up from the bed, using her arms to steady herself. Putting weight on her prosthetic leg, she felt hesitant. *'What if I fall? What if this doesn't work? What if Sam decides to renege on his offer?'*

Self-doubt rose up. *What if this was all a dream?*

She remembered the painful strains she had to endure and the hard work she had put in, being supported by her comrades. She straightened her back and raised her head, determined to succeed. She looked around the room, taking in the surroundings with a new perspective. *I can do this!* She anticipated many more tests ahead…*face them with determination!* Dressed, she headed out with courage and curiosity, prepared to take on whatever came her way. With rediscovered resolve, Mantha stepped out into the sunshine.

"Morning, Sam," Mantha approached and sat on the bench. Penny jumped onto the bench and put her head on Mantha's thigh.

Sam met her greeting with a knowing smile. He poured a cup of coffee and handed it to her. Then he opened his lunch box and pulled out two fresh, warm blueberry muffins with butter and a plastic knife. The cardboard container said 'Dee's Cafe.'

"You already went shopping this morning, Sam?" Mantha seemed surprised.

"Already went to Russia and Japan, tested my new loads, and picked up these muffins. Enjoy! Been around the world and walked across the street." Sam laughed.

'So it was gunshots.' Mantha pulled her legs up on the bench, setting her coffee on her good knee and inhaling the brew. "You made this, Sam? It's pretty good."

Warrior to warrior, Sam gave a half smile.

—

Small-town Saturday mornings offered locals and out-of-towners connection, tranquility, and simplicity. The town of Riverdale awoke with the sunrise. The sky was clear, teens slept late unless they had employment, and the rest drove into town for errands or friendships. The apple-picking season had replaced biking and camping at the river's edge.

Riverdale businesses opened their doors and hung out their flags. Out-of-towners searched the hardware store, small shops, and antique mall, seeking treasures. The town market square served as a hub for local events. Residents and visitors flocked to this gathering place to support local farmers and artisans while enjoying cool fall days crackling with a vibrant, friendly atmosphere. Area musicians played in the small grandstand. The local farmer's market came alive with children laughing in a chase around stately trees and darting into the inclusive park.

Artisans offered fine woodworking, colorful quilts, and warm knitted wool mittens for holiday purchases. Vendors piled freshly harvested three sisters—squash, corn, and beans—high in colors of greens, oranges, and yellow hues. A few red ripe tomatoes remained along with zucchini. Booths brimmed with pies, homemade jams, canned goods, and pickles.

As a Frisbee flew past, Penny suddenly emerged from under the bench outside the garage and chased after it. She ran down the street with her mouth wide open and tongue out while the yellow disc flew high into the crowd. People quickly moved out of the way, leaving an open path for the determined dog chased by a panting old man.

"Penny, stop!" Sam shouted as the pitbull bore down, mouth agape and teeth ready. Oblivious to all but her chase, Penny leaped into the air to catch the Frisbee, slamming her jaws closed on her prize. Penny turned dog grinning to trot back to the garage and laid herself under the bench. The briefly alarmed community resumed calm once they realized the game was over.

Seated on the bench, Mantha chuckled. "You are quite the strike force there, Penny." She sipped her coffee as Sam returned to sit with her, winded. "Not a bad run for an old man, Sam. You're in good shape." She handed Sam his old mug. "Release," she told Penny who let go for Mantha to return the yellow flying disk to the teen.

"Not bad for having one foot already in the grave and a life of eight decades." Sam raised his pant leg, offering his explosive truth.

"You never…" Mantha began.

"Wasn't important. Your old friend Quintel knew; I never thought I needed to share it with neighborhood kids. I had to get my head around the loss myself," Sam explained. "Her name is Liberty," rapping his knuckles on the plastic. "And she is as much a part of me as my skin is. Fate dealt us a complex path, Mantha." Sam smoothed his pant leg back over his prosthesis.

Two people pulled up at his pumps, paid, and drove off. "Out-of-towners," he mused. "Locals would have come over or said hi," he continued. "Life throws unexpected curve-balls at us whether we like it or not. It's not about what we lose. I realized the important part was what I had left: my love for mechanics, my family, and this community." Sam looked directly at Mantha. "I was serious about retiring last night. If you'll have it, O'Rileys is yours. It'll cost you a dollar if you want to buy it. Call it Riley's. Everyone else does since that fool **O** in the light broke. That way, you won't have to fix it."

Mantha took out a two-dollar bill from her wallet. "My dad gave me this when I left to invest in my future. You can't split a two-dollar bill, so let's make a deal. One dollar for the garage and one dollar for half a share in Penny, the Ham Shack, and…" she paused.

"And what?" Sam waited.

"You teach me to shoot left-handed. I heard a gun range behind my bed," Mantha deduced.

"Why do you think that, Captain?" Sam joked.

"Nine millimeters, hot load, counted seventeen in a two-to-one pattern five times, and one on each end."

"Not bad, Captain." Impressed, Sam offered his right hand to shake. "Deal?"

Mantha looked at her thumb with two fingers. "Focus on what's left."

Sam raised his eyebrows, his arm outstretched. "Focus on the present to build your future, Mantha. Deal is done with a handshake."

"Deal." Mantha clasped his right hand with what was left of hers. "To what's left." She tapped her leg. "Calling him Freedom."

"Exactly. That's right," Sam tapped his leg. "Along with my Liberty!"

People continued to stop for gas, pay, and drive off. Penny was settled under the old park bench between Sam and Mantha. The dog snorted and passed gas. "Sam, does she always smell this bad?" Mantha pinched her nose.

"Only when I feed her human food or treats. Penny and her odor will follow you with her tail wagging to fan out the scent!"

Mantha, still grinning at the explanation of Penny's odoriferous aura, was now curious about her surroundings. "Sam, let's get on with it. I'd like to see what my two dollars bought besides two 24-hour gas pumps and a room with a cot."

Sam flipped the office sign to close. "OK, I'll show you. You got a deal. After the tour, you can OPEN YOUR NEW BUSINESS. Let's go, Penny, we got a RILEY Garage tour to perform!" The old man stretched as he stood up to walk inside. He locked the door to begin as Mantha's tour guide for Mantha, her new business and her new home. She could 'Open' Riley's today. It was hers.

—

"Can we ride in the squad car again?" Zak begged.

"Nope. You're using those red shoes to walk to town with me. It's three blocks, and as you can see, we have 'the list' from Kate of what we are to bring home." Uncle Ben walked out the door. "So you coming, or will you live in one pair of dirty underwear forever?"

Zak laughed. "I want to ride! Please."

"OK, I need to fill the tank anyway. Climb in, we'll stop at Riley's," Ben drove around the block to Riley's.

"Can I see the lights and hear the siren?" Zak pleaded.

Ben had heard an old friend had returned stateside and was bunking at Sam's. He flashed the lights and gave the siren one blast, figuring curiosity would bring out whoever had returned.

Sam had just opened a garage stall door to let the light in. Mantha jumped and looked through the garage door window. There was the Sheriff's car with a tousle-haired teen jumping out to run over to what was just exposed in the stalls—a 1957 Chevrolet Bel Air owned by Doc Johnson, the high school principal, and a 1940 Ford Coupe owned by Sam.

"FIRE!" Zak shouted. Each adult, all three veterans, alerted, popping their heads up and scanning for danger.

"Where's the fire?" Mantha demanded as the squad car driver walked into the station bay with unspoken but apparent authority.

"That's a real! A real..!" Zak stuttered in surprise, his eyes wide with excitement, breathing in every intricate detail of the vintage beauty. The car's sleek lines, radiant chrome grille, and nostalgic charm left him spellbound. "Blanking, blank, right Uncle Ben? That is FIRE!"

Ben smiled and nodded. "Yes, blanking."

"A blank, blankity blanking blank, real blanking real, 1940 Ford Coupe." Unable to contain his excitement, Zak approached the car his heart pounding with anticipation. Sam and Mantha regrouped.

"STOP!" A voice hollered as Zak reached out to touch the car's metallic surface. Zak's hands flapped up to shield his ears.

"Hey, young man! You admiring my old Ford?" Questioned Sam. He looked like Santa. "Morning Sheriff."

Zak turned, sputtering. "Uh, y-yes, sir. It's amazing. I've never seen a car like this before. I love old cars! Like this real life…real..This… Right here. Right now. Right in front of me!"

Sam smiled warmly at Zak's awestruck enthusiasm. "Well, you have good taste, young man. This is Rosey. This car was my father's '40 Ford Coupe, the epitome of class and style."

Zak's eyes glittered. "Do you, uh, think maybe… You could tell me more about it?" The teen's body gyrated. He clasped his hands behind his back, grandpa style, bobbing up and down on his toes. "Could I touch it? Maybe even sit inside?" Mantha noticed the ever-so-slight bouncing as he spoke. He didn't just talk. His whole body was begging to take in the marvelous machine.

Sam O'Riley paused playfully. "Perhaps I need to know who you are and why the sheriff brought you into my garage."

"I'm Zak!" Exclaimed the boy with a Cheshire cat grin, the same grin Sam's son had once sported before the accident. The sparkling eyes struck a chord of beloved memories from times long ago. Death does not end triggered memories.

"Well then, Zak, are your hands clean?" Asked Sam, noticing Mantha chatting with Sheriff Ben.

Zak looked at his hands, licked three fingers, and wiped them on his pants. He held them up in a 'Don't Shoot' upward position. "They are," he confirmed.

"A young lad with such passion deserves to experience this beauty," Sam opened the driver's door with a hand offering entry.

Zak's face lit up as he carefully sat inside the Ford Coupe. Leaning back into the seat, he closed his eyes to inhale. "It smells old, but... In a good way. I can feel her life."

Sam joined him, sitting on the passenger side, and leaned over, confiding, "That's the beautiful thing about old cars. Each scratch and ding tells a story. This car has seen it all—road trips, family outings, a couple of wrecks, and even a few races."

"Races! Wow, that's awesome. I've never been in a car with so much history." Zak gushed.

As if fueled by a magical magic, Sam began recounting tales of journeys with his car. "My son, Shaun, and I loved adventuring. He adored the rumble of the V8 engine and the wind in his hair as we raced down deserted country roads. We were more than father and son in this car. Shaun and I were buddies during those unforgettable summers." Sam's lower lip pushed up, and he sighed, quietly adding, "But…he passed on."

Zak listened intently, hanging on to every word. His mind painted colorful scenes of those cherished moments. He imagined himself behind the wheel, creating memories of his own. "Did..He….did Shaun die in Rosey?" Zak was curious.

"No, he veered his 4-wheeler to avoid a rabbit. His head hit a tree," Sam exhaled. Zak's question was unfiltered in the same way Shaun would have asked it. Sam switched off the reminiscence. "Come on out, I got work to do."

Zak turned to Sam, his face shining with gratitude. "Thank you, Mr. O'Riley, Sam, sir. This was... The best experience ever. I'll never forget it."

Incredulous, it was like he was looking into Shaun's eyes over twenty years ago.

—

"Sheriff? You have got to be kidding me?" Mantha laughed.

Ben walked over to Mantha with a playful grin, "Well, if it isn't little Sammy Dawson. Welcome back."

If looks could kill, the Sheriff would have been dead. "Call me that again and find out what it's like being on my bad side."

"Riley's could use a woman's touch," Ben straightened the crooked 'Trust in the Lord with all your heart' sign. "A little pink paint and some flowers, maybe?"

"Do I call you First Lieutenant, or do you prefer Sheriff Ben-neeee?"

Ben laughed, "So, what do I call you now, Captain? A lot of life has passed since we last saw each other."

She stood her ground, establishing new boundaries. "You protected me when I was a child like a big brother, Ben, I can take care of myself now. It's now Mantha. Samantha no longer exists. And Sammy Dawson passed on decades ago."

"Okaaaay. Have a blessed day, Ma'am," Ben tipped his ball cap. He sensed her stiffen and understood, recognizing the mental shield to fend off emotion—behavior that bore the mark of battle. "Come on, Zak, we must get everything on Kate's list at Homestead Provision."

—

Sam placed a hand on Zak's shoulder, and a gleam of pride sparked. "You're a good lad, Zak. Remember, there are always passions in life that can bring us joy. Never let anything hold you back from pursuing them, alright?"

Zak smiled. *It was the smile of his son Shaun, his cheekbones pressed into his eyes. It was unnerving.*

"Come on, Zak, we have a laundry list of errands and things to get for you. You'll need to find a job after I cover you for your supplies," Ben brought Zak and Sam out of reminiscing.

"We aren't doing extra laundry, Kate said. I need to gear up for school. Sam, can I come back and see Rosey?"

"Anytime, Zak. Anytime." Sam offered, then realized that he maybe should have set tighter parameters as the words slipped from his tongue.

"Nice to meet you." Zak waved.

"Goodbye, Rosey. Goodbye, ma'am," Zak bid farewell to the 1940 Ford Coupe and the smiling woman. He dreamed of the day he could create his own experiences with a vintage car, as Sam did with his son, Shaun, so long ago.

—

"Nice kid," Sam rubbed his chest.

"Yep."

Sam stood by the blue tarp covering a large object. "Zak reminds me of Shaun. Strong, powerful memories came back as we talked. His walk. His talk. His smile. It is uncanny."

"Yeah, he's a good kid," Mantha shared. "So many like him served under my command, and they served well. Followed orders to perfection. Incredibly loyal. Kind. They were my mighty warriors during our most heated battles. They were not afraid to put their life on the line to sacrifice for a comrade. Just took the right kind of training. I loved them. I felt that same feeling for Zak."

Sam patted his heart. "Yes. Truth."

~5~
SHOP TIL HE DROPS

Standing the test of time, Homestead Provisions was not just a place to shop; Riverdale's small mercantile represented the essence of the community's shared values.

The Brakket family stocked simple, reliable goods essential to small-town living that were reasonably priced and functional. Tourists enjoyed its practical charm. Colorful products adorned wooden shelves; an appealing aroma of wool and flannel gave a down-to-earth welcome to customers. The shelves were neatly organized and stocked with care, and the sizes and colors of clothing on the racks were coordinated to maintain a sense of order. The toy department was filled with classic toys, puzzles, and games. The store was well known for its spectacular Christmas displays: the annual lighting was a town event with free candy canes, cocoa, and photos with Santa, who now happened to be Sam.

The Brakket family took pride in curating a wide and varied assortment of items, ensuring something for everyone. The store's size limited the availability of trends or novelties, favoring utility and convenience for the townspeople who would otherwise travel great distances to shop for necessities. The atmosphere was bustling with people of all ages, from children to the elderly, visiting on Saturdays.

"Good morning, Ben!" Peter Bracket greeted each local patron by name.

"Good morning, Peter," Ben smiled.

"What brings you in today, and who is this fine young man accompanying you?" Peter reached for the list in Ben's hand. "I don't think we've met."

"This is my nephew, Zak, who will be starting Riverdale High on Monday," Ben answered with courtesy.

Zak ignored the introduction and stared at the top shelf with a small display of rockets next to games. Ben turned Zak around by the shoulders. "Earth to Zak, we are here for clothes, not toys."

Peter eyed the list. "Zak, I can fix you up with most of this. Let's get five pairs of socks out of the way first." Peter grabbed a five-pack of white tube socks.

"Are there seams? Are they tight at the ankle? How high are they?" Zak asked pointedly.

"They are socks." Ben's patience was already waning with item number one.

"Same socks the other kids buy here," stated Peter.

"Same socks other kids buy?" Zak questioned, squinting dubiously.

"Same socks," Peter repeated.

"Can I see one?" Zak pleaded as Peter gently opened the package, handing one sock to Zak.

Zak turned the sock inside out and rubbed the seam across his cheek. Then, he measured the height of the sock up his calf. "These won't work. The seams are too big, and they are middle height and squeeze my leg. They are too scratchy. When they squeeze my calf my toes buzz."

"We'll take them. These are fine socks, Peter." Ben was taken aback by this weird response. *'Socks were socks.'* He grabbed a package of white briefs and put them into the basket.

"But—" stammered Zak.

"I told you no buts, and as long as I am paying, it is my way or the highway." Ben held the package of socks and five white briefs. "These are white."

Zak laughed. "You really expect me to wear whitey tighties! Man, they drive me nuts! They're so darn uncomfortable. It's like having a tight grip on my goodies all day long! It drives me crazy! Plus, those elastic bands feel like they're digging into my skin. My stuff can't breathe. It's like a torture device down there!"

"I see," mumbled Ben, hoping Zak would cut the volume. He noticed a wide-eyed boy about age ten snickering. Ben felt heat rising up through his collar into his face.

Zak was revving up into nonsense. He was now in tears. He struggled to communicate between yelling, gulps of air, and sniffles. "You don't get it. You don't understand. No one ever understands. I can't do anything if my mind is paying attention to itchy, scratchy pressure. I can't go to school and learn. I won't graduate!" His bent arms flipped up by his head and waved like pistons. He dropped to the floor eye level to the astounded ten-year-old hiding under a clothing rack.

Peter knelt beside the dysregulated teen, "Zak, I have a secret stash of items I keep in stock only for VIPs. Seems like you're a very important person." The wailing yielded to hiccups. "I don't have many VIPs." Zak bit his lip and listened. "Yep, you might become our top VIP."

"Let me handle this, Ben," Peter considered, "I have another sock-particular young man who says his socks can distract and overwhelm him. Beats me, but he likes these." Peter handed Zak another sock. "A quality sock helps him focus on other activities or tasks."

"It's not easy for me to find socks that feel good." Zak share cautiously. "The seams, and size, and material can be very irritating."

Peter nodded. "I ordered these special for another student. They are designed to address seamless sensory issues with soft, non-abrasive materials. These socks are created to provide maximum comfort and reduce irritation for customers with sensory sensitivities."

Zak tentatively took the black sock. "Wow, these are perfect. I didn't know they even make sock like this." He rubbed it across his cheek and measured it on his leg. "One problem."

"OK," said Peter.

"No. They are not OK. They are black. I want white," corrected Zak.

"Black is perfect and looks cleaner longer," Ben jumped to speed things up. Peter looked up with a clear I will handle this.

"Have you tried any other types of underwear that might be more comfortable?" Uncle Ben diverted his eyes to Peter, who was grinning from ear-to-ear as he invited Zak to shop further. "Let's look, we have a good selection of novelty boxers. I reckon you can't go wrong with regular boxers. They're loose, comfortable, and allow for plenty of breathability."

Peter offered Zak a variety pack of boxers. "Nothing quite like the freedom and airflow that comes with boxers. Ain't nothing worse than feeling squished up all day long. When it comes to style, regular boxers are where it's at. They come in all sorts of colors and patterns— you can express yourself."

By now the ten-year-old eavesdropper was holding his mouth with both hands to keep laughter from exploding beneath the sweatshirt display. His round cheeks turned red, and tears streamed from his eyes. It was his lucky day to ear hustle an underwear conversation that included the town sheriff!

"Support, schmupport!" Said Zak, not willing to negotiate. "Uncle Ben, I've been trying to upgrade my underwear game lately. I'm thinking about switching to boxer briefs. They have style."

Uncle Ben looked perplexed. He had never thought underwear shopping could take a guy this long. His style was enter, see, bag, and buy, he shopped like his hunted.

Peter offered, "Of course, buddy. Let's find a solution that works for you. Everyone has needs and preferences. I hear you about boxers. They offer little to hold things in place, especially during physical activities. On the other hand, boxer briefs give a snug fit that keeps everything in check but doesn't bind up. I have three pairs of boxer briefs - red, green, and black."

"Aunt Kate said I need five pairs, and I don't like green," Zak shrugged.

"What colors do you want? I can add three to next week's order," Peter suggested.

"Black, no blue, how about more red—" Zak looked around while thinking about the colors he would like.

"Zak, we don't have all day for this. Black is perfect for your needs," Ben turned to Peter. "Please order two black and one pair of white. White briefs are necessary. You can't always wear black or red underwear. You'll get used to them quickly."

Zak opened his mouth to protest, but Ben cut him off. "Zak, I don't have time for this. Peter is telling you what you need, and you need to listen. He said boxer briefs are the way to go."

Zak looked at Peter and then at Ben, taken aback by their assertiveness. "OK, Peter, I'll trust you on this."

Ben scoffed. "Modern, schmodern! There's somethin' timeless about good ol' boxers. They've been around for ages, and folks still prefer 'em. Ain't no need to be all fancy and uptight with those snug boxer briefs. Probably cost double."

"They do," said Peter, pausing, smirking at Ben, "cost double. You'll thank me later. Take a break, Sheriff. I can handle this order." Peter flicked his wrist toward the door, indicating he would continue to handle Zak, and Ben needed a break.

"I reckon it's all personal preference—different strokes for different folks. Just make sure whatever you choose gives you comfort and confidence, Zak. As long as you're happy with what's huggin' your nether regions, that's all that matters. Consider this a loan, and you can pay me back," Uncle Ben compromised. "Peter, you got this. I'll be at the market. Put it on my tab; I'll return later." Ben took a deep breath, relieved to be free of Zak and the clothing problem, and left the store.

The ten-year-old spy under the rack now had his hands planted on his chin in rapt amusement at the performance. Zak grinned at him playfully, holding up his new trophy socks and underwear like a boy the same age as the spy.

———

Lindsay Larkin sold homemade baked goods and jams from a white plastic table with two mismatched plastic chairs at the Saturday market. She was a hardworking, stable woman that Riverdale had come to love. Four days a week, she waited tables at Dee's Cafe, helped Margie with the early morning baking, and supplemented her income at the market. As a single mom, she was raising two teens. Q was a senior and also worked at the cafe. Shay, age 16, helped her mom and volunteered at the Memory Care Center.

"Hello, Lindsay. How are sales today?" Ben greeted her politely.

"Fine, Ben," Lindsay forced. Even after fifteen years of sobriety, Lindsay felt unsettled around the Sheriff. She had experienced too many past encounters to feel relaxed or friendly. The mutual relationship between her and law enforcement remained uneasy.

"A dozen pecan pumpkin cookies and a loaf of your multigrain bread would be perfect," Ben pulled out his wallet.

"Uncle Ben, Uncle Ben!" Zak came running, tripped on a tree root, and landed on the soft bag of clothes.

A cute, wide-eyed teen jumped up to offer assistance. "Are you OK?" The beautiful girl offered Zak her hand!

"I'm OK," Zak stared with his mouth open.

"I'm Shay; who are you?" The girl pulled him to his feet.

"Zak," he smiled eagerly.

"Are you new?" She asked.

"No, I'm eighteen; that's not too new," Zak replied.

"No, silly, are you new to Riverdale?" Shay smiled, covering a near-giggle with her hand, then resting it on her hip, awaiting a response.

"I guess so," Zak answered, turning his head over his shoulder to catch another look as he followed Uncle Ben back to the store to pay the tab. "See ya."

—

"Wow, Peter! That's quite a bill there. Two Hundred twenty-nine dollars and fifty-two cents! I had no idea someone could spend that much money in your store." Ben scratched his ball cap.

Peter laughed, "Don't worry, Ben. Here's Kate's list for Zak, and we've checked off everything except the three pairs of boxer briefs that will arrive next Friday. Homestead Provision appreciates your business, and Zak will be all set for his new school experience."

"Amazing, Peter!" Nodded Ben in appreciation.

"I can't thank you enough for everything. I am grateful for your help." Zak was sincere in his thankfulness.

"Let's get home." Ben opened the bag of fresh cookies for him. "Here, have a cookie, Zak."

As they walked away to the car, Shay waved discreetly behind him. Zak looked back, caught the wave, and was sure he'd made a real friend. He waved back. She was cute.

—

Ben and Zak returned home with shopping bags that Kate unpacked at the dinner table. "Looks good, Zak. Seems like Uncle Ben took good care of you."

"Peter did," Zak said as Ben looked away.

"I got all the paperwork for your high school admission into Doc Johnson. He's our new principal this year," Kate added.

"Doc Johnson?" Ben did not look happy.

"I'll put this stuff in my room." Zak was not interested in their conversation. It sounded too much like how Mom and Dad's tone changed when they talked about him. He bounded three steps at a time up the stairs.

"Mike, you remember him as Mike. He was in my graduating class. He has been going by Doc since his time as a medic." Kate continued, "He's doing an excellent job."

Ben remained quiet, with an impassive expression as if sorting mixed recollections without wanting to delve too deeply into the subject as Kate finished the arrangements.

—

Kate drove Zak to his first day at Riverdale High School. Unlike his city school, grades seven through twelve, middle and high school students were housed in the same building. Upon their arrival, a tall, slender, middle-aged, handsome man smiled a greeting toward Zak and Kate in the parking lot.

"Hello, I bet you are Zak, grade twelve," Doc observed as Zak flipped his hood up, hunched his shoulders, and peered at his red shoes, his feet fidgeted and hands jammed into the front pockets of his sweatshirt. There was no eye contact.

"I've been told you love Astronomy. Well, you sure have come to the right school with one of the best teachers," Doc said admiringly, looking directly at Kate. "Kate was chosen Minnesota State Science Teacher of the Year. That's a mighty special peer endorsement."

Zak flashed a grin at Kate—he did not trust counselors or principals.

Kate blushed. "I have to get ready for class. Thank you for taking this on today, Doc. I know it was short notice."

"Anything for you, Kate." Doc's eyes sparkled as he lingered on her smile. "See you at lunch."

Kate's smile glowed. '*They are good friends,*' thought Zak. '*Maybe this guy deserves trust.*' He'd wait. He learned early on to watch carefully as words and actions did not always match. People tricked and surprised him. He thought of the girl at the market. He was thankful he had met Shay and hoped to find her at school. Transitions to new environments or experiences made his stomach tighten into a knot.

"Where's the bathroom? Where's the lunchroom? Who are my teachers? Do I get PhyEd?' Zak strung together sentence upon sentence as if he was afraid to lose a thought through a conversation. He seemed anxious, in reality it was his way of gathering information.

"Quiet," responded the principal. "I will answer all those questions in my office."

Zak followed Doc Johnson to his office, where he signed admittance papers. He tried to listen as Doc rambled. The man described classes, schedules, and school rules. ...*blah blah blah blah blah blah.*

Zak watched the girls' gym class run cross country. Doc's office had a big window. His mind floated. He had learned to mask by pretending to pay attention to lecturing teachers with brief, polite replies. "Uh-huh. Yes, mmm. Thank you, I appreciate that," Zak inserted occasionally.

The principal droned on ...*blah blah blah blah.. blah blah blah.*

"Yes, sure, okay, I can, uh huh," he camouflaged, his mind elsewhere.

"Do you like astronomy?" Doc Johnson leaned forward with hands wide open.

The man's face suddenly came into view, and he genuinely listened. Zak's head snapped up toward the principal.

"The only class we have is with Ms. Jordan. Can you handle that this semester?"

"Of course I can!" Zak's head was cleare and hyper-focused as Doc rattled off his new class list.

"Your transcripts state you need seven credits to graduate. Your high school coursework must include at least the minimum state credit requirements. I've set you up for a first-hour Supportive Study Hall, which should give you time to catch up with assignments before your day starts. We will get the tough stuff out of the way. You'll be one credit short, and our school has a special work project program you can use to fill in. I believe we can make that happen, Zak."

"Work project?" Zak cocked his head; he owed Uncle Ben a chunk of change.

"Riverdale High believes in getting our students work-ready. You earn your final credit when you get a part-time job and keep it all year. If you can prove you can work, you deserve to graduate. A high school diploma is worth $10,000 additional each year of employment. If you work until age 65, you can plan to make one-third of a million dollars more than a non-graduate in your lifetime. It's worth the effort."

"A million dollars?" Zak drooled. His brain was at full attention now.

"Statistics state about $350,000," the principal continued. "The rest of your classes are Communications, Astronomy, Algebra, Civics, Art, and Health/PhyEd."

Doc handed a thick, overwhelming package to Zak. *… blah blah blah blah blah blah. A fresh start, a new family, and do over. Find a job.*

"Second hour Algebra starts in 20 minutes. I'll show you the library; to wait. Algebra is in Room 3 and is right across the hall."

—

The library display was filled with science books, a fabulous fungi book, an even better book on rocks, and another big window where a beautiful cheerleader walked past in a uniform with the word Rockets across her chest. Zak followed her bouncing hair with rapt attention like a crow riveted to the sparkle of a shiny bauble. *Was his school really called the Riverdale Rockets? The girl was captivating. She had a warm smile and seemed friendly.* He needed more friends. He followed her.

The girl suddenly did an about-face. Her voice unnerved, "Weirdo, are you stalking me?"

Zak dropped his gaze to his red sneakers and shuffled his feet. "No! I..I..I'm looking for the Algebra room. It's my first day. Could you help me?"

"I'll drop you at the classroom door." She said curtly. "My name is Missy." "Follow me."

Zak moved in too close for comfort. "My name is Zak."

"You're in my space bubble, dude; step back." She rolled her eyes, shook her head in disgust, pointed at the Algebra door and disappeared.

Zak was confused. "I never saw a space bubble. Girls? She started out friendly." He said to himself as he walked up to the teacher's desk.

"Well, hello, Zak. Doc Johnson informed me that you would be in my class today; here is your book, and I have you sitting right in front of my desk." Zak liked front-row seating as the only distraction he had was the teacher.

The teacher began: "Remember, algebra is like a fancy way of solving puzzles using letters and numbers. Instead of adding or subtracting, we use letters called variables to represent unknown numbers. It helps us find the numeric value of these variables and solve complex problems even when we don't know what actual number we will find when we first start out. Algebra lets us work our way there to the right number."

Puzzles and mysteries intrigued Zak, so he tried to listen. This was the third time he had taken an Algebra class. He hoped this time, the learning would stick. The teacher wrote on the whiteboard. "It can be tricky at first. Algebra follows specific rules called the order of operations. We start with parentheses and then do any calculations involving exponents or roots. Next, we multiply or divide from left to right. Finally, we add or subtract from left to right as well. Following these rules helps us solve algebraic problems step by step."

Zak missed words as he worked on his lyrics. Too many steps uncoupled in his mind. He could follow the rules if shown what to do in sequence, a step at a time. A student raised his hand.

"Yes, Q," said the teacher.

Q stated, "That makes sense. It sounds like algebra is about using the proper steps, then operations to find the correct answers."

Zak could not hold his quiet. "Exactly! It may seem complicated, but the more we practice, the easier it gets."

Q added, "It's useful in real-life situations to solve problems with unknown quantities. It helps in understanding patterns and relationships in numbers. Algebra is a power tool."

Zak looked at the teen in the back of the class; that was one smart dude! An astronomy book was on his desk next to the algebra book. Aunt Kate taught the only astronomy class. He would check Q out. Intelligent people were often crucial to his survival. His heart leaped through his chest as he followed the boy named Q into astronomy. Students pointed at him and whispered about him with their hands over their mouths. '*I know they are talking about me!*'

Ms. Jordan said, "Zak, you can sit in this middle desk."

Zak froze, planting his back to the wall, hoping to be swallowed. "I can't sit there, Aunt Kate; I mean, Ms. Jordan, ma'am."

Student's snickered. "Oh, I am sure you can sit there. Just walk up and sit down."

"I can't do it, ma'am," repeated Zak.

Ms. Jordan stood like a tin soldier, pointed at him, and motioned him to MOVE NOW to that desk. Her eyes were locked on her nephew.

Zak's brow furrowed. Reluctantly, he walked to the desk and passed by eye-rolling students. Q, who sat in the far back corner, stretched. His crossed legs stuck out from the desk, and he locked his fingers behind his neck. He gave Zak a wide smile.

Zak sat as Ms. Jordan began teaching on the ionosphere. He locked his ankles around the chair legs.

"The ionosphere is a layer of Earth's atmosphere that contains charged particles called ions. It starts around 37 miles or 59.5 kilometers above the surface of the Earth and extends up to several hundred kilometers. The ionosphere is divided into different layers, each with unique characteristics."

Zak tapped his fingers on his desk. His aunt continued teaching. "The Sun's energy is the main source of ions in the ionosphere. Sunlight contains ultraviolet radiation that ionizes the atoms and molecules in the upper atmosphere, creating ions. These ions are positively charged, while the electrons released are negatively charged."

Zak sat on his hands, bouncing with the pulse of the flickering overhead lights. His heart pounded. He strained to capture every word as if gluing a mental picture together.

"The ionosphere plays an important role in our everyday lives. It affects the propagation of radio waves, allowing long-distance communication through the reflection and refraction of these waves. This enables various forms of wireless communication such as radio broadcasting, satellite communication, and even GPS navigation."

Zak gripped his wiggling chair seat, his ankles shaking.

"Furthermore, the ionosphere is responsible for the phenomenon of auroras. Auroras occur when charged particles from the Sun interact with the ions in the upper atmosphere, causing them to emit colorful lights. These lights can be observed near the Earth's poles, creating breathtaking displays known as the Northern and Southern Lights."

Q put his hand to his chin in understanding as he watched the new student's erratic behavior. *'Symptoms of over-stimulation,'* he surmised. *'Perhaps asking Zak where he could sit to learn best would be a practical and helpful solution.'* It was a logical conclusion to what he was witnessing.

"Due to its ability to reflect radio waves, the ionosphere also plays a role in meteorology. Scientists can use the ionosphere to study the movement of large-scale atmospheric waves and monitor changes in the upper atmosphere, helping in weather prediction."

"In summary, the ionosphere is a layer of the Earth's atmosphere filled with charged ions," Ms. Jordan continued as Zak's desk shook like a rocket ready to launch.

Zak fidgeted. He wiggled. His legs rattled up and down, pumping wildly underneath his desk. He could see Kate looking at him, but he couldn't understand what she was saying anymore. Student attention moved from the lecture to Zak, who looked as if he and his desk were ready to blast off.

"It affects the propagation of radio waves, causes auroras, and aids in meteorological studies." Ms. Jordan continued.

Zak's legs jiggled like pistons, pumping faster, higher, wilder, until he and the whole desk tilted over, crashing to the ground. Zak lay tangled in a pile, complete with scattered notebooks and texts, beneath his desk on the floor as all eyes locked onto him like a herd of piercing headlights. He couldn't make out the whispers around him or grasp what his Aunt Kate was saying until…

"…Launch sequence aborted. Captain Zachary Jordan, please return your rocket ship to its launch pad. This amateur craft lacks the speed, propulsion, and fuel capacity to break through Earth's ionosphere, rendering it a potential hazard upon re-entry. Thank you for the demonstration."

Zak looked around. Suddenly, the eyes passing judgment offered approval. He lifted himself and righted his desk. "Permission to relocate to a westerly launch pad, Ms. Jordan?"

"Permission granted." Kate offered Zak a smile as he dragged his desk toward the far side of the classroom. Students cleared a path as he resettled in the front right corner, away from the window and nearby seats.

—

Q remained after class to talk to Ms. Jordan. "Um, excuse me, ma'am. I may have an idea about what happened to Zak today. Sitting at that desk would've been difficult for me, and I can relate to it because I used to act similarly when I was younger. You see, the light right above that desk is fluorescent, and being neurodiverse like me means that it creates a sensation of movement in my world. I tried my best to synchronize myself with that movement when I was younger."

Q squared his shoulders, turned, and walked out.

Ms. Jordan froze, absorbing this newfound insight.

—

Thankfully for Zak, the next class was art. The assignment was to illustrate a mechanical item. Zak immersed himself in rendering a detailed rocket blasting off into the ionosphere. His drawing abilities were exceptional.

"Wow, you really can draw good," admired the boy across the table.

"Are you related to Ms. Jordan?" Asked another.

"Yeah," said Zak.

"Man, that was the coolest thing I ever saw a new student do. Did you guys plan that rocket ship demo this weekend to wake us up?" Questioned another curious boy.

"Not really," Zak's response was flat as he returned to adding depths of shade to his rocket. Soon the smell of spaghetti sauce lost his concentration, and the bell rang. He followed his nose and a mob of students to the lunchroom.

—

Mrs. Jordan cleared her desk and took a moment before joining the faculty for lunch.

As she exited, the principal, Doc Johnson, blocked her door. "Kate, I need a word with you. The lunch room is buzzing with how you handled your nephew throwing his desk in your room today."

"What happens in my classroom is my business," Kate tried to exit through the open side, but Doc blocked her.

"Everything that happens in your classroom is everyone's business. And you know that, Kate. Welcome to the modern school."

"I need to be trusted to handle my students my way."

"Your nephew needs to be handled. Period. What if that desk would have hit another kid on the head?"

"It didn't." Kate retorted.

"But, if..." Doc pressed as Kate threw her hands in the air. "I'm on your side, okay? Let's get him graduated and out of our lives. See you after school."

"After school?" Kate questioned.

"Committee meeting," Doc smiled.

–6–
ALIGNMENTS &
ASSIGNMENTS

ak focused on the scent of spaghetti, trying to ignore the bodies, smells, and sounds of the lunch line. He honed in on grabbing two extra garlic breads.

"Do you have lactaid milk?" Zak asked.

"No. We got this!" Blurted out a large boy dispensing the cartons. "We got milk!" The boy grinned, proud of his meme memorization.

"Is that all?" Pushed Zak.

"We got milk!" Repeated the boy.

Zak took the milk, mumbling, "They'll be sorry." The unfamiliar environment bombarded his senses with a cacophony of stimuli—harsh fluorescent lights, echoing chatter, and pungent smells. Zak's heart raced, his stomach churned as he stepped into the crowded seating area of the cafeteria. He squinted his eyes at the maze of a room for an open seat: lights flickered and bounced from floor to ceiling. Mouths chewed and chattered. Sounds crisscrossed. Smells collided.

"Too many people. Where can I sit? Who can I sit with? Where is the bathroom? Too many faces," Zak muttered aloud as he tried to navigate the overwhelming new environment and gather the visual markers he needed to orient. He was desperate for information and swam through the overload with self-talk. What seemed zoned out and expressionless to teachers and therapists was thought integration to focus. It was uncanny. Through the labyrinth of sensory chaos, he finally recognized Q.

Zak carried his tray to that table where the teen sat peacefully, absorbed in a book, oblivious to the surrounding world where Q found solace in the back corner of the lunch room. It was the darkest cafeteria area and it lined up with the teachers' tables. The other students referred to the area leper colony table. It was a safe place for Q to refuel his introversion bucket before returning to the battle of people-crammed classrooms and chaotic hallways.

Gathering his courage, Zak stopped behind the table, trying to access the boy's name from his brain. 'His name was a letter.' Zak whispered, 'a b c d e f g h i j k l m n o p q q q q Q...' "Q!" Zak barked.

Q was so startled that his rear lifted, his arms flailing, and he almost choked. His book departed his hands and just missed landing in his spaghetti sauce. *Who was barging into his domain?!* Then he recognized Zak.

"Hey, could I sit with you?" Zak placed his tray on the other side of the table and performed a short breakdance.

Q sharp brown eyes met Zak's gaze. He typically struggled with unexpected social situations, but he managed a slight smile and offered Zak to join him. The breakdance created a chuckle. *"Impressive,"* thought Q, *"And ballsy."*

Zak returned the smile and sat. Q rolled his spaghetti precisely with his fork placed on his spoon. Zak chased his noodles and used his bread to sop up the sauce. Q drank his milk in sips, and Zak gulped all 8 ounces in one chug with a throaty burp finale. Q gently patted his clean lips with a napkin. Zak wiped his face on his sleeve.

The girl from the farmers market, whose mom made the best cookies he had ever tasted, joined the table, chirping, "Hi, Zak, remember me?"

"How can I forget you? You saved my life!"

"Do you remember my name, Zak?" The girl tested.

Zak's mind went blank. He remembered meeting her. He remembered her hands. Why didn't he remember her name?

"That's OK, Zak, I'll help you. Listen! Lay (she pointed her fingers down and along the table). Day (she made an "o" shape for how the sun crosses the sky down to the horizon, signing "Day"). Play (her pointer fingers became the conductor's hands). My name is... she repeated the actions–lay (she pointed her finger down and along the table), day (she motioned to the sun crossing the sky), play (the pointer fingers became conductor's hands), and my name is —" the girl paused with eyebrows raised.

"Shay!" Shouted Zak. "Your name is Lay-Day-Play Shay!"

Shay's face radiated. "You are remarkable, Zak. Remarkable."

Q wrinkled his forehead. "Dear sister, how did you create such a mnemonic?"

"Q, it is how my brain works to get unstuck," answered Shay.

"Explain, I am interested," offered Q.

"I use my body to remember rhymes. Mama always says, 'There's no rhyme or reason to how I think,' so I took her 'no' out and added the rhymes to the reasons," replied Shay.

"Quite interesting, I shall delve deeper into that," remarked Q.

Zak watched the conversation like a sports match. "It works. Shay, it works for me, too. Except I rap," Zak said.

"Like poetry," stated Q. "Rhythm with rhyme."

"Show me!" Shay clasped her hands in anticipation.

Zak stood on the table bench, wiggled his body to get a good position, and let loose. He walked up and down the bench. The teachers took notice as he took a deep breath and exploded. No one knew, Zak's experience in three failed Algebra classes created his lyrics.

"Yo, listen up, let's break it down

Time to rap about the math in town

Algebra's the name, equations it's game

Gonna show you how it all became the same!"

Zak jumped upon the table. The trays rattled and clattered. He twirled, pointing directly at Q and then Shay. The wide-eyed Algebra teacher turned to watch.

"Solve for X, that's the first step

Keep it balanced, not totally inept

Add, subtract, do the multiplication

Divide it all. That's an equation."

Zak stepped down to the bench, elbows out, hand syncing to the strong beat of his riff.

"Now, let's solve for unknowns.

You got this, I got this— WE got this.

No need to fret or miss

You got this, I got this — WE got this.

Combine like terms,
Simplify with ease
Gonna make math flow
Like a gentle breeze."

Q outright laughed as Zak jumped, both feet landing back up on the lunch table. Shay grinned and squealed. Zak had full memory moments for each line.

"Solve for X, that's the first step
Keep it balanced; don't let it slip
Add, subtract, do the multiplication
Divide it all. That's the equation of persuasion."

Zak jumped straight off the table as all the teachers gaped at the lunch show. Students left tables to watch.

"Quadratic equations, they're a little tricky
'cause they're a little bit sticky
Use the quadratic formula way,
Gonna conquer math without delay."

And he remembered his chorus repeated the same way.

Shay chimed right in with him.

"Solve for X, that's the first step
Keep it balanced; don't let it be inept
Add, subtract, do the multiplication
Divide it all. That's the equation."

The music teacher, head bopping to the rap next to the math teacher, noted a bridge.

"Algebra, we rock this game
No matter the variable, we can tame
So put your hands up, let's shout it out loud
Algebra's math wows our crowd."

Then, back to the chorus, the same movements now synchronized with Zak, Shay, and three more rap-loving students.

Q analyzed and memorized the rap in silence.

"Solve for X, that's the first step

Keep it balanced; don't let it be inept

Add, subtract, do the multiplication

Divide it all. That's the equation."

Zak lunged back on the top of the table, engulfed in his performance.

"Algebra, it's about the unknowns

But with these tools, we won't be in a groan zone!

Remember the rap. It's your guide

Mathematical genius, you have arrived!"

Surprised by staff, Doc Johnson let the behavior slide. The Algebra teacher applauded. Ms. Jordan smiled. There was something enchanting, yet quite frustrating, about that young man.

"That was cool, Zak. Can you show me how to do that? What are your next classes?" Shay was blown away.

Zak pulled out the crumpled paper. "Communications. Civics. Health/PhyEd."

"I also have Communications next and Health/Phy Ed last," said Q.

Shay batted olive green eyes, "We have Civics class together. I can come to get you at Communications. We can walk together."

"Let's go, Communications class starts at 12:45." Q was already moving toward the door. "We can't be late."

"It's not 12:45 yet," said Zak.

Shay reached out her hand. "Silly, you gotta do zoom-to-room time. Let's go." She jumped up childlike. "See you soon!" She blew him a kiss.

"She blew me a kiss. Oh, blankity blank blank, she blew me a kiss," Zak whispered, awestruck.

"I believe, sir, that my little sister has, shall we say," Q paused, "the hots for you. We must traverse now to class. It is inappropriate to be late for a class at Riverdale High. You could end up with an after-school detention ticket."

Zak followed Q, whispering, "She blew me a kiss. Oh, blankity-blank, she blew me a kiss."

—

Communications class was divided into three semesters–speech, debate, and drama. This semester was a speech. The room had large windows with natural lighting but was too high to see outside. Instead of desks, the classroom held tables in a horseshoe with two rows.

Q's table had an empty chair, so Zak sat there. Having Q by his side comforted him. When he did not understand, Q asked the precise question to help him understand. He hoped Q was his friend. The Communications teacher had been sitting next to the Algebra teacher in the lunchroom and clapped. "Zak, I would like you to come to the front of the class."

Typically, if he'd been called to the front of the room, he had been disgraced, dismissed, or humiliated. He knew that teachers were capable of more hurtful bullying than the students. He looked at Q for guidance. Zak's feet burned into the floor.

"Safe," Q mouthed.

Not wanting to repeat the rocket experience in this class, Zak carefully pushed back his chair, triple-checked for clearance, and plodded forward, his head and shoulders drooped shrinking to classmates.

"Zak, I saw something exceptional today in the cafeteria. We are studying speech and this week, types of speech using poetry to communicate through history. Today, my assignment was to find, memorize, and analyze a poem by Emily Dickinson. Do you know who she is?"

"No," Zak answered.

"You may sit here next to me." The teacher sat in a chair next to Zak. Zak did not feel quite so singled out sitting on an equal level. "We are going to team teach this, Zak. I will tell the class about Emily Dickinson, and you will bring us 150 years into another style of poetry speech. I will stop in the middle of my teaching and ask you a question. As my team member, are you willing to answer?"

"I guess so," said Zak, crossing and uncrossing his feet. He glanced at the teacher who was looking at him. "I mean, yes."

The teacher read, "Emily Dickinson was an American poet who lived from 1830 to 1886. She is widely regarded as one of American literature's most influential and innovative poets. Dickinson was born in Amherst, Massachusetts, where she spent most of her life in relative seclusion."

She paused, "Zak, do you know what year you were born?"

"2006."

"How many students here were born in 2006," asked the teacher.

"Wow, half this class shares your same birth year, Zak."

"During her lifetime, Dickinson wrote almost 1,800 poems, but only a handful were published while she was alive. After her death, her sister discovered an extensive collection of her writings and arranged for their publication. Her poetry is known for its distinctive style, characterized by short lines, unconventional punctuation, and often exploring themes such as nature, love, and the mysteries of life and death."

"Zak, do you ever write down your poetry?" Asked the teacher.

"Yes. So I remember to use my lines later."

"How many students have written and never shared small or large poems? Or thought of a rhyme in your head and never shared it?" Asked the teacher. Every hand raised.

"See, Zak, every student in this class is interested in rhyme like you. Dickinson's poetry, unique in form and content, displays a profound sensitivity, keen observation, and a deep engagement with the complexities of human emotions. Her work often delves into themes of mortality, nature's beauty, the self, and the spiritual quest. Her poetry reveals a deep understanding of the world around her. Her poems often employ vivid imagery and metaphors to evoke a sense of wonder and to capture the essence of everyday experiences."

Zak noticed Missy at the side back table. She was so pretty.

"Dickinson's contribution to American literature and poetry can't be understated. Her innovative style and profound exploration of human experiences have earned her a secure place in literary history. Today, she is considered one of the most significant poets of the 19th century, and her poems continue to captivate readers with their emotional depth and thought-provoking themes."

"Zak, today you shared one of your poems with us in the lunchroom," nodded the teacher.

Hearing his name snapped his brain away from the girl. "Huh? Yes, of course." He shared his best smile, sat straight, and breathed deeply through his nose.

"Today's lesson will be to find a poem by Emily Dickinson and discover the chorus. In poetry, a chorus refers to a recurring group of lines or a stanza that regularly appears throughout a poem. It is similar to the concept of a chorus in music or theater. The chorus serves as a refrain, lending the poem a sense of rhythm and repetition."

"Zak, does the poem you shared today have a chorus?" The teacher encouraged.

"Yes. Yes, it does."

"And why did you put in a chorus, Zak?"

"I used it to repeat an important part and connect it," Zak continued.

"Yes, exactly. The purpose of a chorus in a poem can vary depending on the poet's intention. It may provide a thematic element or serve as a commentary on the main subject of the poem. The chorus can also act as a unifying or reinforcing element."

"Zak, what is your poem about?" He asked.

"Algebra."

"Why did you write a poem about algebra?"

"I hate algebra." Zak shared as students laughed. "I didn't understand it, and I needed to. Algebra is not going to stop me from graduating. Writing rhyme helps me remember things."

A few students clapped softly, and some gave thumbs up. From his seat, Q smiled in approval and nodded.

"Thank you for being transparent, Mr. Jordan. Would you stand up and share your chorus with this class? Who would like to hear Zak perform?" All hands raised. "Looks like you are on, dude. Stand up and show us what you've got."

"Are you sure?" Zak stood up and wiped his sweaty palms on his jeans. He looked up at the teacher.

"Yes, I am sure you will do great, Zak." The teacher assured him. "Typically, a chorus will have consistent wording or structure, though it may be modified slightly each time it appears to fit the specific context of the poem. The repetition of the chorus emphasizes its significance and can create a memorable and impactful effect. Zak, I believe the poem you recited in the cafeteria was captivating. You're on Zak."

Zak twirled as he spoke, danced, and commanded the floor.

"Solve for X, that's the first step

Keep it balanced; don't let it be inept

Add, subtract, do the multiplication

Divide it all. That's the equation."

The students applauded!

—

"Give it to us one more time, Zak, and whoever wants can chime in," offered the teacher. "I invite anyone who wants to stand up to move!" Six of the students dared to stand and chime in.

Zak began. Three more students stood. Q stood, which energized Zak's performance, and by the last stanza, everyone but the icy, cool cheerleaders were participating. That pretty girl sat with her arms crossed over her embroidered Rocket's patch.

"You may all be seated, the teacher continued. "Choruses in poetry can take various forms, such as a single line repeated throughout the poem, a distinct stanza appearing at regular intervals, or even an entire poem repeated verbatim. The use of a chorus can enhance a poem's overall structure and musicality while adding depth and resonance to its themes. Poetry helps our memories, and when rhyme or song is added our memories are enhanced even more. If I say—the wheels on the bus." The teacher's head bobbed. "And you say—"

"Go round and round," said the students, some added more verses with Zak getting totally into it and singing with abandon.

"You can see how this works. Speeches and sometimes single words spoken in history trigger a bigger message for those in the know. Now it's your turn. I will write the assignment on the board. You have all just participated in an interactive chorus. Thank you for helping me demonstrate this, Zak. You may sit down."

She wrote:

1. *Find a chorus in an Emily Dickinson poem.*

2. *Listen to your heart and write your own modern chorus for your life today.*

The bell rang, and Shay, with her beautiful green eyes was waiting.

"Can I carry your books, Shay?" Zak asked.

Shay handed over her books as Missy passed. "Weirdos," she hissed with a sneer, her hair bouncing as she pranced away with the other cheerleaders to her next class. She no longer wore her cheerleading sweater, under the sweater bounced a flimsy crop top.

Q raised his lip, a dog ready to bite, and a rumble sounded from the back of his throat.

~7~
CIVIC DUTIES

Zak swaggered walking Shay to class. He was grateful the only available desk was by a naturally lit window. There was no artificial overhead lighting. A day full of buzzing sounds made his head fuzzy. Buzzy-fuzzy made learning more difficult. Shay sat across the room.

Zak wasn't sure what Civics was, but if he had to take it to graduate and make more money, he was all in. If the class included Shay, he would make this work. The Civics teacher was a pretty female wearing an outfit with just the right amount of thigh when she sat at her desk, and Zak had a perfect line of sight. She remained seated as she taught, and Zak didn't take his eyes off her. To the teacher, it appeared she had his full attention, which, in one way, she had.

"Class, open your books to page 57. We will take turns reading and then discussing what we have read. We are moving along well with the U.S. Government Foundations. Today, we study your rights and responsibilities as a United States citizen. I want you to feel prepared to understand and handle these as they relate to our government, politics, and citizenship. Whoever in this classroom is already 18 years old, please stand?." Three students, including Zak, stood up.

"Who will be turning 18 before January 1st? Please stand." Nine students were standing.

"How about June 7th, Riverdale High School graduation day?" Out of thirty students, only six remained sitting; Shay was one of those six. "You may all sit down." The teacher went on.

"What do you think are the rights of a U.S. citizen?"

Zak excitedly raised and waved his hand. "My dad told me when I am 18, I can do whatever the hell I want." Students snickered.

The teacher smiled. "Zak, while it's great that your dad allows you more independence as you grow older, being a U.S. citizen comes with various responsibilities and rights. Rights include freedom of speech, religion, the right to vote, and the right to a fair trial. These are important for protecting our liberty as individuals. With rights comes the responsibility to obey the law, pay taxes, and participate in the democratic process. Citizenship is about enjoying our rights while honoring our obligations as members of a society. It's like we do here in our class, but on a more powerful scale: when everyone contributes, we succeed!"

Zak grinned mischievously. "Well, I guess I'll have to wait to explore those rights fully! But yeah, it's important to know our rights and responsibilities as citizens. Thanks for explaining it, teacher! I guess that 'doing whatever I want' does not mean everything."

"Everything, Zak, is a pretty broad term. Today, we'll cover individual rights and freedoms, such as freedom of speech, religion, assembly, and equality under the law. I want each of you to understand this well because with rights come important responsibilities. From there, we will move into civic participation and activism when individuals work together. I want you to understand the importance of civic engagement, community service, advocacy, and how change happens peacefully."

The teacher read from the top of page 57. "The rights and responsibilities of a U.S. citizen can be broadly categorized as follows." Then she paused and said. "Shay, will you read number 1 under Rights?"

Shay read slowly and steadily, pronouncing each word carefully. "1. Freedom of Speech: Citizens have the right to express their thoughts." She struggled with the next term. "And Op-onions."

Someone laughed. That kid had no right to laugh at Shay! Zak wanted to pull the kid out of his seat and slam him to the floor.

"O-pin-ions," corrected the teacher.

"Opinions," Shay continued. "And ideas without fear of government censorship or…" she paused.

"Reprisal," assisted the teacher softly.

"Reprisal," mirrored Shay.

"Class, let's break down the language, starting with the right to express our thoughts."

Zak raised his hand and yelled, "So that means the jerk that laughed at Shay has the right to do that?"

"So that means the weirdo by the window has the right to call me a jerk?" The boy retorted.

"You just called me a weirdo!" Zak shouted.

"You called me a jerk first!" Shouted the other teen. "Jerk!"

"Weirdo!"

The teacher placed two chairs three feet apart at the front of the room. "Boys, come, be seated, and remain silent."

Both teens sat silently, but continued to make underhanded expletive gestures and faces.

"Let's use this argument to review how freedom of speech works in real life. I will facilitate a respectful and open discussion about your differing viewpoints. Freedom of speech, a fundamental right in our society, allows us to freely express our thoughts, opinions, and ideas. One way to explore this concept is by hearing different arguments and perspectives. We now have that opportunity to hear two thoughts and opinions right before us."

"Zak and Scott, the principles of freedom of speech begin with a respectful and thoughtful debate. Zak, would you like to present your argument?"

"Wow, like Judge Judy. Cool. Make this make sense: 1. Shay has been asked to read. 2. That puts her on the spot, and, for me, when that happens, my heart beats faster, I get a dry mouth, it is hard to think, and harder to talk. 3. What Scott did was not kind."

"Thank you, Zak, for sharing your perspective. Scott, it is your turn to present your argument."

"OK, OK. This is hard. I am also a poor reader and struggle like Shay. I laughed to relieve my tension. I do it a lot because it helps after I make mistakes. But I didn't mean to hurt her."

"Thank you, Scott, for presenting your viewpoint. We just witnessed both students exercise their right to freedom of speech: each expressed their opinions. What they said arose from their different experiences. Remember that freedom of speech protects everyone's right to express themselves, even when their opinions differ. In respectful dialogue, we hear each other out. It means listening with patience, then speaking about our own experience, so we can really learn what is different and what we have in common to weigh our choices about what to do," explained the teacher.

"Now, let's open the floor to the rest of the class. Please remember to be respectful when sharing your thoughts and listen attentively to your peers. You can agree or disagree, but let's focus on a constructive discussion based on freedom of speech, hearing others' points of view, and critical thinking."

"Shay, would you like to say something?"

"Yes, I would. Scott's laughing made me feel more nervous. I wanted to quit, but I kept going because you encouraged me. You did not criticize or embarrass me. It felt good when Zak stuck up for me, but now that I know Scott struggles, too, I understand he wasn't trying to be mean. I get so nervous. But now…I realize it's not just me."

"How many students here struggle with something? I will be the first to raise my hand," offered the teacher. Every hand went up, including Zak and Scott.

"Who's willing to share their struggle with the class so we can use our freedom of speech to understand and support one another?"

"Hey Scott, I got mad because I struggle with a lot of things …so many I don't even know how many. The hardest thing is knowing something one minute, and then whatever I knew…disappears." Zak's voice quieted with eyes downcast. "Sorry, I called you a jerk."

"It's OK; I am sorry I laughed at you, Shay," Scott admitted. "And Zak, you're not a weirdo. Sorry, I said that when I got mad."

Everyone struggled with something hard, even though it was not a special education classroom! Out of the thirty students, all hands were raised for laughing at the discomfort of another. Seven had reading difficulties. Ten struggled with math. One student had trouble making friends, and then nine more jumped on difficulting in friendships, as they were no longer alone. Two students had food allergies; one disclosed he was a Type 1 diabetic.

"Freedom of speech is vital in a tolerant, democratic society. As a freedom it can be abused when we call others names, or it can allow positive understanding and change when we dare to speak up and share our point of view. Freedom of speech protects everyone, including students, who want to express their thoughts, debate respectfully, and understand diverse perspectives. For homework, please write a paragraph about what you learned today. And Shay," nodded the teacher, "I want to acknowledge your hard work and effort, especially with your reading.

It may be challenging sometimes, but remember that every small step you take toward improving your reading brings you more success. You're showing determination and a willingness to learn, and that's incredibly commendable. You're doing so well!"

Several students repeated similar sentiments on their way out of the class. "Shay, you're doing great." "Way to go, Shay. That was brave."

Zak reached down to give her hand a supportive squeeze as Q stopped by to lead him toward the gym. Q waited to enter, as Zak ran ahead.

—

"Hey Zak, do you need a gym uniform, or did you bring clothes?" Asked the deeply tanned gym teacher wearing a ball cap and dark mirrored sunglasses. "The weather is great today, and we will be playing soccer. Do you know the rules of the game?"

Zak shouted, "I LOVE soccer and I have gym clothes in my pack!"

"Well then, dude, suit up!" Mr. Thompson held his large whistle. "I EXPECT EVERY MAN ON THE FIELD BY THE TIME THIS WHISTLE BLOWS AGAIN." He gave a loud, sharp chirp for emphasis.

Zak quickly threw off his pants and hoodie and pulled on his shorts and t-shirt. He beat everyone outside to the field and ran a half-lap to get his mojo going. Aunt Kate was smart to cue him to bring shorts and an extra T-shirt in his backpack for phy-ed.

The vibrant green soccer field stretched out before me, a well-maintained natural grass playing surface. The air was brisk and fresh, and the sun was still warm for a late autumn day. A large, old, weathered wooden fence separated the soccer field from the football field. Soccer remained a less accepted sport than historic American football, as indicated by the concessions and two triple-row metal bleachers on each side that shouted privilege for the football team.

As Zak peered through a hole in the fence to see the larger football field, he noticed the sparse seating of the soccer field and knew that family, friends, and supporters gathered here, dedicated to cheering on their players. Everyone assembled, with the home team parents sitting next to the opposing team, as many folks knew one another or were related. The grandeur of the American Football field to the right, with a bandstand, dimmed with the warmth and camaraderie of neighborly competitor acceptance of the close-knit communities.

In a burst of energy, Zak scaled the fence and was about to leap over it onto the sporting event track. The track's rubber surface promised cushioned footing and enhanced performance. However, a glance around made him reconsider. The distance he would have to walk back to the soccer field was not worth the shortcut, and he decided against it.

Riverdale Rocket Football embodied the spirit of the community. Friday night lights illuminated the high school stadium, drawing crowds from rival teams. Friday football nights were packed: families ate hot dogs, drank sodas, and bought bags of chips, popcorn, and candy while turning out to support their team. A busload of rival supporters arrived energized and ready to cheer from their bleachers..

———

Unlike Zak, when Q entered the gym, his anxiety rose, and his stamina tanked. He despised gym class! The noisy, smelly percussion was a non-stop sensory assault.

The 'thwack' of rubber balls echoed off the wall, reverberating with shouts from all directions. He struggled with the blinding halogen lighting and overwhelming smells of sweat and used gear. Q escaped to the locker room to hide in a toilet stall. The whistle blew. He covered his ears in agony at the shrill vibrations scorching through his body. He pulled his knees to his ears as he cowered, rocking and groaning. Even hiding in a closed restroom stall with a secure metal bathroom door, the sharp sound attacked.

Q's body was so acutely oversensitive he had gone out of his way, managing to avoid physical education classes for three years. This was his final year, and there was no way around it. Q had enough credits to complete high school, but he needed that last credit from the gym to graduate. At least he would be outside today. He dragged himself out to the soccer field, hoping to avoid involvement. Mr. Thompson tried his best to help each student, and Q appreciated that, as previously, he had been humiliated and shamed for his neurodivergence. The tall trees surrounding the field swayed gently in the breeze, providing natural shade and a tranquil backdrop for the athletes. He noticed birds chirping and leaves rustling. He tried to focus on that.

———

Zak jumped down to warm up with high kicks and push-ups. He overlooked Q, who crept onto the field, cringing at the geese poop spread from one end to the other by the birds who had gathered on the grass. Physical education was Zak's passion, and so far, Zak's first day went pretty well. He was jazzed and ready to play soccer. Soccer was his favorite way to expend immense energy. He was in the zone. The players converged in midfield. Zak gazed at a pair of metal goals standing tall at each end of the field, anchored firmly to the ground. The netting looked sturdy, not saggy. If he were the goalie, it would give him an adequate challenge to protect his team's territory while the opponents tried to shoot the ball past him.

"Hey Coach, I am pumped for today's practice! I can't wait to show you what I've been working on!" Zak exclaimed.

"That's the spirit! I can see your energy level is through the roof today. What have you been practicing lately?" Asked Coach Thompson.

"I've been practicing my dribbling skills, specifically the inside-outside move. I think it's gonna be a game-changer for me," Zak shouted.

"The inside-outside move is an effective way to deceive opponents. Could you show me what you've got? I gather you have played before," encouraged Coach Thompson.

Not waiting to answer, Zak launched into dribbling, quickly alternating use of the inside and outside parts of his foot to manipulate the ball and shift direction. He changed speeds from fast to slow to fast.

"Your technique is impressive, and your quick footwork makes it difficult for defenders to anticipate your next move. I'm glad you're putting effort into improving your skills. Run over to the goal. I want to see your skills there," ordered Coach Thompson with another sharp report of his whistle. Q shivered and covered his ears, shrinking into the background while Zak, oblivious to the noise, engrossed himself, readying for play.

"I want to be a striker," protested Zak, allured by this position in the excitement of finding the back of the net.

"Get your butt to that goalpost now! You could be my ball boy if I WANT!" Barked the coach. He was clearly in charge and no longer playing. "Peterson, you're my striker, opposing team."

"But," whined Zak.

"Geezy," Scott Peterson raised his voice an octave. He was the kid in the civics class who'd called Zak a weirdo. There was still a grudge.

The coach blasted his whistle. "I don't accept buts! Say what you mean and mean what you say, goalie. Go now!"

Q, desperate to stay out of the way, fled across the field. Desperate to avoid actual involvement in the game, hoping to ride it out as a ball boy.

Zak bolted over into position as ordered. He did not yet realize that Mr. Thompson was the soccer coach, and Scott was a famous local striker who bore a grudge. Strikers are responsible for scoring goals, making them the focal point of any team's plan of attack. Zak assessed Peterson's speed, agility, and technical skills for maneuvering the ball as play began.

Knowing the explosive outcome, it dawned on him that maybe goalie wasn't such a bad idea. Zak's stomach rumbled. He felt the volcanic eruption in his bowels from the lactose-laden milk he had drunk earlier at lunch. A gaggle of geese honked as they flew overhead. A few landed to graze behind the net. Zak took his position, keeping a keen eye on Peterson.

During the game, Zak proved a formidable force for Peterson. Peterson deftly directed the ball away from an oncoming defender, creating space to assess the chance to attack. Then, with pinpoint accuracy, he delivered a perfectly weighted pass, lofting the ball gently over the defense directly into the path of his teammate. This precise pass set up his teammate for a slicing shot on goal that could decide the match. As the teammate received the pass to his chest, it dropped into the ready position, immediately setting itself up for a powerful strike. In an instant, Peterson took his lightning shot at the net! The ball soared through the air, with tension charged as students gaped.

Zak, eyes hyper-focused on the ball, stretched out like a panther, extending his reach. Time seemed to slow down as the ball hurtled towards the net. The Rocket's star striker had crafted the perfect setup. In a sublime display of skill and execution, the ball met the hands of the goalie just as the geese erupted in a bold blast of honking that masked a noisy explosion in Zak's bowels.

With a firm grip on the ball, Zak thwarted Peterson's attempt, leaving the students dumbfounded by the save. Zak stood tall, a smile of triumph on his face, his relief hidden by the distance between him and his peers, who were blissfully unaware of the invisible cloud of flatulence that had accompanied his heroic moment. Q smiled.

—

Aunt Kate stood outside the boy's locker room. "Hey, Zak. How did Day One go?"

Zak looked at his feet. "OK, I guess."

"Well, for day one, you made quite the impression," Kate smiled.

"I have an hour after students leave to prepare for tomorrow. You can do your homework in my room."

"Don't have homework," mumbled Zak.

"Yes, you do. I know of two things you have been given to do," said Kate. "Let's return to my room while I finish my work."

"I don't have to sit at that desk again, do I, Aunt Kate?" Zak asked.

"No, of course not," Kate shook her head. "Is there a better place for you to sit?"

Zak tried a couple desk spaces and chose the front desk where Ms. Jordan stood to lecture. "This desk space is perfect."

Aunt Kate tilted her head, "Please tell me more, Zak. I want to understand how your desk turned into a rocket ship."

Zak was hesitant. "You mean that I can tell you?"

"Yes."

"OK, OK, OK! Wow, really, like wow!" Zak was beside himself.

Kate placed her hands on her chin and leaned toward him.

"The light above that desk makes my head rattle. The ceiling buzzes like swarms of bees live inside those long, skinny light bulbs. My world bounces. I can't think. I can't read. I can't sit still." Zak recognized Aunt Kate was listening.

"What makes this desk space better, Zak?"

"I am right in front. There is no light right above me. Only five people can bug me instead of eight. I can pay attention," Zak paused. "Aunt Kate, can I ask you something? What made you think of making that crash into a rocket launch?"

"It fit into what I was teaching. It was a bit more dramatic than normal, but memorable. Something tells me the ionosphere will never be forgotten in my class," she chuckled. "Thank you for trusting me enough to share. You can sit here tomorrow."

———

Hi, Lindsay!" Mantha sat at the back table at Dee's, in a chair facing the door.

"Mantha, it's great to see you. Can I get you something?" Lindsay served hamburgers to another table of guests and quickly returned to take her order.

"Just a coffee and two pieces of Margie's famous Honeycrisp Apple pies to go." Mantha smiled. "Cheddar cheese on the side please."

"Sam loves that pie. Did he order you here, or are you surprising him?" Lindsay poured coffee into the beige mug. "Don't forget his cinamon ice cream."

"Surprise." Mantha smiled and lifted her coffee, smelling the roast and savoring its warmth.

"Well, well, well! Will you look at what the cat dragged in?" Lindsay turned, then bristled and scowled as the patron arrived.

Doc Johnson walked to Mantha's table and sat down. He ignored Linsay and did not have an invitation. "Great to see you, Sammy." A flirtatious smile crossed his lips as he commanded, "Lindsay, get me two hamburger plates and package the same takeouts: sweet potato fries and coleslaw."

Lindsay glared and set her jaw, meeting Mantha's eyes.

"Hello, Michael. My name is now Mantha." Mantha said flatly and focused on her mug. She preferred to dispatch the intruder to oblivion.

"And I have dropped Michael for Doc. It is Doctor Johnson now." He added, "I have my Ph.D. I am the principal at Riverdale High."

Mantha gave the briefest nod as an almost invisible wrinkle of disgust passed her lower lip. Lindsay dropped off the two plates of burgers. Doc ducked his head lower to make eye contact. Mantha stiffly froze him out in impassive refusal.

"It's been so long since we've sat together in this cafe. Same table. Same chairs. Exact placement," Doc crooned. "Remember."

"Not the same people," Mantha said with quiet authority.

"Oh, but we are the same people," Doc pressed. "We could start over from where we left off."

Lindsay watched from afar with the tension of a guard dog ready to lunge as she cut the pie, packaged it, and added an empty to-go box.

"Where did we leave off?" Mantha emphasized with cold irony. "My 4.0 GPA got me into West Point. If I remember correctly, your GPA was too low to go. I don't think you can slide in here and expect a relationship. Don't try to seduce me now because I am disabled. You are delusional. I have more grit with fewer body parts than you tried when I was seventeen."

Lindsay held back a poker face snicker as she set down the empty box and two pies. Mantha packaged her dinner and laid down a twenty-dollar bill. "Good night, Doctor... uh, Johnson," she said as she got up, adding a downward glance below his belt line for emphasis before warning him off with a direct stare of ice.

"Your to-go order is ready," Lindsay said coolly. "You'd better get it home before it gets too cold." Doc finished his dinner slowly, eyeing Lindsay with contempt.

—

Doc arrived home to find Nicole pour and then gulp her second mixed vodka and ginger ale. "What took you so long? Missy and I were waiting. You said you were coming straight home." She sipped.

"I brought you your dinners. It was busy at Dee's tonight, I had to wait." Doc rolled his eyes. He sighed at her insignificance hoping to shut down further discussion.

"Where's your dinner, Daddy?" Missy asked.

"I'm not hungry." He handed Missy the cardboard box. "Eat!" He gave her a dead stare and Missy knew from his look to avoid further conversation. She hated when his eyes dilated and seemed to pop out of the sockets ready to pounce.

"Why try? It's pointless." Missy thought. She stopped by the cupboard to snatch something to drink as her parents' voices in the parlor grew louder. Missy left, desperate for refuge as unwanted feelings welled up.

~8~
COOKIES &
DREAMS

The rhythm of Zak's schedule flowed with the cycle of his body. The freedom of first-hour Study Hall with Q allowed him to complete homework he'd forgotten. Astronomy in his newly assigned desk helped with his focus, art allowed him to relax, and PhyEd expended his pent-up energy.

Missy however, was a distraction and it didn't help when she removed her cheerleader sweater. Whereever he was going, Zak turned and followed her like a puppy.

Missy about-faced furiously and caught her dad's eyes watching at the end of the hallway. "Ouch! You swatted my butt."

Zak was shocked. "I did not!"

"You hit me!" She wailed.

Doc came in hot pursuit to save his darling. He chased Zak down and grabbed his arm. Zak turned to swing. In shock he stopped seeing the other end of the gripping hand was the principal. "Both of you into my office NOW!" Doc roared.

"But Daddy, he hit me," she pouted. "I didn't do anything wrong."

"Both of you! Into my office now!" He growled in finality, shooing them into his office. He loudly shut the door.

"Mr. Johnson, I didn't..." Zak stammered.

"It's Doctor Johnson, and I am the ONLY one with permission to speak. Sit!" The principal scowled at Zak. He side-glanced at Missy.

Zak sat, "I ..."

"Day three, you lie about inappropriately touching a sixteen-year-old girl."

"I ..."

"Day one, you threw your desk on the floor in Astronomy class."

"I ..."

"I AM still talking! Do you hear me?"

"Yes," groveled Zak.

Missy snickered and Doc handed his daughter her a pink zipper hoodie. "PLEASE put this on NOW. And zip it up!"

"But Daddy!" Missy pleaded, "It doesn't match what I am wearing."

"What you are wearing is inappropriate. Both of you out now! We will speak more on this when I get home, Miss-s-s-sy," hissed Doc Johnson. "You should be grateful. What if this was fabricated in your head?" Doc turned away from his daughter.

"Zak, I do not want to see you again today. Do you hear me?"

Zak's shoulders rose to his ears. He did not trust this man. Once again, a person in authority dismissed his reality, not letting him explain what happened. He was made to feel guilty for something he had not even done. He would stay out of his way, even if he had to hide.

—

Adding Zak into the mix of Shay and Q incited gossip about the strange trio as they drew closer together as friends. Their mother, Lindsay, was a classmate of Doc, Kate, and Mantha at Riverdale High School. Years later, Lindsay remained among the working poor in Riverdale, a fact that didn't define her but only fueled her determination. In her youth, she was a wild child known for her love of partying and her rebellious nature. She got pregnant in high school and then had a second pregnancy after graduation. No one knew what fathers. Her pregnancy and the birth of Shay was a turning point that led her to sober up and turn her life around. Despite her past, she had been sober for fifteen years. Lindsay had worked at Dee's Cafe baking pastries and bread, cooking, and waiting tables since she was sixteen. She sold produce and home goods at the local farmers market. The Riverdale community loved Lindsay's attentiveness, cooking, and baking.

Lindsay, Shay, and Q lived in an old double-wide trailer home on the edge of town just down the road from Riley's Garage. After settling down to raise her children, she earned the respect of skeptics as her children grew to be courteous, kind, and thoughtful youngsters. She clearly looked out for them and had taught them to look out for each other. At the far end of the family's five acres, Lindsay ran a boneyard filled with a maze of empty semi-containers. Previously an enormous truck garden, it was now a rental space for three local trucking companies that treated it as an all-purpose repository for bulk metal, tires, and other materials. Lindsay collected rent money.

—

Aunt Kate continued to help Zak learn new skills in place of rash re-actions and impulsive comments. She tried to focus him on the positive aspects of a small community where these social dust storms could pass if one kept their wits and handled themselves better next time. It seemed an uphill battle, there was always some new eruption. Once she got wind of the school lunch whole dairy milk situation, she provided Zak juice boxes. The juice was warm and he explained he liked things either hot or cold. Aunt Kate gave him the teacher stink eye and he knew better than to open his mouth. Uncle Ben found Zak an old bike, relieving Kate of chauffeuring. It wasn't a fancy bike, but it had working tires and brakes and since the town was small would get him where he needed to go.

—

Aunt Kate picked up a banana from the Ala Carte selection for teach-ers in the lunchroom. Zak noticed Doc saunter up behind her. He put his arm on her shoulder laughingly. Zak ducked under the table.

"Zak, what are you doing under the table?" Shay asked.

"Doc doesn't want to see me for the rest of the day, so I am hiding until he is out of sight. Keep watch for me!" Zak peered between the ta-ble top and the bench, seeing Missy drop her bag of carrots on the floor.

"All clear, Zak," Shay whispered.

Zak slid out, run and ducked under Missy's table to fetch the dropped carrots. "EEEeek, you weirdo! What are you doing looking up my skirt!"

"Hey! No, no, no!!!!! I was getting your carrots when they fell." Zak quickly got up and tried to run, accidentally throwing the carrots onto the table as he backed into Scott Peterson. Scott's tray crashed onto the table as he raised his fist. With his arms flailing, Zak unintentionally connected hard with Scott's cheekbone. He stopped Scott's fist in acci-dental self-defense and interrupted the impending assault.

"Fight! Fight! Fight!" the students shouted. Zak hurried back to his table, but rumors and gossip quickly spread throughout the school, leading to suspicions, assumptions, and general drama. Although entirely untrue, there was just enough plausible illusion. The gossip mill went into overdrive and shook the school. Zak was simply relieved to avoid the principal. Students chattered, embellished his escapades, and talked about him behind his back. To Zak, that was nothing new.

Thankfully, the first week Zak attended the new school only lasted three days. Thursday and Friday were the State Teacher Conference.

———

"Looks like you boys will have a weekend to yourselves," Kate announced after supper. She tapped her lips and folded her cloth napkin. "I've made a large tater-tot casserole that should last you until I return home. There's a vegetable tray and fruit platter. I bought two dozen pumpkin pecan cookies from Lindsay. Zak, you can ride over to pick them up at the trailer. She will be baking them fresh and they will be ready tomorrow morning."

Zak looked up. "Happy to help."

"That's the spirit, Zak," Uncle Ben nodded. "Kate, we will be fine. I am looking forward to a guy's weekend."

A horn honked, and Kate grabbed her bags. "Gotta go. Doc Johnson offered to carpool three more teachers. It will be nice to ride instead of drive this year." She kissed Ben sweetly.

Ben hugged her. "Have a great time, honey. See you Saturday night." Tossing her bags over her shoulder, she waved to Zak and shut the door.

"Zak, bus-S-S, please," Uncle Ben accentuated the SSS, "but do not bu-S-T the dishes." He emphasized the ST.

Zak let out a nervous laugh. His dad would have been furious if he saw him intentionally break his aunt's dish. Although Ben was unhappy, his uncle even helped him clean up and he didn't explode in anger. Zak also didn't feel threatened and at the mercy of punish every time he did something his father called stupid. Zak carefully picked up the plates and cups and placed them on the counter.

Uncle Ben opened the dishwasher. "In this house, we have a routine. After supper, I expect you to bus, rinse off, and put the dirty dishes here. We run the dishwasher, add the soap, and turn it on. Then, we put the clean dishes away before bed to start fresh in the morning."

Ben went to watch TV, leaving Zak with a sense of responsibility and the importance of daily chores.

Zak crammed the dishes into any available space. He placed silverware on the rack, arranged bowls and cups face-up to catch water, and mixed Aunt Kate's wooden utensils in with the pots and pans. He did not rinse them. A blue bottle of dish soap sat by the sink. He squirted some and then added more for good measure. After taking a second look, he filled a bowl halfway, hoping there was enough soap. He closed the lid and turned the dial to pots and pans cycle to ensure they got clean. The note inside the door read, utilizes high temperature and increased water pressure to effectively remove tough, baked-on food residues and grease.

"All done, Uncle Ben. I want to ride my bike. Is that okay?"

Ben mumbled something that sounded like "Sure" and fell asleep in his recliner; the movie he'd started to watch droned on without him.

—

Zak rode to Riley's Garage to see if he could find out where Q and Shay lived. He swerved his bike into Riley's, where Sam and Mantha sat on the bench. "Hi, Sam! Hi, Mantha! How is Rosey?" He hopped off and squatted for Penny to greet him. She jumped up on his shoulders and licked his face.

"Rosey's fine. Looks like Penny likes you," said Sam.

"Do you know where Lindsay lives?" Asked Zak.

"Easy peasy, good buddy, just keep riding that way. Her trailer is on the right side at the end of that road," Sam responded.

Zak flapped his right hand to determine which side of the road was right to make the correct turn. "Thanks, Sam!"

He asscended the road to find the old house trailer, weathered by time and the elements. Tall grasses with wildflowers of asters and black-eyed Susan's surrounded it and reached up like a dust ruffle. The old double-wide was endearing despite its imperfections. Its once-vibrant exterior had faded and patches of peeling paint revealed the aluminum underneath. The roof sloped with a dip in the center. Clothes hung on a line. Bustling tan and red chickens pecked around a weathered red shed by a giant woodpile. An apple tree laden with fruit hung heavy alongside a vegetable garden with squash and pumpkins.

The trailer windows bore marks of numerous repairs—screens sagged, and some glass showed long cracks. Windows were open and bakery smells wafted.

"Cookies!" Zak tossed his bike into the high grass by a bush. A forked dirt driveway pitted with puddles ended at a small wooden deck needing stain. *"Wonder where that road goes,"* Zak's mind blinked as he ran up the steps to knock on the door that Lindsay answered.

"Hi, are you Lindsay? Are you Shay and Q's mom? Are they home? Are you making cookies? Do you have any now? My name is Zak, and I live with the sheriff."

Lindsay wiped her hands on her apron. "Goodness, you have energy. Come on in. Q works at Dee's, and Shay is at the library."

"Do you have cookies?" Zak wiggled. "The pumpkin pecan cookie kind? Aunt Kate said I could pick some up if you have any."

"I thought you were coming tomorrow morning to get them. No worries, they are just cooling now, and you can take a plate," Lindsay offered. "Have a seat while I fetch them."

Zak sat in an oversized, soft, gold floral-patterned chair. The faded upholstery was worn and patched with thick silver duct tape on one arm. Maple wooden paneling on the walls and a wood-burning stove provided warmth. The setting sun filtered through the curtains, casting a soft glow. Lindsay handed Zak a green melamine plate filled with cookies and covered in plastic wrap.

Zak took the plate. "Thank you, Ms. Lindsay. Tell Shay and Q, hi."

"I will, Zak; now hurry home before it gets dark."

Zak stepped outside. He heard crickets striking up their evening songs. An owl hooted. Most of the sky was cobalt blue. He saw tiny glimmers of greens and some purples as the sun set. Zak had never seen such a sky. The bustling city lights he grew up under masked this miraculous glory.

"Cheek cheek cheeka cheek!" An albino squirrel sat on a fence post in front of him. Zak carefully held his plate of cookies and followed the little critter as it scampered down the narrow, pitted road. He stopped at a large stand of trees upon a slight rise, and there below, he spotted an incredible array of huge, multi-colored containers under that incredible magical sky. Pressing the plate of cookies against his chest, he ran down the hill to explore.

Soon, he was surrounded by overgrown vegetation in a long-forgotten world. Many of the once sturdy metal structures now bore evidence of the passage of time and neglect. Zak approached a container with a rusted exterior. "What a great hideaway this could be!" He ran from container to container, going deeper into the maze. He jumped over barrels and old car parts to arrive at one unremarkable blue container with peeling paint. A rusty cut-off padlock lay on the ground.

Curious, Zak opened the creaky double doors to enter a compact but versatile space. The interior of the cargo container relied on natural light seeping through the small windows high above. Graffiti and faded artwork graced the walls. Someone else had discovered this hideaway. Somebody had piled a blanket in the far corner. A TV tray and mismatched chairs made a private spot to hide from the world. There were old candles, an empty cracker box, and candy wrappers. "I wonder whose secret place is this?" Zak was intrigued. The echo of his voice answered *"is this...is this?"* Then the container became silent.

Zak walked over and sat on the blanket, soaking in calm. He peeled back the plastic wrap, taking just one cookie. Streaming light from high above lit the plate. "These cookies are so delicious!" The container echoed back, *"...delicious....delicious."* He ate another, then a third. Light faded as the container darkened. He ate cookie number six, and then seven, eight and nine, living in processed bits of time, drifting in delicious moments. Zak licked the cookie bits off his lips and opened the double doors.

He was transported into the expanse of a green and pink sky. The lack of artificial light allowed the Aurora Borealis to come alive against the darkening blue. The enchanting lights amazed him. The hayfield shimmered, inviting him to dance, swaying in ethereal hues. His body moved with grace and joy as he stepped out into the field, lost under the flickering sky. With each leap and twirl, his breath filled with wonder. He felt at one with its Creator and he danced until he could dance no more. Exhausted, he returned to the container, finished all but one of the cookies, and fell asleep.

—

The dishwasher's setting for pots and pans created the perfect storm in Sheriff Ben Jordan's home. The half-full bottle of blue liquid dish soap stood sentinel as a tsunami of suds gathered force in the heavy agitation cycle as Ben snored. Churning and whirring, the magical blue liquid cut through grease and grime, creating an abundance of bubbles. Slowly, the suds rose into a frothing mountain of pressure inside the dishwasher. The emergency release opened the dishwasher door, unable to contain the pressure cooker of soapy hot foam and water. A torrent of bubbles burst forth, rushing through the kitchen like a river breaking its banks. The foam filled the entire kitchen, engulfed in a sea of soapy suds, then flowed into the great room where Ben peacefully slept in his recliner. Suds found their escape routes through open crevices of heat ducts and area rugs and rose up the walls and out window sills. Piles of suds reached into the living room, the hallway, and the bedroom. Ben and Kate's home had become a sudsy water park. The suds meandered down and rose in waves of bubbles up Ben's chair, covering him like a snowy blanket.

When the foam reached his nose, he sneezed. Ben startled upright, still groggy from his post-supper stupor. He roared, "Zak! Get down here NOW!" No answer. "Is this some kind of joke?" He bellowed. "Where are you?" Sheriff Ben stood on his porch looking like an abominable snowman of foam. "Zak, when I get a hold of you, I'm going to kill you!"

Sam and Mantha had walked to the market square for a leg stretch and heard the roaring commotion from the typically peaceful neighborly sheriff. "Sounds like the sheriff is making terrorist threats." Mantha laughed.

Suds leaked out of Ben's open kitchen window and beneath the sills of doors bubbles flowed. This was funny on television. In real life, she almost wet her pants! "Ben, you need help? I'm calling 911 to see who can volunteer to help you clean up this mess. What the hell did you do?"

Sam could barely spit out the words between chuckles as he dialed. "Jill, we've got a situation at the sheriff's. His new kid must have dumped liquid dish detergent in the dishwasher. We don't know where the kid is now. Soap is everywhere. The Sheriff's gonna need a volunteer clean-up crew."

Jill laughed. "Goodness! It sounds like a mess. I'll dispatch for help. This is a way better emergency than a fire. Let's see who shows for this one. I can put out an alert for snow shovels."

Filled with a local sense of humor, the deputies and volunteer firefighters showed up, grinning from ear to ear, alongside a curious Riverdale Times news reporter. Word of this foamy escapade spread through Harris County, and before long, large numbers folks gathered outside the Jordan's house. Most were eager to witness the unscheduled foamfest. Parents chuckled, kids shrieked in delight, and everyone soon joined the bubbly extravaganza.

Sheriff Ben managed to turn off the overflowing dishwasher and, together with his neighbors, cleaned up the colossal mess. Armed with snow shovels, leaf blowers, shop vacs, mops, buckets, and laughter, the community teamed up for hours of sponging, wringing, and dumping buckets. Eventually, the suds were out of the house and into the yard where children giggled in bubble throws. Hills of soap-foam lay drying, scattered about the yard—still no Zak.

"Zak!" Ben shouted into the air to reduce the building stress and heat remaining in his chest.

A burly volunteer guffawed. "Why, I never thought I'd see you so squeaky clean, Ben! So, I heard you are the sheriff?"

Ben glared at the man, recognizing him, but blanked on his name. The man was new in town, probably that big guy Kate had mentioned who worked at the school.

"Clever! Quite the housecleaning method before the wife returns." He held out a huge hand. "Nice to see you, soap and all; it's been years since boot camp. John Mason, do you remember me?"

Finally seeing the irony of the situation, Ben laughed as he returned the handshake, "Been years, John. Nice to see you again."

"Ben, Zak came by the garage hours ago. He rode up to Lindsay's place." Sam shard.

"I'll take Penny to Lindsay's to check things out." Mantha offered. John did a double take toward Riley's new owner. Ben and Sam both noticed, Mantha did not.

"Penny, let's find Zak. Come on." Mantha chuckled not noticing she had turned her right cheek toward John Mason, who nodded and gave a secret salute.

"Want some help?" he offered.

"Carry on, I got this." Laughed Mantha.

—

Mantha knocked on Lindsay's door and was greeted by her old friend. "Hi, Lindsay," she smiled.

"Wow, Sammie, I am so glad you're back home! It's been since high school graduation. Q told me he served you at the cafe this week. And then I loved your line at Dee's wtih Doc. He never stops." Lindsay dried her hands on the dish towel. "I'm glad to see you."

"It's just Mantha now. My world's changed. Let's catch up later. Have you seen Zak?" Mantha was on a search, and there was no time to chat.

"Zak? Yes, I sent him home with a plate of cookies before sundown." Lindsay caught on, concerned.

"He didn't come home. No one's seen him," said Mantha. "Do you mind if I look around your property? His bike is outside."

"Sure, no problem," Lindsay stepped onto the porch. Penny alerted to Zak's bike and ran down the dirt road and over the hill into the container maze. "I think the dog knows something about Zak. She sniffed his bike and then took off. I'd follow her. Do you want me to join you?"

"Stay here, I'll call you if I need more help, give me your cell number." Q and Shay arrived on bike to join the search. "Woo woo woo woo!" Penny returned to bark at Shay and Q.

"Let's go!" Called Shay. They raced to the cargo containers

Mantha shouted. "Zak!" There was no answer.

Shay stopped as she rounded the bend to enter the container garden. "Whoa! Look at all the pretty lights! It's like they hug me, all warm and tingly. This is the most beautiful thing I've ever seen!"

Penny remained in the lead as they ran through the container calling for Zak. Q stopped captivated by the swirling lights. His attention to detail allowed him to notice the variations in color, intensity, and patterns. "The vibrant hues blend like a symphony. The purple is deep. The green like a graceful river. It rains upon us in streaming ribbons."

Mantha listened to each teen with her heart. Q's analytical mind sought to understand the visual array, while Shay's emotional perception embraced the magical quality of the sensory experience. Emerging from the rusty structures to the big field the sky danced.

"Wooo, wooo, woo!" Penny brought them back to their task at the unlocked and partially opened container. "Wooo, wooo, woo!" The dog entered first as Q opened the door. Zak rubbed his eyes as the dog ran to the remaining cookie, claiming it as her finder's reward.

"Zak, dude, are you okay?" Shay asked.

Zak yawned. "Did you see the dancing sky, Shay? Did you feel the sky move you?"

"Yes, yes! YES, I did!" Shay giggled and twirled. "They are still here!"

Mantha called Lindsay. She called Sam, "Mantha's got Zak. He is safe. Penny found him in a cargo container." And Sam told Ben.

"Would you kill him for me?" Ben growled, relieved but exasperated

There was a piece of him that harbored a secret hope that the boy had taken off, never to return.

Sam laughed. "Mantha's bringing him home. You go to bed. We can deal with this in the morning."

Ben stayed on the porch to await his arrival. Seeing him return reset Uncle Ben's bellowing, "Get to bed. NOW!"

"Did you just get out of the shower, Uncle Ben?" Zak said puzzled.

"I said—and will not repeat it—GET TO BED. NOW!" The Sheriff's command could be heard two blocks away. Zak scrambled inside, left his empty plate on the counter, and ran up the stairs to bed.

———

It was Thursday morning, Zak day seven, zero six hundred hours. Ben woke to the smell of fresh coffee. A neighbor must have programmed the pot for the morning. He poured a cup. It was a clear day, and every window sparkled. John was right. The cleanliness of their house would surprise Kate.

Last night was the first time he awoke chest-deep in soap suds! He left the muddy green plate sitting on the pristine counter. It looked like a dog had licked it. Ben opened the dishwasher to add the plate. The dishwasher was empty and sparkling clean; somebody had washed all the downstairs windows, and the floors were shiny. Ben laughed at the irony. Somebody had washed ALL Kate's knickknacks. He ran his finger along a shelf, then across the top of the refrigerator. There was no dust. His home had the "guests-are-coming" holiday shine. Kate was going to be quite impressed!

He stepped out onto the porch and picked up the daily newspaper, featuring a larger-than-life, monstrous snowman with soap suds flying from his bare chest. In all his years as a first responder, there had never been such an elaborate photo even for significant events. The two-inch bold headline read "Sheriff Ben Finally Comes Clean." Last night's suds spectacular was going down in the Riverdale history books. The results of the suds flood scoured his house, fertilized his grass, and got him front-page attention. Sheriff Ben was the town's favorite topic the month before the elections. He was sure the whole county had heard or seen the story, which was seeping into outlying areas.

The one-half-inch subheading humorously exclaimed, "I'm going to kill him!" A mix of emotions flooded in. The coverage might have been humorous if he hadn't been the focus, and if it had been about someone else. The headlines were catchy, and he certainly had a commanding military voice that was hard to miss when raised. Most people just obeyed. However, the subheading bothered him. He had indeed said it. He had said it more than once, loud and proud like a roaring lion. The picture captured him beating his chest as soap suds spewed forth.

'Nothing like making a memorable splash.' Zak had lived in his home for less than a week, and because of this nephew, Ben made the front page in an election year in what amounted to a cheap but ideal advertisement for any potential adversary without campaign funds.

Sadly, even after a night of sleep, he wanted to scream in utter frustration when he thought of Zak. *'But,'* thought Ben, *'When someone says 'I'm going to kill him,' it is generally not meant to be taken literally. People say things like this at the moment to vent anger or frustration. It's not meant as a genuine threat of harm.'* True, he had used strong language to vent his frustration, but with no actual plan or severe intention of ever harming his nephew. Did THAT need to be called out for public attention as a subheading?' It made him uneasy.

This was the first time his actions had been displayed—AND he was half-dressed, bellowing from his porch like King Kong on steroids. He knew from complex professional experience that people had been incarcerated for such behavior if it happened at the wrong place and time— saying such things distressed and alarmed people. He had learned that the hard way years ago in a potential child maltreatment case containing threats of whooping, beating, and killing. Even rhetorical statements were promptly suspected by authorities. He understoor the cost of such statements and seldom stooped to this low level in public. He confined remarks in jest to private banter with his comrades at the VFW.

Ben focused on work and readied his gear quietly to not wake the sleeping tornado in his office. He dressed and suited up in full gear, with his twenty-pound duty belt, firearm, handcuffs, baton, pepper spray, and radio. Ben stuffed his notepad and two pens in his shirt pocket.

Sheriff Ben Jordan didn't have the energy to check on Zak. His recliner was still damp. He was a modest man who tried his best to handle being the butt of local jokes. He slipped out the door quietly, and being the sheriff, he took his take-home car to the station only two blocks from his house. He had no energy left to face the nemesis in his office.

—

Q repeatedly heard the infamous bubble story. Locals laughed so hard they cried; some rushed to the restroom for tissues. He couldn't wait to get off work, finish waiting tables, and stop by the Jordan home to see if all the bubbles had dissolved. In his black patina shoes, he ran down the street, across Market Square to find Zak barefoot and bed-headed, standing on the porch.

"Whoa, Zak, did you just wake up?" Q was incredulous. "It's Thursday, 14:15 hours central standard time! I've worked an entire shift. I must thank you, dear friend, everyone in Riverdale is in a good mood and my tips quadrupled. You and Sheriff Ben are the talk of this town."

"Huh, yeah, huh?" Waking took some reboot time, and Zak's brain was not fully connected to the day. He shook off the internal cobwebs.

Q sat on the steps. Zak yawned, stretched, and rubbed his eyes. His eyes watered. "I was dreaming about something that might have happened yesterday, but I don't remember." Zak said.

"You can tell me," offered Q.

"There's a gorgeous cheerleader. She's called Missy. After the last class yesterday, she invited me to become a cheerleader for the football team. I told her yes. They have cheerleader practice at the park tomorrow. That was before Coach Thompson asked me to be on his soccer team. I want to do both."

"That's a conundrum," said Q.

"What kind of drum?" Zak stretched.

Q droned, "A conundrum is a challenging problem difficult to understand or solve. It may seem contradictory or paradoxical, leaving people feeling puzzled or confused. I find conundrums particularly challenging because I prefer clear and logical solutions."

Zak looked at Q. "What? Say it in English."

"Certainly—it is like a riddle or a hard puzzle. Like, if there are two opposite things you want, but you only get to pick one," explained Q.

"Exactly, bongo, conga, conundrum. It sounds like a snare drum to me," said Zak. "Can I only pick one activity after school?"

"Yes. How could you do both? Be prepared, Zak. It might be a prank. Those cheerleaders are mischievous. From what I've heard, their pranks are harmless. But they like causing trouble. They do it for fun," shared Q. "Their jokes put you on the spot. They've hidden my library books, pens, and assignments. When I panic, they laugh. It's worse when I go off like a firecracker. I don't trust them."

"I told the coach I would be a cheerleader and gave up soccer. I told Missy, 'See you at the park!'"

"Sounds fishy to me, Zak. You don't know those girls from Adam," warned Q.

"Who's Adam?" Puzzled Zak.

Q burst out laughing. "Zak, you are too funny! I've got to get home and help Mom with market preparation. May I call you friend?"

"Call me Zak. Friend is not my name. You can call me Z or ZMan."

"Most certainly, yes." Q covered his mouth before he exploded with laughter again. He loved Zak's wit. "Hey, when you get dressed, walk on over. I saw your bike lying in the grass in my yard. You'll need to get it if you want to ride it. We can go explore the containers."

"Thanks, I thought I lost it," yawned Zak.

—

The long weekend for the Minnesota Educator Academy (MEA) offered a yearly break Minnesota teachers and families looked forward to. It happened every third Thursday in October when the fall colors peaked. Families planned an extended fall weekend of pumpkin patches and apple picking, and thousands of teachers assembled in the Twin Cities , The annual conference dated back to 1861 with MEA conference attendance entirely voluntary. There was no financial compensation for the fuel, food, or lodging. Participate was for the joy, camaraderie, learning, and sharing of professional experiences. With the pandemic finaly over, two thousand members of Education Minnesota had eagerly signed up, a testament to their dedication and professional passion.

Doc, Kate, and two other Riverdale High School teachers looked forward to a hiatus from Riverdale. Doc secured his private hotel room while the ladies joined forces, saving money by sleeping in two king-size beds. The elementary school team of eight drove separately. Other educators stayed home. Some accessed virtual learning. Most rested and reset by spending time off with their families.

Every year, Kate looked forward to this event and only missed two conferences due to the pandemic in her twenty-year teaching career. She had carefully selected her classes. Among her packed schedule were topics including suicide prevention, trauma-informed intervention, classroom management, and one course she had no interest in but chose to take anyway—*Prenatal Alcohol Exposure and Consequences for Learning and Behaviors.* It was her last class on the first day, and she sat near the front of the room. She was excited to get out and enjoy the cosmopolitan culture of the big city—street music, art galleries, white linen dining, maybe even a symphony—all things that were not Ben's idea of fun. She listened intently as the presenter began.

"Let's introduce you to a new student named Tim. The first day in a new school can be overwhelming and nerve-wracking for students, especially if they have sensory issues and Fetal Alcohol Spectrum Disorder (FASD). While their disability may not be readily apparent, their behaviors are noticeable. Any child with prenatal trauma may have issues and instances of hidden surprises. Alcohol, as a solvent is the most aggressive, fentynal, and meth follow closely behind. "

"Tim steps foot into the high school and is immediately bombarded with a barrage of sensory stimuli—the buzzing of conversations, the sound of lockers slamming shut, the smell of multiple scents mingling, and the bright lights that flood the hallways. For someone with sensory issues, this can be quite overwhelming and cause anxiety or even meltdowns. He has a meltdown that arises from the limbic system, which malfunctions when he becomes overwhelmed. His episode is not intentional but severe and unexpected; the behavior can be quite alarming for everyone around. A meltdown is a limbic storm that can take hours of recovery, though not noticed as a need by onlookers. It is not a temper tantrum for an unmet need. I recommend you research this further."

Kate set up her laptop and started taking notes.

"Because no one can visually see Tim's neurological differences, no supports or accommodations are in place to help him navigate this new environment. Tim might show various behaviors throughout the day: difficulties with impulse control, problem-solving, memory, attention, and social interactions. His challenges, the symptoms of how his brain works differently, give us the key to unlocking his needs and open creative ways of accommodation. Tim may struggle to follow instructions, find it hard to focus, have difficulty making and keeping friends, or have impulsive behavior that makes him seem younger than his age. The core of Tim's struggles is that his threshold for stress is more vulnerable, and when his brain fatigues, his symptoms get worse. We can't consecrate an asthma attack to make it stop, and the same thing is true for Tim's symptoms. His episodes and problems with learning, focus, and interaction are involuntary, the result of neurological glitches he has no 'inhaler' for."

"Confabulation, can be puzzling for educators and it is not 'crazy lying.' It's a symptom of neurological compromise where the person fills memory gaps with emotional content to tell a story, but the facts don't match up. People with brain injury from FASD struggle to recall information accurately. They may answer 'yes' or 'no' when asked if they were present at certain events, even when evidence shows otherwise. It is helpful to think of confabulation like a movie trailer for an emotion: feeling is what comes across in the clip, though the context is incomplete for the date, time, or place and how the whole plot goes. The brain skips steps in an attempt to connect a chain of experiences. In addition, elation, fear, or defensiveness interferes with recall, the time and date stamping which organizes the filing system of memory. The feeling is real; the file parameters are garbled and details like people, places, and things may be confused, switched, or made up. If in defensive mode, confabulation escalates to involve vivid accounts of imagined events, with the individual believing the story because it feels true to them to create an emotional picture. The person's story can be emotionally 'true' but factually an amalgamation of cognitive files because of damage to memory function. Confabulation is the brains desperate attempt to fill in the blanks from inaccessible memory. On the other hand, lying is deliberate deceit motivated by a desire for personal gain, avoiding consequences, self-protection, or manipulation of others and will remain consistent over time.

"Imagine you ask a student, 'Did you take the cookie?' Who answers sincerely, 'No, I don't eat cookies' despite the cookie being in their hand with a bite out of it and chocolate around their mouth. A liar would know better than to say that because the facts are obvious. The student with brain injury from FASD doesn't see the mismatched pieces. You must realize here that confabulation happens to all of us."

"It is important to note that provoked questioning with heightened stress may increase this unintentional behavior, as the individual may want to please the questioner. It is best not to avoid posing forced-choice questions. A forced-choice question has no option for a neutral response or contextual description. Educators and family members need to understand these dynamics as a team. You may discover it better to ask the student to draw what happened and then draw two ideas they can use to solve the problem it created."

"Teachers and classmates can learn to understand the neurodiversity this student faces. Over time, a student like this becomes more familiar with the new high school and builds relationships as we help them find strategies to cope with their sensory issues and neurological challenges. The school community must work together to create an atmosphere of acceptance and understanding, enabling the new student to thrive academically and socially. At present we can expect one child in most classrooms, as the children born during Covid19 enter school, we will see an uptake in numbers."

———

Kate took extensive notes on her laptop, her mind filled with jumbled impressions of Zak. She reflected on the stories she had heard about him at family gatherings, the strange things she had witnessed, and her current experiences of living with him. She considered seeking insight from Doc, the Riverdale school principal, and her old high school flame. She was glad that Doc had returned and believed he would make an excellent principal.

Kate noticed Zak's behaviors were similar to those of Tim. She glanced backward and saw Doc sitting at the last table, his pen in his mouth in the same pose he used as a high school senior. She considered talking to him about this and reminisced about relying on Doc in high school to find answers to tough questions. She was once "that girl" the quarterback chose, and her status was elevated by his attention. She remembered being the center of attention during her teenage years as his showgirl, which was a source of pride for her. She felt a surge of excitement, recalling that feeling of being valued. He was her prince charming before Ben. She was surprised when Doc's family returned to Riverdale, and he accepted the principal position. She had grieved when he and his mother severed all connections to her small town after his father's murder and graduation.

———

The presenter continued. "Recognizing possible prenatal alcohol exposure in your student population can be difficult because we often look at their behaviors as bad choices versus symptoms of brain and metabolic injury that cause more extreme reflex behavior and other atypical patterns in the course of daily living. Fetal Alcohol Spectrum Disorder also referred to as FASD, is invisible 90% of the time. According to the Centers for Disease Control or CDC, it affects one in every twenty students. For many, it makes for a lifetime of living in the mental processes of concrete operations versus transitioning to abstract reasoning. The pandemic statistics of children possibly born exposed prenatally to alcohol is set at one in seven. School districts, employers, and communities must be ready to understand and support these people who are all around us and want to contribute to society in positive ways too."

"Are there any questions?" Many hands went up as Kate's mind spun, reviewing memories, assembling thoughts, and connecting possibilities.

—

Zak was relieved to find his bike and even happier to hang out with real friends! He rushed up the stairs to get his sneakers. He avoided his new socks. He ran off without eating toward Riley's Garage. Penny rose on her hind legs to look out the window. She perked up, hoping to see her favorite tabby cat. Her nose lifted in a sniff. *No cat. Boy. Car boy.* Typically, people drove into the garge. They didn't run. The slap slap slap of a runner was uncommon. *Yes, it was him. A good person. She liked him.* Penny chuffa-chuf-fa-chuffed and charged out the door with a huge pitbyull smile to greet Zak.

Zak froze. His arms flew up and crossed to protect his face. He was sure he was going to die. A blood-curdling scream rose from deep in his belly and grew as Zak expelled all the air he had in his diaphragm. The dog sat three feet in front of the teen sounding like he was being mauled. '*Someone seriously is being hurt*' Mantha thought as she worked her way out from under the car.

Penny sat in silence watching the boy writh on the ground. "Come here, Penny. It's alright. Go find your bed." She pointed and the dog arose and went to the garage. Zac lay curled in the garage's entryway in a fetal position, gulping gasps of air while choking back sobs. The screaming stopped. Mantha had seen this before. "Hey, good buddy, how are you doing? Tell me about it." Mantha tapped softly but firmly, pressing her hand to Zak's shoulder. The teen's wide eyes barely focused. He stared upward, unsure what was happening. "Did Penny jump on you?" Mantha asked. "Are you okay?"

Zak felt the ground with his hands, trying to get oriented, and slowly sat. "She… she…scared…me," he struggled for words.

"I bet she did. Penny is big and fast, and she likes you. I bet she was running to say hello. Would you like to see her in a non-scary way?" Mantha asked softly. "She thinks you might have another cookie."

Zak slowly nodding in agreement.

"Penny, check in," Mantha ordered. Penny ran directly, plopped herself in front of them in a perfect sit with paws a few inches apart, and showed a calm, alert expression as if awaiting the next cue. "Would you like to pet her, Zak?"

Zak returned a timid half smile. The dog nuzzled the boy, and soon, they tumbled together like pack brothers. His complexities intrigued her. *Zak could become somebody with the proper training.* Mantha watched. This kid was endearing like so many of the other privates Mantha had known. She missed the young men and women who served under her and often became her favorite with their loyalty and uncanny abilities.

Zak, charmed by the dog's play, grew courageous and stood. "Down, Penny." Penny downed. "See, I could be a dog trainer!"

Mantha held her collar.

"I gotta go, see you," Zak left as if nothing had happened.

"See you later, Zak," Mantha answered.

"Alligator!" She heard him shout.

———

Doc watched for Kate as the conference ended. Even in middle age, she remained a fine-looking woman. "What did you think of the last class, Kate?" He asked.

"I kept thinking about Zak," Kate answered.

"Me too. I was wondering if you'd like to talk about it. We could enjoy the city like old times. Have dinner with me tonight. I'll buy," he offered. "I am happy to share what I already know."

"I would like to hear your thoughts to get some ideas, and I don't want to discuss a student in front of other teachers." Kate met his eyes. "I'd be happy to join you for dinner."

They exited the conference hall into the gloaming of the early evening. A talented saxophonist played jazz, the setting sun sparkled from his brass. Doc added money to his box.

"I don't know enough about FASD after what I heard today," said Kate.

"Let's compare notes at the restaurant. We can make it an early dinner so you get back to the ladies before lights out," suggested Doc.

Kate's eyed the art gallery sign.

"Would you like to go in?" Doc asked.

Kate smiled.

A sense of nostalgia wash over her, as they walked through the gallery door. Doc was so unBen. The contemporary art pieces came alive under the soft lighting, and she could not help but feel excited to explore art with Mike again. She was surprised by how easily they fell back into their old routine, laughing at insider jokes.

Their eyes met and Doc put his hand on her side. "I've missed this," he said softly, as his hand played at the taper of her waist. "I've missed us. Let's get something to eat."

The restaurant was within walking distance between the conference center and the hotel. Doc took out his smartphone to reserve two tables in an exquisite restaurant with white linens. The ambiance was subdued: the perfect place to talk and reminisce. "Order whatever you'd like, Kate, my treat." His eyes exuded confidence and charisma. Kate ordered a filet mignon, baked potato with sour cream, and a Caesar salad. Doc ordered a Porterhouse with the same accompaniments. He also ordered a bottle of fine red wine.

They discussed Zak briefly, laughing about how she saved the boy's confidence and kept the class on track after his desk mishap. Doc treated her like a princess and it had been years since they had shared a fine dinner alone. She had dated Doc in high school when she was a cheerleader, and he was the quarterback. Then, the year before Ben returned from the Gulf War, they had dated once briefly when he had flown into town from down south, then life happened and the lost touch of each other.

Doc placed his hand over Kate's and whispered. "What happens in the cities stays in the cities. It always has." She felt the wine warm from within. Kate remained incensed about Ben's commitment to his brother without her input. Her body relaxed, remembering fond memories with Doc, murmuring secrets of laughter and pleasure. They had dated without consummating a relationship. It was wrong—so wrong—but no one ever had to know.

"Let's go back to my room for a nightcap," Doc beckoned with a seductive smile. "No one has ever made me feel as good as you do, Kate."

—9—

ACCOMMODATIONS

Zak tripped on his shoelace as he mounted his bike and twisted into a leap that fell short. Hee rolled onto the grass, got up, swiveled, picked up the bike, and slid it thoughtfully beneath a bush where no one else would be hurt by it lying there.

Seated on a swing in the garden, Shay watched the crazy manuever and ran to greet him. "You want to sit on a swing in the garden or go back to the containers and poke around?"

"I came to get my bike… think Q wants to come?" Asked Zak.

"I'll go get him. He's probably reading some old book." Her eyes rolled. "Let's check all the containers and see if others are open."

"I only found one because it was getting dark," Zak explained. "Let's go back to see what we find. Maybe we'll see the dancing lights again."

Shay fetched Q, and the three set off into the container boneyard. The wind whistled through the steel jungle.

"Tag, you're it!" Grinned Zak, tapping Shay on the shoulder. He careened around a container and dashed away. The game of tag had begun, and the rules were simple: no hiding, no boundaries. The entire cargo container boneyard was their playground. They darted among the towering containers, their laughter echoing through the metallic maze.

"I'll get you!" Shay laughed, her voice sparkling with excitement. Her joy was contagious and brightened anyone's day. Shay was a whirlwind of energy, curious, and playful. She was filled with a boundless zest for life.

Q's analytical mind mapped the environment, memorizing the layout of every container and noting its colors and sizes. He predicted where his friends would go next and strategically positioned himself to intercept them.

Interesting, Shay had the unexpected advantage. Her uncanny ability to find unconventional paths gave her jackrabbit agility. She zig-zagged away, evading capture at every turn. Her impulsivity was a superpower in this chaotic game.

Zak waited patiently for her path, sometimes tricking her into a soft collision with his gentle tag. Free and wild, time flew by, and the sun dipped low in the sky. The threesome gathered in the shadow of the blue unlocked container, gulping ragged breaths.

"It's like a giant maze in here," Q exhaled wide-eyed.

Shay exclaimed, "I love playing tag with you guys. It's so much fun!"

Zak nodded. "We make a great team! Q, your memory helps us plan, and Shay, your energy keeps us on our toes."

"SQZ, we are the monogram masters," declared Q.

"The what?" Asked Zak.

"The Monogram Masters," repeated Q. "SQZ! I've been thinking about something that can make our friendship even more amazing. We create a group, a special group, and call it the 'Monogram Masters or use the secret code 'squeeze.'"

Curious, Shay tilted her head. "Monogram Masters? What's that, Q?"

"Good question, Shay," Q replied with precise enunciation. "Monograms are like puzzles, patterns, and codes. Each of us, with our unique abilities and quirks, is like a puzzle piece. Together, we create a unique and beautiful pattern."

Zak frowned. "I'm not sure I get it, Q. How do abilities fit into this group?"

"Great question, Zak," Q turned to his friend, eyes lighting up. "Here's the thing: I'm good at seeing patterns, remembering details, and organizing things. Zak, you bring immense curiosity, creativity, and an unstoppable energy. Shay, you've got the gift of empathy, understanding people, and sensing emotions like no one else. Together, we form a powerful team. I see what others don't, Zak explores what others can't, and Shay makes amazing connections—she brought us together!"

Shay's face lit up. "So, it's like a puzzle with three pieces that all fit together?"

"Exactly!" Q exclaimed. It's not about fitting in with others; it's about each of us fitting together as a team, but doing it by being precisely ourselves—interlocking in a way that makes us unique and unstoppable. We each have an initial in the 'monogram,' and combining them, we create a 'masterpiece' of friendship and collaboration."

Zak jumped gleefully, understanding the significance of Q's proposal. "I see it! I SEE IT! I like it, Q. I've always felt like I didn't fit in, but maybe I do in our Monogram Masters. If I had paper, I could show you what I see."

Shay peered up from inside the container. "I found a journal and pen. Show me what you see!" The journal was hidden under a blanket and pillow, which Zak hadn't noticed the night before. "Here, we'll just take one page. No one will know," Shay whispered, carefully tearing out a sheet and handing the paper and pen to Zak. She noticed the name, Michielle, on the first page.

Zak sat on the old, worn floor, sketching an amazing Monogram. He connected his S to Q and Z, and the three letters made a pattern.

"Zak, we are invincible together!" Exclaimed Q, unable to contain his excitement. It's incomparable. Nothing can stop us now!"

"That's pretty, Zak. It is us! It is the three of us," rejoiced Shay. "We are all for one and one for all, like in the movies."

"Hey, it's getting dark," Shay announced. "The stars and moon are already out! We should head home now to be safe."

"It's better to be closer to home when it gets dark outside. Let's plan to meet and come back soon in the daylight," Q added.

Zak stretched out his arms. "Do you see it? Q, do you see it? This is where the sky dances! This is our rocket's launch pad."

Q was mesmerized as the sky lit up in his imagination. He gazed into the luminous expanse of the darkening night. "Zak, have you ever noticed how the stars form patterns in the night sky? I've been studying this constellation wheel, and it's fascinating." He pulled a cardboard circle from his pocket. "This star chart helps me understand the positions of constellations in the night sky at different times of the year. They visually represent how the stars move throughout the seasons. Constellations are like a giant cosmic stargazing dot-to-dot puzzle."

"All I see is a bunch of sparkles mixed up in the sky. I look at the moon. The moon is like a giant glowing cookie in the sky," Zak laughed, recalling the delicious cookies he had eaten here not too long ago.

"The moon is pretty cool, but constellations are like stories written in the stars. This wheel helps me find them." Q showed Zak his wheel. "Have you ever looked at the night sky and tried to find constellations and their stories?"

"I've tried, but the stars are just little blinking lights. What do you mean dot-to-dot and stories in the stars? That's wild! Like the man on the moon? The moon is made of cheese?" Zak held his hands up in a V, placing the rising moon right into his palm. "So, show me a story!"

"How about I start with the most brilliant and spectacular star group in the sky? It is called Orion. Almost every ancient culture had stories about him—the Hunter, the Great Warrior, the Loyal Shepherd of Heaven. You see, we all see the same sky and the same stars, but depending on our culture, our stories vary. This one is easy to find because of the row of three bright stars that make up Orion's belt or, in Spanish culture, "Las Tres Marias," which means the three Marys." Q pointed to the row of three bright stars in Orion's belt. "People in history connected the dots to create pictures that make sense to where they live. These same stars in Indigenous Australian Wergaia culture think of it as two hunters named Yuree and Wanjel who pursue a kangaroo."

"I see them. I see the belt in the sky!" Squealed Shay.

"That's very good, Shay. Orion is the cosmic hunter or great Shepherd in the sky. Those stars are called Alnitak, Alnilam, and Mintaka," listed Q, tapping each finger.

Zak watched the moon in his hands.

"I think the belt stars are treasure gems," Shay looked skyward with a sparkle in her eyes, imagining the jewels of heaven.

Q grinned. "The middle star is called Alnilam, which means pearl. The outside stars' names mean belt. We wear a belt around our middle; look up and down, Shay, and you will see a trapezoid, like a four-sided slanted box. See the brightest star on the upper left, the shoulder? Its name is Betelgeuse, a red super giant and one of the largest known stars in our galaxy. Betelgeuse and Rigel are the brightest stars on Orion's shoulder and foot. As super giants, they are nearing the end of their lives. Betelgeuse will eventually explode in a supernova."

Hearing the bug form got Zak's attention, "Beetle Juice, explode? Supernova? I saw that movie once. Show me." Q carefully guided Zak's eyes to see the belt and the bright star. "Yes, yes, yes! Q, I see the belt and 'Beetlejuice.'"

"Betelgeuse," Q laughed, catching Zak's misunderstanding. "Betelgeuse is spelled B E T E L G E U S E. It sounds similar, close enough if it helps you remember. Astronomers believe it is a thousand times larger than the sun and over 600 light years away from Earth. When Betelgeuse explodes, the brightness and the energy will outshine the entire constellation. It could leave behind a neutron star or a black hole."

"Wow. I can connect the dots. I see the square around the belt. Shay, can you see the rectangle shape? Where is his sword?" Zak asked.

"Straight down from the center star, the pearl is in the belt and connects to the knee. That line represents his sword, and a compact cluster of three stars above the shoulders marks his head. We are lucky it is so dark tonight, even with the moonshine." Q's eyes turned to the night sky.

Zak squinted at the moon and moved his fingers to create a heart frame, "What does Orion hunt? Maybe he plays hide-and-seek with the stars."

"Greek mythology tells about a battle between Orion and Scorpio; they did not get along well and were sentenced to remain in the stars, with Scorpio chasing after Orion. Scorpio lives mostly in the southern hemisphere and Orion in the northern hemisphere. It is rare to see them together." Q played with his wheel to see if he could discover when they might simultaneously be in the northern sky. "The Earth completes a full rotation on its axis in 23 hours and 56 minutes, four minutes less than the commonly accepted 24-hour day. Consequently, the stars appear to rise, cross the sky, and set approximately four minutes earlier each night, leading to an hour earlier in 15 days and two hours earlier in 30 days. Facts are not always the complete truth; they change over time, experience, and culture. Truth, however, remains true."

"You want to play a game with the moon?" Zak was bored with talk.

Q was intrigued. "Sure, what kind of game?"

Zak held his hands up as if cradling the moon. "Imagine you can grab the moon with your hands. Feel its glow and warmth. It's like playing catch with the biggest ball ever."

Q paused, mirrored Zak's movements, and visualized. "That's a unique game. I'm holding the moon in my hands, feeling its energy."

Shay was excited. "Right? It's our moon, and we can make up stories about it. Maybe it's a secret giant cookie waiting for us to discover." She giggled toward Zak.

"That's fun! Imagine we take a bite out of the moon. What flavor do you think it would be?" Wondered Zak.

Shay grinned. "Definitely chocolate chip. It's the best moon flavor."

Q nodded. "I like your game. Maybe one day, we'll find a way to share our stories with the stars and the moon. Some ancient cultures saw constellations as guides for hunting and navigation. Like hunters tracking bears, they'd look at the stars to find their way."

"There are bears in the sky?" Asked Zak.

Q continued. "The bears are called Ursa Major and Ursa Minor. I just read a passage in the Book of Job at Sunday's service: "He is the maker of the Bear and Orion, the Pleiades, and the constellations in the South. Ursa Minor, or the Little Dipper, is a constellation located at the celestial north pole. The star at the end of its tail is Polaris, which is also known as the North Star. Due to Polaris being a fixed point in the sky, Ursa Major and Ursa Minor are visible most of the year as they rotate around it. Ancient people navigated using the North Star."

"I thought Polaris is a snowmobile," laughed Zak, picking out choice words from Q's very wordy explanation. "Or an ATV!"

"I see the Big Dipper," shouted Shay, colliding her outburst with Zak's words.

"The Big Dipper is not a constellation on its own but rather an asterism—a recognizable pattern of stars within a constellation. In this case, it is part of Ursa Major, the Big Bear," expounded Q.

"Hunters tracking bears? I bet those bears had their own stories," Shay laughed.

Q was into this. "Absolutely! Imagine the bear constellations telling tales of brave hunters and daring chases in our maze. It's like a cosmic game of hide-and-seek between the stars and the bears. And the bears hid a significant secret. It was called the drinking gourd in code used by enslaved people seeking freedom via the Underground Railroad in pre-Civil War America. Slaves used their knowledge of astronomy, coded language, and oral traditions to resist ownership and seek freedom. Have you heard the song, *Follow the Drinking Gourd*? It seems like a simple work song to be sung in hot fields. It actually contained coded information to know markers, rivers, and departure timing."

"Wow, that is so cool. It is like secret missions in the stars. I got an idea," Zak interrupted. "While holding the moon, we could be on a quest! Like, we're star hunters on a mission."

Q cocked his head. "That's a cool twist! We could navigate through the night sky, using our constellation wheel as a map, tracking the bears' journey among the stars."

"We could find the bears' secret hideout like our container to have starry celebrations." Zak expanded.

Q grinned. "I love the way you think, Zak. Our moon-holding adventure became a cosmic quest with bears and starry celebrations. It's like a story only the Monogram Masters would co-create."

Zak exclaimed, "Exactly! Our own story in the universe!"

"I love holding the moon," Shay marveled. "And Orion might be the great Shepherd instead of a hunter. He might guide the bears and keep them safe. He shines two brightest lights to lead them in the dark."

Q was thoughtful. "Sometimes our imaginations can create the most incredible tales, even among the stars and bears. One day, our tale may become its constellation story that shines brightly in the night sky."

Shay clapped her hands, crushing her moon vision. "That would be extraordinary!" A flash streaked through the sky. "A falling star! A falling star! Make a wish! Quick!"

Zak's stomach growled so loudly he scrunched his eyebrows at Q. "Q, you are so funny. None of us have tails! Man, am I hungry! I forgot to eat today."

"I'm famished!" Q admitted. "I need to eat soon and I must stick to my routine and have dinner at a certain time. If I go home now and stick to my meal schedule, I will be at my best for our next adventure."

Shay stepped out of the container. "Let's go home. Mom bought a new bottle of ketchup! I can make noodles and hot dogs."

"3-2-1...blast off!" Zak shouted while Shay zigged through the container maze toward the double-wide trailer. Q ran straight down the main path. Zak careened around a container corner to chase Shay.

—

The Veterans of Foreign Wars (VFW) post in Riverdale was a lively social center where veterans connected over drinks and shared experiences. It was a welcoming environment where members enjoyed cold drinks, chatted about their service, and formed new friendships. The post provided a space for veterans to open up, support each other, and bond over their unique experiences. It was a place where they could reflect on their sacrifices and the impact of their service as a shield protecting their loved ones from the horrors of war. Mantha was welcomed home with hearty handshakes and genuine smiles. Most everyone said the same thing—"Sam, I can't believe it's you! It's been too long!" She replied, "Mantha, my name is now Mantha."

Most saluted. "Yes, ma'am, Captain Mantha." They acknowledged her correct rank and title. This gesture conveyed their respect and professionalism, a silent tribute. No one probed about her injuries. They didn't need to. The unspoken understanding was that she was home, and that was all that mattered. Ben settled in to join Sam and Mantha at the table. He ordered a beer. Sam had water. He wasn't sure what Mantha was drinking.

Conversation moved forward to welcome her home, sharing stories and reflecting on their experiences and the bonds they had formed. The reunion was a warm gathering of brave but modest citizens, their deep resonance known only by those who had returned from the brink of death into life again. Mantha, unfamiliar with all the enlisted Riverdale had sent overseas, was soon surrounded by more comrades. A former combat medic in Vietnam was now a local doctor. A translator in the Gulf War was teaching high school English. A military engineer who owned a highway construction service was active in FEMA. Life had changed, but the bond remained. From boot camp to county sheriff and teacher. New ownership of Riley's. Some bore apparent physical injuries. Others showed nothing on the outside. But all carried the weight of memories in a mental gear trunk, packed away, apart from everyday community topics of conversation.

John Mason's hearty slap on Ben's back was a testament to the camaraderie that filled the room. Ben held his tongue to not spit out his beer as everyone ribbed him about his Sudscapade. With Kate out of town, he had dropped by the local VFW Friday night steak fry event, knowing the razzing would be fierce. The large room was abuzz with the comforting discourse of fellow veterans. The walls were adorned with military memorabilia, flags, and photos of veterans in uniform.

One table pushed into two, and two moved into four as drinks flowed. For $9.99, a steak seared from rare to well done, with sides of a baked potato and iceberg lettuce with cucumber, tomato, and ranch dressing, was served.

———

After a long day at the education conference, the street concert, the art gallery, a lovely meal, and a lingering nightcap drink in his hotel room, Doc walked Kate back to her hotel room. He kissed her hand slowly and gently. It was the early wee hours and the ladies had long been asleep. She tiptoed shoes in hand.

———

Shay had learned to cook simple meals and was proud of her skills. She gathered the necessary ingredients: a few packs of instant ramen noodles, hot dogs, and two pots to boil water. Her focus and dedication were evident as she followed each instruction carefully.

Shay read aloud and rechecked the directions on the ramen package, to focus her mind and dull Zak and Q's chatter. Talking to herself helped organize her thoughts, like a damper on the sound of a gentle rain tapping against the roof. Her words quieted the surrounding stimulation even though random words slipped in and snagged her interest, disrupting her attention. She hated messing things up. She popped in her earbuds to add a stronger filter to stay on task.

"1. Bring 2 cups of water to a boil in a pot." She paused. "I need two times," she said as she used her mother's 1 cup glass measuring container. She added water from the faucet to the hot dog pan. The water soon boiled on the natural gas burner.

"2. Add dry noodles into the pot, breaking it up to soften. 3. Cook for 3 minutes, stirring occasionally." Shay turned the head of the plastic rooster kitchen timer to set it for three minutes. Then she added the ramen to the pot, stirring the noodles occasionally.

"4. Remove from heat. Add ramen base packet." She paused. "Add two." She opened each package using her front teeth, shook it into the pot, and stirred it well. Then she carefully placed the hot dogs into the boiling pot while Q and Zak sat at the kitchen table, chatting about their adventures at the boneyard and what they could do with rockets as the Monogram Masters.

Then they watched with fascination as Shay managed all the steps and cookware. She seemed to make the pots and pans fly as the kitchen filled with the comforting aroma of boiling noodles and hot dogs. Shay drained the noodles and served them in three bowls, each topped with a steaming hot dog.

"5. Garnish if desired," she read aloud filling three soup plates and adding a ketchup drizzle with a sprinkle of Parmesan cheese from a green plastic container. "Here you go, guys!" Shay beamed as she placed the bowls in front of Q and Zak. "I hope you like it! I decorated your hot dogs and garnished the noodles with some cheese."

The three friends dug into the simple yet delicious meal, enjoying the warmth and camaraderie of the moment. Ramen noodles and hot dogs had never tasted better, and the hungry boys appreciated her efforts.

"Shay, this is really good! Thanks for cooking for us." Q complimented and then suddenly stood and rushed out the door.

"Is he sick?" Asked Zak.

"I hope not," Shay grimaced.

Q returned holding greenery. "Hey, I've added a twist to our delightful dinner to make it more gourmet. I've picked fresh chives to garnish the noodles. It's a simple upgrade, but it adds a burst of flavor you might like. Shay, do we have any butter and garlic?" Q took out his Swiss Army knife and used the little scissors to snip the chives.

"Maybe—I'll look." Shay opened the frig. "I found the butter!"

Zak checked the cupboard. "I found garlic powder."

"Bring me the garlic, and I'll add it to the butter. I can microwave it," instructed Shay.

"Then pour it on top to enhance our meal!" Offered Q.

Zak added, "Monogram Masters have some serious cooking skills. It's fun hanging out with you." Shay blushed with appreciation for her contribution to the team.

"Hey Zak, I've got a fantastic idea for something fun." Q shared. "I know this TV program I think you'll enjoy, and I'd love for you to watch it with me. It's called 'Cosmos: A Spacetime Odyssey.' It is hosted by astrophysicist Neil deGrasse Tyson, a renowned scientist and public speaker. This program serves as a follow-up to Carl Sagan's original 'Cosmos: A Personal Voyage.' It is deep and explores various topics related to space, astronomy, and the universe. I have watched it many times."

"Wow, sounds cool. I love astronomy," shared Zak.

"Like ten times, but I'll watch it again with you, Zak," cooed Shay.

"That's obvious," Q grabbed the remote. "It covers the history of scientific discoveries, the nature of the cosmos, and the wonders of space exploration. The series combines stunning visual effects, scientific explanations, and engaging storytelling to make complex topics accessible and captivating for viewers. It's a compelling choice for anyone passionate about space and rocketry."

The show opened with ethereal music accompanied by pulsating orbs of orange and red, which blurred into an image that looked like an eye. Zak hopped over the old high-back sofa and dropped onto the avocado and floral-patterned cushions. Q raised his eyebrows, tilted his head, and sat appropriately at the other end of the couch, smoothing wrinkles out of the fabric. Shay walked around and plopped down very near Zak, but not quite touching.

Lindsay, Shay and Q's mother, arrived home after cleaning up and closing Dee's Cafe. She had given Margie a night off. "Zak, you better head home. It is getting late. I don't need the sheriff knocking at my door looking for you tonight. Shay, it would help if you had a shower tonight, and I expect that cooking mess to be cleaned up before you go to bed. Q, turn off the lamp. We don't have extra money to waste on electricity, and you've already got that TV on."

"Good night, Ms. Larkin," Zak gave her his best grin.

"Good night, Zak. Call me Lindsay, or Mama L, or Mom." She grabbed a bag of potato chips and vanished into her bedroom at the rear of the trailer.

—

Zak rode straight home, deep in thought of what he should call Q and Shay's mother. He eventually settled on Mama L.

Sheriff Ben arrived home just as the light to his office—Zak's new room became dark. Noting the bike set against the porch, he went inside to relax. *'For the moment, all seemed well.'*

-10-
PRANKS

Lindsay slept late into the day. She had good kids who were grown enough to fend for themselves through the MEA weekend. She had decided to pick up the night shift, giving Margie time away from the cafe in the afternoons and evening. As the employee scheduler, she offered Q her morning shift Thursday through Saturday. Her son was happy to oblige and this opened weekend night hours for sleepy high schoolers. Dee's Cafe was closed on Sundays. It also opened the Monogram Masters evenings to hang out.

Lindsay typically left home on Friday morning before Q or Shay rose for school. Margie's Soul Food Friday breakfasts had made Dee's Cafe famous. Q knew from Mom's conversations that Fridays were the busiest mornings in spring and fall. Local farmers and harvesters met at day-break to plan the weekend, compare notes, and fuel up with more than a hearty meal. Business owners shared weekend plans.

Q awoke. It was 4 am, and he had heard from Mom that his boss, Margie, now in her mid-seventies, was up before the crack of dawn bak-ing and preparing Dee's Cafe for the day. Ever since he could remember, Q had an innate desire to help others. He woke with a strong urge to help those in need and Margie's kindness toward him was evident. He decided to arrive early at the café to assist.

Once a week, Margie prepared her signature down-home breakfast featuring dried beef or sausage gravy over his Mom's must-have fresh buttery southern-style biscuits. The fluffy scrambled eggs perfectly ac-companied the crispy fried protein-packed catfish, chicken wings, thick bacon, or home-cured sausage. For those familiar with Southern sides, there were smoky collard greens, creamy grits, and sweet potato hash. A separate plate of moist and mildly sweet cornbread, a Margie specialty, with or without jalapeños, was a complimentary treat with the first cup of purchased coffee. It was always served alongside local butter, honey, and two kinds of fresh jams also made by Mom. And if these options weren't enough, guests could add their favorites like waffles, pancakes, or French toast to complete their meal. Margie's recipes were a testament to her dedication and passion, perfected over a lifetime. Regardless of the day's weather, the atmosphere was always warm and inviting, filled with the comforting aromas of baked goods, coffee, syrups, and the cheerful hum of conversation.

Riverdale seemed deserted except for the vibrant hanging plant baskets of Fall colors. Q strolled down the street, past Rileys, and into town. Each step of his surprise mission was filled with excitement and nerves, but his unwavering determination and sincere intentions propelled him. The town was quiet, its street lights dim until activated.

He arrived at the quaint café before dawn and peered into the window. Margie was bustling between the kitchen and the tables, preparing for the day. Q carefully tapped on the window.

Margie startled. "We don't open until 5:30. You gotta wait," she shouted, shaking a rag. "Do you see an open sign anywhere?" She ignored the window tapper and strolled around the tables, turning down chairs. There was in no rush. Anyone with the audacity to interrupt her morning baking and breakfast feast creation was going to have to wait for service. She pushed back the closed sign to get a better look.

"It's me, Margie. I came to help." Q voice twitched.

Margie peeped through the blinds and unlocked the door. "Well, I'll be. What brings you here, Q? A whole hour and a half before we open?"

"Good morning, Margie. I've risen, and I'm shining. I expect the harvest crews to stop by for your famous Friday breakfast. I decided I'd relieve you from both the setup and the serving. Won't they be surprised to see an 'early morning care with a flair.'" His shoes glistened, his white shirt was pressed along with his black slacks.

Margie laughed. "Q, you are a delight! You give an old woman an early morning laugh. Do you know my son shares your name?" She wiped her hands on her apron. "Someday, I will tell you about him; he's a big lawyer in Alabama. You are right; I need your help. Now get to work."

Q smiled as he pulled down chairs, added paper advertisement mats and rolled silverware. Margie disappeared into the kitchen to get down to business. Q heard her singing hymns with vibrance.

The café's doors swung open and hot freshly ground coffee floating into the street. Mom was right, Friday breakfast was an event. In a time when the pressure of harvest completion loomed and the weather was holding out, Q fostered a morning atmosphere of caring service. Q's eyes sparkled, catching Margie's approving smile and occasional thumbs up. He was tuned into details—a customer's life matters—a unique hat pin, a handwritten notebook, or even a sorrowful feeling concealed beneath a masked smile. Guided by inate empathy, Q asked questions that revealed his sincere interest in their stories without crossing boundaries.

"I have your order; it will be right up. I checked the weather. It will be cold, dry and sunny. Dry weather firms the ground, allowing your farm machinery to traverse the fields without getting stuck. It also prevents excess moisture from damaging the crops or causing muddy conditions that could make harvesting difficult. A clear day with plenty of sunlight will help crops dry out faster after harvesting. Dry conditions and ample sunlight promote ripening, producing better flavor, color, and nutritional value in harvested crops. We want quality, not spoilage. That is a fine hat pin with a trout! Does it have a story? I'll get you fresh coffee." The human encyclopedia tended to each diner's details.

He focused on empty cups and glasses. Each was promptly filled as men and women laughed about the most fantastic trout ever caught, past harvest success and failure, and planning the projected progress. Hardscrabble customers felt heard and seen, their souls uplifted through simple conversation, and their bellies filled for a solid day's work until the sun went down.

—

Zak woke hungry. The house was empty. The large red-numbered digital clock in his new room said 8:00 am. The stairway handrail offered the fastest route to food. He rummaged through the refrigerator, his eyes landing on a substantial, untouched potato-topped casserole and a bowl of red jello adorned with marshmallows and fruit. His hunger overrode any concerns about the food's origin, and he grabbed a spoon from the third drawer he tried, leaving all three ajar. Zak opened the dishwasher, spotting his green cookie plate. "Oh, well," he muttered, deciding to forego the plate and dig into the center of the casserole, avoiding the crusty edges. He despised anything crusty or crunchy as those textures bothered his over-sensitive mouth.

He looked at the round clock with moving arrows over the sink.

Those pointers were called hands as if he didn't know what hands were. And 3 was 15 and 9 was 45 and 6 was 30. It was all silliness. He grabbed his baseball cap, facing it backward to avoid the brim. He scooped a spoonful of red gelatin into his mouth and then pushed in a second scoop. Zak left the spoon half-dripping with jello on the white counter before heading to the park. He had to be at the park by 9:00 am for the cheerleading practice Missy invited him to join.

—

Sheriff Ben arrived home hungry, thinking about Kate's hotdish. He missed her. *What luck he had that she was still single when he returned stateside to begin his civilian life.* Kate handled sensitive issues with consideration and fairness, and so did he. Her compassion comforted him, while his integrity provided her with security and a loving lifestyle. Compassion and integrity were paramount in people-oriented careers like teaching and law enforcement. Their home and marriage were places of order and refuge for these two community servants.

Zak's bike was in the same place as when Ben had seen it the night before. He noticed a large red pool at the top of his front steps. A footprint carried the bloody red down every other step. Ben bent down to examine the situation. Step two contained a mini marshmallow. The red marshmallow prints led away from his house. He scratched his head. He felt inclined to bellow his nephew's name at the top of his lungs. He held back. That had not worked so well, and regardless of the pressure he felt to release another tirade, Ben had no intention of becoming the subject of another article for the local paper.

He stepped over the footprints, avoiding what he now surmised was red gelatin. The doorknob was sticky. *'The neighbors had wiped everything down to a shine.'* The mess was incredible. *'I need my gloves? My porch looks like a crime scene!'*

Hours ago, his home had been shining! He walked lightly toward the kitchen. The refrigerator door was ajar, and the dishwasher was open. The Red jello dessert with many less marshmallows had melted to a liquid, staining his white Corian counter with deep scarlet pools. The potato casserole looked like some animal had gnawed the center out of it! Red jello was stuck on all the cupboard and drawer handles, and more had dripped into the utensil drawer, covering all the spoons.

He had never played the role of a father before, but he had often seen people at their worst. He was a war veteran, had worked as a paramedic, and served as a deputy police officer. He was the county sheriff, for God's sake! He was a son, brother, and friend. He was the husband and lover of a wonderful woman. He closed his fists and raised them high, screaming, "Uncle!"

Ben dropped to his knees and prayed, "Lord, Help me figure this kid out! Amen," he started with square breathing and a ten minute plank. He finished with 50 push-ups. Then he took a coffee mug and poured in the gloppy remains of jello. He selected one of the slimy spoons from the opened drawer, rinsed it off, and then calmly ate around the crater of the casserole. *"Might as well eat it cold. Why waste a spotless plate?"* He shrugged. A sad surrender overcame him. He gazed at his kitchen, feeling incredulous! Ben returned the plate to the cabinet shelf and shut the door. After removing the gooey spoons–every red dripping utensil resembling a spoon in every size they owned—he closed the drawers and placed them all in the dishwasher. He wiped down the drawer. He shut the dishwasher after he added the 'right kind of soap' and started it at its normal wash cycle. It whirred quietly in the background.

He was hungry, and food was food. He gulped the liquid red gelatin and floating white globs, drinking it from the service bowl. *"If Kate ever found out,"* he ate along the casserole's edges. Regaining his domestic bearings, he covered the food and returned it to the fridge. Unlike Zak, he shut the door after triaging the worst of the mess.

Ben wiped down the counter and all the handles, including the front door knobs on both sides, and washed the steps. He had no idea how to get the bright red stain off his counter or remove the red from the white paint on his porch steps. Kate had planned just a simple and easy lunch. He missed her now more than ever. He searched on his smartphone, 'How to remove red stains from white counter.'

———

The choice between cheering with beautiful girls and playing on a boy's soccer team was easy. Zak was so stoked he sprinted breathlessly to the park! No one was there but a young mom pushing a toddler on the swings.

Zak's love for cheerleading at home was a well-known fact. Every Friday night, he watched cheerleaders from the local high school perform at the football games. He stood in front of the cheerleaders with pure admiration. He yearned to be part of their lively and spirited team, but the fear of rejection kept him trying out.

At Riverdale High, the Wednesday before MEA, he had watched the cheerleaders practice. They had noticed him admiring their performance and that Zak had perfect form when he mirrored their cheers and stunts. Missy, the perky teen, had approached him to try out and join. After all, they could use the strength of a man, and having him cheer with them would add diversity. She had even patted him on the back and said, "See you there, Zak, city park Friday. 9 am. Be there or be square. We have a pep rally next Friday afternoon, and I'd love for you to join us as we prepare an amazing surprise!" Zak was overjoyed and had agreed without hesitation.

He was at the park, on time, and waiting determined not to be a square, He loved surprising people. He sat under the big tree. Then he climbed the giant slide. He pushed the merry-go-round and went around until he fell, arms spread to watch the world spin. He lay looking at the clouds twirl in the blue sky. '*Still, no cheerleaders.*' Missy said 9 am, City Park. He had done his part. He was unsure what went wrong.

"Beep beep ba beep beep!" A small red-honking car filled with giggling girls drove by. Zak rolled to his stomach to watch the commotion. "Fake out! Psych! Gotcha! Pranked!" Shouted the catty car-full. They roared off laughing at Zak's gullibility.

"Blank, blank, blankity, blank blankets!" Zak pounded the ground. He almost shouted out his street language, but he did not want to be arrested by Uncle Ben. He rolled over, gathering rocks and throwing them at the old tree. He despised being made fun of. His heart sank. His dreams shattered. Tears welled up in his eyes as frustration consumed him. He hated those girls. *How dare they do this?* He stood and ran towards the containers, humiliation tensing every fiber of his body and ravaging his self-worth.

Zak bolted past Riley's garage, with Penny bursting out to meet him, barking. He didn't stop. Penny barked harder and gave chase. The dog was determined to catch up to be part of the game. Mantha stepped out to investigate the commotion and runaway dog chasing a red-faced, frantic Zak! '*Here we go again,*' she thought, recalling his previous episode as she joined in chasing another screaming, barking parade.

Breathless, Zak tugged open the empty container and collapsed in the furthest corner, He wrapped into the soft blanket. He rolled into a fetal position, sobbing. Penny caught up. The dog came close to join him, sniffed, and then curled into a ball with her head on Zak's thigh.

Mantha stood in the doorway, taking it all in. She waited. And then she waited awhile longer. Whatever trigger caused this explosion was severe. It would take patience and silence before she could pull out details. She watched the restless body settle. The gulping breaths became rhythmic. Zak fell asleep. She decided not to abandon him. Forty-five minutes later, Zak rustled. Penny put her paw on his arm and gently licked the boy's cheek. Softly calling from the entry, Mantha ventured. "Hey, Zak, it's Mantha from the garage. Remember, Rosey? Rosey the 1940 Ford. Is everything alright?"

Zak sniffled. "I hate them! I hate them! I hate them! I believed them. I hate myself!" He moaned. "They thought it was hilarious. I want to hurt those girls. Pay them back for messing with me." He was shattered with humiliation.

Mantha approached at a snail's pace, crouching low. "I'm here for you, Zak. Tell me what's been going on. Sometimes it helps to let it out."

"It's just…" Zak's voice trembled with a plaintive fury. "I thought it could be different. That coming to Riverdale would be a do-over. I can't stop thinking about… all the times I've been tricked or set up. It's like there's a Monster Truck in my chest that wants to drive out of my mouth and run over every one of those evil people!"

"You feel angry and hurt. It's tough to start all over," Mantha shared. "I'm starting here too, and I don't know how to handle it either."

"You don't?" Zak perked up enough to briefly meet her gaze before he averted his eyes again. She crouched a few feet away and paused.

"I understand, Zak. It's normal to have strong feelings after some of the things we have lived through," Mantha shared. "Riverdale is my childhood home. Everyone knew me because I grew up here. But…I came home a different person. I lost a leg and fingers; people look at me differently now. My face is different, too. I feel so changed. It's hard to put into words. But I am different inside, not just outside, and I don't know what to do."

"I'm different, too. I know I am," confessed Zak. "When I was little, I thought I was an alien."

Mantha took two steps closer, turning sideways and facing the wall, not Zak. Direct eye contact would be too much. She didn't want him to feel raw and exposed. Penny nuzzled the teen. "Penny likes you, Zak. I'd say you are fully human. I feel alien in my changed body. There were times as I healed, I thought my body was trying to kill me. But you know what, my fighting spirit didn't let it."

"I've got a fighting spirit, Mantha," Zak stated vehemently. "And I want to kick those girls in their blankity-blank blanks."

"Blankity, what?" Mantha sputtered, caught off guard by his phrase. Despite the somber conversation, she felt a soft chuckle rising.

"Uncle Ben said he'd put me on house arrest if I kept using the f' n-heimer or the s-house words. He's the sheriff, and he has a gun. He might even like doing it," Zak paused. "Arresting me. Throwing me in jail."

"Oh, Zak, you…!" She caught herself starting to laugh but stopped short, wanting to be sure he'd feel laughed with, not at. "Gosh… you make me want to laugh sometimes, and I need to laugh more. I get what you mean, though. Since you're new, you try not to goof up or get in trouble here in Riverdale. They trick you, and it makes you feel small. Getting mad… it's like an overcoat to protect you because something hurts." Mantha smiled gently as she turned to face Zak and sat down. She sighed and let her prosthesis show above her sock. She reached out her injured hand. "Would you mind helping me up," she asked softly.

Zak noticed the red area where her fingers had once lived and saw the plastic above her shoe. He smiled warmly, and came forward to help Mantha. He reached out for her hand, steadying himself to stay strong. "I like helping people. Here, Mantha…"

"I know you do. I see the kindness in your eyes." Mantha rose, not needing his help but knowing Zak needed hers. She made sure to let Zak take some of her weight. "How would you like to help me at the garage? You could wash and shine the cars I fix up. Clean the office, maybe go out and wash car windows?"

"I could. I could! I would be good at that!" Chirped Zak. "I owe Uncle Ben a pile of money. Would you pay me?"

"Yes, of course, I'll pay you. Let's go talk to Sam," Mantha encouraged with gentle confidence.

—

The cheerleaders entered Dee's Cafe in high spirits. Their cackling caught Q's attention as they discussed a prank they had played on the new student. It seemed hysterically funny. Q was busy with his duties but couldn't help but overhear as one of the cheerleaders, Missy, gleefully recounted the details as her friends joined in with raucous sarcasm. "Oh my gosh, guys, that prank we pulled on the new kid was hilarious!"

Her blonde friend chimed in. "I know, right? I can't believe he fell for it so easily. He was clueless!"

"I can't stop laughing just thinking about it! Did you see the look on his face after we honked and told him we were joking," snickered a girl with red hair.

"Oh, it was priceless! He looked like he couldn't believe it was happening," a brunette slapped her leg and dissolved in laughter.

Q's broccoli boiled. He had warned Zak yesterday. The cheerleader's offer was too good, but Zak ignored the warning. Q pictured taking a tray with four glasses of water, feigning to trip, and dumping the whole tray upside down in the middle of the table. He added extra ice, then he thought better of it. He would take the high road. At Dee's, his job was to serve.

"His reaction was epic!" Howled Missy.

"He didn't catch on!" Cackled the redhead.

"He waited for three hours! That's a new record!" Howled the cute blonde, breathless with laughter.

"He's probably still trying to figure out how we do things at this school," Missy sneered arrogantly. "We've never had a boy cheerleader. Why would we want one now? Pfft, he's got a thing or two to learn about who's in charge here."

"Excuse me, may I take your order?" Q's voice was as frosty as the ice water. "Here… are four waters… and your utensils."

"Oh, it's the Ass-Burger kid. What do you want from us?" Missy dismissively flipped her ponytail.

"My name is Q, and I will be your server today. Have you decided on your order? If I remember right, two cherry shakes, a chocolate malt, and one dreamy orange float," Q said with flat precision.

"Wow," the blonde said. "Do you know who gets which?"

"Of course, Missy, pardon, yours is the only name I know. As usual, you will want a cherry shake, fries, and a cheeseburger with two pickles. Your friends, I remember by hair color. The blonde gets one dreamy orange float, sweet potato fries, plus a cheeseburger with fried onions. The redhead always orders a Sasquatch burger with cream cheese, green olives, chips, and a chocolate malt. Oh yes, lest I forget, I will put three sweet pickles on the side. Hmmm and to the brunette. Do I know you? My dear woman you are priceless." The girls were impressed.

"And me?" Challenged the brunette.

"Your order's easy: a cherry shake and a California burger. Don't forget the tomatoes, lettuce, and mayo. Oh, and make sure the burgers are piping hot," recalled Q. "Is there anything else? I know each of you better than you know me. And since you did NOT ask, my neurodiversity is listed in the DSM as Level One Autism, previously referred to as Asperger's." Q pivoted on his heel, heading back to the kitchen.

"Creepy," frowned Missy.

"Yeah, he's so weird." The redhead smacked her gum while insulting him. "What a nerd!"

Q imagined leaving the burgers until they were cold and the drinks until they melted, but proper service was his job. He choice a different tactic. He placed each specialty drink with the appropriate cheerleader. "Pardon me…. uh, can I talk to you young ladies for a moment?" Q asked with his customary courtesy.

The four girls raised their eyebrows as they sipped their drinks.

"It concerns what you did to my friend today. He was excited to help you at the pep rally. I don't think he deserved that prank. It was….." Q's voice was dispassionate. "RUDE." Q puckered his lips, raised his left shoulder, and looked catily at the girls.

"Ah, who cares? It was all in good fun. Besides, pranks are a rite of passage in high school, right?" the brunette challenged.

The cheerleaders exchanged looks, tilting their heads in agreement.

Q pivoted to fetch the burgers. He returned slowly with one order at a time. "I shall start with the piping hot California burger; don't forget the tomatoes, lettuce, and mayo." He held it out of the brunette's reach, paused, and stepped back.

"Maybe it didn't seem harmful to you, but for someone like him, that prank was distressing. He finds unexpected situations hard, and you young ladies, I MEAN girls, set him up pretty badly."

For emphasis, he set the plate clack before the girl, who pulled in her chin and shot him a "whatever" look.

"I shall stroll to get the next burger, so I do not drop anything." With his back toward them, Q smirked, walking as slowly as possible.

The brunette had already chomped down half her burger when he returned. Q held the Sasquatch burger with cream cheese and green olives on a plate piled high with ridged potato chips above her head and said crisply, "For the redhead, your lunch is served. It's important to consider the impact of your actions on others. Not everyone reacts the same way, especially people with neurodiversity. It's about empathy and understanding." Q positioned her plate in front of her with an impassive but direct gaze.

"Neuro what?" Asked Missy.

"Diversity," Q repeated. "Respect for differences is the point." He returned to the kitchen and brought the last two plates. "I did not let your lunches get too cold, though I could have…JUST A PRANK." He placed the plates with a purposeful 'clack' on the table before them. "It would mean a lot to my friend if you'd apologize to him. It would show that you understand you hurt him and are sorry for being mean."

"Haha! Seriously?! Your friend needs to toughen up. It was just a harmless joke," exclaimed the redhead, rolling her eyes.

"Oh, come on! We were having some fun!" Complained Missy.

Q stared intently and said nothing. He didn't move a muscle.

"Look, we didn't mean any harm… so… what do you want us to do?" Whined the brunette.

Q remained motionless.

The blonde jumped in. "Apologize? Seriously? That seems like a lot for something so simple."

Q scowled. "It may seem like just a prank to you, but it's not so simple to him. Everyday interactions are challenging, and such situations are hard on his confidence. Your 'simple prank' added to someone else's 'simple prank' that you don't even know about. Each prank build upon the next which builds upon the next. Being the target of pranks is rough. How many pranks occur before there is a complete explosion? If you are the target of jokes repeatedly, the dominoes line up, ready to fall with the right push. What happens when a push becomes a shove and more than a shove? How many people get hurt, then? Do you think being in a new school is easy for him? Have you ever wondered how violence happens?"

"FINE, we'll apologize. But this doesn't mean we won't pull pranks anymore." Missy slurped the dregs of her shake as loudly as possible to show her contempt, one side of her lip raised high.

Q cleared the girl's dishes. "You could find ways to have fun that don't hurt other people. Being considerate of those around you can make a big difference. It takes the same amount of effort to be kind as it does to be cruel. Think logically. If cheerleaders don't improve school spirit, who will?" He noticed the girls smiles droop.

Q lifted the remainder of the plates and silverware from the table and, with his usual flair and rote smile, stated, "Thank you for dining at Dee's Cafe."

The cheerleaders stared after him open-mouthed, eyebrows cocked as he walked away.

—

–11–

ON TIME OR . . .

Riley's garage pretty much ran itself with 24/7 pay pumps and vending machines and that's all most people saw unless they had a vintage car to restore to its original beauty. Sam ran a successful car wash with old-fashioned equipment and a loyal local customer base for years. The car wash industry changed as time passed, and modern automated systems became more prevalent. Three pristine bays on the freeway exit now existed at the never-to-spew-from-Sam's-mouth Rodeo franchise. FREE WASH WITH FULL FILL bragged the highway sign. Sam faced a dilemma—evolve or close. He had already moved away from oil changes and engine repairs to doing things he loved using his high interest in technology with a tendency to think outside the box.

Driven by curiosity and passion for new hobbies, Sam re-purposed his car wash into something unexpected. *Why not turn the car wash into a ham shack? What about an indoor shooting range? It was too dang cold to shoot between fall and spring for the old veterans. Unconventional?* For Sam, it was the perfect combination of his interests to keep his skills sharp and give back to the community. There were so many parts he could re-purpose. Washer roller sponges became soundproofing for indoor range walls. The car gear tracks worked brilliantly to create moving targets. He spent weeks setting up the remote control system. He put everything he didn't want or couldn't use outside by the pumps with a FREE sign for someone else. Everything disappeared. Sam immersed himself in research. Current ham radio operations had changed with technology, and safety protocols for indoor shooting ranges were mandatory. He sought expert help to ensure the transformation met regulation.

The car wash bays were ample, and the open spaces divided perfectly for his project. One side housed state-of-the-art ham radio equipment with towering antennas outside to ensure smooth transmission. Soon, a few passionate ham radio enthusiasts joined Sam's venture, and a small community formed around the Ham Shack. They gathered every Friday morning for breakfast at Dee's, exchanging radio signal stories from around the world. They assisted at nonprofit events and helped with emergencies when communication was essential.

The new indoor shooting range boasted soundproof walls and advanced safety systems to ensure a secure yet enjoyable experience for both experienced shooters and those new to the sport. Sam diligently followed all regulations to provide a safe platform to build skills under professional guidance. On the day of the private reopening, the VFW members were astounded to see the once-familiar car wash transformed into a unique hub for activity. The exterior remained charming and unassuming. The classic Riley sign's **O** remained missing above the subtitle Dazzling Details. Sam added another sign, 'The Smokin' Ham Shack.' His passion for ham radio and shooting was infectious. With his stories and deep expertise he sparked interest and excitement. Young and old found joy in learning from each other in this unexpected meeting ground. It wasn't just a place to communicate or practice shooting; it was an integral part of the town's culture, a hub of knowledge, camaraderie, and entertainment for the veteran community. It brought people together, fostering a sense of unity and shared purpose. It was a beacon of hope, symbolizing the community's resilience and adaptability in the face of change. Sam's Ham Shack and Riley's Range became synonymous with the old man himself.

Mantha, now the owner of Riley Garage, had yet to tour Sam's 'car wash.' He had not offered to share it.

———

Zak and Mantha walked with Penny back from the boneyard to the garage. "I'm excited to have you join our team, Zak. Before we start, I want to review your job responsibilities and expectations. Is that alright with you?" Mantha began.

"Wow, a real job, yes! Thank you for giving me this opportunity!" Zak wiggled with excitement.

"You will be great. Your responsibility will be to assist in detailing cars. You can use the car wash area. You'll be responsible for cleaning the interior, wiping windows, dusting surfaces, and shampooing carpets. Think you can do that?" Mantha asked. "Always remember I will inspect what I expect."

"I'll do my best." Zak stopped and then stammered. "I have t-t-trouble remembering things. I may need reminders."

This impressed Mantha, "I appreciate your honesty. Don't worry. We'll work together to make sure you're well-supported. After my brain injury, I used visual aids, checklists, and verbal reminders to help me remember tasks and processes. We can work this out together."

"I do real good with notes and reminders," Zak added.

The garage was empty. The door was unlocked. "Sam! Sam! Are you here?" Mantha shouted as she walked into the detailing area.

"Wonder where he is?" Zak's head went from side to side. "Maybe he's in the car wash."

Mantha tipped her head. "Let's check it out. Here's the key."

Zak ran to the door. "The door is open, Mantha." He entered. "Wowzer! Check this out! This ain't no car wash? Whoa! James Bond stuff!" Sam wore a black headset, which made him deaf as a doorknob. Lights flickered, knobs, dials, and switches surrounded him. "Star Wars! I'm transported!" Zak raised his arms and bowed low.

Amidst this mesmerizing symphony of colors, the glowing amber of the digital display emanated a warm welcoming aura that drew in Zak. He stood silently behind Sam, yearning to participate in this captivating communication process. The glossy black buttons and switches shimmered with intrigue as though they were the secrets revealing invisible threads binding radio waves to the ionosphere.

"Dang, Sam, this is no slouch setup." Mantha was awestruck. She now understood the antennas living on the garage's flat roof. "As I live and breathe!" She thought of her limited field operation setup. This was like a command central… she shook her head. Mantha had been pleasantly surprised at the resilience of O'Rileys with its many updates, was astounded at the primo Ham set up in front of her. Her eyes widened at the intricate details of the boards of technology surrounding the walls behind the unassuming doors. *Seeing was believing.* Next to a black rotary dial telephone was a tube station from the fifties.

Old and new puzzle pieces began connecting for her. Her mind raced from past to present to past, reliving the communication training across the world. Clearing her head, she saw Zak's starstruck expression and realized that was exactly how she felt the first time sitting in a similar chair in training. She stood ear hussling Sam's conversation.

—

Each week, Sergeant Reg and Sam met on the airwaves to rag chew with a cup of coffee.

Sam: I can feel the skip rolling in today! This is going to be one heck of a ride! Reggae, let's roll.

Mantha and Zak looked at each other, watching in fascination.

Reggae: *(Chuckling)* You got that right! It's like riding a wild wave on the airwaves. Let's see who we can tune into.

Sam: Roger that, partner. This skip has got my radio crackling. We need someone to answer our call.

Reggae: Let's see what's out there. Ah, I'm picking up a signal!

Sam: Awesome! What's the signal strength? Is it as strong as the desire for a piping hot cup of coffee on a chilly morning?

Reggae: Heck yeah! It's blasting through like a lightning bolt tearing through the night sky. You won't believe it!

Sam: Don't keep me in suspense! Who do we have on the line?

Reggae: *(Clears throat)* This is Ham 1 and Ham 2, calling out into the vast void of the atmosphere. Come in, come in, and let your voice dance on the airwaves!

Unknown Voice: *(Crackling with energy)* This is Ham 3, answering your call with gusto! It's like meeting long-lost friends at a bustling carnival. Over!

Sam: Ham 3, great to hear your voice! It's like stumbling upon a buried treasure in an exotic jungle. How are you?

Ham 3: I'm riding the skip waves like you! It's a symphony of signals out here, and stumbling across fellow hams is magnificent. And dear sir, I am in an exotic jungle as we speak. October is one of the best months to visit the beautiful capital of Brazil—Brasilia.

Reggae: Absolutely, Ham 3. It's like finding a hidden oasis amid a vast desert. Incredibly, we can connect across such vast distances.

Ham 3: *(Laughing)* You're right on the money, my friends! The skip truly opens up a world of possibilities. So, where do you hail from, adventurous hams?

Sam: Broadcasting from the heartland of North America, with towering cornfields and friendly folk. Trees are ablaze with color.

Reggae: Hailing from the hustle and bustle of the big city, with skyscrapers reaching for the clouds and a symphony of car horns playing in the background. Sirens of first responders careen around blocks and corners. We're in a top-floor apartment with a roof garden.

Ham 3: Wonderful! It's like the merging of two distinct worlds. Ham radio brings people together like butter on warm toast.

Sam: That's the magic of it, my friend. Hand in hand, we are united by the power of the airwaves and our shared love of Ham.

Reggae: Aye, Ham 3. Nothing quite like this tapestry we weave with our voices. Let's keep riding the skip, my friends, exploring. 73.

Ham 3: You can count on it! Here's to memorable conversations and unforgettable connections. Over and out! 73.

Sam raised his arms in the air as conquest. He removed his headset. "Well, I'll be. I did it! Brazil!" He swiveled his chair around, surprised to find Mantha and Zak. "What the hell are you two doing in here?"

"I came in to see the car wash. Mantha hired me to help her with the car details. I was looking for buckets, and hoses, and stuff." Zak's eyes bounced all around the equipment. He was beyond impressed.

"Wow, impressive." Mantha stammered. "Are you… VietW65? Was that Sarg65?"

"Well, I guess the cat's out of the bag," snickered Sam.

"What color is the cat? I'll go find it," Zak offered.

"Maybe," Sam ignored Zak's comment. "And you, my dear, Desert Rose! Face-to-face is better than a ham skip."

"What's a ham skip?" Zak pulled up a rolling chair.

"Ham skips occur due to a phenomenon called ionospheric propagation. The Earth's ionosphere is a layer of the atmosphere. It contains charged particles reflecting or refracting radio waves from the Earth's surface." Sam's hands made waving motions. "Skip propagation occurs when these radio waves are refracted or reflected to the ground far beyond the normal line-of-sight range. It is not an everyday occurrence."

"You mean like the northern lights?" Asked Zak.

"Yes, there can be a correlation between ham skips and Northern Lights. The Aurora Borealis is caused by interactions between the Earth's magnetic field and charged particles from the sun, which create colorful displays of light in the polar regions." Sam's hands were now palming an invisible Earth's north and south poles.

"I saw them dance in colors last week, Sam. They were in the field by the old containers," Zak shared excitedly. "I danced and twirled with them. It was fantastical!"

"They don't often come this far south. Northern Lights often indicate increased ionization in the ionosphere," added Mantha. "This higher ionization can create favorable conditions for skip propagation in certain frequency ranges, allowing ham radio signals to travel further distances. Many hams have reported increased skip propagation during periods of heightened auroral activity."

"You know about this too, Mantha?" Zak's face alight with wonder.

"Yes, Zak, I do, and it appears that Sam and I have been Ham buddies in past skips." Mantha looked intently at Sam.

"The universe creates no accidents." He gave her a knowing nod.

Zak burst out with a sudden revelation. "Mantha hired me. I'm working for you both now! When do I start?"

"First thing tomorrow," said Mantha.

"You will be inside this door before 0- 9 - 0 - 0 on your clock. " Ordered Sam. "You know about Lombardi time?"

"Yes," said Zak. "I mean no, I mean yes about the clock and no about Lombardi."

"Vince Lombardi was an American Football Coach for the Green Bay Packers in the 1960s. He is well-known for his discipline, dedication, and attention to detail. Lombardi time means you arrive here early daily, ready to work and perform at your best. Like Lombardi, I expect excellence from you," Sam instructed. "You understand?"

"Yes, Sam. Lombardi time it is!" Zak face went blank.

Sam noticed the look; he had seen it before in his son. "I think Mantha made a good hiring choice," Sam said, agreeing. He liked this kid and wanted him to succeed.

"What time is Lombardi time?" Zak whispered.

"Leave your house when those numbers say 0 - 8 - 3 - 5; that will give you plenty of time to walk here before 0 - 8 - 4 - 5." Sam explained.

Mantha pointed to a stack of index cards. "Let's write this down." She proceeded to write Zak's first work checklist:

0 - 8 - 0 - 0 - Get out of bed, dress yourself, then brush your teeth.

0 - 8 - 1 - 5 - Eat breakfast - *(Put your breakfast on the table before*
you go to bed. It's Easier than finding it in the
morning with brain fog.)

0 - 8 - 3 - 5 - Be out the door and walking.

0 - 8 - 4 - 5 - Arrive Lombardi time.

Mantha glanced out the window as she handed the paper to Zak. "Looks like your first customer service opportunity! There's a little red car filling up with gasoline right now."

Zak walked out to make a difference and was horrified to find Missy and her cronies at the pump. He turned to face Mantha and mouthed, "Blankity, blank blank!" He started to bolt.

Mantha grinned. "You want the job? Let's see what you can do." She handed him a blue jumpsuit. "Suit up, private. Show me your stuff!"

Zak glared as the jump suite tangled in his legs. After working the legs straight, he noticed her kind eyes and sweet smile. "Yes, ma'am, sir, captain." He saluted, pulled in as much air as he could and held it evacuated in loud raspberries.

"There is more than one way to face your enemies, Zak. Go! Stand tall," Mantha commanded, then watched as she silently cheered for her young trainee.

—

Zak tip toed to the red car. "Would you like your windshield washed to get a clearer worldview?" He asked with a smile.

Sam and Mantha, ready to intervene if necessary, leaned on each side of the doorway.

"Oh, pleeeee-ze," snarked Missy with a dramatic roll of her eyes. "I am sure we'd all love a clearer view of you and your ass'burger friend, Q."

Zak's body language changed as he lifted the dripping squeegee. He pulled back the long-handled tool with the soft, absorbent sponge designed to loosen dirt and debris. It was in a striking position, and Sam readied to jump into action, but Mantha reached her arm across his path. "Wait, let's see what he does." Zak turned his face to Mantha. She smiled and gave him a thumbs-up hoping she was right. Her past experiences with challenging Army privates took them up the higher road.

Zak doused the front windshield with water. The soapy liquid cascaded down the glass. He stepped back, leaning into the car.

Zak gave the girls a mischievous grin. "Welcome to Riley's, where we aim to serve everyone KINDLY." With a swift movement, he placed his right foot on the bumper and lifted his left. He shifted his weight, causing the car to rock, but not scratch it.

The girls rolled down their windows and leaned out. "Zak, are you doing?" Missy's voice pierced the air. "I'm telling my dad!"

Zak gyrated. *"Yo, Yo, Yo".*

Mantha held Sam back. "Wait." And then it came!

"In the aftermath of your cruel prank,

I felt anger and sorrow; my spirit sank,

Disillusioned and broken, I stood alone,

But little did you know, my strength would be shown."

"You thought you could break me with your deceit,

But you didn't see my fire beneath,

I may be hurt and wounded, but I won't stay down.

From the ashes, I'll rise with a righteous crown."

Zak put his face close to the glass as the girls jumped their heads back in to watch. Mantha laughed. Sam cocked his head.

"You can't break me, I'll defy your game,

Angry, disillusioned – I'll rise just the same,

Every setback is a lesson, every tear a fuel,

With determination, I'll break free from the fool."

"I was blinded by trust, cause I count friends dear,

But a prank brought betrayal, the thing I fear,

Deep down, my resilience grew, grew, and GREW.

With a force to guide and help me start anew.

To rise from the hurt lit by inner fire,

with each step I take, your prank expires....

pppsshhhhhhhhhh...mic drop!"

Zak fell off the bumper and onto the ground, laying silent. The cheerleaders' flat noses pressed into the two closed windows. Then a burst of energy sat him upright. He raised the tool into the air.

"I'll channel my anger into strength and growth,
Harness the pain. Let it fuel my oath,
To rise above the hurt, ignite my inner fire,
With every step forward, your prank will expire."
"Wounds can run deep, I won't let them define.
My spirit is unbreakable. It'll continue to shine,
Through the anger and disillusionment,
I'll find my way to a brighter future,
where I'll proudly say:"

He ran around the car. Stopped. The he slowly and expertly squeegeed off the front windshield.

"You can't break me. I'll defy your game.
Angry disillusioned, I'll rise just the same;
every setback is a lesson, every tear a fuel,
With determination, I'll break free from the fool."

Zak appeared to trip over the long handle. The cheerleaders leaned in expectation of a treacherous fall and laughed. But with a sudden twist, he was up and ready for the next stanza.

"I may stumble on this crazy journey I'm on,
But with every challenge faced, my resilience will dawn,
Not trusting now, I choose who gets in,
Learning from the past, stronger from within."

He stood tall, the squeegee flanking his side.

"So watch as I rise from the ash of your prank,
A phoenix reborn, a spirit you can't rank,
I'll find my peace, prove that I'm enough,
I am not broken. No, I am strong and tough."

He spun around and went to wash the back windshield.

"You can't break me. I'll defy your game.
Angry and disillusioned, I'll rise just the same.
Every setback is a lesson, every tear a fuel,
With determination, I'll break free from the fool."

The girls cranked their necks, following every movement. Q had completed his shift at Dee's and stood behind the gas pump watching the shown, he whooped with support.

Mantha clapped and shouted, "Encore!"

Zak put the squeegee into its holder.

"To all the pranks and pain that tried to hold me back,
You may have left scars, but my strength won't crack!
I will rise above & reclaim my power,
For I am a fortress like a mighty tower."

"Girls, your car has some serious mechanical problems. Your engine has a case of dehydration. Your tires are exhausted and need rotation. Your oil is old and time for the station. Have a good day." Zak turned and walked back to Mantha and Sam. The little red car, now with shiny and squeaky clean glass, spun out of the station without comment, leaving rubber on the pavement.

"That was brilliant, Zak! Their use of the term ass-burger was quite advanced for them. I am surprised they connected those dots. I am glad you are mightier than their mischievous pranks and shallow words. Your rap, by the way, was exceptional," Q murmured, with a bit of pride for his friend.

"I am waiting for the other shoe to drop." Sam gruffed.

"Did you drop the first one, Sam?" Zak asked. "Am I in trouble?" Sam stood in the doorway, looking unhappy.

"Don't worry, Zak, Sam's bark is worse than his bite," said Q.

That comment did not help Zak. "Sam's not a dog, Q. You know that."

"Zak! Riley's is in the business of taking care of vehicles, not jumping on bumpers to give girls a scare. It's best not to prank back," Sam scolded.

"An eye for an eye, and pretty soon the whole world goes blind. Do you want to work here? You will treat every car with respect, regardless of the human inside. That 1957 is Doc's car, and Doc is her dad. You know the school principal? I'd treat that car with respect."

"I must sit down. You wear me out, Zak, and that's good. Pranks, regardless of how innocent, can create great hardship," Mantha added. "These are not my words but the words of a young man. God rest his soul. Promise you won't laugh. My heart only remembers a small piece of this, but I remember the life I shared with this young man."

"Yo, let me tell you 'bout a prank that went down.

My friend got fooled, turned the squad around,

Thought it was all fun, just a harmless joke,

But little did we know, it'd leave him broke."

"Started as laughter, a playful game,

Then it turned darker, causing him pain,

I watched him suffer with a riot inside,

I see that prank as the cruelest ride."

"He spiraled in sadness, his smile turned gray.

Internal turmoil he couldn't chase away.

I watched his soul suffer, a riot inside,

Realizing now, the prank a cruel ride."

Do you know what it takes to be kind?

Pranks hurt the soul and mess up the mind.

It's important to think about what impact we make.

A prank isn't fun when it makes a heart break."

Mantha pursed her lips like she was blowing out candles. She scanned her audience. "My private lost his life. It took a lot of work to pick up the pieces and heal the whole squad. Another private shared this at his honors ceremony. I don't tolerate bullies. I know the depth of this pain. Please don't laugh at me. Ignore my Emily Dickinson style."

"Choose compassion, kindness plants seeds,

Walk each day with integrity,

Build new bridges, make friendships grow.

Let's ditch the pranks. Let connections flow."

Mantha slowed at the final line, letting the words sink in.

"Lame, Captain Mantha, Ma'am, yes, but the truth." Zak dared. "The Monogram Masters will try. SQZ go!"

"Squeeze?" Mantha lifted her lip.

"Shay, Q, and Z!" Q fist-bumped Zak. "SQZ, go! Seriously, that is an amazing idea! We can make a difference and create an inclusive environment by standing together. Sam, is Zak working for the rest of the day, or can we hang out?"

"I AM his boss, Q." Mantha paused... Sam smiled "Day one done. Get that suit off, and I will see you…" .

"0 - 8 - 4 - 5! Lombardi time!" Zak grinned. "I remembered!"

Sam glanced at Mantha, who shrugged her shoulders. "The pain management doctor told me to write up index cards to describe exactly what to do when I'm in medium to high pain, so there was no guesswork. Just thought it might help Zak, too."

~12~

~12~
GETTING CLEAN

"Let's go find Shay," suggested Q. "She volunteers at the memory care center today. I bet she'd like to play tag at the boneyard. Those steel containers are amazing. Or we could ride bikes. Or we could try a different game."

"Sounds fun," Zak agreed. "I need to run home and get my bike. I should probably check in with Uncle Ben. I'll meet you at your place."

Zak opened the front door of his new home and was surprised to find a pile of mail on the floor. That was unusual. Mail didn't belong on the floor, at home mail arrived in a little rounded box. Distracted by this oddity, he picked up the envelopes and flyers and accidentally kicked a letter under the boot bench. He set the mail on the counter. He was famished— "Kate's casserole!"

Sweating from his run home, he plopped on the floor in front of the an open refrigerator door. He placed the glass dish in his lap and dug in eating only the middle to bypass the crusty rim. His heart sank when he discovered the gelatin dessert was gone. He craved the mini marshmallows. When the refrigerator door alarm blared, he hastily returned the glass dish to the shelf and shut the door. Thirsty, he grabbed the spray hose, stuck it in his mouth, and gulped, disregarding the overspray pooling on the kitchen floor. He left the hose hanging in the sink basin and dashed off.

He had not seen Uncle Ben for over a day, so he left a note. His mom had always asked him to leave a note so she knew his plans.

He took an envelope from the stack of mail and jotted:

At Q's C.U. Z.

p.s.
I got a job.

Zak rode off to find Q and Shay. He continued into the boneyard to their container fort. There was a lighter on the grass, and he flicked it to spark. The dry grass ignited, and he stomped it out. He caught movement in the woods, aligning the boneyard. Someone was watching him. He left the lighter and went to find Q and Shay.

—

Shay curled up on the sofa to write in her journal. Q busied himself envisioning transforming the boneyard into a vibrant playground. It was now was a dangerous mess. He drafted a list of items related to the shipping containers. A treasure hunt would be a great way to clean up the whole area.

FIND

1. *Old equipment parts*
2. *Paper and cardboard*
3. *Wooden pallets*
4. *Metal scrap or scrap materials*
5. *Industrial barrels or drums*
6. *Used tires*
7. *Wire or cables*
8. *Broken locks*
9. *Plastic containers or bins*
10. *Discarded building materials*

"Shay, wait for Z, then come down to the boneyard. I've got a surprise for SQZ." Q wanted to arrive ahead of the others to create spaces for each item on his list and prepare the game. He was soon engrossed in setting up the activities he wanted to share with the Monogram Masters.

Shay stood on the porch. "Zak, are you here yet?"

"Right here!" Zak had been engrossed in watching ants build a hill at the back of the trailer, and he missed Q's departure.

"Q's waiting for us. Tag, you're it!" Shay shouted.

The boneyard seemed empty. "Hey, Q, we're here; where are you?" Zak yelled.

"I'm setting up a treasure hunt. Perhaps more rightly called a scavenger hunt," Q gestured to them. "Here are the rules to play: There are 10 square areas where you will bring your finds. We each own a corner of each square. Your corner has Z - Q - or - S created with white stones. I took the time to find one correct item for each box. The person with the most finds wins an extra scoop of the chocolate ice cream Mom bought." Ice cream was a rare treat in the Larkin home.

"Do you understand the rules?" Q handed Zak and Shay each a list. "Are you ready?" Q's arms swooped downward, creating a rush of movement. "Get set. GO!"

Shay and Zak raced as they rolled two industrial barrels. Their eyes scanned nooks and crannies. Random old vehicle parts remained steadfast even when they all pushed, pulled, and rolled. Old tires were stacked. Zak created a giant cube. Piles of wire and old gear rose. Wooden pallets created corridors and towers. Zak climbed, bracing himself between the containers, and scrambled to the top for a bird's eye view. "Come up here! You can see better!"

"How did you get up there?" Shay called back.

"Simple, just put your butt on one side and your legs on the other and sit-walk up," directed Zak.

Shay tried. "I'm too short! My legs aren't as long as yours!"

"I'll come down and help. It is pretty cool up here. You can see a long way off." Zak dangled his feet off the edge, lowered himself until he was hanging by his fingers, and…

"Zak, be careful! Don't hurt yourself!" Q warned.

…Dropped thudding to the ground as his legs hit the mud and slid from beneath him, leaving him straddled, rump down in a puddle of slime. The new jeans Zak had planned to wear to work in the morning were caked brown right in the area one would not want such a wet stain. He tried to extract himself without spreading mud everywhere and it was not going well.

Q saw the fall, blinked, puffed his cheeks, then pressed the air out with a pop of his lips, making a sound like a 'splat.' "Game over!"

"Oh no... Zak, it looks like you exploded in your pants." Shay exclaimed!

Zak reached around to his backside, only to extend the greasy mess from the rear to both hands. Muddy goo was everywhere. He grimace with embarrassment.

Q quickly focused on Zak. "Oh no! Are you alright? I noticed you fell. Do you need help getting up?"

"I could use a hand. Thanks for offering!" Zak reached out his blackened, greasy hand.

Q stepped back to assess. "Just a sec. Alright, let's get you on your feet. Can you reach out your hand towards me but not touch me? I will do the work."

Zak extended one hand towards Q.

"Great!" Q considered the next step. "I will gently grab your clean wrist and slowly pull you up. Just let me know if you feel any discomfort. Use your legs for strength." He leaned over slowly, anchoring his stance with his knees bent to drop his center of gravity and use his body as a counterbalance. "Zak, straighten your legs."

"No problem at all. Nice and easy, now. I'll have you standing in no time." Q gradually pulled Zak upright to balance without getting messy.

"Thanks." Zak stood without toppling. "You're a real friend."

"Way to go, bro!" Shay admired.

"Phew, that was a lot harder than I thought. I can't believe I ended up in a puddle of mud!" Zak moaned. "My new pants!"

"Don't worry about it. Accidents happen, and the important thing is that you're unhurt," Q pulled a white ironed handkerchief from his pocket to wipe the dirt from his fingers. "Muddy grease can be quite stubborn to clean off, but I think we can do a reasonable job with it. Let's start by wiping your hands on some dry grass."

Zak bent over to wipe his hands on the grass and smeared the rest on the container with a big ZAK leaving mud on the ribbed metal siding. He reached down to get more mud and finish under his name writing 'Was Here' in a giant scrawl.

Aghast at the additional mud retrieval, Q turned away after noting a freshly charred area below the graffiti. "Let's return to our house and get that mud off you and your clothes. We have a washing machine. We can hang your pants to dry." Q strategized.

"Zak, you'll have to take your pants off outside so I can hose them off. Mom does not play with mud in the house," Shay grinned.

"Ummm..." Stammered Zak.

"Don't worry. I've got a big brother and seen boys in underwear before. Or you can go back home to your sheriff uncle like a swamp thing," Shay jabbed him with her finger.

Q fetched a threadbare towel inside the trailer and held it as a curtain. "Turn around, Shay, Zak needs some privacy."

Zak kicked off his shoes without socks and dropped his pants, extracting his legs like a reluctant spider stuck in glue. Shay snatched the pants, and flung them onto the gravel to hose off the soil. Between rinses, she scrubbed them with the blue liquid soap she hastily grabbed.

Q was surprised. "Zak, where did you get that red underwear?"

"The store in town."

"They're boxer briefs. I had them ordered special. Red was not my color. But it works for you," nodded Q. "Here, wrap the towel around you. It is more modest, especially since Shay's here."

"Thank you for helping me clean up, guys. I appreciate it."

Shay sighed, scrubbing a more challenging stain. "We can line dry them until they stop dripping. Then we will bring them in the house when it gets dark to finish drying. Outside will be too damp."

Q answered. "You're welcome! I'm glad we could assist you. We all need a helping hand sometimes. Is there anything else I can do?"

"Ice cream?" Zak suggested.

Shay threw Zak's pants on the clothesline. Zak wrapped in the towel, followed Q into the house.

Q looked quizzical; ice cream was part of the game, and they did not finish it. "We did not finish the game."

"You said we play your game and get ice cream. Either no one won, and we get one scoop of chocolate each, or we all won because we worked together," Zak rationalized.

"Of course. I understand how unexpected situations can change the rules and be overwhelming. But I am unsure about the ice cream; we never finished the game."

"Q, we played the game, and an accident happened. You better get used to that with me. I get into accidents and mess up a lot, and my body sometimes has a mind of its own. I lose my balance when I lose my focus. I tried my best…" Zak paused with a shrug. "Ice cream?"

Q answered. "Yes. Accidents happen. I don't always have the best coordination or balance, either. But I try my best, as do you."

Shay added. "To do our best despite challenges, I vote for one scoop each." She held out one finger in the air.

"Two scoops!" Zak chimed in, mimicking Shay's idea but holding up two fingers.

Q put his finger to the tip of his nose. "Mom bought the ice cream as a special treat for us. Monogram Masters survived the game and the shame." He paused, turning his head between Shay and Zak. "Two scoops it is!"

"Hurray!" Shouted Zak.

"Yes!" Shay cheered.

"I announce, that the game is paused and we can return another time." Q stated.

"How about we find a new game to play inside while Zak's pants dry?" Offered Shay.

———

Ben noticed his mail on the kitchen counter when he arrived home. He surveyed the stack, eager to find the first allowance check from his brother David for Zak's room and board. There was nothing but bills and a note from the fertility clinic stating another 'no go'. Oddly, someone had written on the backside. 'Zak. Of course, Zak' They had prayed for a child. They had not prayed for Zak!'

At Q's C.U. Z.
p.s. I got a job.

Why did Zak call him CUZ instead of Uncle? And where did Zak get a job? Ben grabbed a glass for a drink of water and slipped on the slick water dribble left on the floor.

"Doggone kid!" He hissed aloud. He opened the fridge, finding the casserole with the hole in the middle significantly enlarged and the plastic covering the dish wadded up and left on the shelf below. He wiped up the water and drove to the local sub shop, where he sat for a couple of hours chatting and catching up with some locals on news other than the suds-capade and his nephew. The camaraderie of friends lightened the load as it grew late. His heart toward Zak had softened. They were near the end of surviving a momentous weekend without Kate at home. Ben decided to drive up and check on Zak, probably still at the Larkin trailer. He spotted Zak's bike half hidden under the bush by their porch. He stepped out of the squad car, hopped up on the small porch, and knocked briskly on the door.

Shay answered, shouting, "It's the sheriff!"

"Tell him I'm not here!" Snapped Lindsay from in the house.

"Mom says she's not here," shouted Shay through the door.

"I don't need your mother; I am looking for Zak!" Replied Sheriff Ben, hearing a commotion coming from the window near the high bushes. He spotted a pair of long bare legs in red underwear hit the gravel and scurry down the road as fast as untied red shoes could run.

"Never mind; it looks like I found him. Sorry to bother you. Have a good night," called Uncle Ben as he jumped back in his squad car. He turned on the blue lights without sirens and pulled up quickly alongside Zak. He rolled down the windows and bellowed, "ZAK, GET IN THE CAR! What in the world happened back there? Why are you running down the street without your pants?"

Zak tried to catch his breath.

"What on earth were you doing?" Uncle Ben chuckled, Zak's red shoes matched his underwear. He had no pants. "Get in my car. NOW!"

Zak quickly clambered into the backseat behind the cage for protection from the roaring lion behind the wheel with a gun in his belt. "Sheriff Ben, it's not what it looks like! I was at my friend's house, and there was a crazy mix-up. While we were watching videos, the pants vanished, and you showed up; I panicked."

Uncle Ben's eyes furrowed, and his eyebrows raised almost to his hairline. "Vanished? All right, son, take a deep breath and tell me exactly what happened. And….where are your pants now?"

"Well, we were having a great time playing video space games and laughing. But then we heard this loud crash from another room, which scared us. Shay ran to the door. Things got chaotic, and somehow, my pants disappeared. I couldn't handle it. I was going back home," Zak sputtered, making no sense, shivering and hugging himself while rocking.

"Hmm, sounds like quite the situation. Did you try asking your friend for help to find your pants before bailing out the window?" Uncle Ben watched him on the squad's rear view mirror.

Zak continued quickly. "I panicked, Sheriff Ben. I just had to get out of there. I knew my room at home was safe under the desk."

"I'm glad our home is a place of comfort. It's best to stay calm and slow down in moments like these. Jumping out of a window without your pants is impulsive and can hurt you. It's alright, Zak. I want you to learn the importance of safety. Now, let's try to find your pants and sort this out. Do you remember where you left them in your friend's house?"

Zak answered sullenly. "They might be in Q's bedroom. Or Shay may have put them in the bathroom. Or maybe they are outside."

"I want to ask why...." Uncle Ben stopped himself and suggested, "Hmm...well... Let's head back to your friend's house together. We'll talk to them and ask them to help locate your pants. I'll make sure everything gets resolved. Asking for help is a good option." Ben did a U-turn, shaking his head in wonder. In all his time as sheriff, he'd never brought anyone without pants into his squad car.

"Thank you, Sheriff Ben, Uncle Ben, sir. I promise I'll handle situations like this more responsibly in the future."

The sheriff pulled up the drive for a second time; Q and Shay had been looking out the curtains, "He's back, and he's got Zak locked up in the backseat!" Shay panicked.

"He has just traversed the last porch step." Q squared his shoulders and opened the door. "Dear sir, what do we owe the pleasure of this return visit?"

"I need Zak's pants." Sheriff Ben said bluntly.

"Dear sister, will you be so kind as to get Zak's pants?" Q turned to look at Shay.

Shay played along. "Of course, my dear brother." And off she hustled in her fleece sweats to collect the wet jeans. She returned quickly, "I apologize for their dampness; I washed them the best I could with the hose and dish soap; we have no dryer."

"Thank you. I...he needs them. I appreciate you helping Zak." Ben tipped his hat awkwardly and held the still-dripping pants. He returned to the car—still confused about what on earth had happened. By now, the same Zak, who did not seem to sleep at night, was curled up and snoring in the back seat, looking lost and innocent in his red underwear and shoes. "I'm here to support you, buddy. I don't know who you are or what planet you're from, but I will ride this part of your life journey to graduation with you, come hell or high water." Ben's thoughts and feelings conflicted; he would pick the story apart at some point to get the truth. It was too late to rustle more feathers if he wanted to get sleep.

———

Being free from the confines of the school and small town community to laugh and share was a welcome relief. Having completed the full-day MEA conference on Thursday, Doc, Kate, and her friends spent Friday shopping and enjoying various museums and reviewing local educational attractions for potential field trips. After a long day, they enjoyed a final dinner together.

Kate's eyes met Doc's, filling her with warm, excited feelings. Always the gentleman, Doc walked the four women to their hotel room and wished them a good night, lingering on Kate's smile as she slowly closed the door. Bedtime came early with plans to eat the complimentary hotel breakfasts and return home by Saturday noon.

———

Zak, dressed in pajama bottoms, but wearing the same T-shirt, pulled a folded note from his front shirt pocket, thankful he had not left it in his now-washed pants.

He read aloud: "0 - 8 - 0 - 0 - Get out of bed, dress yourself, then brush your teeth. 0 - 8 - 1 - 5 - Eat breakfast - *(Put your breakfast out on the table before you go to bed. Easier than finding it in the morning with brain fog.)* 0 - 8 - 3 - 5 - Be out the door and walk 0 - 8 - 4 - 5 - Arrive Lombardi time."

"Nice jammies, Zak," said Uncle Ben. "Got any Saturday plans?"

Zak looked at his checklist. "I need to be out that door," he pointed to the front door. "Walk to Riley's by 0 - 8 - 3 - 5, and Sam said I need to be at the garage by 0 - 8 - 4 - 5. He calls it Lombardi time."

"Sam hired you? That's awesome!" Praised Uncle Ben.

"No, Mantha hired me, and Sam said, OK," Zak corrected.

"Would you like some hot chocolate?" Uncle Ben placed the wet jeans into the laundry room dryer. "These should be dry by morning."

Zak gave a broad-toothed smile. "I like hot chocolate!"

"Kate should be back by noon tomorrow. She will be quite impressed that you got yourself a job," smiled Uncle Ben, then paused. "Zak, can I ask you something, and you will tell me the truth?"

"I'll try," shrugged Zak, sipping his cocoa.

"Why did your pants get wet?" Asked his uncle.

"I..." He paused. "Don't answer why questions. Why puts my mind into a house of mirrors like a fun house at the state fair, so I can't answer you." His face flushed.

"OK," said Uncle Ben, believing Zak was genuinely trying to answer. "Let's try again. How did your pants get wet?"

"That's easy. I was on top of the container at the boneyard and getting down to help Shay, but my hands got tired. I fell in the mud, and Q helped me up. Shay hosed down my pants, and she scrubbed the stain." One breathless sentence. "I couldn't wear them all muddy and wet!" He threw his arms up and bent at the elbows, his fingers extended. "And you probably would be mad if I came home with mud and brought the mud into the house. Right?"

"No, you couldn't wear them muddy and wet. And yes, mud would have made me probably madder than the bubbles," Uncle Ben agreed, shaking his head slowly as he drank, wondering how any story could get so mixed up. He was sure there was more information; Zak was telling his truth in snippets as if he were a cameraman and not the participant. "Kate will be home tomorrow. We did it, Zak. We got through our nights alone." Ben put up his mug, "Cheers!"

"Cheers!" Zak clinked his uncle's mug.

"Do you need help waking up in the morning?" Asked Uncle Ben.

"I can do it myself." Zak began to read. "The list says 0 - 8 - 1 - 5 Eat breakfast.

"OK, then let's put your breakfast out on the table before you go to bed. Easier than finding it in the morning with brain fog." Ben got up from the table. "Do you like cornflakes?"

Zak nodded. "How did you know I woke up in the fog?"

Uncle Ben ignored the comment and continued. "The bowls are in this cupboard. Here are the spoons in this drawer." He handed Zak a bowl with a spoon. "The sugar is in this bowl." Uncle Ben tapped the sugar bowl. "The milk and orange juice are in the fridge. After you eat, I expect everything to be cleaned and in the dishwasher before you walk out that door."

Zak nodded. "Do you want the milk and orange juice in the refrigerator, Uncle Ben? You said everything clean and in the dishwasher before I walk out the door."

Uncle Ben looked over his cocoa mug, "Thank you for clarification. The dishes - the dirty dishes - the ones you just ate from - the bowl, the spoon, the empty glass from the orange juice go into the dishwasher and I will add the soap and start it."

"Okay, got it."

"The orange juice that is left and the milk will be returned to the refrigerator. And since it is my day off, I expect you to be quiet and let me sleep. You understand?" Uncle Ben added.

"Yes, Uncle Ben. Clean up my mess after breakfast, and don't wake Uncle Ben up or else something I do not want to know about will happen to me." Zak rehearsed.

"Exactly. Good night," sighed Uncle Ben, departing to his room. He paused momentarily to say something else but thought better of it. It was another one-of-a-kind day, and Kate would want to hear every detail.

-13-
SMOKIN' HAMS

Zak woke early for his first day at Riley's. The clock said 0 - 6 - 0 - 0. He checked his paper from Mantha. **#1   0 - 8 - 0 - 0 - Get out of bed, dress yourself, then brush your teeth.**

He tried his best to remain quiet to let Uncle Ben sleep. *Would Mantha be mad if he got out of bed earlier? The note said at 0 - 8 - 0 - 0, he was to get out of bed.* He counted ahead on his fingers, figuring out 2 hours and 45 minutes left before he had to be at Riley's. *That was Sam's Lombardi time.* He counted ahead on his fingers, figuring out 2 hours and 30 minutes left before he had to be out the door. *Mom was always glad when he got up early. To follow Mantha's orders, he could always go back to bed so he could get out of bed at 0 - 8- 0 - 0.* Zak got up and tripped over his nicely folded and dried jeans in front of the den door.

Zak wanted to make a good impression, Mom always bugged him about the importance of a shower so he turned that faucet. It was loud, big, and wet. "Yikes! No! No, No!" He shrieked, leaping out of the shower. Uncle Ben, jolted by Zak's yelp, stirred in his sleep. However, the sound was not enough to fully rouse him. Nothing Zak did surprised him anymore; a single yelp was not enough to disrupt slumber. Only sustained commotion warranted his full attention.

For Zak, the sensation of the water, was akin to being poked with a hot fork. It was unbearable. He hated water and wind. They both assaulted him. At least baths weren't pokey. He shut off the shower, opting to fill the tub. He added shampoo for bubbles. "I just need to soak," he muttered. By now, water had spilled all over the floor around the tub. He slid down and submerged to wash his hair. "Gotta look good." He forgot he hated water on his face. "Yikes, No! No, No!" He screamed, desperate to wipe the water out of his eyes.

Uncle Ben heard the next ruckus, grunted, put his pillow over his head to squelch the noise, and fell asleep.

Eventually, the water grew so cold that Zak peeled himself out of the tub, wrapped himself in a towel, ran a toothbrush over his teeth, and raked his wet hair into place. He picked up his clean jeans folded on the dryer and returned to his room for fresh underwear, socks, and a T-shirt. He also hated socks but knew he was expected to wear them. He grabbed his black sneakers, as he didn't want his red ones to get any dirtier.

He reread his note from Mantha and checked the time on the clock: 0 - 7 - 0 - 0. He decided to dress early and then go back to bed as he watched the numbers slowly click toward 0 - 8 - 0 - 0.

He reread the note. One was done.

#2   0 - 8 - 1 - 5 - Eat breakfast - *(Put your breakfast out on the table before you go to bed. Easier than finding it in the morning with brain fog.)*

#3   0 - 8 - 3 - 5 - Be out the door and walking

#4   0 - 8 - 4 - 5 - Arrive Lombardi time

He decided to eat breakfast early. Mantha wouldn't care. He rode the railing and landed with a thud on the bottom of the stairs in front of Uncle Ben's door. Again, Zak's noise jolted Ben awake, making it evident the boy was up and getting on with his day. Since the thud signaled a landing, not an emergency, Ben chose burrowing undercover and was determined not to rise until the door slammed.

The alarm on the refrigerator door announced that Zak had gotten to the milk and orange juice. It was now 0 - 8 - 3 - 4, and as the last number changed to a 5, the door slammed.

Ben was fully awake, he took a deep breath. *Time for coffee.*

—

Sam and Mantha sat on the bench with Penny, awaiting Zak's arrival. *It was 0 - 8 - 4 - 0!* "I'm impressed," exclaimed Sam. "You beat Lombardi."

Zak beamed as he knelt for Penny to greet him.

"Good morning. I need to commend you, Zak. You handled those cheerleaders pretty well, and now here you are, bright and early, ready to go," greeted Mantha. Let's get to work. I made you a checklist for each activity. The checklists are laminated, so you can write on them when you finish them and I will wipe them off after I inspect what I expect. If I don't like the quality you will get the card back as a do over. I added a key ring so you can flip easily through them to get to each activity." She handed Zak the half-inch package of index cards.

"Cool!" Zak flipped the cards while playing with the keyring.

"Zak, here's a wipe-off marker; it's your tool to mark your progress and completion of each task. Choose five cards each day until you have done all of them. Yellow cards are everyday! There is only one of those. Here is the basket to put your completed cards. Make sure you keep the cards left to do on the keyring and hand it here before you leave for the day." Mantha turned it over to Sam.

"We will inspect your work afterward to ensure we're meeting our standards," emphasized Sam, highlighting responsibility and standards. "Zak, your main priority is customer service. I trust your ability to be kind and helpful to ALL our customers. Your role is crucial in maintaining our reputation and ensuring customer satisfaction," reminded Sam, emphasizing the words trust and crucial with his hands.

"Let's start by choosing just one card, Zak, for your first activity, and follow the tasks as listed," instructed Mantha.

Zak chose to sweep the garage. Mantha had a picture of the north wall. The listed tasks said: 1. Sweep 2. Scoop in dustpan 3. Empty the dustpan in the trash.

"This one is easy," he nodded and proceeded to sweep the area in the photo. After comparing the image and looking around, he found Mantha. "Mantha, you can inspect what you expect," Zak was proud.

Mantha walked over to the area. Zak was right. The area shown in the photo location was swept to perfection. Perfection right to the edges where the image ended. Mantha pointed to the unfinished areas. "What about all this?"

"It's not in the picture," smiled Zak.

Mantha was thankful she had seen this sort of literal response before. As a captain, she had initially stormed at the privates who behaved this way. Then she learned, for some strange reason, the very thing she cherished—that of following explicit orders was precisely what they did. She learned to give orders differently to meet her goals and achieve her desired results. "Zak, may I borrow your marker?"

"Sure, here." Zak handed Mantha his blue marker.

"Your work was perfect," she complimented. "Now, step two, since you know what to do, is to complete the floor of the whole garage." Mantha drew arrows out from the photos. "The arrows mean the whole floor."

"No problem, Mantha Captain Sir, I mean ma'am." Zak immediately got to work on completing Task #1. He moved quickly on to Task #2. Then he disappeared.

—

"Where did Zak go?" Sam stuck his head in to see the garage floor and laughed.

"He was here a minute ago. I thought he went to get the shop vac and a bucket," Mantha noticed the Ham Shack door ajar and motioned to Sam to look. Sitting on Sam's swivel chair, with Sam's headset was Zak. Mantha put her finger to her lips. "Shhh. He's talking."

Zak's natural voice: "Hey there, fellow Ham! How's your day going?"

Squeaky voice: "Greetings, my ham friend! Thank you for making my day quite splendid. How about yours?"

Lower voice: "Oh, it's been quite eventful! I had a little adventure in the kitchen. We got to chew on some delicious vegetables and a slice of apple. What about you? Have you had any exciting experiences lately?"

Squeaky voice: "I enjoyed playing with an old toilet paper roll. Hamster heaven, I tell you!"

Lower voice: "Toilet paper rolls are the best. I love rolling around and hiding inside them. It's like having my very own little tunnel. Speaking of tunnels, have you explored any new ones lately?"

Squeaky voice: "I discovered a hidden passage behind my cage the other day. The path led me to a secret stash of tasty treats. I couldn't believe my luck!"

Zak: "Wow, that's incredible! With secret tunnels and hidden treats, you know how to live the high life!"

Zak took off the headset. "Naw, not right. Try again, Zak."

Sam looked wide-eyed at Mantha and whispered, "Shaun did a show like that forty years ago, almost verbatim. Amazing! He changes voices like Shaun."

Zak put the headset back on.

Zak: "Ladies and gentlemen, Delightful Detailing here with Smokin' Hams. We've brought two hams to our studio, one smoked and one brined, for a one-of-a-kind conversation. Let's dive in! Smoked Ham, can you tell us about yourself?"

Smoked Ham in a low guttural voice: "Thank you, Zak. I come from a tradition of slow smoking over hardwood. I'm known for a rich, smoky flavor and a beautiful caramelized exterior. My meat is tender, juicy, and bursting with delightful smokiness."

Zak: "That sounds delicious, Smoked Ham. Now, let's turn to Brined Ham. Can you please introduce yourself?"

Brined Ham in a high squeaky voice: "Of course! Thank you, Zak. Unlike my counterpart, I am soaked in a flavorful brine solution. The flavors go deep into my meat. I am naturally juicy. I am praised for my moist texture."

Zak: "Excellent! Smoked Ham. What are your strong points?"

Smoked Ham: "As a Smoked Ham, I bring a unique depth of flavor to the table. I am a choice for those looking for a rich and smoky taste for sandwiches or soups. I love sweet glazes."

Zak: "Brined Ham, tell me more."

Brined Ham: "Being brined, I adapt to herbs, spices, and seasonings to tantalize every bite. You can choose a tangy mustard glaze, a sweet brown sugar glaze, or a zesty citrus marinade, and I'll bring out the best flavor."

Zak: "Well, Hams, you have been accommodating. Thank you both for sharing tips! One last question each. Smoked Ham, what makes you stand out on the holiday table?"

Smoked Ham: "My smoky aroma brings a sense of warmth and comfort to any gathering. I'm often the centerpiece!"

Zak: "And now, Brined Ham, what is your appeal?"

Brined Ham: "Well, with me, your taste buds gain an explosion of flavors on the 4th of July."

Zak: "Thank you, Smoked Ham and Brined Ham, for this enlightening interview. May you continue to please diners for years to come!"

Smoked Ham: "Thank you for having us!"

Brined Ham: "My pleasure!"

Zak put down the headsets. It did not appear he had twiddled any dials or turned any knobs—it was all pretend.

Sam shook his head with wonder. "He belongs here, Mantha. They say the third time's a charm—first Shaun, then Kevin, and now Zak. Let's work together to give him purpose and community. Maybe this time around the tree I get it right. I guess I might just have the gift of another chance."

Mantha and Sam backed away so Zak did not know they were eavesdropping. "Don't let me forget to tell him that working the radio needs licensing, and except in an emergency transmission without a license, is up to a $10,000 fine." Sam said. "Your military license does not count."

Mantha smiled, "Guess I better get a civilian license, eh, Sam?"

—

Zak emerged from the base station, pushing the shop vac stacked with a five-gallon bucket perched on top and holding the still dripping behind him mop. He was humming, and then singing, and then rapping , and then talking. He spent the day vacuuming, cleaning, and polishing.

Mantha asked him to vacuum the front of the 1957 Chevy, Zak vacuumed only the front, no more, no less. It was precisely what Mantha asked for. "Great job today, Zak. I'll see you Monday at 3:30 p.m. after school."

"Yes, you will," confirmed Zak. He was energized by being helpful. He was near cool cars and friendly people. There would be a paycheck!

Mantha heard the slight squeal of the vintage freezer door as it worked to slide open. The chatter, banter, and laughter of young men intensified.

"Everything inside is one dollar, Q. You want an ice cream sandwich?" Zak reached in to get one for himself.

"No, thank you. I prefer a green freeze pop." Q nuzzled the head of the wiggly Penny, who sat quickly in hopes of a treat.

"That will be two dollars, boys." Mantha rumbled from under the dark blue metal flake 57 Chevy. "Shut that door, don't let my cold out!"

"I'm not gonna let your cold out, Mantha. It's a deep freeze, and the cold lives in the down part, not the up part," Zak challenged. "Cold falls down and hot floats."

Q noticed the vintage car. "You are restoring a metal blue-flaked 1957 Chevy? I've been researching old classics, particularly 1957 and 1956 Chevys. Both are iconic and sought-after cars, but there are differences."

Mantha rolled out on the dolly. "Who are you?"

"I'm Zak's friend, Q. We'll hang out this afternoon. I am stunned by this vehicle!" Q oogled. "The 1957 Chevy is often called a "Bel Air" model, known for its distinctive tail fins and chrome accents. It has a futuristic and exaggerated design. This was popular during the late 1950s. The 1956 Chevy, on the other hand, has a more conservative design with smoother edges and a less prominent tail fin."

"I like the flair with the tail fins." Zak bit the ice cream sandwich, "Tail fins are way cool."

"What else do you know, Q?" Mantha was curious.

"There are some differences in the engine options. The 1957 Chevy had several engine choices, including the famous 283 cubic inch V8 engine, which was quite powerful for its time. On the other hand, the 1956 Chevy, had a range of engine options, but none as powerful as the 1957 model's V8. In terms of performance, the '57 Chevy had an edge." Q seemed to know his stuff.

"This is a V8, Q," said Mantha. "And what else do you know?"

"Well, the interior designs of both cars were quite similar, with stylish dashboards and comfortable seating options. However, the 1957 Chevy had advanced luxury features, like optional power windows and seats, which were not as common in the 1956 model. The '57 Chevy might be a better choice if you were looking for sophistication. May I ask who owns this car, or would that be intrusive?"

"Doc Johnson, the school principal," replied Sam. "Your knowledge, Q, is quite proficient."

"Thank you." Q appreciated the acknowledgment. "As I understand it, the 1957 Chevy had a limited production. So, it's rarer and considered valuable among collectors. The '56 Chevy had higher production numbers, making it slightly more accessible and less expensive. Overall, both cars have a unique charm and are appreciated by car enthusiasts."

"Do you know the value of a car like this?" Asked Sam.

"A 1957 fully loaded Chevy in pristine condition, fully restored and well-maintained can have an estimated value ranging anywhere from $50,000 to over $100,000 well above the pay grade of any school principal," Q licked his green freezie before it dripped.

—

Kate snuck up from behind with a mid-waist grab after Doc dropped her off at the house. Ben wearing shooting muffs to blow leaves into a huge pile had not noticed. He startled and turned off the blower.

"Where's Zak, and why isn't he helping you?" Kate loosened her embrace of the formidable leaf wrangler.

"Hey, Honey, you're a wonderful sight for sore eyes! Zak? Oh, he's working with Sam and Mantha at Riley's." Ben chuckled, "I can't believe it, but he got himself a job." He hoped the good news would wash away the lingering tension from how the whole arrival of his nephew into their lives had unfolded. In her absence, it had dawned on him that he'd roped her into this mission and not given her time to weigh in or make a real choice. He was used to taking the lead as the sheriff and he hadn't meant to sideline his better half. He hoped she'd be reassured he had made the right decision. Kate was his guiding light, and he believed there was nothing she couldn't handle. He paused, waiting for her reaction.

"That's surprising," said Kate giving a half nod. "How were your days together?"

Ben was surprised he was speechless. He didn't know where to begin and he had wanted to vent and rant. So much about Zak didn't make sense. Overwhelmed and wanting quiet with Kate, he decided to keep things brief. "It went fine. Zak's made friends with...," Ben's s voice trailed off. "Lindsay's kids."

"Thank God they are not like their mother was at their age," Kate said with a wry smile.

Ben smiled back in agreement. "True."

———

Doc pulled up to Riley's garage to fill the tank. Zak ran out to greet him. "Hello, Mr. Johnson, sir. May I wash your windshields? I know you didn't want to see me the rest of the last day at school, but you need to know you will see me a lot here. This is my job. It will be my final credit to graduate."

"My name is Dr. Johnson. Yes, to washing my windshields. I am happy to see you are making yourself useful," said the principal. "Working at Rileys until graduation will qualify for you last missing credit." Zak beamed as Doc paid for his gas. "Can you fill my tank too?"

"Yes, sir, doctor sir. I will fill your tank." Zak watched as Doc left to get an update on his prized 57 Chevy.

Mantha looked at Sam. "Thought Zak was off the clock."

"He is," sad Sam. "He's a kind kid. I like his spirit."

"Good afternoon, " Sam welcomed Doc. "How was your trip to the cities?"

"I did well there. I made some great connections. How is the detailing coming? I'd like it completed by mid-November for Thanksgiving and the St. Paul holiday car show," said Doc. "This beauty of mine should really make a splash. I'm glad you're taking good care of her," he gave Mantha the slow once over. "It's about time she started working on my beauty. I expect nothing but perfection, you know." He looked back at the woman he had tried to conquer in his youth standing in the shadow of the hoist and casually smiled. Mantha did not reciprocate.

Q soaked in particulars while listening to the conversation. Mantha appeared ready to attack but held back.

Sam redirected the conversation, "Your vintage car is quite beautiful. I can assure you that WE will do our best to restore it to its former glory. What specific issues or modifications would you like us to address?"

Doc almost hissed. "Oh, where do I begin? I want every single part of this car flawless with attention to the tiniest detail. This car reflects my impeccable taste and status in the Minnesota State car community."

Q wondered how long Mantha could stay silent. She remained poised as Doc carried on, oblivious to how his arrogance was imposing on others.

Sam knew Doc, having tried to communicate with him before. "I completely understand your desire for perfection. Restoring a vintage car requires great attention. I promise we will meticulously inspect each component, from the engine to the upholstery, ensuring everything is in top-notch condition."

"And does SHE know what SHE is doing?" Doc asked pointedly. The principal's rudeness was not what Q witnessed at school. The man was the king of professional and expected social behavior at Riverdale High.

"Mantha comes highly recommended. Her experience, skills, and education surpass mine," Sam had iron confidence in his voice. He held his tongue wanting to add, *Mantha has more expertise than you have manners.* Even with Doc and his rudeness, Sam remained a firm adherent to the customer comes first.

"Excellent. I expect MY exterior to sparkle like a diamond, so don't spare any effort polishing this girl. Microfiber only! Make sure MY engine purrs like a contented lion. Nothing less will suffice." Doc surprisingly added a compliment. "I like the new color."

Mantha noticed Zak returning to the Doc's SUV with a clean microfiber towel. She smiled, knowing Zak found them by climbing upon the blue square tarp to reach the high shelf with the sealed package. In doing so, Zak peeked under the tarp. "Wow, a four-wheeler with a helmet. Cool beans!" Then he ran out to finish the job. He was off the clock.

"Rest assured, Doc. I'll ensure the exterior is flawless. As for the engine, it will be a roaring success." Sam upheld a sense of calm.

"I'm glad to hear that," Doc continued. "The interior better scream luxury. People should feel envious just sitting inside her."

"Your wish is my command," Sam made a big deal out of it. "I'll ensure the upholstery is pristine. Your passengers won't be able to resist the allure of the car's interior."

"It's not just any ordinary vehicle; it's an extension of my unmatchable persona!" Doc oozed arrogance. "I hope you understand the privilege of working on my car."

Sam wanted to vomit but replied diplomatically, "I understand your attachment to this car and your desire for it to announce your presence. A car like this beauty warrants regard. Rest assured, Mantha and I treat every car we work on here with utmost care and respect. I'll put my heart and soul into restoring it to its best possible condition, rendering it a testament to your exceptional taste."

"That's more like it. Just remember, when people see this car rolling down the street, they will know they're in the presence of perfection and, by extension, my superior example," sniffed the pompous principal.

Mantha stood Tin Soldier still. Q stared, stunned by this display of self-aggrandizement by a person he had respected until this moment. *There was a whole other side to Doc* and it gave him a queasy stomach.

Zak missed the show because he also washed Doc's SUV headlights, side mirror, bumper, and soft toweled off all the streaks.

Sam remained composed as Doc would pay them an acceptable sum for the work. "Your vision is clear, and I'll do everything I can to bring it to life. My goal is to provide you with a restored vintage car that impresses others and gives you immense satisfaction whenever you sit behind the wheel."

Doc laughed. "I suppose I can enjoy myself, too." Then he returned to his more modern SUV and drove away.

"Have a lovely day," Mantha sneered when Doc was out of earshot.

Q laughed at her momentary sarcasm.

Penny huffa huffed, even she knew.

"So what just happened?" Zak asked. "Did I do something wrong?" "No, Zak, you did everything right. Thank you for going above and beyond. Now you boys get out of here and have some fun on this late Saturday afternoon," Mantha shooed them toward the door.

Sam announced, "Hey, just in case you can catch it, tonight is another Aurora Borealis event. You may find it interesting."

"I've seen them!" Zak beamed. "Let's go to the boneyard and finish that scavenger hunt. Then, we can be at the right place to see if the lights dance again. That is FIRE!"

Sam and Mantha grinned at each other, knowing Zak meant: "super colossal stupendous!"

—

By the time the sun began to set, the teens had accumulated 15 old tires, ten pallets, a pile of 2x4s, a couple of sheets of plywood, four industrial barrels, a stack of plastic containers, cement blocks, glass blocks, a large pile of metal scraps, wires, and cables. They picked up random screws and nails and put them into separate containers. They checked every container and all the containers were secured except the rusted blue one on the edge of the field.

The off-loaded containers stood almost proudly, interlaced by trails of adventure. The Monogram Master's work was admirable. The area that had looked like a dump now looked like a fantastic play area. A few sizable old car parts remained scattered. The rusted, too-heavy pieces would serve as obstacles to avoid.

"We can't move this one," Shay grunted. "It's too big to push even to the side."

"It's okay, Shay, we can use it as a hurdle in our races," Zak offered.

"Let's go wait for the lights. We can open up that last container. Let's sit by the Rocket Launch Light Dancing field," encouraged Shay.

"I like the name you gave to our field, Shay," said Zak

Then as they approached the blue container, they heard sobbing. The Monogram Masters hushed and huddled together. "Shh," whispered Q. "Someone is crying."

The container doors were closed, and opening them would create squeaks and squeals. They sat outside, motionless, listening, and hoping to learn more. "Should we just let her cry?" Shay worried.

"I don't know who it is, but they sound so unhappy." Zak whispered.

"Let's offer help." Shay's brows knitted in concern and empathy.

"What if she wants privacy and no one to know?" Q disputed. "What if we are best off respecting her business?"

"I think we should blast in and save her," said Zak. "Like Mantha saved me when I felt so bad I didn't know what to do. She helped me a lot." Zak noticed the lights go on in the house at the far end of the field, and then abruptly, the shades were pulled. The hiding girl continued sobbing.

The northern lights arrived dancing in the sky, but the experience did not feel the same. "Dear God, Creator of all these lights, we must do the right thing. Help us!" Prayed Shay.

Silence. Silence was scarier than crying. Zak reached for the rusty doors and wrestled them open with a grinding groan. Peering into the dim light, he made out a slumped form. His mouth fell open in surprise. It was Missy!

—14—
CHANGE OF HEART

Missy Johnson lay on the floor in the back of the off-loaded container wrapped in the fleece blanket. She had vomited and smelled awful. Next to her was an empty bottle. It had been filled with vodka. She was non-responsive.

"Oh my goodness, it's Missy! We need to do something!" Shouted Shay. "Missy, Missy, wake up."

"This is serious. We need to help no matter what she thinks of us," Zak trembled. "She made me so mad! But…this is not good. She needs help."

"She does need help. We must try to stay calm," Q stated evenly. "Let's think, we need a plan. Mom has our only phone, but she's at work. It's up to us! Shay, you comfort and talk to Missy. Zak, you are the fastest runner. Run to Riley's and get help! Have them call for an ambulance! I will stay here in case Shay or Missy needs more help."

Zak let out a sharp breath. "Let's make sure she's safe. Can we drag her on her blanket to the front of the container so the ambulance people can get her out easier and we can breathe fresh air?" Q's eyes bulged at the horrific scene.

"Q and I can do that, Zak. Run now! Run like the wind!" Shouted Shay as she pushed to get him moving.

Zak ran like his life depended on it, banging Riley's door and screaming, "Mantha, Mantha! Help me! Missy is hurt!" The garage was empty and locked, as two cars pumped gas.

Zak ran to Dee's Cafe and crashed into the first table, which was Uncle Ben and Aunt Kate. "Help! Help! We need help! Missy is hurt in the container boneyard! We need an ambulance!" Zak's arms flailed as his heart raced.

Uncle Ben wrapped Zak in his arms, taking command while giving firm comfort. "Margie! Call an ambulance! Zak, slow down and tell me what's happened?"

"She was crying. We didn't want to bother her, so we sat outside the container. And then everything went quiet, and we thought maybe she went to sleep, but she smelled horrible, and there was an empty vodka bottle next to her. It was a big bottle, and it was empty! EMPTY!" Zak tried to show how big the bottle was. You need to help me, Uncle Ben. She's not moving, and we can't wake her up!"

"Zak, you come with me. We'll lead up in the squad. Do you know exactly where she is?"Ben spoke urgently in a low, steady tone, guiding Zak out the café's door.

"The ambulance is on the way, Ben. What address?" Margie shouted from the kitchen.

"At the end of Larkin Trail, Margie. Where are Q and Shay, Zak?" Urged Lindsay as her throat tightened. Mantha left her meal on the table to support her.

"Q and Shay stayed to keep Missy safe. They're in the last blue container." Gasped Zak.

"Margie, tell the ambulance to meet us up at the old shipping container on Larkin road," Ben shouted ushering Zak out.

"Lindsay, we'll get the kids back safely," Mantha consoled, their eyes met. A lifetime of experiences had separated the two women. Lindsay gave a weak smile, nodding with agreement. "Zak, is she in the container I found you in?" Mantha asked/

"Yes." Zak said weakly.

"Ben. I'll ride with you," said Mantha.

———

Missy lay next to Shay who gently held her. "I'll stay by her side, Q. Look around for clues if there is anything that could have harmed her. See if she could have taken anything—pill bottles or blister packs. We do that at memory care when something happens." She touched the girl's face, tapping her cheek urgently. "Missy, it's Shay. I am here to help you. Can you wake up? Missy!"

Q encouraged, "Make sure she keeps breathing, Shay, and monitor her. We don't want this to worsen. I'll check her journal. I'll let you know what I find." Q paged through the journal, scanning for clues.

"Once the EMTs get here, let's try to help." Shay made soft circles on Missy's face with her finger, "We don't want her to die! Something must have hurt her real bad for this to happen."

"Absolutely. We can show kindness, even if it's just from us. We have a chance to help her." Q flipped through her journal and stopped. He stepped out of the container and opened the door wider to increase lighting and ventilation.

'… feel so hurt and frustrated'

'This is exhausting. Why do they always argue like this? They're so busy blaming each other that they don't fix anything. They don't listen to each other. All they do is make me and everyone else miserable! Grown-ups! Where is the empathy and respect ?! All I want is for them to fix their problems so we can have some family again. Everyone thinks I have the perfect family. Hah! Little do they know. I can't have anyone over with them fighting all the time. I feel so alone. I can't stand it any longer.'

Q read another page and quit. He knew Missy's parents. He had counseled with her father at Riverdale High. The feeling he got at Riley's returned even louder in his solar plexus. He tried reading the last entry…

'…shocked, hurt, and betrayed'

'Oh my god, I can't believe this is happening. How could they do this to our family? I thought they loved each other. I thought they were happy. I feel so betrayed. It's like everything has been a lie. The thought of my parents being with someone who isn't each other, it's just… I can't even put it into words. I don't know how to handle this. Our family is falling apart, and it feels like there's nothing I can do to stop it. I want to be able to trust them again, but right now, it feels impossible. I want to sleep forever.'

Q put the journal down. These were Missy's private thoughts. Her personal space. He would not betray her. He knew enough and would leave her confidential information alone.

"Shay, I think Missy has been hurting for a long time. I think this is where she comes for refuge from her family. Her home is just across the field, so it is an easy walk. How is she?" Asked Q.

"Q, I am all wet, Missy just peed on me. She peed a lot!" Shay whispered in a panic, her arm was already covered with vomit.

Zak careened around the containers, followed by Uncle Ben and Mantha. The sirens of the ambulance blared in the distance and then stopped unable to go further. "I got 'em! I got 'em!" Zak called out. "Help is coming!" Ben and Mantha surveyed the boneyard for potential threats and were surprised to see it cleaned and organized.

Mantha signaled to Ben with a raised hand that she would reach out first, female to female. She approached Shay and bent down to look at Missy, gently shaking her shoulder. The girl was out cold, completely unresponsive.

"Dear God, please help her," Shay prayed as she shivered from being wet. Q put his hand on Missy's foot and prayed silently. Zak watched.

"Missy, Missy honey!" Mantha called loudly, but it was ineffective. She checked for signs of life. Her breathing was shallow, thankfully there was a pulse. She nodded to Ben, letting him know. She positioned Missy on her side, supporting her head and neck, to prevent choking on vomit or any potential airway obstruction. She examined Missy's arms and wrists for cuts; there appeared to be no injuries. The girl's breathing was irregular and jagged.

"Here they come, here they come!" Shouted Zak as he bounced anxiously in place. The tension of the emergency sent his energy through the roof.

"Thank God," said Mantha, understanding the seriousness.

The paramedics made their way in and assessed her vital signs, administering oxygen through a mask to ensure she had sufficient air to breathe. "How much do you think she drank?" John Mason asked the teens.

"We don't know; we just found her," said Zak, running back to get the bottle. This was not here before; she must have brought it."

"We will treat for the worst case of alcohol poisoning," said the female paramedic as John did a sternum rub with no response.

"She's not breathing. We need to revive," ordered the female EMT. "Initiate cardiopulmonary resuscitation (CPR). Clear the area and make space for us to work," John ordered. Ben, Mantha, Zak, Q, and Shay stepped out of the way.

The female EMT placed the barrier over Missy's mouth and put her hands over the teen's heart. "Prepare the defibrillator."

"She's back!" John Mason exclaimed. "Her pulse is rising." They placed Missy on the stretcher and carried her out to the ambulance stopped on the other side of the immovable car part.

Zak watched the green lights with purple streaks mix with red spinning ambulance lights racing away. A car drove up to the distant house. Lights popped on. Three figures, two embraced—he thought he knew who—the night turned somber as everyone returned to their homes, hoping for some news of the teenager. The northern lights glided away, leaving a clean, moon-free night.

"Mantha, you want a ride?" Ben offered.

"Naw, I need some solitude," said Mantha. "I will walk Shay and Q home."

Zak hopped into the squad, vibrating with nerves while sitting shotgun in the front seat, still shaking from the evening's events. He had to sit on his hands to still them. "Do you think Missy will be alright, Uncle Ben?"

"I hope so, Zak. I hope so."

———

Mantha guided Q and Shay along. Noticing Shay's trembling, Mantha removed her camouflage green hoodie and dressed Shay. She suspected Shay's shivering stemmed not only from the traumatic experience but also from being soaked in Missy's bodily fluids. "I am so proud of you all," commended Mantha. "Without your quick thinking, Q, Shay's warm body, and Zak's fast feet, we may have lost Missy. Young people often don't have a clue about the damage alcohol can do."

"Really?" Shay said softly.

Mantha draped her bare right arm over Shay's shoulder and pulled her close. "I have lost exceptional military men who over-drank like Missy did. Tragically, they lost their lives because friends didn't intervene. They hid behind laughter until their comrade took his last breath. Alcohol poisoning is no joke."

Q noted Mantha's long scar and missing fingers. He saw his mother running toward them, and though he was not comfortable with hugging, he embraced her back. It was the first time in his life that he molded into her body. Lindsay noticed the change in his embrace and took the opportunity. "I love you, Q."

Q echoed back, "I love you, too, Mom." Lindsay felt his sincerity.

Mantha held Shay and gazed at Lindsay. Though she had never been a parent, she was an Army Captain and a leader. It meant being there for your soldiers who often faced difficult circumstances. She had to be empathetic and understanding like a family would by offering a supportive presence to help those under her leadership navigate challenging times. She saw fierce strength and independence in Lindsay and respected her fortitude.

Lindsay glanced over with appreciation and smiled at Mantha. "I packed up your dinner. Sam took a to-go box. Would you like to come to our house for a cup of coffee to warm up?"

"Thank you, and," Mantha said with genuine regard, "would love to."

—

Kate arrived home to find Zak and Ben seated at the kitchen table with cocoa in hand.

"Hi honey, where were you?" Ben was grateful she was home.

"I drove up to Doc and Nicole's to offer support and help them prepare for the hospital. I knew you were busy at the containers."

"That was sweet. Thank you for doing that." Ben kissed her cheek.

"Aunt Kate, get some cocoa and hang out with us," said Zak.

"Sounds good," sighed Kate as she scooped cocoa into a cup and poured the hot water. "Zak's got some fast feet. His speed made a big difference in saving Missy's life tonight."

"Everyone made a difference. That's what having a community and being neighbors is all about." Ben agreed.

"I suppose we're all life together, aren't we, Uncle Ben?" Zak reflected. "Just yesterday, I was angry enough to want to hurt Missy. But then we found her so sick, and how close she is to dying. Now I see her as a person and I care about her."

"Every individual deserves to be seen as a person, Zak," Ben explained. "As sheriff, I have to keep that perspective at the forefront. Everyone's life path has its twists and turns. What I witness is just a moment in time, not the complete story."

Zak lowered his eyes. "My entire life feels like one big tangle." He swirled his hot chocolate to chase the marshmallows with his tongue.

Ben and Kate, new to parenting, exchanged glances of bewildered amusement, unsure how to respond to Zak's introspection.

—

"Shay, get those clothes off and into the washer. I need you in the shower first with wash and rinse. Then, draw a hot bath and soak. You have to warm up." Lindsay ordered. "Your sweats are folded in the laundry basket and ready for you." Lindsay grabbed two mugs and poured hot coffee from a thermos. She motioned Mantha to sit and shooed Shay off to clean up. Q immersed himself in his latest book.

Seventeen years had gone by since the two women had sat in Lindsay's grandpa's old double-wide trailer. They reminisced over cups of coffee, reflecting on everything that had transpired between them.

"Mantha, you were always the courageous and determined one. The day you got acknowledgment of a West Point scholarship, I got two little pink lines on a pregnancy test." Lindsay sipped her brew. "The trajectory of our lives took such different directions."

Mantha put her coffee down, "We sure had fun those last high school years. Have you been working at Dee's the whole while?"

Lindsay laughed with irony, "Yeah, Margie pretty much adopted me after my parents discovered I was pregnant, and my grandpa kicked me out of this old trailer. I named my son after her son. Do you remember Quintel? He was such a sweet person. He was always the girl's friend but never the boyfriend. What a kind guy. It was tragic what happened to his sister, Tasha."

"Life is filled with tragedy, Lindsay. One day, you're a K9-handler and Army captain in a foreign land, and the next, you wake up with a Purple Heart and accolades for exceptional bravery in the line of duty. All it takes is one misstep."

"Sometimes, a misstep becomes a true joy. What mother has better kids than mine? It doesn't matter to me that I live on the other side of the tracks with two illegitimate but perfectly legitimate-to-me children. They are my world, and they make me proud," Lindsay glowed with gratitude. "You know, I always admired what you did. I mean, standing up in rank with tough men."

"Lindsay, I need to say something. I faced my battles with the whole United States Army surrounding and behind me," Mantha paused. "You stood your ground, right here, against stigma and gossip—no team at your flanks. You raised two perfect fledgling neurodivergent adults. How did you do it? I am equally in awe of your resilience and unwavering love in providing for your family."

"We are a family, and we are better together than apart. We love each other, and the little things we do show it. I respect my kids, and my kids respect me. We take turns getting angry. If I am having a bad day, they give me space, and if one is having a hard time, I do the same for them. We work to keep each other out of defense mode. It takes all three of us to run this place and make ends meet. Every one of us is different; the world runs best like that. We embrace our differences and use them as strengths. When I step up my Lindsay ego for control and power, I might get my way, but we all lose. Life's battles show up daily, and we don't get to pick and choose."

Mantha raised her right hand. Lindsay noticed the missing digits. "We make choices at the moment that can bring a lifetime of consequences."

"We sure do! I was young and alone, thinking I needed to have sex to be loved when Q arrived. His father's genes placed him on the spectrum, and seeing the world through his brilliant mind has been a real blessing. I was knocked up and then knocked down by the community. I started using booze as my pacifier. Shay was born while I was drinking. It is my drinking that gives her that special shine but also her challenges and tough struggles. I can't take back my past. I quit drinking when she was born and have not had a drop since. I try each day to do one good thing for myself and each of them. I guess you can say I've been resilient."

Mantha raised her coffee mug, "To friends and resilience!"

"To friendship." Lindsay took a long, slow sip. "I see Shay's glimmer in Zak."

Mantha nodded. "Me too."

—

Zak tossed and turned, thinking about Missy, the alcohol, and the fact that the ambulance could not get past that unmovable rusted car part. The four-wheeler in the garage had a ball hitch! He knew how to stealthily exit his room. He knew where the chain was, as well as the gas. The key was under the helmet. He could make the boneyard safe in emergencies if he could borrow that four-wheeler for a moment. Mantha was the problem as she slept in the garage. He had to wait until the garage was empty.

—

Missy regained consciousness on Sunday morning, her body a catalog of pain. Her head throbbed mercilessly, nausea overwhelmed her, and a sharp ache radiated between her ribs. The light assaulted her sensitive eyes, forcing them shut. A slight movement revealed a minor rib fracture, sending waves of discomfort through her torso. She could hear her father's voice conversing with someone nearby, but when she tried to lift her arms, she found them securely restrained.

Instinctively, Missy retreated into a familiar coping mechanism - dissociation. She allowed her consciousness to drift away from her physical form, observing the scene from an imaginary vantage point above. This was a skill she had honed during difficult times at home, a mental escape route to a sanctuary within her mind. In this self-created refuge, Missy found solace. Here, she could shield her innermost thoughts and emotions from the harsh realities of her situation, much like she did when writing in her journal. This mental hideaway provided a sense of safety and comfort, allowing her to temporarily distance herself from her current predicament.

She heard footsteps, too many footsteps, and then a severe voice. "Alcohol can disrupt the normal electrical signals in the heart, leading to irregular heartbeats or abnormal rhythms. The amount of alcohol Missy drank was lethal."

Missy continued to drift, listening but not participating. She kept her eyes closed; she had hoped for lethal.

"We are giving her fluids. Alcohol is a diuretic, which increases her urine production; in addition, it gives her severe diarrhea. We are working on correcting the dehydration causing her electrolyte imbalances to avoid organ dysfunction. Missy arrived in myocardial depression. Her blood alcohol content was 4.6; without the intervention of her friends, she might not be here," continued the voice.

"Friends, what friends? No one knew about her secret sanctuary, her precious place of seclusion." Missy floated.

"High levels of alcohol depress the heart's function, leading to reduced contractility and a weakened pumping ability. This decreases cardiac output, which is the blood pumped by the heart per minute. She quit breathing. Her heart stopped. We are thankful this happened after our paramedics arrived."

She heard her mother sniffle. "Will she be alright?"

"Alcohol poisoning is serious. In extreme cases, it can be fatal if not promptly treated. Like I said before, her friends saved her life."

"Who?" Doc, demanded.

"We don't have that information. We do not believe there is brain damage. Severe or repeated episodes of alcohol poisoning can cause permanent brain damage, leading to cognitive impairment, memory loss, and other neurological problems. Thankfully, she has had no seizures."

"Brain damage? Seizures?!... My poor baby," Nicole sobbed, overwhelmed by the shocking realization. Missy was surprised by her mother's display of concern. Over the past few years, Nicole had become emotionally distant, burdened by her own struggles. Missy had masked the pain of this abandonment with a facade of shallow extroversion, striving to be the ringleader and control those around her, yet feeling numb and dead inside.

"I can take her clothes home to wash," Nicole offered desperately, searching for any way to make a difference.

"Her clothes? We cut them off. I don't think you would have wanted them; they were quite messy," whispered a female. We had to put them in a hazardous waste bag. They are burned by now."

"My favorite Pink outfit!" Missy shouted, *"YOU CUT MY CLOTHES OFF AND BURNED THEM?!"*

"She's awake!" Proclaimed her father.

"Clothes can be replaced; we can't replace you," soothed her mother.

Missy felt a wave of nausea wash over her. "I think I'm going to be sick," she managed to say before vomiting. The acrid smell filled the air as her hospital gown became soiled. A nurse quickly attended to her, providing a fresh gown and gently cleaning Missy's face. As the nurse changed the bedding, Missy weakly asked, "Who was with me?"

Her father, looking worn and worried, replied softly, "We don't have that information yet, Missy."

-15-
NEW BEGINNINGS

As Doc and Nicole exited the hospital, they presented a united front, holding hands. When their SUV arrived, Doc made a show of opening the door for his wife, the picture of a caring husband. Once inside, he assumed a rigid posture, hands gripping the steering wheel at the textbook 10 and 2 positions. The facade crumbled as soon as they were alone.

Doc cleared his throat, turned to Nicole, and unleashed his pent-up anger. "How could you let this happen?" he hissed. "If you'd been a better mother, our daughter wouldn't have tried to end her life!"

"How can you say that?" Nicole gasped. "This is not my fault! It's heartbreaking for both of us. We need to support her instead of blaming each other."

"I thought I'd raised her better," he said with an exaggerated laugh, flashing a practiced, insincere smile. His tone shifted to one of controlled disdain. "You're the one who couldn't handle parenting."

Nicole marveled at his ability to switch emotions so abruptly. Her own laughter, rare as it was these days, always faded gradually. "That's unfair," she protested. "She's been struggling for months, and you've ignored the signs. Blaming me won't help."

She recognized the familiar pattern of their argument, a well-worn path they'd trodden countless times since the honeymoon phase of their marriage had faded. Exhaustion settled over her like a heavy blanket. Her shoulders slumped in defeat as she gazed out the window, her eyes unfocused on the passing scenery.

"I just can't believe you didn't see the signs. I thought you were paying attention. This reflects badly on my reputation as a principal. If you loved me, you would've paid closer attention." He lectured to the back of her head. She knew the guilt trip smile he would plant on her face.

Nicole refused to make eye contact or engage physically as she spoke. "It's not your fault as a principal or mine as a mother. We need to come together to support our daughter during this difficult time. It's about her, not us. I don't think either of us truly know her." Doc's expression hardened.

"You can say what you want," he challenged. "I'm the new principal, and I don't want this affecting my professional reputation. Your incompetence now makes it look like our family is dysfunctional. We can't even control our child's behavior!"

"Our focus must be on Missy's well-being, not your reputation. It's not about what others think. I feel all of us need help. We can get through this together." Nicole's voice was weary, almost plaintive.

"Phhhffff," exhaled Doc. "Easy for you to say." Doc slowly shook his head, tilted his chin as he turned his face, and rolled his eyes to the sky. *There she was demanding things again, as if his advice wasn't good enough. He was the professional, after all. Didn't she realize how good she had it? She had never had to work. Her only jobs were to be his wife, the mother of Missy, and keep up the house. Now she even had access to a car, she could drive Missy's.*

Nicole felt Doc's ambiance hurl at her even without words—*you're so stupid, you are never good enough, why are you even in my life?* Doc never raised his hand to her, but his words beat her down with rejection, disapproval, and critisim.

—

Zak was up early, especially for a Sunday. "Uncle Ben, do you think we could visit Missy at the hospital today?" he asked.

"Sure, after church?" Ben suggested.

"Church? Church is boring," Zak replied, rolling his eyes and looking away.

"How do you know it's boring if you've never gone with me?" Uncle Ben reasoned.

"Maybe our church isn't boring."

"It doesn't make sense to me. It's hard to focus and understand what's happening," Zak said, staring intently at the chicken napkin holder. Ben, recognizing the intensity of Zak's gaze, knew from experience that direct eye contact often overwhelmed him, making it difficult for Zak to listen. For Zak, who relied on reading body language, face-to-face interactions could be too intense, even without words.

"Look at it from a different perspective. Church can be a place where we find support, learn about our spirituality, and connect with a caring community." Ben suggested.

"So, it's like social media visiting an old building?" Zak asked

Kate snickered behind her coffee mug. "Lindsay takes Q and Shay."

"Tell you what," challenged Ben, "You try it this Sunday, and I will drive you, Q, and Shay to the hospital to check on Missy."

"Are you bribing me to go with you?" Zak ventured.

"I guess," Ben replied with good humor. "It's part of our community."

"What do you mean, you guess? It is or it isn't. I guess it is, maybe, and mostly. Just use yes or no. I don't want to feel overwhelmed. What if it's just all this talking, and it's boring? Can I leave when I want?"

"How about we sit together, and I explain things to you if you have questions," offered Ben.

"Shay dances and sings in the worship team," Kate added.

"She dances at church?" Zak was shocked.

"And sometimes Q is up front reading for us. He's an excellent reader. Plus, I know everyone at church today, we call that our congregation, will pray for Missy to heal. You can be part of that." Encouraged Ben.

Zak put up one finger, "One time, and you make it make sense." He put up two fingers, "Two friends get a ride to see Missy."

"Deal." Said Ben. He put out his hand.

"Deal," replied Zak, reciprocated with a clasp.

—

Doc pulled up to the church entrance. "I'm heading back to the hospital to oversee Missy's care. You can't be too careful. I'll pick you up after the service."

As Nicole stepped out of their luxury SUV, she spotted Kate. "Kate, thanks so much for coming over last night. Doc's worried about the situation. He's going back to the hospital to ensure everything's handled properly. He couldn't even attend church today."

"That's what friends are for. You know how much I care about your family," Kate reassured her, noticing Nicole's tired, puffy eyes.

Nicole found comfort in Kate's small kindnesses. Doc felt like a distant memory now. Her upbringing in northern Florida contrasted sharply with this tight-knit Midwestern town, leaving her feeling like an outsider.

Zak trailed behind Ben, keeping close.

"Who's with you today, Sheriff?" Smiled Nicole, inquisitively.

"This is my nephew, Zak. He's in his final year at Riverdale High and recently joined our family," Ben introduced.

Zak offered a quiet "Hello."

"It's a pleasure to meet you, Zak," Nicole said, extending her hand in greeting.

Kate added, "Zak and his friends were the ones who found Missy last night and got her help."

Nicole gasped, her hand flying to her mouth. "Oh my," she exclaimed, tears welling up. She then grasped Zak's hands in hers. "I-I can't thank you enough," she stammered, overcome with emotion.

Zak, uncomfortable with the sudden physical contact and intense reaction, felt his body tense. He wanted to pull away but found himself frozen in place, unsure how to respond to Nicole's unexpected display of gratitude.

—

Doc approached Missy's hospital bed, his face a mask of concern. "Good morning, Missy," he said, his smile not quite reaching his eyes.

Missy opened her eyes briefly before shutting them again, unwilling to face him. Leaning closer, Doc whispered harshly, "I can't believe you'd embarrass me like this. What were you thinking?"

Missy remained silent, wishing she could disappear. "Always making the wrong choices," Doc continued, his voice low and menacing. "Stop being so dramatic. This attention-seeking behavior needs to end."

The nurse entered, and Doc's demeanor changed instantly. He kissed Missy's forehead, saying sweetly, "I love you, honey." His smile to the nurse seemed genuine. Before leaving, he whispered one last barb, "You'll never measure up."

Missy winced, biting her lip to keep from crying out. The nurse, misinterpreting Missy's reaction, said, "Oh, Missy, you must be in pain. I've brought something to help."

Doc exited with a false cheerfulness, "Bye, sweetie. I'll be back later."

Missy held her breath, lips pressed tightly together as the nurse offered her medication, saying, "This will make things better."

—

Doc's immaculate vehicle pulled up just as church let out. Ben noticed fresh mud on the fender as Doc lowered his window. With a politician's smile, Doc greeted him: "Ben, thanks for your help last night. I heard you were at the containers for Missy. She's doing well and will be home later today."

Ben approached the car. "Good to hear, Doc. Make sure to thank the medical team, the kids, and Mantha too. They did the heavy lifting. I was just there."

"Give yourself some credit. You need it after that suds fiasco last week," Doc chuckled. "Saw the photos in the paper." He sped away, leaving a cloud of dust.

"No need," Ben muttered, choosing not to engage. He noted Doc's odd mix of compliment and jab, then rejoined Kate, Zak, Lindsay, and her kids.

"Uncle Ben, can I hang out with Q and Shay today? We're all free," Zak asked.

Lindsay offered, "I'd be happy to host everyone for lunch. Hot dogs, beans, chips, and pickles."

"I love hot dogs!" Zak exclaimed. "Especially with ketchup and mustard!"

"Me too!" Shay chimed in. "I like how you said 'decorate.' Makes eating more fun!"

Q turned to his mother. "Mom, can I go to the library? I want to research something. Save me lunch. I'll only be an hour."

Lindsay laughed, knowing better. "I've never seen you spend just an hour there. Those chairs must be magnetic! Walk home when you're done."

"We can give you a ride if you three squeeze in the back," Ben offered. "Lindsay, Kate has lunch planned, so we'll have to pass on your kind offer."

"I'm not passing it up!" Zak declared. "I'm having hot dogs."

"Go ahead, Zak. I'll pick everyone up for the hospital visit later," Ben reminded him.

—

Q delved into research at the library. While they had a TV at home, a computer was a luxury they couldn't afford, let alone monthly internet costs. His mind was still reeling from Doc's behavior at the garage and the revelations from Missy's journal and suicide attempt. Concern drove him to action, but he knew he needed to proceed carefully.

He began by exploring online forums, blogs, and articles about surveillance techniques. His research covered covert observation methods, recording devices, and other tools used by professionals. He also browsed reputable equipment providers' websites. Comparing his findings to what he had available, Q took stock: his backpack, a notepad and pens for documenting observations, a flashlight for low-light situations, spare batteries, zip ties that could serve as makeshift restraints, a basic first aid kit, and his amateur telescope.

He considered bringing his 50x amateur telescope to the container boneyard to watch the sky and the house across the field. It was a clear distance without trees, and there was no light pollution, so the magnification might work. Still, a telescope is primarily designed for observing celestial objects such as stars, planets, and galaxies rather than terrestrial objects in a neighborhood. Binoculars or a camera with a zoom lens might be more practical for such close-range observations. However, he didn't have either. Q read about scouting areas effectively and observing from a distance; "you may acquire a pair of binoculars with zoom capabilities. These will enable you to view potential targets or areas of interest without getting too close. You also decide to include a monocular in your gear. Its compact size makes it handy for discreetly scoping out objects or people with minimal movement."

He read further on how to capture crucial visual evidence. It would take investing in a covert video recording device. The sites advised: "Use careful consideration in selecting a high-resolution mini video camera that is small and inconspicuous, with motion activation and night vision capabilities, making it perfect for discreetly recording any suspicious activities. Opt for a miniature digital voice recorder with noise cancellation and long battery life for audio recording. This device will help you document conversations or collect audio evidence without drawing attention. Check with the laws in your state on recording devices."

Covert action went deeper regarding communication, focusing on obtaining a set of lightweight, inconspicuous wireless earbuds with long battery life and high-quality sound, allowing one to have a discrete line of contact with team members. "Consider adding a small handheld radio scanner to your backpack. It will enable you to tune in to local emergency frequencies, law enforcement transmissions, or even private communication channels, providing further awareness of potential events or incidents." He imagined equipping a team of sorts.

His backpack was big enough to hold all the gear except his telescope. Q printed out all the information saved the links for future purchases, and headed home.

—

On Sunday afternoons, Ben usually visited local adult patients at the hospital, albeit voters, to chat and say hello while the Monogram Masters strolled down the long hall, past wheelchairs and medical carts, to Missy's Room number 49. Today he also took the teens.

The door was open when they entered. Missy was curled into a ball, crying softly, with the white sheets drawn up to hide her face,

Shay put her hand on Missy's shoulder, "Hey Missy, we came to say hello and see how you're doing."

Missy opened her eyes, not recognizing the voice. She was shocked. "What are you losers doing here?" She groaned.

Q looked at Zak. Zak looked at Shay and then Q and burst into laughter. Zak's laughter was so contagious that pretty soon, Shay was laughing, and then Missy started laughing, unsure why. Finally, Q could not help himself and started laughing, but he had to interject. "May I ask you, Zak, what you find so funny, especially in a hospital room?"

"Missy said it upside down. We are not the losers. We are her savers." Zak continued to laugh as tears streamed down his cheeks. He held his belly. His laugh was contagious. "Sometimes people like Missy get us all wrong. They don't understand."

Missy laughed, "You losers are my savers?" She fell into hysterics.

"I hated the police, and MY saver is Sheriff Ben! It's crazy." Zak continued to laugh.

"Savers never look like what or who you expect," commented Q. "And my saver is you, Zak because we are so opposite and so the same. No one makes me laugh like you."

"And my saver is you, Missy," grinned Shay, "Because you helped me become a better person and press through my hurt to find kindness even when I didn't want to."

Missy sat up, her cheeks wet with tears. She was suddenly serious. She gulped and then stammered, "So...You mean...You guys found me? And...Even after I've been mean to you..." She was full of mixed feelings and wasn't sure what was happening here. *Why would they care about her when her own family didn't even understand how she felt? Had they found her journal and read all her private thoughts? Was this a prank they were pulling to get back at her? Could she trust them?*

Q ventured, "I've observed that individuals who have been hurt in the past sometimes hurt others. They repeat what was done to them. We don't know why you were mean to us. We saw how mean you were to yourself, though. That bottle of booze was empty. We thought you were going to die. We don't think you should die just because you act mean. We think someone must have been mean to you first, causing you serious emotional pain."

"I've realized that when my feelings are hurt, I tend to dwell on them," Shay confessed, looking at her brother. "Sometimes those feelings resurface, and I lash out at you or Mom. I get snippy and picky. It's not something I'm proud of, but I never made the connection before."

Q nodded thoughtfully. "I've noticed that when someone feels offended, it's like they put up an invisible barrier around themselves. Unless there's a shift in energy or perspective, that barrier stays in place and grows stronger over time, becoming increasingly difficult to break down."

"That's cool, Q," Zak was excited. "I see it! I see it! But when you have the right sword, you can poke right through!"

"I think you mean words, Zak. We no longer use swords. It's important to recognize that everyone has struggles that affect how they interact with others. Shay and I have each other in our family for support, but Zak is starting all over alone in a new family. Missy. We don't know your life, but we understand that something must be difficult, or you wouldn't have drunk a whole bottle of vodka. You almost killed yourself."

Zak added, "That makes sense, Q. I get confused and frustrated often, and when I do, I hurt others without realizing it. I melt down and don't even know until it's over. It's not an excuse but a how-come. My mom and dad were sick and tired of me. They were glad I went to live with Uncle Ben and Aunt Kate. Dad called me his pain in the ass."

Missy watched as Zak spoke. She held onto each of his words, "I didn't want to hurt anyone else, just me...I...I don't know how to stop the hurt...in me. I don't even know why you guys care."

Shay expressed, "I mean, no one is perfect, right? But at least we can care about other people because maybe we aren't the only ones having a hard time. I have challenges, but I learn and grow from them. Maybe it's just how we all deal with what hurts us that matters. Helping you made me feel better. I believe making friends is endless. It's like love. The more you put in or give out, the more you get back."

"Missy, would you like to become part of the Monogram Masters? We imprint goodness on the world, knowing everyone struggles."

Missy was perplexed. Shay's meaning of love could not be the same love she felt at home, "I'll think about it." She drew in a deep breath, "I'll consider it."

"You don't have to think, Missy, you just have to be," Zak shrugged.

Sheriff Ben poked his head into the room. "It's Good to see you sitting up and chatting, Missy. Come on, kids, it's time to go home."

———

Doc and Nicole picked up Missy, who was discharged because of Doc's reassurances she would be monitored. Missy locked herself in her room and stayed in bed, avoiding the acrid air of tension that pervaded the household. Nothing had changed.

———

Ben returned the kids to the trailer. Zak and Shay engaged in dominoes. Q packed his bag. "You want to go to the container? I thought I'd bring my telescope."

"You have a telescope? That is so cool. I always wanted one," Zak said, holding his domino in midair. "I have a rocket," he added.

"You have a rocket! I have always wanted to build a rocket. A rocket that would fly so high it would take my telescope to see it!" Exclaimed Q.

Lindsay shouted from her room, "Bring a black garbage bag, a bucket of warm, soapy water, and a big sponge. The container will need cleaning if you want to keep playing there. We can wash Missy's blanket here after you bring it home!"

"Thanks, Mom, that's a great idea," Shay called back, fetching cleaning supplies and preparing a bucket of water.

"Shay, don't forget the cleaning gloves," Lindsay exclaimed, "You're going to need them. Take both pairs. We can get new ones at the Dollar Store."

"I'll carry the bucket for you, Shay," offered Zak.

"I'll get the trash bag," volunteered Q, wearing his backpack with his telescope. "I have masks in my first aid kit. We might need them."

"Good idea, thanks," nodded Shay.

—

Back at Riley's, Sam and Mantha worked on Doc's car, "So Sam, since I own the garage now, and we share a dog, a Ham Shack, and a closet in your old car wash, are you going to let me see what you have in the range? Or am I not a member of your private gun club?" Mantha looked over the open hood.

"You own it, Mantha. I just haven't had time to give you the proper introduction. Come on, you want to take a look?" Sam winked, and Mantha wiped her hands on her towel. "The police shoot here once a month on Sunday nights; the team will be here tonight."

If Mantha was astounded at the base station setup, the shooting range surprised her even more. It was pristine, soundproof unless you were sleeping next door, and 75 feet long. It was wide enough to shoot targets or practice tactical scenarios. It had exceptional filtration to remove the residue and a secure area for bullets down range. Someone had set up a scenario that looked like a retail store with two active shooters and seven customers. The shooting looked difficult. The goal was safety first for all citizens and neutralizing active shooters. The active shooters had a variety of remote trajectories: straight-on, stationary, path-crossing, and random. Sam's remote control system picked out which movement each officer engaged in, changes in times of daylighting with shadows, and varying volume startle sounds. No scenario was ever the same. This prevented later shooters from planning strategies based on previous engagements.

"Wow. This is incredible."

"You want to try the scenario? I'm intent on stopping training scars."

"No, I'll wait until the police have completed and pasted their targets at the end of their match," Mantha was a right-handed master shooter. She was not as confident with her non-injured hand. "Can I watch tonight?"

"Of course, you can watch. Ben intends for his officers to make split-second decisions with the least force. A training scar that happens with only range practice can put even expert shooters into reaction versus response, which is too dangerous for community living," shared Sam.

"Sam, I have an appointment at the VA next week. Would you be willing to join me?" Mantha asked.

"I'd love to. It's been a long time since I had a friend to accompany me to medical appointments. Let's spend the day. There are some places I want to share with you."

———

Equipped with gloves, masks, and cleaning supplies, the Monogram Masters gathered in front of the weathered container door. Just as they were about to open it, Q hesitated. "Mask up!" His eyes widening with caution.

Shay, always eager for adventure, brushed off the warning. "Come on, it's probably fine!" Determined, she opened the heavy doors as the putrid smell instantly assaulted their senses. It hit them in a tsunami of ICK!

Q gagged, turned on his heel, and walked into the field for some fresh air. Zak and Shay pinched their noses, the stench permeating even through their masks. They exchanged uneasy glances but were determined to complete their task. The masks offered little relief. Missy's bout with alcohol poisoning had left a lingering odor of bile that filled the entire space.

"This is really gross," Zak groaned.

"If we want to use this cool space, we have to clean it up," commanded Shay, undeterred by the disgusting mess. She took a deep breath and put on a pair of disposable gloves to protect herself from germs. She grabbed a few paper towels, carefully removed the solid chunks of vomit, and disposed of them in a plastic bag that Zak carefully held with one hand. He held his nose with the other and sealed his mouth tightly shut.

With the majority of the mess cleared, Shay prepared to tackle the stubborn stain and lingering odor. She had brought a spray bottle filled with a homemade solution of equal parts white vinegar and water.

As she aimed the bottle, Zak interjected, "Hold on, Shay! Let me do it!" His nose wrinkled in anticipation.

Q remained outside, keeping his distance from the unpleasant task.

Zak, now armed with the vinegar solution, enthusiastically sprayed the stained area. "Pew, pew, pew!" he exclaimed, dancing around as he worked.

Shay chuckled, "We need to let it sit for about 20 minutes to work its magic. Let's go outside and look at the stars."

Grateful for the fresh air, Shay and Zak frolicked in the field under the night sky. Q sat at the container's edge, his telescope pointed across the field. As he observed his friends twirling beneath the shimmering sky, something unexpected caught his eye near Missy's house. He kept this observation to himself.

Zak and Shay returned breathless and laughing as Q redirected the lens, looking at the night sky through his 50x lens. He was uneasy about what he had witnessed.

It was time to start the cleaning process. Shay grabbed a clean cloth and gently scrubbed the stained area, careful not to apply too much pressure. The vinegar solution worked wonders, gradually lifting the stain from the surface. Shay continued scrubbing, occasionally blotting with fresh paper towels to absorb any excess liquid. Zak, now holding the garbage bag with both hands instead of pinching his nose, helped out.

The dedicated team worked tirelessly to restore the container to its former state. As hours passed and day turned into night, the container slowly transformed from a dingy, odor-filled nightmare into a clean, blank canvas ready for new adventures. Zak disposed of the dirty water, while Shay aired out the container.

They stood back to admire their hard work, the sky shimmering with wondrous green gyrations. Shay felt relieved as the stain and odor completely vanished. She wiped the surface dry with a clean towel, and even Q noticed the difference.

"Hey, Q, do you think we could use your telescope to keep an eye on Missy and make sure she's safe?" Zak asked, pointing the telescope toward the field where two blurry figures embraced. "It's too blurry."

"We need a pair of zoom binoculars and a monocular, Zak."

"What's a monocular?" Zak put the two empty bottles into a black bag. Shay put Missy's blankets into another.

"A monocular is a compact and lightweight optical device used for seeing distant objects clearly with one eye. It is essentially a small telescope you hold in your hand and has a series of lenses that magnify the image of faraway objects. It allows you to see more clearly at different distances with an adjustable focus. This makes it useful for bird watching or stargazing." Q hoped Zak did not register that he had already attempted to use his telescope in every direction.

"Or watching out for Missy," confirmed Zak. "I'll check with Uncle Ben. He has everything."

~16~
NOBLE PURPOSES

By mid November the fields and grasses were brown and crisp. The sun set before 5 o'clock and the little town of Riverdale began spending more time indoors with fireplaces adding extra warmth to homes reluctant to turn on the furnace. Kate stopped by Dee's to pick up an easy night's dinner—chicken pot pies. It had been a long school week and Doc wasn't helping the situation.

"Hi Kate, how's the school year going," Mantha, was also waiting for a pot pie pick up.

Noting the attempt at small talk, Kate blinked her eyes, "It's going well. Wish I could say the same about the new charge we have in our home."

"You mean Zak? I love that kid! He is such a hard worker, so upbeat and funny. He makes me laugh. I am so glad I hired him. Work experience will get him the final credit he needs for graduation. That kid has untapped potential." Mantha shared.

"Thank you for hiring him, Mantha. You didn't have to, you know. He can be trouble," Kate warned.

And before Mantha had time to answer...

"My my my, if it isn't my two most beautiful women in the world." It was Doc's voice edging closer behind them.

"Flattery will get you..." both women recited.

"Everywhere," said Kate.

"Nowhere," glared Mantha.

———

Zak wasn't home, which was okay with Kate, she needed adult time with Ben. Zak's pot pie could reheat in the microwave. Ben and Kate sat before their hearth, sipping a Merlot and eating on TV trays. "I heard about the soap suds disaster," began Kate, taking a small sip as Ben looked over with a sheepish dip of his chin. "Saw your picture in the local paper at school. You made quite a splash. Do you want to tell me what happened?" She cocked her head to the side, waiting with her wine glass in mid-air.

"We had a neighborhood crew cleaning party," Ben evaded. "Did you even see how the windows sparkled in our home?" Ben lightened his response to match his shrug.

After returning from an elevated educational conference with advanced topics and captivating discussions, she was unnerved to find their private refuge front and center in the local news. Her husband had been on display like some soapy cretin from a drunken Frat Party. "Something is broken in that kid. Are you sure you want him to sleep in your den?" Kate challenged again.

"Why not? I'm getting to like him," Ben shrugged again, looking at Kate.

"In class, he asks question upon question. I answer the question, and he asks the same question again." Kate took another sip, voice rising. "Then he says, make this make sense. And you know what, Ben? I can't."

Ben chuckled, thinking back to Kate's casserole with the crater in it and the red jello crime scene kitchen. Life with Zak was nothing if not a surprise. He hadn't even mentioned apprehending him in red underwear running down the road and thought he'd best remain quiet on that.

"Are you laughing at me!" She faced him. "I need this to make sense. There is something very different we have to deal with here. Zak is not like other kids his age. There's a two-week workshop in the cities on pre-natal alcohol exposure. I took a class on this at MEA. I keep thinking, could this be what's wrong with Zak?"

"I'm not laughing at you or your concerns," soothed Ben. "I don't see anything that wrong with Zak. I see something different than typical. He's not like most young men, that's true, but—I don't know him well enough yet. I have seen and heard glimmers of selflessness and empathy from the locals. Zak is not a deliberate troublemaker or a mean-spirited guy. He does make me look at myself and how I see the world with new eyes and it is quite the adventure."

"Well, I don't trust him. He makes things harder, and I need them stable and smooth," she bristled, grabbing the blue checked fleece chair blanket. "I'm going up to check on him and give him this." Kate made her point known, and she was done.

Ben stretched as he rose from his chair, taking his last sip. "I'll join you, and then I'm heading to bed."

Kate was still frustrated with Ben, but how could anyone stay mad at that man forever? He was her knight in shining armor.

—

School began to sit better with Zak. Friendship with Shay and Q eased his loneliness. Q as his 1st hour study partner made an immense difference in completing assignments and becoming test-ready.

He enjoyed living with Uncle Ben and Aunt Kate and appreciated his new home. They were quite different from his parents. His aunt and uncle had a straightforward approach: as long as he acted like an adult, they would treat him as one. He didn't seem to frustrate or anger them constantly. Though he was still learning their expectations, he felt a sense of accomplishment with them.

Working for Mantha and Sam at the garage was fulfilling for him. He made strides in maintaining order and cleanliness while assisting customers. Interacting with adults was often easier for him than navigating social situations with peers, such as in soccer or cheerleading. Meanwhile, Missy kept her distance from the Monogram Masters as she recovered, and Q, Shay, and Zak chose not to disclose what had happened, believing it was Missy's private matter

Zak observed his Uncle Ben's love for the law. And he realized that his father and his uncle had two very different jobs. His father, the lawyer, was busy debating and finding faults and pieces he needed to win trials. In contrast, Uncle Ben focused on building relationships, with the community's safety and well-being at the forefront of his actions. When Zak discussed the incident with Missy, Uncle Ben offered sage advice: "Hard things happen to people. It is our job to respect that all people make mistakes. We all have things to learn, and that is easier to do when others act kind and fair-minded." Despite facing challenges, Sheriff Ben always chose the high road without making a fuss. Zak's respect for his uncle grew as a result.

Riverdale began to feel like home to Zak. He enjoyed having friends and spent every free moment outside of school with Shay, Q, or Riley's.

—

Doc arrived home with three burger takeouts. Nicole watched a movie with Missy curled up on the sofa. "I stopped and got burgers. I figured you would not be cooking me dinner tonight, Nicole." He scowled at the wine glass in her hand.

Nicole looked up. "Thank you, that was thoughtful."

"You could have been more thoughtful. Get up and clear off the table so we can eat," Doc ordered.

Nicole glared. "Just a second until the commercial, we are at an exciting part of the movie." She did not want an argument. *Must you be so rude? You are so polite in public.*

"You can see a movie anytime. Dinner is getting cold."

Nicole rose to set the table with plates and tableware, Missy at the right side, Doc in a face off in head table position. "Table's cleared." *TV trays and eating out of the boxes could have work as well, we wouldn't even have to look at each other.* She knew her thoughts did not matter.

"Good, here's your food." Doc handed each person a box. Missy glared at him, took her box, and headed to her room. "Where do you think you're going, Missy? We are eating as a family tonight."

The teen opened the cabinet, putting something into her sleeve. Doc noticed the bulge as she charged out the door, shouting, "What family?"

"Nicole, you need to manage your daughter." Doc snarled.

Dinner was eaten in silence, with Doc sitting in his favorite chair. *There it was again. Takeout. He certainly took everything out of them.* Nicole did not look up except to sip her wine.

———

Q finished wiping the tables, stacking the chairs, and rolling the silverware perfectly for the morning shift. Dee's closed at 8:00 pm, and the library closed at 9:00 pm. That meant he had between 35 and 40 minutes left for quick research. Silently, he removed his white apron, hung it on the hook according to habit, and quickly took his leave. "Bye," he said. "If Mom calls, tell her I am at the library."

Margie wiped her hand on her apron, "Where else would you go?"

———

The more Q learned, the more it felt like he was sinking into a world of intrusion—the lines between privacy and prying blurred. A weight of responsibility settled deep inside him of ethical dilemma. Getting the necessary gear was a pipe dream. Everything cost so much money, especially for all the cool things he discovered on his Internet forays. They were powerful tools permitting accurate surveillance with serious consequences for their misuse. Aware of the severe implications, if acquired, Q vowed to use them only for noble purposes. What was happening to Missy? Why? He logged his discoveries into his brilliant brain. *God, I'd love to try some of this stuff.*

He sped home on his bike to share what he learned with Shay and Zak, playing dominoes on the kitchen floor.

—

Uncle Ben and Aunt Kate were asleep when Zak tiptoed into the house to discover the chicken pot pie in the frig. It was cold and he liked cold or piping hot food. He didn't like middle anything. Middle was like a maybe or a mostly. As far as he was concerned middle stuff gave no indication of what really needed to be. Zak carried the food upstairs to his room. He forgot the spoon and ran back to get it along with a juice box. He had not spent much time in his room, and as he ate, his curiosity got the better of him.

He admired Uncle Ben's office, which was now his. The room was tucked away in the upper reaches of the Jordan home. The double-hung windows opened to the back porch roof, allowing him to come and go as he pleased by simply hanging over the edge and dropping two feet. He had already checked the area for mud or dangers and found none, unless he got caught. Though he had no reason to leave now, it was a potential secret escape route, reminiscent of detective shows or superhero movies.

A large cabinet stood against one wall, filled with doors, drawers, and shelves containing remarkable items he had only seen on television. A closet housed a tall, locked safe. His eyes widened as he surveyed the cabinet. Unable to resist his urge to explore, Zak opened one door after another. The first door revealed a box of old police badges glimmering in the dim light. His eyes sparkled with excitement as he imagined the stories behind each badge and the courageous events they represented. His curiosity piqued, he carefully lifted objects and put them right back where he found them, adhering to his father's rule: "If you touch anything, you are to put it right back where you got it." His father, an attorney, expected everything to be orderly and precise, and Zak followed this rule diligently.

The bookshelf cabinets were filled with crime books, photos, photo albums, and police memorabilia. His heart raced with excitement as his curiosity overwhelmed him. Like a crow drawn to glittering objects, he craved the thrill of discovering novelties. His eyes darted from one item to another, scanning for anything that caught his attention. Gently, he picked up a photo album and began flipping through its pages. Inside were pictures of his mom and dad, himself as a small child, his dad and Uncle Ben hunting and fishing, and holidays at Gram's. He missed Gram and her cookies.

Zak moved onto the desk. The desk drawer was slightly ajar, tempting him to uncover its hidden treasures. He carefully slid the drawer open with bated breath and discovered a leather-bound notebook. Its worn pages were filled with handwritten notes about closed cases from ongoing investigations. There were intricate maps and sketches of crime scenes. Secrets and mysteries captivated his imagination. He was thankful the notes were printed as he could not read cursive. One tab said, Unfinished Business. *Hmmm...that was intriguing.* The first date was 2007—Zak would have been a one-year-old. The notes talked about a teen his age named Kevin, who worked at O'Rileys. He went to Riverdale High and was a run-away who lived with the Jones family. *Who were the Jones family?* This was great bedtime reading. He placed the notebook exactly where it had been.

Unable to resist, he examined them closely. A wave of excitement washed over him as he imagined himself as a master detective, solving complex puzzles and uncovering secrets with these very tools. The drawer was deep, and in its farthest corner, he discovered a miniature camera cleverly disguised as a pen. He marveled at the device, his mind racing with thoughts of thrilling undercover operations. He envisioned himself gathering evidence like the detectives in his favorite crime shows and apprehending dangerous criminals.

After pocketing the secret camera pen, Zak was struck with a pang of guilt. Though this was now his room, he realized his actions were wrong—he was invading his uncle's privacy and taking things without permission. With a heavy sigh, he slowly returned the pen camera to its original spot.

Zak couldn't contain his excitement as he carefully closed the desk drawer, ensuring everything else remained as he had found it. A whirlwind of emotions flooded his mind—his heart raced with a strange mix of thrill, guilt, and inner conflict. The mundane school books on the desk stood in stark contrast to the world of intrigue he had just been exploring.

———

Ben rustled awake upon hearing Zak arrive home. Despite Zak's attempts at a stealthy, tiptoed entry, his movements were loud. The young bull in Ben's china shop had arrived. Ben listened for the microwave to ding, but it didn't. Instead, he heard the thuds of footsteps above his head, loud enough to wake Kate.

"It's just Zak; it seems he can fall asleep anywhere but in a bed. I have to check on the shenanigans in my office," Ben whispered as he rose from his bed.

"You need a reason to go up there. I'll get the blanket, and we can deliver it," Kate decided, taking the fleece blanket off Ben's chair.

———

Zak continued to explore his new surroundings. His room, once a chaotic mess, was now neatly organized. Uncle Ben had taught him about Riverdale's litter fines - a hefty fifty dollars - which applied even to his own room. This real-world lesson prompted Zak to adopt new habits: making his bed each morning, placing dirty clothes in the basket under his bed, and folding clean clothes in the footlocker at the bed's end. He even arranged his four pairs of shoes underneath, with his favorite red sneakers at the far left.

Suddenly, he heard footsteps followed by a sharp, sheriff-style knock on his door. Zak quickly slid into Uncle Ben's chair and repositioned his algebra book. "Come in," he called out, looking up. He felt relieved that he had strategically placed his textbooks and note paper on the desk as a prop, just in case of unexpected visits. It worked perfectly. Zak was determined not to disappoint his uncle or jeopardize their growing relationship.

"I brought you a warm blanket, Zak. Don't want you to get cold," Kate said as she entered, carrying a thickly folded blue and white checkered bundle. She offered it to Zak while discreetly surveying the room.

"We thought we'd come up and say good night. I'm glad you're here, Zak," Uncle Ben smiled warmly.

"I was studying," Zak replied, aware that 'study' was a fitting word, given that Uncle Ben referred to his den as a study.

"You've certainly made life more interesting," Kate remarked, averting her eyes as she struggled to address Ben's awkward mission.

"Oh, uh, thank you," Zak stammered, rising to accept the blanket, feeling his face flush. Kate noticed the notebook on the desk, surprised to see three algebra problems correctly solved. Ben scanned the room, finding nothing out of place. Satisfied, he reached for the doorknob.

"Good night, Zak," they said in unison as they closed the door.

"Good night, sleep tight," Zak responded, one of his habitual phrases whose meaning he'd always wondered about. With a pang in his heart, he was thankful for Dad's years of training—everything was back exactly as he had found it.

He unfurled the blanket and curled up in bed. He tried to sleep, but restlessness consumed him. He longed to explore that closet further. He slipped out of bed, tiptoed to the closet, and gently slid open the door, clicking on the dim light.

On the floor were black work boots. In the corner was a wooden box. He lifted the lid, discovering three binoculars and the monocular thingy. These were some of the things Q wanted to find. 'I found them! Q won't believe this!' Zak lit up inside, thinking of Q's surprise at the tools.

Next to the box was a metal container filled with surveillance gear. *Did Uncle Ben have secret powers like Clark Kent?—or maybe he was more like James Bond,* he thought. Zak carefully examined each piece of equipment. The thrill of adrenaline rushed through him. His breathing quickened as his heart raced with anticipation of the discovery. He loved solving puzzles and uncovering secrets, and now he had a collection of real spy tools at his fingertips. With this equipment, he could become an actual spy and unravel mysteries that had long remained unsolved! *I can impress Q. The Monogram Masters can save Missy from hurting herself again.* His heart broke for Missy. He was sure that embarrassment was causing her to ignore the Monogram Masters.

———

The next day, Sam and Mantha rose early for the northbound drive to the VA hospital. The sun was deep in sleep. It was a drive Sam had made many times over the past decades. It was Mantha's first. She pressed her back into the truck seat and looked straight ahead with her mouth closed and jaw tightly set. For over a hundred miles, she made no sound. Nor did Sam. They had experienced similar injuries and life changes. It was why he was driving them to see her physician today. Why he outright gave her the business without asking for anything but truth and friendship in return. Perhaps he was not retiring. Every day, Sam arrived at their now shared garage with fresh coffee, conversation, and counsel.

Sam turned off the freeway and veered off another exit onto the route toward the Humphrey terminal. "I hate these diamond interchanges. Why can't they keep things status quo?" It was the first words spoken in one hundred miles and Mantha could safely answer without emotion.

"It eliminates left turns, Sam, and that saves lives, no to mention it gives a longer viewing distance," Mantha shared as rows of headstones emerged on her right side. This visit to the national veterans cemetery invoked a heavy mix of memories loaded with emotion. Mantha stared at the over a quarter million pristine white tombstones with solemn respect. They prompted a profound sadness. So many silenced futures, with only memories remained for Gold Star families. Sam and Mantha's injuries sustained in combat were a constant reminder they survived.

"There is solace in knowing you returned home," Sam whispered. "I am here for you, Mantha." Sam understood this vital passage. It was a journey through time, reliving the horrors of war and paying homage to fallen comrades who had made the ultimate sacrifice. He parked the car, and they walked with each step echoing the weight of scars and struggles for stripes and stars. Sam noted Mantha's eyes linger on engraved names and dates. Underneath each held a story. Above each left behind a loved one-size hole in their hearts.

Even decades later, a tumultuous storm welled within him, Comrades' faces flashed through his mind—laughter, brotherhood, the alliance of a shared duty. War stole indiscriminately from all sides. Soldiers fought for what they believed to be their truth or what they were told to do. A still, small voice whispered: Truth is truth. It is factual. Possessed truth is merely perspective. War stole life from human beings passionately wedded to their perspective. Standing on a sorted belief on how best to live. Killing over group belief.

A curious equation formed in his mind.

In a cemetery, humans learn truth from truths and life from those who gave their lives for their beliefs. Truth faced him now: beliefs kill, beliefs heal.

Cemeteries ask: What do you believe?

The pain of lost friendships, a wound seared deep into Sam's heart. It lingered after sixty years.

Sam paused, his voice heavy with the weight of his past. "Sit, Mantha, you are alive. Beneath us, a quarter million interments bear witness to the passage of time. We must carry on."

Mantha, now seated, gazed at the solitary headstone, its weathered surface and enduring presence a testament to the resilience of life. "I want you to meet my mentor, Gunner Hunter, who guided me back to life. He was my anchor in the storm. It is good to be alive. Mantha, you and I, we are still standing."

"Fifty years ago, Gunner was like Jesus to me, and he had lost his son, my best friend, Josef." Mantha traced the star with her left index finger, looking warily at Sam. "Jesus was Jewish, too, Mantha."

Mantha read the inscription:

STAR

Gunner

Hunter

SGT

US ARMY

WWII

FEB 15 1924

OCT 3 2008

Mantha fixed her gaze intensely at the world around her; she had deliberately distanced herself from all organized belief systems and institutions as she dedicated herself to the cause of humanity. As a child, organized anything, including religion, was not a family norm. Paying rent, food, and keeping the heat and lights on were real and immediate. School sports cost money, and movies or restaurants were buildings to drive past to get to Rileys for fuel to go to work. Her proud parents were not the kind to accept handouts or be considered charity cases. Her calm demeanor reflected a deep-seated wariness. She found it difficult to support a system in which individual egos were exploited to control and manipulate others. Over time, she had witnessed an overwhelming amount of suffering and anguish resulting from human ambitions and their deviation from the true intentions of any higher power. Due to the conflicts between religious groups, she had nearly lost her life.

Sam continued, "When I returned, I hated everything in Riverdale. I didn't trust a damn soul, and I let people know. I used alcohol to medicate my losses. I returned from 'Nam with a messed up heart and head. The parts of my body that remained out country were soaked in Agent Orange spray. I had no feelings and no job. My skills as a jungle foot soldier with radio experience amounted to nothing in Riverdale. I lost my foot and I had no radio. To make it worse, my friends were planted at the National Cemetery. I had survivor's remorse. The three of us deployed to 'Nam—I was the only one who came home. Small-town folk bury the pain. I was a glow-in-the-dark neon sign of that reminder every day."

Mantha traced the star with her scarred right hand, narrowing her eyes at Sam in a challenging gaze.

"Grave markers reflect one's faith. The Hunter family departed from Odessa, arriving during the pogroms in 1903. They Americanized their name, kept their faith hidden, and settled safely in our small community. They attended the Lutheran church, provided food for potlucks, and embraced farm living. They worshiped with us and prayed with us. Their children went to school and meshed with the rest of us. When World War II arrived, Gunner joined the Army and enlisted as a protestant. He soon found himself in the European Theater, thankful his dog tags held a cross. MaLu, his wife, fought hard to change that star because of his paperwork. Simple wrong designation—a checked or unchecked box—something so insignificant can ripple through one's life and carry on in death."

Mantha listened as her fingers traced the six points on the star.

"MaLu, Gunner's wife, dedicated her twilight years to working with Operation Benjamin, an organization committed to honoring American-Jewish soldiers who risked their lives for democracy and freedom. Her efforts focused on replacing Latin Crosses with Stars of David on the graves of Jewish soldiers mis-registered in places like Normandy. This work gave her life profound meaning. She ensured that her son, Josef, my best friend, received his star in 1969, even before the operation officially began. By the time she passed away, the VA had updated its policies, allowing next of kin to request specific emblems for headstones if they were not already available. Today, there are sixty-one emblem choices, each grave telling its own unique story. The VA no longer questions the individual belief systems of any eligible veteran or their family members"

A somber gathering under a nearby canopy paid respects to a fallen soldier, their grief palpable. Sam bowed his head, his hand trembling as he touched Gunner's cold, polished stone. Memories resurfaced, vivid and raw—Gunner's laughter, his warmth, the bond forged between brothers in arms. "Thank you, Old Man," Sam whispered, standing to salute. "I shall carry on. Boots are tied and ready."

Sudden gunshots startled Mantha as seven military members fired three synchronized volleys. Smoke lingered from this show of respect and honor. She turned to the flag and fallen, then saluted. The haunting melody of 'Taps' pierced the silence, played by Sgt. Reg, whom Sam recognized.

The mournful notes resonated with Mantha, filling her with bittersweet sorrow and pride in her service. The sound echoed among the rows of tombstones, a solemn tribute to those who had given everything for their country and convictions. "Sam, I will," Mantha paused, "I will carry on."

Standing on the hallowed ground of the national cemetery, surrounded by the invisible presence of the fallen, she felt a wave of peace wash over her. She realized their shared purpose - to serve their country's spirit and principles, honoring those who came before. Connected through time, she felt her shoulders relax and exhaled slowly, feeling lighter. She was no longer burdened without a cause.

"Climb in, Mantha," Sam said. "We can't be late for our appointments."

———

Mantha and Sam attended their respective doctor appointments at the same clinic. Sam's doctor confirmed stability in his ongoing battle with cancer, which had been triggered by Agent Orange exposure. "Not bad for an old soldier, Mantha. The labs are clear. I've been in remission for almost 18 years. I am blessed."

"They're offering me a titanium socket, Sam," Mantha beamed. "They said I'm ready for a more durable, lightweight, and permanent option." She lifted her hands for a high-five. "It's already in the works!" Her enthusiastic gesture drew attention in the lobby, and patients saluted and applauded.

"Lunch is on me, Mantha," said Sam. "Let's celebrate! Then, we'll visit the haunts of the Hardware Men. Do you remember launching all those rockets in the big field? We have a few hours before my next appointment. I was thinking about Zak. I bet he would like to build a real model rocket. You're welcome to join me."

Mantha's mind wandered back to her childhood, running in golden fields with her father and Sam's son, Shaun and his friend, Ben. At O'Riley's they built countless rockets. Sam invited the neighborhood and then some. They were joined by Sam's friend Emmett, and his son Michael Johnson. Kissy, their tag-along preschooler, and Trapper. John Mason from the Hanover Falcons, a rival school, and his grandfather, who lived in Riverdale. John mounted friendly competitions against Sam's rocket team. They built rockets with dual engines as each tried to attain higher altitudes. Such fond memories. Snapping back to the present, she felt refreshed and inspired.

Mantha let out a whoop, "I'm in. Let's DO this!"

—

Mantha had given Zak a key to the garage and asked him to check on Penny after school. She used a large key fob in bright neon red and attached it inside his backpack so it would be hard to misplace. She handed him four index cards with tasks. One was for entering and exiting the garage, the other was for how to take care of Penny, and the last one listed steps for cleaning the front entrance.

His first card gave security directions with a note, 'Lock the door behind you and do not let anyone inside.'

Buttons confounded Zak, and he usually pushed them randomly until they worked. This was often a big mistake, so he carefully pressed the buttons for the entry lock in the exact order written—slowly, firmly, and double checking before he pressed. The camera whirred above his head, locking onto him. He smiled, waved, and gave an okay sign. Then he carefully opened the back door—**Bee Beep, Bee Beep**.

Penny pranced over to greet him. Her smile was wide, and her tail wagging. His heart raced. What if he needed to be faster? He had practiced the alarm reset with Mantha. Now, he was alone. He touched his heart, telling himself, *"Be calm, heart, you can do this."* He punched in the numbers—**beeee-eeeeep** and then silence.

"Whew, Penny, I thought Uncle Ben would show up. Mantha said that would happen if I didn't do it fast enough. Sam's alarm calls the police. Card one is done." He told the dog and read the second card labeled

"Penny" in bold, listing three points:

1. Let the dog out to go potty and then play in Sam's backyard.

2. Play ball with her for 15 minutes so she can run.

3. Refill her water bowl and her food dish if empty.

He unarmed the system again to let Penny out and threw the ball to play with her. Zak was done playing long before the dog wanted to quit. He urged, "Come on, girl, let's get you a drink." Penny followed him as Zak checked to ensure she had food and fresh water. He found his marker and crossed all three tasks off the list. "Card two is done."

He read the third card, 'FRONT ENTRY.' It had four tasks.

1. Sweep the front entrance and empty the debris into the trash.

2. Pack the garbage from the cans into the big can and empty it into the dumpster by the back door.

3. Return ALL the trash cans to where you found them.

4. Wash all windows and dust sills.

Zak swept as Sam had shown him, which meant cleaning behind and under everything. He carefully positioned the dustpan over the trash to shake off the dirt and debris. He dumped the front trash bin into the dumpster in the back of the garage. He was glad he had left the system unarmed. He returned the trash bin precisely to where he'd gotten it. Zak found the next can and did the same. Penny followed. He found another. And another. And another. 'ALL' was underlined, so he hoped he was finding ALL of them.

He peeked under the square blue tarp in case a trash can was hidden to check on the four-wheeler and get a better look. "Whoa, Penny! It's still here." Zak picked up the helmet and put it on without strapping it. "The keys were under the helmet! FIRE!"

Zak peeled back the tarp, finding no more trash cans but what looked like a perfect opportunity. "There's a hitch, and here's a chain. This could move the big car parts in the boneyard. The ambulance guys won't have to carry anyone out if they get hurt!"

Zak turned the key, and it sputtered. He checked the gas, and it was empty. He scoured around, finding four red gas cans. He used a little gas from each to keep from leaving one empty. He would refill what he used later when he got his paycheck. He would take the 4-wheeler out quickly, clear the path at the boneyard of those big car parts, and put everything right back where he found it afterward.

"Tap-tap-tap." Zak jumped. He hurried to return all the red cans and carefully replaced the tarp.

"Tap-rap-tap!" This time, it was louder. Maybe it was Q or Shay. "Rap-rap-rap!" It sounded like the window glass could break.

"Open the door!" A man's voice shouted.

"No!" Zak refused, following Mantha's instructions. He slid to the floor to remain unseen. "No one is here!"

"You're there, and I said, 'OPEN the door.' I want to see my car!" Doc's voice raised.

"I can't!" Retorted Zak.

"I said, 'OPEN the door.' I want to see my car!" The voice raised.

"I won't!" Shouted Zak.

The man banged louder. "Where is Sam?"

"None of your business!" Zak felt cornered. "Get out of here!"

"You can't tell me to get out of here. You have my car!" The man was determined to manipulate the boy.

"I don't have your car. Riley's is closed!" Zak was trying his utmost to maintain the guidelines he was given. "Mantha said no one can come in. You are a NO ONE!"

"You're in trouble, boy. You remind me of that creep, Kevin, that Sam hired years ago! I can put you away, too." The man stomped to his car, slammed the door contemptuously, and sped away.

"How can he put me away, Penny?" Zak turned off the lights and slid to the floor. "It sounded like the principal. What a creep." Zak was shaking. "What did he mean, he could put me away too? Where would I go? And who else did he put away? One of the cars is Sam's, the other …"

He didn't want to think about it.

Penny nuzzled him, "Maybe I heard wrong, like at school when I need things repeated." Penny put her paw as Zak lay his head on the dog. "Penny, we did right, didn't we? Mantha is the boss, and she said it right here." Zak pulled out his card. "Do not let anyone in. And THAT WAS AN ANYONE!"

Zak held Penny.

Sleep only came easy for him if he was overwhelmed. The boy and dog nestled together, exhausted.

———

"Have you seen Zak?" Kate asked Ben, placing dinner on the table. "He drove more than one teacher crazy at school today. And Doc thinks he is stalking his daughter, Missy."

"I haven't seen him. Why would Doc think that?" Ben asked perplexed.

"Doc said he's overheard Zak's comments," frowned Kate. "I mean, would you say to me, 'You have a radiant smile; it brightens up my day?'"

"I might," Ben grinned playfully, "say it to you." His eyes twinkled flirtatiously with his wife.

"Ben, stop it. I'm serious," she interrupted firmly. "Doc said he saw Zak following Missy down the hall like a dog chasing a ball. He overheard him say, 'Missy, you have an incredible sense of style. I like how you look in your outfits.' I mean, really!" Kate was clearly exasperated.

"Do you think he meant it in a sexist or lecherous way? Missy does dress exceptionally well," Ben said, scooping up a steaming ladle of soup, and grabbing another of Lindsay's fresh baked sourdough bread. He wanted clarification, recalling Zak and his friends' concern over Missy's well-being during the container incident. Given Zak's somewhat awkward immaturity, it seemed unlikely he was being intentionally inappropriate.

"Don't make light of this! Doc told me he saw his daughter push Zak away and say, 'Buzz off, bucko. Leave me alone.' She smiled when she saw her father watching, and Doc made sure she was doing the right thing by nodding and giving her a thumbs up."

"I can talk to him, Kate. There are always two sides to a coin, and the truth might be in the middle," Ben said, blowing on his hot supper and inhaling the spiciness of the peppers and tomatoes.

"You and your idioms," Kate scolded. "That doofus, I don't trust him."

Ben narrowed his eyes. "What's gotten into you?" *That was an unusually sour comment coming from his wife, especially given her years of experience with students.*

"I just liked it the old way," she crooned, "with just us."

This puzzled him. "It will be just us again in six months," reasoned

Ben. *So, that's the bone she's got to pick with the boy? Her critical attitude was growing, whereas he was settling, which was the opposite of what he'd expected.* "I think having Zak here is good for both of us. Shakes things up a bit, and makes us GROW." He chuckled while taking another slice of bread, recalling that hole Zak had eaten out of the last casserole when Kate was gone. Still funny!

"You think THAT's funny?" Kate sneered.

Ben had just put a forkful in his mouth, "Naw, the casserole is funny." Chewing, talking with food in his mouth, and biting a hole in the bread like Zak had done his breakfast toast and with the last casserole. "I was laughing at how Zak ate the last casserole, is what I meant." Ben mumbled.

Kate pouted, sighed with audible exasperation, and withheld further comment as she ate. Ben cleared his dish, rinsed it, and put the plate in the dishwasher.

Kate piped up, "Whose green plate is that?"

"Zak brought it home, I don't know," Ben replied.

"Well, you just don't take somebody's plate!" Kate scolded. "I mean, it breaks up the set." She was not about to let this slide. "Gross!" She said with disgust. She was picking a fight but couldn't let it go.

"Okay, I'll talk with him," Ben said, lifting his hands in a truce. "He's a challenge."

"Talk TO him!" Barked Kate. "He's mayhem on legs!" She pushed her plate away, left it on the table, and marched off to their bedroom, slamming the door behind her.

"Yikes!" Ben exclaimed under his breath, bewildered by her outburst. *What in the world was going on with her? This can't be just about Zak living with them;* he sensed something deeper he couldn't quite put his finger on. Years in law enforcement had taught him to trust his instincts but not to get ahead of himself. He took a long breath and decided to give her space to calm down.

—

Having completed her appointments, Mantha joined Sam in his leadership group. The practice of medicine with veterans had changed with the severe injuries of soldiers returning from the Middle East. Sam had started the narrative therapy program back in 2010. He appreciated how veterans helped each other put intense and catastrophic experiences in context so they could heal, rebuild their lives, and reenter the community. Narrative therapy was story-based and effective, though it needed better integration into mainstream medicine.

"I'd like to introduce my business partner, Captain Mantha," Sam informed the familiar faces he trusted. "She will be joining me today."

"Welcome, Captain," they greeted her with regard.

Sam noticed Mantha relax as he began to speak. "I know this is unusual. Today, I'll share instead of counsel. Before it gets harder for me to talk about... It involves the death of my son. Shaun was my biological child. He died almost twenty years ago. The loss still hurts." Sam paused, his voice heavy with emotion. "Shaun died at age twenty-six in a 4-wheeler accident. He was a good driver. To this day... I'm not sure exactly what happened."

The group listened intently, as Sam rarely shared anything beyond his counsel and encouragement. "I'm sharing today for two reasons. First, I want to finally get this story off my chest. Second, I'm usually the one listening and counseling. Today, I want you to realize that even sixty years later, I'm just a person like you. I survived Vietnam, as you know. I regained my place in my community, but losing my non-military child as a young adult triggered complex, layered emotions. And I've just met a new young man who is triggering me. I want you to know I understand more than just the battlefield. I also understand your lifetime of reentry at home."

Sam took a deep breath. "Shaun was born prenatally exposed to alcohol; in other words, he had Fetal Alcohol Spectrum Disorder or FASD. After Nam, my wife and I drank quite a bit, and well... Seems like sex and drinking go hand in hand, or should I say..."Everyone caught his drift, knowing what he did not need to say. "Shaun was a kind person. He was fun and funny. He was generally rather impulsive. However, once he learned to drive or use a tool, he did it well every time. I trusted him and considered letting him drive my vintage car because he was so careful."

Sam continued, his voice heavy with emotion. "I know Shaun's motor coordination was sometimes uneven. He could over-correct as a driver, which usually caused no real problems. I was told a rabbit had jumped across the trail, and he swerved to miss it, plowing head-on into a tree... That killed him. I went there... I checked that space out repeatedly. It had been muddy, and a rabbit would have left tracks. I found none. It would have been like Shaun not to hurt an animal because he loved them. But it struck me wrong that I found no paw prints after Mike told me about the event."

"Mike, his passenger, survived but suffered a traumatic brain injury and had to be in a rehab center. On the other hand, it would have been like Mike to scare the animal or even prank Shaun. Thinking about this many years later, I believe there was more to the story. Mike was the only son of my best friend, Emmett, and his wife, Sally. It gets worse. Not long after my son's death, Emmett, Mike's father, and my best civilian friend was murdered. I lost both my only son and best friend within the same year. Thankfully, Mike came through his rehab with flying colors."

Sam swallowed hard, continuing his story about the losses he'd experienced, including his comrades from Vietnam. He spoke about Kevin, an employee convicted of Emmett's murder, whom Sam believed to be innocent. He drew parallels between Kevin, Shaun, and the new hire, Zak, noting their similar behaviors and challenges.

As Sam described his unease about Mike's (now Doc's) behavior around Zak, Mantha tried to connect the pieces. She recalled privates in her troupe she suspected had fetal alcohol syndrome, and her particular incident involving the IED and the young private who died trying to save her dog. Suddenly triggered, Mantha shouted, "STOP!"

The group surrounded her with understanding silence. When she opened her eyes, she saw concerned faces instead of glaring hospital lights. Her body was tense, eyes darting.

Sam gently soothed her with his voice. "Captain, you are back. You are alive. You are safe."

"That Private who died trying to save my dog... He was so like Zak!" Mantha buried her face in her hands. Tears ran down the deep scar on her cheek.

—

Sam and Mantha returned to Riley's, surprised that the back door was unlocked and the alarm was off. The garage was dark. Penny, who usually greeted them excitedly, had not. They entered cautiously, padding to the front, unsure of what they'd find. Mantha spied Penny and Zak in the corner. The dog rustled, but the boy did not. They rushed over to where they lay.

Mantha gently touched Penny first, who kept watch over the youth. "Zak—Zak, are you alright?"

"Huh?" He yawned, "Yeah, huh? What time is it? I fell asleep."

Mantha wanted to say, *"I guess you did, and you left the door open and the garage unlocked. What are you doing sleeping here?"* But she did not.

Sam observed in silence as Mantha asked, "What happened, Zak?"

"Doc, doc, doc—at least it sounded like Doc—you know who the school principal." Zak trembled, recalling the uncomfortable exchange. "He wanted to come in, and I said no. Then he yelled at me, and I told him no because you said no. I told him to go away. I told him no one could come in. I told him he was a NO ONE! He told me I was a creep, like Keith? Somebody? Maybe the name was Kevin and it was someone Sam had working here before me? Anyway, he said he'd get rid of me too. Where did that guy go? Will I have to go there, too?"

Sheriff Ben arrived at the front customer door of the garage, and Sam let him in. Penny greeted him jumping at the front door, being opened by Sam.

"Hello, Penny. Have you seen Zak?" Ben leaned down to scratch Penny's ears.

"Hi, Uncle Ben," came a quiet voice from the floor beside Mantha. "I fell asleep. I came to let Penny out and clean the front area after school."

"This is a mighty hard floor to sleep on and probably cold. How about you come home and get to bed," coaxed the Sheriff.

"Okay," said Zak. "See you tomorrow, Sam, Mantha, and Penny."

"See you later, alligator," Sam nodded and watched him go, still thinking about his son with his thoughts turning to Zak and what Doc said… getting rid of Kevin… and now threatening to get rid of Zak. A chill ran down his back and goosebumps rose on both arms.

"After a while, crocodile." Zak smiled quietly, recovering himself after Doc's unpleasant tirade.

"Don't skip a beat, parakeet," Mantha quietly added, noting the Ben had his arm around Zak's shoulder.

Zak felt comforted with the weight of Uncle Ben's arm. He was unsure of what to do next so he rested in his uncles strength. "Uncle Ben, Doc seems angry no matter what I do. I don't want to mess things up with Mantha or Sam. I have a real job now, and they count on me. I'm being the best me I can be."

Uncle Ben looked lovingly at Zak, "You are Zak. You are being the best you, you can be and I see that."

———

"Looks like these will have to wait," Mantha said, taking out two rocket kits from the shopping bag. One was an Estes Big Bertha, designed to reach about 500 feet, and the other a more advanced Estes E2X Ascender Rocket kit, capable of soaring over 3000 feet with a booster.

"Hey, Zak!" Mantha called out as the Sheriff and the boy headed home. "Bring Q and Shay to the garage tomorrow after work. Sam and I have a surprise for you!"

Zak responded with an enthusiastic thumbs up, spinning around in a full circle. Mantha noticed Ben affectionately ruffling the boy's shiny hair.

———

-17-
CAUGHT

Ever since Zak snooped through the Sheriff's office, his fascination with the world of law enforcement, spies, and superheroes had grown stronger. His curiosity overrode his worries. There was so much left to explore! Proper equipment would give the Monogram Masters a way to uncover what made Missy feel desperate at home, even though she kept up a tough front at school. She mostly avoided him. He tried his best to be kind and sweet and thought hard about things to say that could help her. Zak understood from experience that trust is hard, especially when someone knows something about you that you don't want anyone else to know.

Zak was excited about his discoveries but decided to keep them secret for now. He resolved to use the spy tools responsibly—only to uncover corruption, protect the innocent, and bring justice where needed. In his mind, being a spy meant gathering information for the greater good. He imagined his Uncle Ben would understand this was an important secret mission, after all he might be like Clark Kent.

When Zak found binoculars and a monocular in his closet, he felt a sense of accomplishment. The monocular was exactly what Q had mentioned needing. Holding the devices filled him with intrigue and excitement. Testing the monocular, he could clearly see license plate details on cars down the block. Each new tool sparked his imagination about uncovering hidden truths and becoming a hero. He planned to secretly read the notebook of unfinished business at night by flashlight.

The Monogram Masters were meeting Saturday to play tag and watch for the northern lights again. Thursday felt far away, and the lights hadn't reappeared yet. With darkness coming earlier each day, there was less time for outdoor games. Zak was eager to start investigating with his new spy gear.

He packed a pair of binoculars and the monocular in his backpack. He put on his shoes without tying them and borrowed the pen from the desk drawer, promising himself to return it later. Early Friday before dawn, he quietly climbed out the den window and jumped into a pile of leaves below. Driven by his passion for justice, he ran to Q's house to knock on his bedroom window and share the equipment.

—

'Tap. Tap tap. Tap Tap Tap'

Q heard the noise and peered out the window at Zak, holding up two pairs of binoculars and a monocular. "I got 'em!" He mouthed.

"Where?" Q asked, his voice quiet with awe.

"Uncle Ben," Zak answered.

"Wow, this is astounding. Sheriff Ben is letting us use these?!" Q was astounded.

"We can try them out tomorrow with your telescope. I gotta get back into bed. See you," Zak rasped in a coarse whisper and ran off.

Q held the new equipment. The thought of utilizing these tools for covert operations and solving mysteries fascinated him, yet he knew that these tools were not to be taken lightly. A sense of unease crept over him. He contemplated the gravity of balancing the need for information with the potential risks and consequences that could arise from discovering evidence of harm. Guided by his moral compass and fueled by his passion for justice, he would wield his spy tools with care and precision, making his mark in the covert realm of espionage.

Q examined the binoculars more closely, realizing they were equipped with high-quality lenses and night vision technology. These advanced features allowed him to peer into the darkness and observe hidden activities.

He watched as Zak ran home through the pre-dawn shadows. Remarkably, he could even make out the small text on the Riley gas station sign. These were clearly no ordinary binoculars. Carefully, Q placed the binoculars and monocular into his backpack on his desk, next to his telescope. He knew he had some important decisions to consider regarding this unexpected gift.

Meanwhile, Zak had made his way back home. He climbed onto the rain barrel, then pulled himself up onto the porch roof. Within minutes, he was back in bed, fast asleep.

—

Mantha eagerly anticipated Zak's arrival at work after school on Friday. The boy had been enthusiastically discussing his rocket projects, and when he brought in his attempt to show her, it was unfortunately beyond repair. She knew the Estes Big Bertha would be an excellent introduction to rocketry, and the open field where the kids played in the boneyard would serve as an ideal launching area for beginners.

After carefully considering various options at the hobby store, Mantha and Sam had decided the Big Bertha was the best choice for impressive yet manageable launches. Both had personal experience with rocketry—Sam had built a Big Bertha with his son Shaun, while Mantha had constructed her own with her father in her youth.

As children, she and Shaun had flown their rockets together. Shaun's was sparkling red because he had sprinkled it with silver glitter. Hers was a brilliant solid Maxfield Parish blue.

She hoped the Monogram Masters would feel the thrill of the slow, realistic liftoff propelled by powerful standard Estes engines. She looked forward to watching it return from its 500-foot journey back to earth, landing softly with its 18-inch parachute. She placed the Big Bertha in a big white shopping bag and had Sam store away the more advanced rocket in the safe closet so Zak could not discover it.

—

With Kate driving him to school early, Zak had no bus altercations and now his bike offered the same opportunity of non-connection. Q helped him with homework, and he appreciated the help. He never meant to get into trouble; like Uncle Ben said he was the best he could and he was a good person—well almost.

Algebra test-taking was stressful, and he hoped to get Q to look up. Zak turned around to see how Q was doing. When he rotated his head his eyes had to refocus because of the overhead fluorescent lights and that took a minute. When Zak could finally see, Q's head was down and he was writing on his test paper.

"Uh hem," he smelled the hot breath of a towering figure, "Mr. Jordan, may I ask exactly what you are doing?"

"Just looking," Zak's face turned red from being called out.

"Cheating is a violation of school conduct," said the teacher, who picked up his paper and swiftly marked it with a large red X and an F.

"You can't do THAT!" Desperate, Zak blurted. "I was looking!"

"That's how you cheat," admonished the teacher. "You look. I am done with you here. You can go to the office and see Doc Johnson."

Zak wanted to avoid the principal, like Missy was trying to avoid him. He was shaking in his red shoes and he walked to the office as if on a sticky mouse trap. It took ten full minutes to walk two hallways.

"My teacher sent me to see Doc Johnson," mumbled Zak.

"Dr. Johnson is busy. You can sit here until he can see you," the secretary looked up briefly from her computer.

The loud black circle clock ticked as Zak watched the secondhand go around the circle. He began counting each revolution… one…two… three— …ten. The bell for the next class rang, and Zak got up to run out the door. He did not want to miss Astronomy.

The secretary stopped him. "Not so fast, young man. You are here for a reason, and you will stay sitting right here for that same reason."

"Huh?" Zak sat down.

"The cat's out of the bag on you, son," the secretary looked over her glasses that we now on her lower nose. "Your actions are speaking louder than your words."

"What cat? I never put any cat into a bag," Zak was irritated. "Why are people saying I do all these things I don't do? I can't be late for Aunt Kate's class."

"I think you mean Ms. Jordan," sniped the secretary.

Zak continued to count revolutions …thirty-nine …forty.

The office door opened. "Mr. Jordan, I am available to see you now. You may come in," a snide smile curled on Doc's lips. "Take a seat, Zak. Pick anyone." The principal gestured.

"I don't need to take a seat," Zak said, scanning the chairs. The principal's voice grated on him.

"I don't have anywhere to keep it."

"Are you trying to be funny?" The principal asked curtly. "Sit down."

The tone reminded Zak of the voice from the garage that had scared him. "Why didn't you just say that if you wanted me to sit?" Zak asked.

The principal's eyes narrowed. "Tell me why you didn't understand what I said."

"You REALLY want to know?" Asked Zak.

"Yes, I do," his body language appeared to be curious and sincere this time.

"Okay, you told me to take a seat. How come would I take a seat from your office?" Explained Zak.

"How come? Why did you think that?"

"You want the truth, or you want me to play you? WHY questions send my mind into a house of mirrors. I don't do WHY questions because I cannot answer them. So I do. HOW comes. How come this happened? How come that happened? Not why. You understand?" Zak's voice raised with exasperation. His skin crawled being this close to Doc.

"Okay, so why…" the principal said in a placating tone. "HOW COME you cheated on the algebra test today?"

"Blankity Blank Blank!" Shouted Zak. "I did not cheat. I looked!"

"Cheating and insubordination are going on your school record. You're done for the day. You are a piece of work, Zak."

"I do work!" Said Zak.

Doc glared over his desk, "There is an issue, Zak, we need to discuss."

Zak had heard that tone of voice from his father—the very same word, "Yes, sir. What, sir?" He answered, shrinking himself to blend into the chair.

"I noticed you've been paying attention to Missy," said Doc.

"I keep checking up on her," said Zak.

"Clarify what you mean by 'checking up'?" Pursued Doc.

"I've been trying to find out more about her."

"Do you know your behavior crosses boundaries. It can be intrusive or even harassing? It's crucial to respect others' privacy and personal space. What do you hope to achieve?" The principal leaned in.

"I haven't talked to her much," Zak calmed.

"It's crucial to remember that people choose who they want to engage with and how. Respecting their boundaries is essential," Doc instructed, a Cheshire cat grin on his face. "Our counseling office is always available for guidance and support. Don't hesitate to reach out if you have further concerns or need assistance. Let's work together to foster healthy relationships and appropriate boundaries within the school." Doc leaned back in his chair, signaling the end of the conversation. "I'm giving you three days of in-school suspension. You can pick up your assignments but cannot attend classes until next Wednesday."

"But what about lunch, PhyEd., and art?" Zak asked.

Doc cocked his head with a dismissive smirk. "That's your challenge. Let's see how you handle it. It's a better alternative than expelling you." His smile widened into an eerie sneer, clearly enjoying the situation. "Now, what would your Uncle Ben think?"

Doc lectured while Zak listened passively. "In-school suspension is the consequence of cheating, which violates academic integrity and Riverdale High School's code of conduct. Since you were caught or suspected of cheating, I support the teacher's decision," Doc said, locking eyes with Zak.

The principal leaned in and extended his arm across the desk. "The purpose of this consequence is to give you time to reflect, and we expect it to discourage such behavior in the future, if you can, Zak." He handed Zak a paper to sign, acknowledging the cheating and insubordination.

"Sign here to accept my offer," said Doc. "I will inform Kate, and I'm sure she will inform Sheriff Ben." Doc smacked his lips and raised his eyebrows, holding all the cards.

"You may report to the nearby suspension room now. I will be happy to escort you."

Zak signed, feeling he had no choice but to comply.

—

"Mr. Mason, Mr. Jordan is here until Wednesday for INSUBORDI-NATION. He was CHEATING," Doc spit. "I am sure you will help Mr. Jordan with this." He turned and departed from the makeshift room, a storage closet emptied to become Mr. Mason's office.

The buzzed-haired, large, muscled man nodded, "No problem, we'll get along just fine. Zak, pick a paper from Jar One and Jar Two. Then, pick a ticket from Jar 3. These are your extra exercises and assignments for today."

Jar 1—"25 push-ups," Zak read aloud. He pulled another from Jar 2 and put the paper into his right pocket. Then he pulled a paper from Jar #3 a placed it into his left jeans pocket. He did not like tickets and hoped Mr. Mason forgot about Jar Three.

Mr. Mason, like Uncle Ben, was big, fair, and rugged. Zak stared at skulls, maidens, and curly word tattoos decorating Mr. Mason's bulging biceps. "Cool art!"

The massive man with muscles and no neck looked into his face.

"Push-ups? Is that PhyEd? Today was going to be outside. Blankity Blank! Can I put on my gym clothes?" Zak knew he might get sweaty and wanted to be prepared.

"What are you going to do next, Zak?" The voice boomed.

Zak gazed around the tiny closet-like suspension room. There was barely room for a table, a chair, and a large Mr. Mason. There were no windows. The lights began to bother him. "I will get down on the floor. Now. Right now. And I will follow your orders."

"Is there something you do not understand?" Growled the giant.

Zak took a deep breath, dropped his backpack onto the table, got onto the bare, hard floor, and wedged against the legs. "Okay, okay, already," he said, looking at the dirtyt floor, with furballs and a paper clip.

"Do you know the next step?"

Zak's arms pumped down and up, down and up. He did not let the paper clip touch his nose. "12, 13, 14…" The room was stifling. Mr. Giant Man did not move. When Zak reached push-up 22, his shoulders and arms burned. He wobbled. Breathing quickly with heart pumping, he compelled his body to complete the final three. Then, he fell flat on his stomach, causing the paper clip and lint to swoosh forward. They swirled around Mighty Mr. Mason's hard-toed boot. Zak rested.

"Do you have more assignments? Get up." The voice instructed.

Zak took time before moving. "Now? Blankity Blank Blank All this is just for looking?" This experience was puzzling. Zak rose, careful not to touch Goliath, inches away and blocking the door. "Okay, Mr. Mason, sir, what is my next punishment?" Zak's eyes blinked quickly; he tilted his head down and away from the throbbing ceiling.

"I don't see any punishment. I asked you to pick one piece of paper from three jars. What's next?"

Zak pulled the paper from Jar 2 out of his right pocket and read, "Jar Two: Write multiplication tables starting with 0x0 through 10x10, ten times each. That will take me forever!"

"Plenty of paper and a jar of newly sharpened pencils you can use if necessary. Do you want to do anything else right now?." Offered Mr. Mason.

"No." Answered Zak, sitting at the plain wooden table filled with carved gouges, initials, and swear words. He ran his finger around the blankity-blank grooves. Big Guy was now leaning against the cement block wall, clearly bored.

"How do I start this?" Zak stared at the bald man. His head was beginning to pound, and he rubbed his temples.

"You can start with zero times zero. Here, let me do one set." Mr. Mason wrote a row of zero equations, with each equaling zero. "Now you add nine more rows of what I wrote. And when you are done, you will begin with 1 x 1."

This job was immense. It could take days. He drew one, slid his pencil over, and added another one, slide/add one slide/add one until the paper had ten ones across the page. Under those, he printed a one, two, three, four, five, and so on to ten. XXXXXXXXXX was next. He became a robot writing in repetitive movements until the pencil tip became dull, fuzzing and smearing each number he wrote.

"Mr. Mason, sir, I need another pencil, please."

A shadow descended over Zak. "Here" and Mr. Mason left the room.

Zak needed a bathroom break and a drink of water. Where was the teacher? He would just stretch his legs to get away from the glare of the lights. He lifted his long arms above his head and yawned. He needed air—a quick walk to the bathroom would be good. Zak rose and opened the door to the hallway—no teacher. The bathrooms were down the corridor. The water fountain was on the way. Zak gulped the water before entering the boy's room. Even the bathroom had fluorescent lights! *No teacher, whew.* He closed his own eyes, trying to relax for a moment...

BAM, BAM, BAM! Zak's eyes shot open. He jumped from the toilet seat in the closed stall. "You were not permitted to leave the room. Get back now," Mr. Mason's big boots pointed toward him from under the stall.

"Sorry, Mr. Mason, sir! I needed water." Zak stammered.

"This is not the water I'd advise you to drink. Get out here now. It is not a suggestion!" A broad chest stretching a tee shirt to its seams met him. Zak was led back to the lifeless room of numbers, erasures, a headache, and two sharpened pencils. "There is no second break."

Another class bell rang.

—

Zak had missed the last half of Algebra, all of Astronomy, and the next class was Civics. Zak looked up meeting Mr. Mason's eyes, "Mr. Mason, sir. Do I have the right to free speech in America?"

The bushy eyebrows raised, "Yeah, you do."

"And Riverdale is in America, and Riverdale High School is in Riverdale, so that's like multiplication tables, right?" Queried Zak.

The bushy eyebrows now were on a very deep ridged forehead. The giant's large hand was on his chin, wondering where was this going. "How?" He grunted.

Zak mirrored putting his hands into his chin, "Freedom of speech lets individuals express ideas, debate, and get a deeper understanding of hard issues. Isn't that what multiplication does, too? I mean, it goes from one person to two and then four until it is more, and more, and more."

"Continue…" Mr. Mason wanted to find out how was connecting these dots. He did not know how much physical activity helped Zak think even when the lights assaulted him.

"Okay." Zak continued,"you learn to solve problems with multiplication, and by having more and more people share their ideas and how come they think that, without being scared or stopped, everything works better. When my friends and I share ideas, we get bigger and better ideas."

"Okay," Mr. Mason sat and crossed his big leg over his other boot and put his hands behind his neck stump. "I see. You may continue…"

"Well, it doesn't matter what number you are. You can still live and work on the multiplication table. And that's the same with people. It doesn't matter your shape, size, age, or color. You can still say what you need to freely. Your background does not matter."

Mr. Mason moved his hands before his face, covering his mouth. Zak recognized that as the signal for another person's thinking and continued. The teacher did not interrupt Zak's train of thought, and because of this Zak could continue to link ideas together. When people kept their mouths closed and didn't stomp on his words, good things could come out of Zak's mouth. Zak paid attention to the little things others did not notice to remain safe in his world.

"Okay, so when you multiply two times four, you get eight. Consider what happens if you multiply two people's ideas four times. That means you can get eight differences. And that is a whole pile of choices to pick and choose and mix up. So both multiplication and freedom of speech make people smarter."

Mr. Mason said, "Okay."

"So, multiplication offers friendship in numbers, and freedom of speech offers friendship with people. The numbers bridge the gaps, and the words the people speak bridge the missing pieces." Zak paused. "Based on America's Freedom of Speech, could I ask you a question?"

Mr. Mason tried hard not to laugh. This was most certainly the most creative approach a student had undertaken, "Yes, based on Freedom of Speech, you may ask a question."

"Do I need to read the last ticket in my pocket?"

"I would pull it out and read it, Zak," Mr. Mason smiled.

"Jar Three Ticket: Ignore Jar One and Jar Two."

Zak's eyes popped open. "You tricked me!"

"No, I just told you to take out three pieces of paper. You tricked yourself." Mr Mason said.

"You mean I don't have to finish the 7, 8, 9, and 10 tables?" Zak asked.

"If you don't want to, don't," said the teacher. "The ticket gave you a free ride."

"I will finish them after lunch. Can I go to lunch, sir?" Zak asked.

Mr. Mason nodded. "I will escort you. I know you sit next to the teachers. Feel free to sit next to Q and Shay. Nice job this morning, Zak. You have proven yourself, and we will resume this afternoon with the other in-school suspension students in the larger room. But no funny business, you hear me!"

"I can finish the tables, right?" Zak asked.

He was sure he saw a sparkle in Mr. Mason's eyes. "Only if you want to. I expect you to read ALL my directions before you start any assignment in the future."

"I do want to finish and yes, I will read ALL your directions from now on."

–18–
NOT AS IT SEEMS

Aunt Kate exited Riverdale High School boiling over, "What is this I hear about you cheating in algebra? I can't believe you would do something like that! I put your bike into my car! I will drive you to work. We need to talk."

"I was just looking. Doc called it in sub-ordi-nation or something like that," said Zak.

"That's not what I heard. Cheating won't get you anywhere in life. You need to learn the material and put in the effort to succeed," lectured Aunt Kate. "I understand you may have felt overwhelmed, but cheating is never the right solution. It undermines your learning and your trust in teachers and classmates. Can you explain what the consequences are?

"Doc gave me an in-school suspension for three days," Zak looked at his untied shoes. He was beginning to think he may have really done something wrong. *Looking at Q was not wrong. Looking around, maybe.*

"Three days?! Consider yourself lucky. Mr. Mason is no joke. He will straighten you out. You deserved a more severe punishment. This is going on your permanent record, which could affect your future," ranted Aunt Kate as she dropped him off at Riley's. "I will save you some dinner for after work. I want you home tonight. No going out after what you pulled."

"Okay, Aunt Kate," said Zak. "Thank you for the ride."

Kate continued. "I want you to realize that cheating has disciplinary consequences which hamper your growth and development. It's crucial to take responsibility for your actions and learn from this experience. No, going out after work; I want you home to think about this tonight."

"I think you already said that. I will come right home," said Zak.

Think about what? This whole thing was already said and done hours ago.

—

"Mantha, can I tell you something?" Zak peered under Doc's car. "Sure, Zak, what?"

"What does in sub ordi nation mean? I got that today. I don't think it's good?" Zak asked.

"Insubordination? Really?" Mantha questioned, "Not usually good. Did you talk back?"

"I told the truth. The teacher lied."

"Did you refuse to do a task?" She queried.

"He said I was cheating and gave me a big red X and an F. I was doing my test. He made me quit."

"Were you cheating?" Asked Mantha, puzzled.

"No, I was looking," said Zak. "Then I told Doc what I was thinking."

Mantha chuckled, nodding, "Yep, sounds like insubordination to me. We can work on this so you don't get yourself in trouble again. Insubordination is what they call it when you disrespect a limit everyone must follow—accepting authority. School is where authority and structure provide order, so can learn together. Otherwise, differences of opinion would make everything too chaotic to focus on the main things we study. Does that make sense? We can work on that so you understand it better."

"Okay," agreed Zak.

Mantha rolled out from under the car and grabbed Zak's shoelaces, "I could take you out by grabbing these dudes. You want to know how Russians tie them?"

"Where would you take me out to by grabbing my shoelaces?" Zak was perplexed.

"Take you out—it's a figure of speech. What I mean is, I could dump you on the ground, spin you around, and hogtie you—take you out of the game, out of what you were focused on," explained Mantha. "Let me show you how to fix those laces. I had to learn a new method, too." She held up her right hand.

"Okay, sure—I get it now," Zak smiled.

Mantha rolled to her belly on the dolly and grabbed both laces of the left shoe, "Watch. Two bunny ears and tie them in the middle."

"That's it? No whip-a-roo' and over here and go there?"

"Nope, two bunny ears and tie them in the middle. Try it."

Zak grinned, made two bunny ears, and tied them in the middle. He was astounded. "I did it!"

"Yes, and you will forever more. Now get to work. I need those windows sparkling clear, you hear me?" Mantha ordered.

"Yes, Ma'am," beamed Zak.

"And that, dear sir, is the opposite of insubordination. That is called obedience or compliance." Mantha paused, "Thank you."

Zak was silent. Mantha was filled with goodwill, and she made things safe. He could soak in everything she taught him.

"And you say back to me, 'You're welcome or my pleasure, okay?'" Mantha coached.

"You're welcome or my pleasure, okay," repeated Zak.

It was a start.

—

Q showed up at the garage to hang with Zak. A few minutes later, Shay arrived on her bike. Sam watched her ride up. "Hi, Shay. Nice to see you. Do you have lights on that bike?" He asked.

"No, it is usually light outside, so I didn't need them," Shay hopped off. "Well, it's not light now. What time do you get off work?" Sam was already looking carefully at the bicycle.

"I start after school and get off after all the dishes are done at Memory Care from their bedtime snacks. It's about 7:30 or 8:00," Shay answered.

"Well, this won't do. Bring your bike in here. Let's fix it together so you are safer after sundown," Sam offered. Shay wheeled her bike to the workbench and cabinets filled with parts and pieces as Sam rummaged around. "Here, got just the part, and since no one is using it or has not used it for probably twenty years, these lights are yours."

Q followed Sam and Shay. "Shay, do you see that? Wow! Those are generator hubs!" Q was already down on his knees, contemplating how this would all work and spoke aloud. "As your wheel spins, the generator hub creates electrical energy that can power various components, including lights. The generator hub eliminates the need for batteries or recharging. As long as you keep pedaling, the lights will remain illuminated. This can be particularly useful where reliable lighting is crucial for safety."

Sam winked at Q. "Would you like to put them on for your sister? I have one for the front and one for the rear. Let's see what you can do!" "Mr. O'Riley, sir, I am so appreciative," thanked Q.

"Mr. O'Riley, we are so appreciative," added Shay. "Let us know how we can help you. Zak, are you coming up to our house?"

"I gotta get home tonight. I promised Aunt Kate I would stay in and think about my insubordination," Zak looked at his tied shoes and then at Mantha. "See you tomorrow!"

"Wait a minute, everyone!" Mantha shouted from the front. "I have a surprise!" Everyone gathered to watch Mantha. She stood behind the rarely used cash register. "Dum da da da Da Da Da Da Da Da Da Da," she sang, slowly raising a large white bag. Then very slowly she began to pull—and stopped. "What do you think it is?" She asked quietly. Everyone was silent. Sam's eyes gleamed. "Estes …. Big Bertha!" She yelled, "Rocket Kit!"

"No way!" Shouted Zak who was now jumping.

"Way!" Shouted wide-eyed Shay with hands clasped.

"Yes," nodded Q quietly with a slight smile. "Let's do this!"

—

Zak came home to the enticing aroma of sloppy joes, accompanied by chips and pickles. He devoured five sandwiches, then placed his dish in the dishwasher as Ben had instructed. He left the cooking pan on the stove, the serving spoon nearby, and the pickle jar open on the table, mirroring how he'd found them. His aunt and uncle were still out.

Opening the fridge, he took a long swig directly from the lactaid milk carton before replacing it and closing the door. On his way to his room, he snagged the bag of chips. Settling into his swivel chair, he rifled through a stack of photo albums. He selected one filled with images of beaches, swimsuits, and palm trees.

The scrapbook paper was yellowed, and the photos were held in place with little black corners that looked like tiny pockets. The first picture shows his mom and dad with Aunt Kate and Uncle Ben in front of a big boat. They were all so young, and it looked like they were having a great time. He flipped the page. The pictures were all so pretty that he pretended he was a part of this tremendous Caribbean boat adventure.

…A picture of his mother and Aunt Kate laughing on beach chairs by a large, long blue pool caught his attention. It looked like they were staying at a hotel. The caption, printed in perfect letters of gold, said, "Amidst the gentle lull of the ocean waves, we set sail tomorrow. Enjoying margaritas to celebrate this next adventure—Two weeks in heaven. January 2006." The picture next to it was his father and uncle sitting on top of a concrete wall, clinking bright green glass bottles; palm trees were in the backdrop.

"A voyage of unforgettable memories—We set sail from the port of Miami. The sun was hot on our skin, and we had shed our parkas" in golden print.

…A picture of his mother in a bikini snuggled on top of his father, holding a glass with a little pink umbrella, featured the caption, "A canvas of relaxation and excitement, adorned with loungers and umbrellas." More pictures followed: pretty glasses, incredible food, blue skies, big ocean water. Uncle Ben in the middle of a climbing wall, and Aunt Kate zip-lining into a turquoise pool. His dad wore cool sunglasses. Zak was surprised to see that Uncle Ben had a tattoo.

…In another picture his mom read a magazine, sipping from a tall glass filled with a pink drink, "Carly, sipping her Zin as Kate baby zip lines on the ship," in gold letters with a happy face. There was a plate of little sandwiches and chicken wings. Pictures of his dad snacking and another of him rubbing Mom's feet.

…Mom was SO PRETTY! His eyes were drawn to Mom in a long gown and Dad in a tuxedo, standing in front of an orange-with-pink sunset on an upper deck. They clinked glasses of tropical cocktails with Uncle Ben and Aunt Kate. "Toasting our friendship and the lifetime of adventures that await us." There were pictures of laughter, dancing, sunsets, and sunrises. There was food, food, and more food than Zak had ever seen in his whole life.

…In one picture his Mom and Dad ate steaks with large glasses of deep red wines, toasting with Aunt Kate and Uncle Ben, "From fine dining to casual buffets, every meal is a celebration of friendship and shared experiences."

There was a dance workshop by the pool, where people swayed to the rhythm of Latin beats. His Mom spun in a brightly colored halter dress. His aunt looked young and beautiful, as Uncle Ben admired her.

"The freedom of the open seas and the joy of being carefree," read that caption.

…There were pictures of coffee on balconies and visits to island markets; the photos continued. Zak wished he was there, running on the beaches, swinging from palm trees, and building a sand castle that touched the sky! Tropical luaus with glamorous masquerades in one long, never-ending party. "Underneath the starlit sky, wrapped in blankets, gazing at the horizon, we embrace our future and our friendship," said the caption of two women kissing the men they loved.

Zak heard footsteps and carefully hid the scrapbook between his bed and the wall.

"Good night, Zak," said Aunt Kate. "Thank you for coming home, as I told you to. Do you need anything?"

"No, I'm good. Good night." Zak replied, preoccupied with the photographic adventure of gentle breezes and Caribbean vistas. He quietly got up and put the book back, down three albums and over one, exactly where he had found it.

—

On Saturday, Ben rose early, put on a pot of coffee, and emptied the dishwasher—his morning routine. In less than three months, they would celebrate twenty years of marriage. He sipped his coffee, reminiscing about their honeymoon on the tropical seas after their double wedding. A ticket for a surprise cruise this winter would make a perfect holiday gift for Kate. She had been on edge lately, her usual good-natured self seeming brittle.

"Hi, Uncle Ben, do you have a job for me today?" Zak asked.

"Uh, what?" Ben almost spit out his coffee.

"A job. Mantha said I needed compliance instead of insubordination and then gave me a job. I washed her windows," Zak explained, "but you're windows are already clean."

"Clean, yep. Huh?" Ben was still catching up.

"Do you have a compliance job for me?" Zak hoped to gain some points and be allowed to hang out with the Monogram Masters. He didn't want his in-school suspension to continue at home.

"Wood," said Ben. "I've got wood to prepare for winter. Come on, I'll show you." He grabbed his coffee cup and walked through the kitchen door to the woodshed. Zak followed closely behind. The woodshed was in disarray and needed reorganization before adding the new wood for next year's burning.

"Okay, here's your compliance job. Pick up all the sticks and stack them in the kindling box. Take the middle size and small logs and put them next to that box. Take all last year's wood and bring it forward. Got it?"

"Got it," Zak looked at the mess.

"You can bring in fresh wood for the wood stove in the great room. Mix the sizes." Uncle Ben picked up a larger log in one arm, holding his coffee with the other, and walked toward the back porch. He balanced the cup on top of the log to open the door. Zak was impressed, "Come on, Zak, I will show you how and where."

Zak grabbed a twig, a branch, and a log and followed as Uncle Ben held the door. Ben showed him the empty metal wood rack next to two recliners. His uncle put his big log at the far end and took Zak's largest piece, laying it closer to the stove. Zak handed him the twig, which went all the way to the other side and added the branch size between them. "Kate likes this just so," instructed Ben. "Stack sizes by sizes. She likes order." Ben laughed. "Compliance means it's done right. When you are finished here, you can do the shed."

Zak got to work. BANG went the kitchen door. Pause. BANG. The sound was so loud it resembled a gunshot! An armload of wood, reaching above Zak's head, came through, leaving a trail of leaves, dirt, and bark to the wood cart.

BANG BUMPITY BANG, the wood dropped. Zak stacked it in perfect order. BANG went the kitchen door again. Pause. BANG. Another armload of wood entered, adding more debris to the trail. BANG BUMPITY BANG. Zak dropped the wood to stack it.

Kate pulled a pillow over her head. 'What on earth? It's 6 am on sleep-in Saturday.' BANG BUMPITY BANG, BANG. She tried to return to sleep. By eight o'clock, she gave up and rose, slightly irritated. With bed hair and wearing her bathrobe, she glared, her eyes landing on Zak as he dashed out the door across a thick trail of nature's debris. Each step spread more leaves and wood bits.

"What the—" she stopped, noticing Ben's sparkling eyes.

"He's practicing compliance," Ben chuckled. "Go check out his work."

"My bare feet already checked out his work. He has made my kitchen into a disaster area!" Shouted Kate. "In addition to destroying my morning to sleep in."

Ben poured Kate a cup of coffee, hoping to soothe her inner beast. "Hey, I'll make us a morning fire, and you can curl up in your recliner with that book you've been reading."

"I gave him my blanket," Kate said as resentment bubbled.

"That was my blanket, and I took it back. Here, take mine, it's yours." Ben tossed his Buffalo plaid thick fleece over her.

BANG, went the door. Zak arrived humming with more firewood, dropping leaves, dirt, and bark on his wood cart trail.

"Don't look!" Said Ben, gently touching her cheek.

"But, I want to look," argued Kate.

BANG BUMPITY BANG! Zak dropped the wood.

"Wait," he coaxed. Sip your coffee. This is a surprise." Ben winked at Zak, who had the cart perfectly filled to the brim with an arranged order Ben had never even accomplished in all their years together. He kissed her forehead, "Okay, now you can look."

Aunt Kate turned her head, seeing a magazine designer home wood cart ready for the photo shoot. "Wow, but…" Then she looked at the trail of debris spread on her floors.

"Zak, that cart is compliance perfect," said Uncle Ben. "I want you to turn around and look at the floor."

"Who did that?" Zak was shocked.

"You did," said Kate.

"I didn't do that!" Said Zak.

"YOU did do that!" Kate raised her voice on the 'you.'

"I brought in the wood. I stacked the wood. I did not make a mess. Look at what I did," Zak said. "The wood did the mess itself!"

Ben stifled a chuckle. He was not sure if Zak was pulling Kate's leg or if he was serious. Regardless, the conversation was funny, and he added fuel to the fire. "Zak's got a point: the wood DID do it. Come on, Zak, let's clean up what the wood did on Aunt Kate's floor. The wood most certainly will not clean it up for us."

Zak giggled. "Mantha would tell me to get the broom."

Zak stood still. "So get the broom," said Ben. Zak did not move.

Ben cocked his head and took a step toward Zak, hoping to create movement. It didn't. Then Zak raised his index finger and curled it up and down, inviting his uncle to come nearby. Zak mouthed, 'But I don't know where the broom is.'

Kate turned to watch, almost cheering for an altercation. Ben caught the vibe, "I bet I never showed you our broom closet; follow me."

Zak mouthed, "Thank you, Uncle Ben." He proceeded to choose the broom Kate would have chosen. With skills learned from Sam at the garage, he swept the kitchen like a pro—behind and between. Mantha had shown him under. Under the boot rack, he found a dirty old envelope he could use for a dustpan. He hadn't see Kate's dustpan.

———

"Going to do the woodshed next, Uncle Ben." He put the dirty envelope on the table, and BANG. He was gone.

———

Ben rose to refill his coffee noticing the dirty envelope dripping debris on Kate's eating table, "Oops, good buddy. You missed this." He went to throw it away and then noticed the address. It said, Benny Jordan? 'What on earth?' Probably another bill, he thought. Curious, he opened it finding a handwritten letter on legal paper in his brother's script. A smaller blue paper fell to the table as he read:

> *Dear Ben,*
>
> *I hope this letter finds you well. I am reaching out to you because there is a strain in our relationship that needs to be addressed. The court case in which I represented the defendant and ultimately won has put us on opposite sides of the law, which I sense has caused tension between us.*
>
> *I have the utmost respect for your work as a sheriff. I understand that your job is to uphold the law and keep our community safe, and I admire the dedication and hard work that you put into your job every day. As an attorney, my job is to ensure everyone has a fair trial and is afforded their rights under the law.*
>
> *I want to take this opportunity to thank you for taking on the task of getting Zak, my delinquent son, to graduate from high school. I know it isn't easy, but your dedication and commitment to ensuring his success are*

admirable. Your role as an uncle and mentor to Zak has shown me the kind of person you genuinely are – caring, patient, and persistent.

I miss our close bond and would like to work towards repairing our relationship. We can move past this disagreement and continue to support each other as brothers. Let's set aside our differences and focus on our love and bond as a family.

I hope we can have an open and honest conversation about this, and I am willing to listen to your perspective and work towards finding common ground. I value our relationship and want to ensure it remains solid and unbreakable.

I love you, Ben. Let's put this behind us and move forward together. I'm sharing some money for Zak's support here.

With love and respect,
Your Attorney, Little Brother David

Ben handed the letter to Kate. "This check more than pays for Zak's clothes."

"Let's start a savings account for his future, Ben," Kate said as she considered the wood pile stacked to photo perfection and her clean floor.

—

Outside, Zak was on a roll, he put twigs and little wood into the box. When there were no more little sticks in the shed, he walked around the yard and picked up every one he could find. Uncle Ben had said all the sticks, and in his understanding, ALL meant ALL. He found long-forgotten sticks under the back porch. Eventually there were no other sticks. He looked in the shed. It was better but different from what Uncle Ben had said for compliance. He hated when his brain fizzled and sparked and didn't remember things. It was blank. He sat on the wooden floor, trying to think. None of his usual thinking tricks worked…until…

Zak raced to the house. BANG. "Uncle Ben! Uncle Ben! I need your help!" His voice sounded serious.

Ben jumped from his book and chair, "Are you alright?"

Breathless, Zak gasped, "I need help! Mantha gives me cards so I know what to do. Can you do that for me?"

"Tell me about these cards, Zak," Ben said earnestly.

"Every day, I get three cards with three things to do. I cross them out when I finish. Then, Mantha inspects what she expects. That's what she says every time. Can you do it for the woodshed?" Zak pleaded.

"I guess," Uncle Ben was unsure of the unusual request.

"No," stopped Zak, "you can't guess: you either do it or don't do it. You have to pick."

Ben rummaged through Aunt Kate's recipe box for index cards and found a black magic marker from the junk drawer. Zak saw all the cool stuff in that drawer. "Okay, yes." Instructed Ben, "Show me how Mantha does it." Ben exited out the kitchen door armed with his marker and blank cards. Zak followed. BANG.

Engrossed in her novel, Kate jumped but caught sight of her kitchen corners. *Goodness, he even swept under the counter toe space.*

———

Mr. Mason drove his dual chassis, black, four-wheel-drive, double-cab truck to fill up at Riley's pumps. Mantha noticed as he washed his lights and windshields. Then he pulled out two red five-gallon plastic gas cans and filled them. After paying, he strode into the station to get an ice cream sandwich, waving as he passed Mantha's surveillance camera and putting two one dollar bills on the counter, "You want one, Mantha? My treat." His walk and mannerisms blinked been-there done-that military.

"Sure, thanks."

"Heard you have a kid named Zak working here," asked Mr. Mason.

Mantha raised her eyebrows, "Maybe."

"Good kid, I like him. He's worth watching out for. I'm John Mason. Nice to meet you." Mr. Mason held out his paw of a hand.

"Remeet," smiled Mantha. "Rival school, five years my senior. Rockets with your gramps when we were little. You sure grew." She did not offer her grip. They also saw each other at the VFW as if John did not remember and EMT at the containers. "Thanks." She raised the ice cream and bit the end off. She held it in her right hand and shared her scarred cheek.

"See you around," John flirted with his deep chocolate eyes.

"See you," Mantha knew that even in this quick encounter, the iceberg of John's life was deep underneath that man's handsome surface.

—

"Impressive, Zak. Did you pick up every stick?" Ben asked.

"Every stick I could find," answered Zak. "Even under the porch."

"Your compliance is commendable," complimented Uncle Ben. "Now, tell me about these cards. How do I do them?"

"Start with what you want me to do next," instructed Zak. "Then write or draw that."

"Okay, I want all the wood from last year brought forward," Ben drew the shed floor, lines, rectangles where the wood was now, and arrows where it needed to go.

Zak beamed.

"You have to stack it so that it won't fall, with the smaller pieces next to the kindling box," Uncle Ben explained, drawing a clear diagram of his expectations.

Zak nodded knowingly.

"Then you see that big stack of split wood? You fill up starting from the back of the shed. Then when it's done, you can hang with your friends."

With a heartfelt smile, Zak accepted the three cards from Uncle Ben, "Thank you, Uncle Ben. I really appreciate your help."

—

Cards were superpowers. Zak now knew how and where and put everything into its place. He ran into the house, 'BANG!' to get the broom. "I need a dustpan!" He shouted.

"Hanging on the door where you got that broom," shared Uncle Ben who was doing push ups.

"Do something about that banging. That boy is giving me a headache," groaned Kate, rubbing her temples snuggled with her coffee and covered in Ben's blanket.

"89, 90, 91."

Zak returned, 'BANG!' with the broom and dustpan and put them right back where he got them.

"Hey Zak, come here," Uncle Ben rose from his push-ups. Both he and Zak had glistening foreheads.

"Yes, sir. What do you need, sir?" Zak acknowledged.

"Do you know about door-shutting practice?" Asked Ben.

"No sir," answered the curious teen.

Ben winked at Kate, "Problem solved. Come with me, Zak." Ben opened the door and helped it shut softly. "Now you try it."

Zak opened the door and let go, BANG!

"Did I do it that way?" Uncle Ben asked.

"I dunno," shrugged Zak, "It's just a door."

"Watch for the difference. It's a puzzle." Ben opened the door and helped it shut softly. "Did you see what I did differently?"

"You didn't let go!" Exclaimed Zak.

"Exactly," said Uncle Ben. "Did you ever do push-ups to learn discipline?" Zak's eyes looked like deer in the headlights. "No need for push-ups. Zak gave me 25 soft door shuts, exactly as I showed you. The next time I hear BANG! It will be 50."

"Yes sir, Uncle Ben, Sheriff, sir." Zak complied without an outburst or bang. "COMPLIANCE!" Zak shouted triumphantly as he shut the door quietly and ran to finish his project.

———

Lindsay covered Margie's shift at Dee's Cafe on Saturday, while Shay and Q spent their day at the Riverdale library. The outdoor fall market had concluded for the season, with the final event being the holiday craft and bake sale held in the community building during Thanksgiving weekend. This event coincided with the monthly co-op bulk deliveries.

The old library served as a sanctuary of knowledge and refuge for Q and Shay, where time seemed to stand still and the outside world faded away. It catered perfectly to their inquisitive natures.

Q found solace in the written word and the vast knowledge available. He enjoyed the warm, golden light streaming through the old windows and the hushed atmosphere. The rhythmic ticking of the large wall clock soothed him, and he appreciated the silent reverence for the wisdom preserved in books.

Shay savored the scent of aged books and polished wood as she browsed the shelves. She found particular interest in art books, gardening guides, and cookbooks.

Q immersed himself in Online research, following his interests from surveillance to rocketry. He became excited about the idea of organizing a school competition for rocket altitude. Inspired by Sam's radio shack, he explored the electromagnetic connection between the ionosphere and the Aurora Borealis.

For Q, the Internet was a vast mind map that transported him beyond Riverdale to anywhere in the world.

~19~
ROCKETS
& SPROCKETS

Zak entered the back door so quietly that neither Uncle Ben nor Aunt Kate noticed. Ben snored while Kate was cuddled into a ball with her book. He stood right behind their recliners. "Compliance!" Zak shouted. "It is time to inspect what you expect!"

Kate's body spasmed so powerfully that her New York Times best-seller shot and spiraled into the air. It spun, pages fluttering across the floor like an awkward paper helicopter as it landed with a thud.

Ben snorted. "Are you done already? I was thinking a man could get a good nap first."

"After that you can nap. I need you to…" Zak's arms raised in the air.

"Inspect what I expect," Ben finished the sentence, still half asleep.

"Right! See, you know!" Zak bounced on his toes. "I need you now."

Ben lifted his cold coffee.

"I need you right now!" Zak repeated. "I am all finished."

"Okay, okay," Ben raised the recliner back and lowered the leg rests. "Gotta get my boots back on." Zak was antsy. He took his time. He watched for Zak's reaction.

"Uncle Ben, use bunny ears. They are way faster." Zak offered.

Ben continued lacing and then made the first loop to tie his boot… "No, Uncle Ben, you're doing it wrong." Kate blurted out a laugh as Ben tied and then double-tied his first boot and laced up his second.

"Stop! Uncle Ben, you can get rid of the wop'a roo overs and under." Zak was so excited he was jumping. Then he knelt beside his Uncle's boot. "Here, let me do it."

Ben watched with amusement as Kate struggled to contain her laughter. He held up his hands in a gesture of surrender, silently encouraging her to continue enjoying the moment.

Zak demonstrated the "bunny ears" method of tying shoelaces, creating two loops and knotting them together. "See? Two bunny ears, that's it!" He explained.

Ben nodded, acknowledging the simple technique.

"Now come out and see what I did," Zak urged, eager to show off his handiwork.

Ben stretched his back and followed Zak outside, with Kate trailing behind in her slippers. To their astonishment, they found the woodshed completely transformed. It was now impeccably organized, resembling a designer showroom. Zak had cleverly disposed of excess wood debris in a five-gallon bucket, which fit perfectly into the kindling box.

"Wow! You did this? Where are your friends?" Ben exclaimed, impressed by the transformation.

"At home, or maybe the library, or Riley's with our new Rocket Kit," Zak replied matter-of-factly.

"No, I mean you did this whole thing by yourself without anyone?" Ben clarified, still in disbelief.

Zak spun around, arms outstretched. "I don't see anyone. I guess it was me."

"I thought you didn't guess," Ben remarked.

"I CAN guess. YOU can't guess," Zak corrected him.

"But I don't have to guess. This is a fine job. It is well done," Ben praised.

"Compliance! I'm hungry. Can I have more Sloppy Joes?" Zak's stomach rumbled in agreement.

"Of course," Ben replied, heading back inside. "Have as many as you want." He glanced at Kate, who stood speechless, marveling at the meticulously organized woodshed. For once, she was at a complete loss for words.

—

The scene at Riley's was bustling, with local vehicles coming and going throughout the day. Sam and Mantha observed the constant flow of traffic, noting who was driving alone and who had passengers. They were amused by the number of people taking selfies in their cars.

"Hi, Mantha," Shay called out.

"Hi, Sam and Penny!"

"Check-in," Q instructed. Penny responded with a perfect front sit, eagerly awaiting pets—there was no jumping and mauling behavior.

"Hey guys, did you come to get the rocket?" Sam inquired.

"We're looking for Zak," Shay added, glancing around.

"He's not here yet," Sam replied, checking his watch.

Mantha explained, "I hope Kate lets him come over today. I know he was supposed to go home and stay in his room to think about his cheating."

Q interjected, "I don't think he was cheating, Miss Mantha. I saw the whole thing once the commotion started. I think he was looking at me as a friend for support because he gets so uncomfortable with pressure. Testing is pressure." He concluded with an empathetic sigh.

Shay sat cross-legged on the ground with Penny.

"May I get a chair?" Q asked. Sam nodded in agreement.

Q retrieved the black folding chair from the entry, wiped it clean with his cloth handkerchief, and took a seat.

—

Kate reheated the Sloppy Joes and retrieved the pickles from the refrigerator. As she entered the pantry to get chips, she realized, "I thought we had chips."

"I ate them," Zak admitted.

"All of them?" Kate asked, bewildered.

"The bag was empty," Zak stated matter-of-factly.

"The bag was full," Kate countered, crossing her arms.

Ben chuckled, "I bet it was both. Full when Zak found it and empty after he ate them!" Zak laughed along. Annoyed, Kate stirred the Sloppy Joes. She found it frustrating to deal with Zak's unpredictable behavior fluctuating from incredibly detail-oriented to oblivious to the obvious. It disrupted her efforts to maintain order and predictability in their home.

Ben winked at Zak, beginning to understand the boy's thought process. He had encountered similar patterns in some of his past arrests. Ben grabbed three plates from the cupboard along with the buns and set them on the table.

Kate noticed the mismatched tableware. "Ben, why are you using that green plate? It doesn't match."

"That's my plate," Zak interjected.

"And where did you get that plate?" Kate pressed.

"Lindsay told me to take a plate, so I did," Zak explained.

Kate scolded, "Lindsay doesn't have enough money to give you her plates. You need to return it."

"She gave it to ME!" Zak insisted, cherishing his gift.

"I'll be discussing this with her, Zak. I'm certain she didn't give it to you," Kate asserted as she transferred the hot meat mixture into a serving bowl and placed it on the table.

"You could have left it on the stove, and we could just dig in," Zak commented. Kate glared in response, clearly frustrated with the situation.

—

"Can we discuss the rocket?" Shay inquired eagerly. "I'd like to learn more about it."

Sam turned to Q, making eye contact and receiving a genuine smile in return. "Q, what can you tell us about it?"

Q's face lit up as he began to share his knowledge. "The Estes Big Bertha is an excellent starter model rocket. It's highly regarded for its fun factor once assembled and launched. Standing at about 2 feet tall with a diameter of 1.64 inches, it's specifically designed for beginners like the Monogram Masters who are just entering the world of model rocketry. The rocket is constructed from durable materials and includes some attractive decals, giving it a sleek and impressive appearance. Would you like me to continue?"

Mantha smiled. "Of course."

"Then, let's talk about its flight capabilities. The Big Bertha uses a single engine, which you must insert in the rocket's middle. The engine powers the rocket to propel it upwards into the sky. The coolest part is that it can reach altitudes of up to 500 feet, which is pretty amazing for such a small rocket. When you launch the Big Bertha, you can expect it to go straight up. It reaches an exceptionally high speed, and you can see it accelerate as it climbs higher and higher. Once the engine burns out, the rocket reaches its peak altitude and descends to the ground. See-ing it parachute down is impressive, and it lands gently." Q recited from what he had read at the library that morning. "Plus, because of its size and eighteen-inch parachute, it is easy to monitor and relocate. That last thing I said was in the reviews."

"I can't wait to watch it soar into the sky and come back down with its parachute," Shay clapped her hands. "Is it hard to build?"

"I downloaded the assembly instructions Online," Q pulled out a perfectly folded set of papers from his pocket.

"Of course you did," laughed Sam, smiling at Mantha. She enjoyed the energy of these teens.

Q continued sharing his knowledge about the Estes Big Bertha rock-et, emphasizing its beginner-friendly design and comprehensive kit. He then paused, looking at his notes before adding, "We'll need some basic tools like glue, sandpaper, scissors, and a suitable workspace. I have scis-sors at home, but we'll need to figure out the rest."

Mantha offered a solution, "I can set up the folding table by our workbench. We have four folding chairs and a rolling stool if we all want to work together. Both Sam and I have experience building a Bertha be-fore."

"That would be fantastic," Shay exclaimed enthusiastically. She then recounted a past crafting mishap, "Mom wasn't pleased when I used sandpaper, glitter, and glue in her kitchen last time. I made quite a mess, which she still reminds me about whenever she finds leftover glitter. I won't be making that mistake again!" She finished with a sheepish shrug.

Mantha suggested, "Let's set everything up for when Zak arrives." Shay fell silent, lowering her head without moving.

Noticing the sudden change in Shay's demeanor, Sam asked, "Shay, are you alright?"

"Yes," Shay whispered with sincere concern. "I just said a quick prayer that Zak isn't stuck in suspension prison for his entire life."

———

"Grace," Zak said as he grabbed three buns from the bowl. He couldn't understand why Kate had taken them out of the perfectly good bag, ex-cept that the bowl made them easier to grab. He speared two pickles with his fork and poured himself a full glass of his special milk.

As Zak chased the pickles around his plate, Kate asked, "Why did you leave the pickles on the table and not put them away after you ate last night?"

"Huh?" Zak looked up, clearly confused.

"WHY did you leave the pickles, Sloppy Joes, and buns out after you ate last night? You put your plate in the dishwasher but didn't clean up anything else," Kate repeated.

Uncle Ben watched Zak's eyes dart around before addressing him, "Zak," he said, catching his attention. "WHY did you leave the food out last night instead of putting it in the refrigerator?"

"I did put it back. I put it back exactly where I found it. The pickles were in the same place, and so were the buns and meat, just like when I got home. They were out, so I left them out," Zak explained.

Kate remained skeptical. She'd had enough of the confusion. "Alright, from now on, if I leave something out for you, I expect you to put it back where it belongs or where you found it." She fixed her gaze on Zak.

"Yes, ma'am, I will," Zak replied obediently, though unsure how he'd determine where things belonged or where Kate had found them. He quickly devoured his three sandwiches and reached for more.

Kate moved to stop him, but Ben intervened, "Zak worked hard. Let him eat his fill." She reluctantly complied, frustrated by her lack of control over the situation.

To her surprise, Zak helped clear the table and loaded his dishes into the dishwasher.

"Hey, Zak," Ben said, pausing. "You're redeemed!"

"Huh?" Zak looked confused, hoping he wasn't being re-something when he wanted to join his friends.

"Redeemed means you're FREE to go and enjoy yourself. In my book, you've made amends and paid your dues," Ben explained.

"I didn't pay anything," Zak corrected.

"Yes, you did, Zak. You gave me your time this morning and exceeded my expectations." Ben made eye contact, touching Zak's shoulder. "Full compliance. Now go before Kate says otherwise!"

Zak dashed out, remembering to close the door gently. "That wasn't fair," Kate glared at Ben. "You didn't consult me."

"Kate," Ben replied firmly, "The way you've been acting, you're not exactly consulting me either." He refused to escalate but felt compelled to address her behavior. Her tension seemed disproportionate to the situation, and she was being unnecessarily hard on Zak despite his efforts.

"Zak, come back and return this plate to Lindsay!" Kate called loudly through the door.

"I can't. It's mine. She gave it to me," Zak shouted back. "The plate came with the cookies!"

—

Zak raced into the garage breathless. "Hey guys, I'm here!" The office was empty.

Shay ran out excitedly. "Thank goodness, we have everything set up for Big Bertha! Come on back!"

The chairs at the folding table held Q, Shay, Mantha, and Sam. "Zak, here, have this stool," Mantha offered.

"Cool!" Zak sat and spun, his knees up to his chin. "I like this!"

The group gathered around the table, each contributing to the rocket-building project. Q had meticulously arranged the parts, while Sam displayed an array of colorful spray paint cans. Mantha had gathered all the necessary tools, and Shay was admiring the decals.

"Zak, what color do you think we should paint her?" Shay asked.

"You're good with colors, Shay. You pick," Zak replied.

"Hot pink!" Shay exclaimed enthusiastically.

Q and Zak were taken aback by the choice.

Sam, amused by their reaction, teased, "You asked, she picked. Hot pink it is. Learn from your mistakes, boys. What color did you expect?"

Q, recovering from the surprise, suggested, "With a Black Monogram Master logo down the fuselage. Zak can draw it."

Mantha addressed the group, "Who's going to prepare her for painting? Someone needs to create an evenly sanded surface for the paint to adhere. Here's the fine-grit sandpaper to gently smooth out the entire rocket body. Pay special attention to any rough areas or imperfections. And here's a soft, clean cloth to wipe away dust when you're finished sanding."

"I'll handle that," Q volunteered. He then turned to Zak, "Could you draw the rocket and show us your layout idea?"

"Absolutely," Zak replied, excited to for the role of rocket designer.

"Here are some supplies: paper, a pencil, a pink highlighter, and a black marker. Let's see what you can come up with," Sam challenged. "And here's the primer for after you're done sanding. The primer helps the paint adhere better, providing a base coat for that hot pink color."

"Shay, you can apply the primer," Q instructed. "Make sure it's evenly coated with no thin spots, runs, or drips. While it dries, we can play tag at the boneyard."

"I want to paint the pink," Shay countered.

"Of course you do," Q agreed. "You can paint that too. The primer is your practice coat. It evens out the surface so the final color coat spreads evenly and dries smoothly."

Shay loved her big brother for giving her this opportunity.

—

"How long before my car is ready!?" Boomed Doc.

"Should be ready Thursday," Sam got up slowly to greet him. "Just a few final touch-ups."

"About time," Doc elongated the word time. "Just in TIME for the holiday car show this weekend." Doc gloated as he walked around his car. Seeing the three teens, he paused and then approached them.

"Hey, can I talk to you three for a moment?" Doc insisted.

"Sure, what's up?" Replied Zak.

"Step outside, I need your help with something vital," Doc requested.

The Monogram Masters looked at Sam and Mantha. Mantha's back faced Doc. Sensing their reluctance, she quietly said, "Go outside, by the bench. We've got your backs. You'll be okay. Sam and I are here."

The teens stepped outside the garage and sat on the bench, which positioned Doc perfectly in front of the video recorder, part of the garage surveillance system kept on at all times. "You see, my daughter recently had a bit of a mishap with alcohol, and we must keep it under wraps."

"It's her business," stated Q. "You are the principal. We have no reason to discuss it; however, we are concerned about her well-being."

"I understand your concerns, but this could ruin her future and my career." Doc continued. "I trust you all, and I was hoping you could keep this a secret for us."

Q spoke. "Mr. Johnson, sir, with all due respect, alcohol poisoning is no joke, and your daughter needs support, not secrecy."

"Q, of all people, I... I didn't expect this reaction from you! You must understand I'm doing what's best for my family." Doc stepped closer to Q. "Right?"

"We like Missy and are worried about her," explained Shay.

"Look, I assure you, she's already received medical attention and is improving. I don't want this incident to affect her future or our family's reputation." Doc spoke softly but with a stern edge to shame them. "Why can't you find it in your hearts to forget about this?"

Zak burst out, "I want to help Missy."

"You! You've already done enough damage, stalking her and scaring her to death. Leave her alone, or else! This is my concern, not yours. And I will take care of it my way." Doc was seething but pulled into a more professional tone. "You don't understand the consequences this could have for all of us." His eyes pierced Zak. "And here I thought you'd be capable of understanding. Enough said." He marched to his car, rubbed his nose, shot them a final look of contempt, and sped off.

—

"What was that about?" Mantha watched Doc speed away.

"I dunno," shrugged Shay and Zak together.

"It appears to me Doc is like the primer on our rocket. Our principal is choosing to hide something important. He expects our collaboration. He's putting on the pressure. He insists we smooth over what happened to Missy so his reputation isn't questioned. He wants us to keep everything secret," Q concluded.

"Touche, Q," nodded Sam. "You are wise beyond your years."

"How would you guys like to go to a movie in Hanover tonight?" Mantha offered. "It will take all our minds off Doc."

"Yes!" Shay shouted.

"Okay, we have to leave in an hour. Make sure you get permission," counseled Sam.

"Doc wants compliments all day, but he ain't getting any from me! He's not a good person. Come on, let's head to the boneyard. TAG, you're it!" Zak broke the ominous spell, tapped Shay's shoulder, and ran.

"I'm going to get you!" Shay swerved to catch up to Zak.

"I'll stop at Dee's and tell Mom about the movie," Q volunteered. "We'll be back in an hour, Mantha. I want to see if the aurora has arrived."

—

"She's been back," observed Zak as they perused the container hideaway. "Unless someone else has been here, Missy returned during the week." The blankets were a mess, three candles had been lit, and there was a large bottle of clear soda.

Q checked the area for liquor bottles. There was nothing but a candy bar wrapper. The journal was gone. "We've got to keep a careful eye on her. I noticed she's been acting differently at school. She seemed worn out."

"We have gym together," said Shay. "I saw bruises above her elbow this week as if someone grabbed her hard."

Q retrieved three optical instruments from his bag. Zak took the monocular, focusing it on the house and Doc's truck. Shay used the telescope to observe cloud formations in the sky, imagining shapes and patterns. Q raised the binoculars to his eyes, carefully scanning across the field towards the Johnson estate.

A small car carrying Missy and her mother departed down the driveway. Doc remained on the porch. Shortly after, another vehicle arrived. A woman exited, delivering a large manila envelope to Doc. He accepted it, then embraced her in a prolonged kiss. This unexpected scene caught both Q and Zak off guard.

Absorbed in cloud-watching, Shay missed the unfolding events. Zak and Q exchanged stunned glances, their instruments nearly colliding. They were at a loss for words, confronted with a situation they wished they hadn't witnessed.

"I can't discuss this," Q said quietly.

"Neither can I," Zak agreed, his voice unsteady.

"What's going on?" Shay inquired, oblivious to the situation.

Seeking a distraction, Zak redirected attention skyward. "The northern lights are starting, Shay. Look, they're dancing. Let's run and dance with them." He needed to process the unexpected scene they had just witnessed.

Q packed up the equipment, his mood somber. "It's time for the movie," he announced.

"I think I'd better head home," Zak whispered, clearly unsettled by what they had observed.

"Take my backpack," said Q, trying to distance from what the gear brought into focus. "Put them back. Zak, I don't want them anymore."

Zak grabbed the backpack and ran, tripping over the considerable car part they could not move.

"Zak, are you okay," Shay offered her hand.

"I gotta get home, and we have to move this before someone else gets hurt." Zak brushed off his pants. "I have an idea."

"Aren't you going with us to the movie? Sam and Mantha will be disappointed," Shay battered her eyes. "I thought maybe we could hold hands."

"I gotta go. This is important." Zak said. "Tell them next time." *This was the perfect opportunity to get his job done with no one knowing.*

Zak entered through the back kitchen door. The house was dark. He felt dirty as if he had seen something he should not have seen. He ate the remaining Sloppy Joe's, making sure his friends had enough time to leave Rileys. He still had the key. He returned everything he had taken from his Uncle Ben. Uncle Ben never needed to know, at least about the equipment.

———

Zak's timing to get back to the garage was perfect. Everyone was at the movies and Lindsay was working the evening shift at Dee's. Since Zak wasn't going Sam had invited Margie.

Zak used his key to open the garage and his index card to turn off the security system. He removed the blue tarp, pulled out the 4-wheeler, and gassed it until it overflowed. Remarkably, the motor started right up, though it was running rough. He grabbed a heavy chain, hooked it to the hitch, and held it as he drove to the boneyard. *That stupid car part had to go.* It had prevented the ambulance from getting in closer to help Missy. *What if someone got hurt again?*

Zak wrapped the chain around the rusted metal and pulled. It moved a bit. He undid the chain and drove up to see if someone was home at the trailer, forgetting everyone was at the movies. He drove back to the boneyard and tried again. He pulled it again, and it moved a bit further. *Maybe someone is back by now*, he thought. He drove back up to the trailer and knocked on the door. No one was home. He sped back down to the boneyard, hitting a rut and flying off. He picked up the helmet, stuck it on his head, and gunned it.

Zak realized he was on his own. He could do this. A part broke off jerking him and sending him flying off the four-wheeler. The helmet sailed into the air, landing in the high, dry switch grass. He rubbed his head. He would do this! It could now pull it to the outside storage space. He was determined. He drove back to the trailer for help. No one was home. *One more try. One more try.* He pulled the large part off to the side and dragged the smaller section further out of the way. Blue smoke was rising from the front of the ATV. He raced back one last time to the trailer to check for help. Blankity blank movie. *No luck, no one in sight.* He bolted back to the boneyard, hooked up the piece, and pulled again. The ATV sputtered, rattled, and POP the engine died altogether. Sam would find out. He panicked. He told himself he'd had permission if Sam knew how come. He had to explain this the right way to Sam. He would fix it. And pay for the parts. Desperate to buy time, he returned to the garage, carefully setting the wood upright with the blue tarp so everything looked in place. He set the security alarm, locked the door, and went home.

—

Exhausted, he fell fully clothed into a deep sleep. Sleep came faster when he did hard physical labor or had conflicted emotions.

–20–
COMMUNITY SUPPORT

Lindsay noticed a faint smell of smoke as she locked the door to Dee's Café. She returned to check the oven, grill, and burners. Everything was shut down. She checked the dumpster in case someone had dropped in a lit cigarette that started to smoke. Nothing. She rounded the building, following the scent. Maybe it was a fall bonfire? She saw a flicker of light in the distance, and her heart raced. The light—huge flaming light—was coming from her property! She dialed 911. ***Thank God the kids are at the movies with Margie!***

Her pulse pounded. The operator assured her help was on the way. Lindsay heard the faint sound of sirens as she ran towards her home. By the time she arrived, the flames had grown, licking the sides of her trailer. The boneyard was ablaze. The fire escalated to a five-alarm crisis—a severe situation requiring all available resources. The call went out requiring assistance from neighboring fire departments.

—

Zak awoke to Uncle Ben shouting at someone on the phone. Then stomping, running, and BANG? Uncle Ben slammed the back door?

Zak rose to check out the commotion. He ran downstairs.

A note on the table read:

Kate and Zak -

Big fire. Have to support. See you soon.

Pray for the family - firefighters -

and first responders involved.

    Glad you are in bed, Zak.

       Love Ben

Zak had no idea how to pray, so he said, "Keep Uncle Ben, the fire-fighters, the family, and the first responders safe. Don't let anyone die or get hurt. I guess this message goes to you, God, whoever you are. Oh yeah, and take care of Missy and…" he could not even say the name of 'you know who.' "The end."

———

Weary and covered in soot, Ben entered the kitchen. Kate was dressed for church and scrambling eggs. Zak sat at the table in what he had worn yesterday.

Kate jumped up from her seat, concerned, "Oh my goodness! You're finally home! Are you alright? What happened?"

Ben sighed heavily while removing his hat and setting it on the counter. "It was a hell of a night, Kate. A massive fire tore through the Larkin place, catching the field ablaze…the boneyard, and even their trailer. Devastating. Thankfully, no one was home. Lindsay and her kids… they've lost everything."

"That's Q and Shay's place. They were at the movies. Is Mama L okay? Whoa, Uncle Ben, what caused the fire?" Zak noticed Ben had used one of 'those' words, the ones that were blankity blanks.

Ben slowly pulled out a chair and sat down, his legs outstretched, his shoulder leaning into the chair back. "We suspect it was a fuel leak. Maybe arson. The fire spread so quickly that it was hard to contain. The whole damned trailer was engulfed by the time we arrived."

Kate brought him a glass of ice water, "Here, sweetie, you must be parched. Did you manage to save anything from their house?"

Ben sipped and shook his head, "No, the flames were too intense. It breaks my heart, Kate. They lost what little they had—everything is gone." His voice filled with empathy, "Being alive is what truly matters. They have each other." Ben reached out to Kate with his dirty hand. She placed her manicured hand on top of his.

"That's so sad, Uncle Ben. Is there anything we can do to help them?" Zak was absorbing this traumatic event carefully.

Ben smiled at his nephew's compassion. "Right now, they need our community's support. We'll organize a donation drive to gather essential items—clothing, food, and toiletries. We'll set up a fund to help them get back on their feet. Someone will offer them a place to stay."

"They can have my bed. I can sleep on the floor," Zak was sincere.

Kate squinted. "No, Zak, we've got enough going here. But the drive is a wonderful idea, Ben. Count me in! We have extra clothes and bedding we can donate. I can rally the townspeople at church today and spread the word through the school."

Ben nodded lovingly. "Thank you, Kate. Your kindness and compassion amaze me. Together, we can make a difference and show them they're not alone."

Zak was excited in helping, "I can speak with the kids at school and tell them what happened. Maybe we can organize some way to raise money for them."

"Your enthusiasm and initiative are inspiring. They'll be incredibly grateful for all the support."

"We're best friends. They are my family! I have to help," Zak declared.

Kate rubbed her husband's neck and shoulders. "You did a good job, Ben. I know it was a tough night, but the fact that no one was hurt is a testament to your bravery and the courage of the volunteer firefighters. Our town will help them rebuild their lives, one step at a time."

Kate removed the bacon from the oven. Zak removed the clean plates and flatware from the dishwasher, first setting Uncle Ben's place.

Ben was exhausted. "Thank you. Riverdale has always been there for its neighbors. This is when we show our true strength."

Kate dished up Ben's plate.

Zak asked, "Uncle Ben, I can make peanut butter toast. Do you want some?" Ben closed his eyes with a weary nod.

Kate kissed Ben's cheek, "My big, brave husband. I'll go set this up at church. Ben, take a shower and change your clothes. You smell awful." She did not invite them to join her at church. "Zak, did you even shower this week? You smell as bad as Ben without the smoke."

—

Zak and Ben ate in silence. Uncle Ben was too tired to talk, and Zak was too stunned and confused. *It was his best friend's house—it was their boneyard!* He emptied the dishwasher, putting everything away in the right places. He bussed all the breakfast dishes, then looked at the dishwasher's emptiness. *Where do I begin?* He remembered what went where adding pieces one after another until everything was in the machine. He grabbed the blue dish soap.

"STOP!" Uncle Ben shouted. The plastic bottle with blue liquid shot into the air.

Zak was startled, "Stop what?"

"Wrong soap!" Ben lumbered over to look at the mess of dishes but was too tired to rearrange the machine. "Use these little packets. It's easy. Put one here. ONLY ONE!" He demonstrated, then handed it to Zak.

"How come you took it out?" Zak asked.

"I want you to practice it yourself. Glad we have two bathrooms. You stink. We both need showers."

"You stink, too," Zak ran up the stairs to wash up. He dressed and left, hurrying to meet Q and Shay on the church steps as they emerged. Uncle Ben was snoring.

—

It had been a long night for Lindsay, Q, and Shay. Margie offered to let them stay overnight in her small semi-furnished apartment above the cafe. Sam had offered his extra bedrooms. Lindsay felt it better to stay at the cafe. "We're alive, all of us. Things are only things. Best thing to do to day is get on with life and go to church."

Church members were surprised to see the family attending. "Where else would I be!" Lindsay proclaimed. Everyone spoke of the fire and who could do what to help.

"Lindsay, I'll organize a fundraiser," Kate volunteered. "Let me know your immediate needs, and I'll see what I can do."

"Thanks, Kate. I appreciate that. Ben and all the responders worked so hard last night. They stopped the fire from spreading across the field and saved Doc Johnson's house." Lindsay looked at Doc.

Doc stepped to the pulpit to set himself up as spokesperson. "I am so grateful to all the volunteers who helped to save our home last night. It was a stellar effort by everyone. I will head up the community drive to help the Larkin family, who recently experienced this terrible tragedy. I'm sure you can all appreciate my expertise coordinating this significant event."

"Good morning, everyone," Kate stood beside Doc. "It's great to see so many people willing to unite and support the Larkin family during this difficult time. I believe we can make a real difference."

"I've already contacted prominent community members and arranged significant donations." Doc interrupted.

Kate cut him off: "Our main focus will be providing support and assistance. It's about their needs. So far, Dee's Cafe has offered an all-you-can-eat spaghetti dinner on Wednesday night. The VFW is using their proceeds from pull tabs this month, and we will use the church's basement as a drop-off and organization center."

"This event will be a shining example of my skills." Doc jumped in, "I am looking for a temporary residence for the family: Lindsay, Q, and Shay—such a fine family."

Sam raised his hand. "Since Deb passed, my home has been just me. I have plenty of room through the winter."

"The apartment on top of Dee's Cafe is not in use," offered Margie. It's only two bedrooms, but cozy and warm."

"Happy to extend my services to demolish and haul," said the owner of the waste company.

"I can help frame a new house…" "plumb the house…" "help with building supply costs." People were excited to give. "Happy to help raise a meal train!" Church members spirited donations for food, housing, and hands-on jobs.

"I appreciate your enthusiasm and dedication." Kate went on," We must prioritize the Larkin family's well-being and ensure they receive the help they desperately need. I will categorize and schedule support."

"Yes, yes. Work with me: we can impact their lives, and that's what truly matters," Doc was in his element.

"We all have different roles, and I'm grateful for each of you. I will meet with Lindsay to outline her family's current needs. Meanwhile, use the back of the offering envelopes in front of you. Write down your ability to provide, add your email, and we will contact you." Kate explained.

"I'm happy to collaborate with you and our church to ensure the Larkin family receives the support they deserve," Doc ensured he was seen as the head of the efforts.

—

Zak sat on the church steps in clean jeans and a hoodie. He was in a whole other world.

"Hey, Zak, you missed church. I sang in the choir today," exclaimed Shay. "Q read 1 John 3 from the New Testament about love."

Zak sat, unable to move, watching Doc speaking with Aunt Kate. His innards twisted every time he saw that man.

"Hi, kids, are you coming over to paint Bertha pink and work on her fins?" Sam walked up to the teens to break the tension.

"Can we go, Mom?" Asked Shay.

"Of course, just don't cause any trouble," Lindsay warned. "Thank you for offering to keep them busy, Sam. They could use a distraction after last night."

"They are good kids," said Mantha. "Easy to have around."

"I better change if we're going to paint," Zak looked down at his clean clothes.

"I'd advise we all change to more appropriate clothing for painting—but we have nothing left to wear." Q scanned the group.

"You can wear my clothes," Zak suggested.

Shay laughed. "I would drown in your clothes, and your pant legs would land at Q's knees."

"I've got shop suits, Lindsay. I'll make sure each of them puts one on," Sam suggested.

"Thank you," Lindsay whispered.

"See you later," sang out Shay. "Mama Alligator."

"Just your luck, Peking duck." Lindsay laughed wearily.

———

Ben was still sleeping when Kate arrived from Sunday service. The church suggestion box overflowed with offers, and almost every envelope had an offer of labor, goods, or money with names, emails, and phone numbers. She had over 100 envelopes and over $1000 from the first appeal. Everything had to remain transparent and accounted for. This was going to take a spreadsheet. She documented each envelope and added personal data. From that information, she began to designate committees and group like interests together.

———

Zak reached Riley's just as Shay and Q walked into the entrance. Sam handed each teen a blue garage suit stating they were apprentice astronauts. Shay rolled up the legs so she would not trip.

Q's shins were bare between black socks and the bottom of his kneecaps. "Try these rain boots on Q. I think they'll do the job. Don't want to take the shine out of those shoes."

"Let's do this in pink," smiled Shay.

"Are you certain you want pink, Shay?" Q double-checked. "

Certain," she was emphatic.

"You're up, Shay! Hot neon pink gloss paint." Sam handed Shay a paint mask and led her to the paint area. "Stand back, boys. This girl's locked and loaded with pink paint!"

Zak sanded fins at the folding table. Q worked on the nose cone. Shay returned with a pink outline on her face like a neon raccoon. "I hope people don't think we're weird if we have to wear the same clothes for three days."

"They probably won't notice. They will notice your pink face, though!" Laughed Zak. "I want to help your family. Maybe we can use our skills in building model rockets and organize a rocket launch fundraiser?"

"That sounds awesome! We could reach out to our school or local community and invite them to watch our rocket launch. We could set up a donation booth where people can contribute funds towards helping us," Q added.

Shay was excited. "We can create flyers and distribute them around the neighborhood, school, and local businesses to spread the word about the event. Maybe the newspaper will write something!"

"We can approach local businesses and ask if they would be willing to sponsor the event. What do you think, Mantha?" Q added.

"Maybe Dee's Cafe could provide snacks or drinks for the attendees, and in return, we could promote their business during the event," Shay chimed in.

"Along with the rocket launch, we could organize a raffle or a silent auction during the event. Neighbors and businesses might donate items or services people can bid on. That way, we can raise even more money for your family." Zak's ideas grew. "Could we have the silent auction here, Sam?"

"Ask Mantha," Sam pointed at the owner.

"I have an idea. I have a great idea. What if…" Zak paused. "What if we challenged our classmates to a rocket contest? Instead of one rocket, we could launch a whole fleet."

"And prizes for the rocket that goes the highest! Or the best design! Or both!" Shay shook her hands by her face. "This will be such fun!"

"I wonder if community clubs would support our cause?" Asked Q. "We can make sure we are clear about where the funds will go and keep everyone updated on the progress. This will help build trust and encourage more people to donate."

"FIRE!" Shouted Zak.

"That's not funny," frowned Shay.

Zak shot her a chagrined look, "Oh no, you're right, Shay. Sorry... I... I wasn't thinking... uh... I... Didn't mean to... sorry...." Zak stared at his red shoes.

Mantha put out her hand for a group high-five. "We can make this happen. We have all winter to build the rockets and the event. Students could get model rocket kits for their presents during the holidays. Your family will need funds in the spring to build a home. Let's do this!"

———

The pieces of Big Bertha were gradually coming together. Although an experienced model maker could assemble her in an afternoon, Sam and Mantha took their time to create valuable learning experiences for the Monogram Masters. They understood this would be the first of many rockets and the beginning of numerous challenges in building, launching, and retrieving them. With Zak's ambitious idea in mind, they knew every detail had to be meticulously addressed. Diligence was crucial to the success of this endeavor.

Behind the scenes, both Sam and Mantha appreciated Zak's vision and focused on linking all the steps to help the teens achieve their goals. They recognized the importance of this project and how much was at stake. By ensuring that each step was carefully executed, they aimed to set a solid foundation for future rocket-building adventures."Have you decided on a launch site for this rocket?" Asked Mantha.

"We can use the field by the boneyard," mused Shay. "It won't look burned in the spring."

"Do you have authorization to fly there?" Queried Sam. "

Authorization?" Zak scrunched up his face.

"What for? It's a rocket, not an airplane!" Asked Shay.

"Exactly, but it's an aeronautic vehicle, and there are specific requirements," Q noted, analyzing the situation. He continued, "I think the field by the containers could be an ideal spot. It's uninhabited, spans at least five acres, and only has a hay crop this season. I haven't seen any airplanes overhead, so it likely isn't in a flight path. Do you think that field is feasible?"

"You've done some research," Sam was impressed. "Using a large field near the airport as a rocket launch site is possible. However, there are certain factors to consider."

"Absolutely. I'm referring to the field just a few miles from the airport. I checked how far on the computer mapping program. It's a wide, open space with no buildings or structures nearby. Additionally, it's privately owned, and the owner has expressed interest in allowing rocket launches."

"Who owns this field?" Asked Mantha.

"Mom!" Interjected Shay.

Mantha chuckled.

"Well, that sounds promising." Sam's fingers tapped his chin in thought. "Privately owned land may be easier to work with, but we still need to keep safety and regulations in mind. Since this is close to the airport, we should consult with aviation authorities and the airport administration to confirm no conflicts with air traffic."

Q fiddled with the nose cone, not making eye contact. "That makes sense. Safety is my top priority." He rotated and turned it over. "How should I approach the aviation authorities and the airport administration to discuss this possibility?"

Sam pulled back his shoulders, chin up. His hand went up to his untrimmed beard. "It's best," he said thoughtfully, "to contact the airport administration office first. They can guide you on the proper procedures. They might put you in touch with the relevant aviation authorities who can advise on airspace restrictions and necessary approvals. I would also check for approvals at the high school football field."

Q was playing right into Sam's hands. "Okay, I will contact the airport administration first. Are there any specific questions I should address when discussing this with them?"

"When speaking with the airport administration, it's important to emphasize safety measures you plan to implement. They will want to know about any notification or permit process you have in mind. It's crucial to assure them that your activities will not interfere with regular airport operations and won't pose a risk to aircraft." Sam explained.

"I understand." Q's mind was quick. "Safety protocols and communication will be a vital aspect of this project. Is there anything else I should inquire about during the conversation?

"You might want to inquire about airport requirements for launching activities near their premises. This could include fencing, clearance distances, or any other criteria they want you to meet." Sam rubbed his beard. "They might have suggestions or recommendations based on their experience regulating such activities in prior years."

"Thank you so much for your valuable advice, Sam," said Q. "Do you have anyone specific I should contact?"

"As Riverdale airport administrator," Sam winked at Mantha. "All clear! You just met with him, and I will appoint Mantha to do the property checkout. If Mantha approves it, I will issue you your permit to fly."

Three right hands flew together in a group clasp. "Go, Monogram Masters! SQUEEZE!" Shouted Zak, Shay, and Q in unison.

"Three are better than one!" Shay flipped her braids. "We're braided."

"A braided cord can not be broken," informed Q. "By intertwining several strands together, the force or tension applied to the cord is distributed evenly among them. This prevents a single strand from bearing the entire load, making it less likely to break."

Zak was excited. "So, even if one strand weakens or breaks, the others will support the cord?" It seemed like Q knew everything about everything!

"Absolutely! The braided pattern allows for load sharing and compensates for weaknesses in individual strands. As a result, the cord remains intact, even if one strand becomes damaged or fails," Q confirmed.

"That's amazing!" Exclaimed Shay. "It's exactly how we work together; we are all different and when braided, we are stronger together!"

"Besides their strength, do braids have other meanings or significance?" Mantha was interested in what Q would say.

"Braided cords often symbolize unity, interconnectedness, and resilience. Weaving together multiple strands can represent the coming together of different individuals or elements to form a strong and unifying whole. In some cultural and ceremonial practices, braided cords symbolize friendship or pledged bonds between people," Q elaborated.

"Like the Monogram Masters," Zak was enthused by how the concept applied to his friends.

"Mantha, you want to check the field out right now?" Shay was excited to move forward.

"Get out of here, all of you," Sam shooed them as Mantha tilted her head. "All four of you!"

———

Yellow tape surrounded the Larkin property. The double-wide trailer stood as a blackened skeleton of what it once was. Charred beams reached like the fingers of a giant hand clawing desperately at the air. The aluminum siding was melted and warped by the intense heat. The shattered windows reflected the pale sunlight with an eerie glint. The partially collapsed roof displayed the stark destruction. Outside, the yard was littered with debris in a razed patchwork of singed grass and scorched ground. Nearby trees bore scars of the blaze, their bark blackened. The aftermath of the fire's fury had left a sad quiet in the ruins of a cozy trailer previously filled with life.

"Look, Mantha, we still have clothes on the line. I have two shirts and jeans. It's a miracle. Look, Q, you've got extra pants, and Mom has her uniform. We are so blessed." Shay was ecstatic.

"Mom is going to be so happy. I'll take them down on our way back to the garage." Q offered.

"I bet Aunt Kate will let you wash and dry them again, Shay." Zak noticed the grey on Q's typically bright white button shirt.

Mantha and the Monogram Masters continued along the charred path to the boneyard and potential rocket field.

"Hey, look, Zak, someone moved that old car part," Q noticed the charred remains of the ATV and he picked up a melted helmet lying in the blackened container. Its outer shell was once a sturdy guardian. "Wow, look at this warped mess. It melted like wax under that scorching inferno."

Zak rubbed his head. It was still sore from the impact of the multiple catapults off the four-wheeler. "Cool," Zak didn't want to let on. He was the one who last wore that helmet. He felt a tight feeling in his chest, hiding the secret of the ATV and car parts. It was bad enough the ATV had quit, he could work with that, but now it was burned beyond recognition. He was puzzled. *"What had happened to start the fire? How am I going to tell Sam? Will Uncle Ben put me in jail?"* He didn't know how to handle this mess he'd gotten into.

———

Finally, the garage was empty, a rare state for many years. Sam had enjoyed the recent flurry of activity but now needed a break. As he aged, he often found himself alone with his dog, Penny. Although he still had energy, it wasn't like the boundless energy of the younger folks. He poured coffee from his thermos and sat on the bench with Penny.

"Good girl, Penny," Sam murmured. "You're the best." He appreciated how dogs were less emotionally demanding than people. He scratched Penny behind her ears as they watched cars pass by. A little red car drove into the pump zone, parking awkwardly between both pumps, too far to actually pump gas and blocking access for half of Sam's potential customers. Doc jumped out.

Sam heard a low growl from Penny. "Oh, girl. I got this. Stay."

"Sam, Sam..." Doc's patronizing tone and hollow grin felt like an undertow. "How are you?" He moved with a serpentine grace, closing in.

"Doing well, thank you," Sam replied politely. "And you?" He noticed Doc's wife and daughter in the back seat.

"I'm running the Larkin fire fundraiser, as I'm sure you've heard," Doc said, staring intently. "I expect you'll be donating. It's a terrible situation for such a low-income family. They had so little, and now they have nothing. I hope you have some empathy for them."

"They have each other," Sam replied, meeting Doc's gaze. "I offered my home. I have compassion and care for others' well-being. I'm not one to talk much about other people's feelings; what do you call that? Empathy? Your car is finished."

Doc glanced at the garage. "About time. I was hoping you got around to the final details," he said, almost hissing.

"You can take it now if you'd like," Sam offered, noticing Penny watching intently. Dogs know things.

"My sentiments exactly," Doc said, edging his hand toward the garage stall housing his 1957 Chevy.

Sam led Doc inside and patted the hood. "Take a good look."

Doc popped the hood and ran his finger around the shiny tires. He examined the mirrors and bumper. "I will take her for a spin," he said, hopping in.

Sam raised the garage door, and Doc quickly backed out, leaving his wife and daughter in the running little red car. Sam approached the vehicle and tapped on the back window, "Shut your car off, Missy."

"Dad told us to stay here until he returned," Missy replied.

"That might be a while. He's test driving his car," Sam said. "How about you come inside, and I'll buy you each an ice cream."

"I guess it can't hurt," Nicole, Doc's wife, decided as she leaned over to turn off the childproof locks and then the car. "No sense wasting gas." She smiled sincerely, hoping Sam would stick Doc with a hefty bill. The thought made her feel genuinely better, perhaps someone else would take him down a peg.

"Exactly my point," Sam encouraged. "No sense charging Doc any more than I already plan to." He was surprised by Nicole's sincere smile as she and Missy exited the car.

It was a warm late fall day; all the leaves except the oaks had fallen, revealing bare branches and open vistas. Despite the approaching winter, early afternoons still held warmth. Penny greeted the women with a good sniffing of their shoes.

"I bet Doc's excited to get his Chevy back," Sam said, trying to start a conversation.

"It's all he's been talking about at home for weeks. Glad to have that conversation over," Nicole responded flatly.

"I think he'll focus on the Larkin Fire Drive now, Mom," Missy said, turning to her mother.

"Well, that will be easier to keep contained outside the house," Nicole replied, looking out at nothing in particular.

—

Twenty minutes later, the 1957 Chevy returned with Doc behind the wheel, a wide smile on his face. His demeanor shifted quickly as he saw his wife and daughter out of the car.

"What are you girls doing out of the car?" he asked suspiciously.

"My doing, Doc. I didn't want you wasting gas," Sam replied, holding the invoice. "Are you ready to settle up? I have the bill ready."

Doc looked at the invoice and frowned. "I'm quite surprised by the amount. It seems significantly higher than we initially agreed upon. Do you mind going over the details with me?"

"This restoration work was no easy task, and we spared no expense in ensuring your car received the best treatment possible. But of course, if you need me to break it down further for you, I'll humor you," Sam offered, feeling offended because he had already given Doc a deal.

"I appreciate your attention to detail, Sam. And the car runs and looks fine. I want to verify that the final amount aligns with the work requested and that there are no misunderstandings. Can you explain each itemized cost on the bill? It would help me understand how you arrived at this total," Doc challenged, initiating another control drama. The veneer of attention to detail was utterly transparent to Sam. Sam was not about to give in, nor was he willing to allow Doc's pompous and theatrical verbiage to distract him.

"My expertise doesn't come cheap, Mike Johnson. You got one good deal here. With this car's shape, the refined V8, and the perfect and authentic turquoise and white paint, it could fetch over 50K on the show market."

"Could you please clarify the basis for these charges in writing," Doc countered, his irritation evident. "I left my given name long ago, and I do not appreciate you using it."

"With your attitude, Mike, it is hard for me to call you by the name of your father, who was my best friend," Sam stood firm. "I assure you, my rates align with the caliber of work I provide. It would be best if you were grateful to have someone of my stature dedicated to this restoration at the price I charged. I did it because I loved your father."

"I agreed upon a specific budget for this restoration project, and I was not expecting such a significant deviation from that. Isn't there any flexibility in the cost?" Doc argued, sensing his failure to manipulate Sam, and his gut churned with resentment.

"Flexibility? Why would there be? This is the exact amount you owe. The charges adjusted each time you arrived in my garage and added more detailing and changes."

"Given the substantial difference between the initial estimate and the final bill, I might need time to review my budget and discuss this. Is there any possibility of negotiating a compromise?" Doc tried again, hoping to bluff if he couldn't outright bully Sam into submission.

"Negotiation? The price I provided is fair." Sam was not about to give in. "In any other classic car restoration shop, you would have been billed double what I charged, but you are my best friend's son."

Doc peeled five crisp one hundred dollar bills from his wallet, "I'll get you the rest. I was hoping for a Black Friday special. It was worth a try. After all, your employee killed my father. By the way, Shaun's ATV is in the boneyard…or what's left of it…probably burned to a crisp by now." Doc sent a final dagger, leaving Sam drawing in his breath to prevent himself from reacting to the inflammatory ploy. He was not about to allow this devious man the satisfaction of a real fight. Sam wrote the receipt, adding 'on account.'

'No, Michael, I believe you killed your father, but I could never prove it,' the old tape silently rolled in Sam's head. The more he had gotten to know Mike, alias Doc, as an adult, the less he liked him. The more he watched Zak's mannerisms and thought process, the more he felt the stinging reminders of his former employee and his son's good-hearted nature.

Sam burned with a desire for justice. Mike Johnson had won that round, but Sam remained unconvinced a man of such poor character would get away with his misdeeds and win the war. Not on his watch. Not if he could help it. 'Fight smarter, not harder,' he told himself. He looked under the blue tarp—it was empty.

-21-
ROCKET POWER

Sam was deep in thought when Mantha and the Monogram Masters returned from the fields. Mantha did an about-face, her brows furrowed. She had been close enough to Sam for the past month to note the new body language. Her professional training kicked in, and registered to discuss later.

"Mantha said yes!" Exclaimed Shay, hoping to get an excited reaction from Sam. There was none.

"That's nice," Sam mumbled.

"Can we glue on the fins?" Shay was undaunted by Sam's response.

"Yes, of course. Let's complete Big Bertha," smiled Mantha as she winked at Shay.

"I think the rocket likes being hot pink." Shay beamed.

"I want to hook up the parachute!" Exclaimed Zak, leaving the twinge he felt at the boneyard behind.

"That's a long way off, Zak, not today. You are at this moment delegated as parachute captain." Mantha said, looking at the instructions taped to the table. "Did you want the nose cone and fins painted white, Shay?" Shay nodded.

Q marked the fin locations on the rocket body. "Shay, can you gently sand the edges with this fine-grain sandpaper to remove rough areas? I marked exactly where I want you to sand. Rounded fin edges create less drag than square ones, and boat tails reduce 'base drag,' which is created to a greater degree by a squared-off aft end of a rocket."

Sam was impressed. "What do you know about rockets, Q?"

"Well, sir, we could discuss this ad nauseam, but I believe the best plan for our first rocket is to follow the instructions. However, according to the Tripoli Mentoring Program Exam Study Guide, the center of pressure or CP is where the aerodynamic lift is centered due to the rocket being at a non-zero angle of attack. For an aerodynamically stable rocket with the CP behind the center of gravity or CG, the lift centered aft of the CG will create a corrective moment to return the rocket to a zero-degree angle of attack. Conversely, if the CP is ahead of the CG, the lift will attempt to turn the rocket around so that the CP will again be behind the CG. This resultant "tumbling" is characteristic of an unstable rocket."

Q's comments flew over Shay's head as she dropped the pile of clothes she was carrying to the garage floor. She carefully took the fins in her hands, ran her fingers over the edges, and began sanding tenderly.

"I see, you know about the Tripoli Mentoring Program," Sam gave a wee smile. "You have answered two of the exam questions perfectly."

"I will handle the Engine Housing," Q applied a small amount of glue to the outer edge of the engine mount tube. He then inserted it into the motor mount ring. "When Shay's fins are dry, I will slide this assembly into the marked area inside the pink body tube, aligning it precisely to protrude out slightly. We have to let the glue dry first."

"Wow, Shay, they look beautiful," Zak admired. "Can we paint the white in the paint station, Sam?"

Sam looked like he was sleeping in the soft chair in the corner, "Go ahead," he mumbled. Mantha took note.

"Thanks, Sam," said Zak, "Shay and I will be careful." He grabbed the white paint from the box.

"Looks like you are back into wait and dry time," said Mantha.

"Tag you're it, Shay," Q tapped her shoulder.

"Let's go watch the stars," Zak shouted.

Q acknowledged, "That's good code language to check on Missy."

"What is?" Shouted Zak.

"Let's go watch the stars."

"STOP! No one goes back to the boneyard. Q and Shay, you need to go home. Zak and I need to talk." Sam had never sounded like this. Zak stood still, his eyes wide. Q and Shay skittered off.

"Wonder what that was about?" Shay whispered, frightened.

"Don't know," Q said.

—

"Zak, I have something important to ask you." Sam seemed grow in size and importance.

"Yeah," Zak looked at his red shoes.

"Did you take my four-wheeler?" Sam was not playing.

Zak was silent, and Sam tried again. "Can you explain why you thought it was OK to take the four-wheeler?"

Zak tried to gather his thoughts. "Well, I saw it in the garage, and no one was using it. I was going to ask, but you were at the movies, and I wanted to use it to get this car part out of the boneyard. It was the part that stopped the ambulance from going in to help Missy, and she was back at the boneyard this week again! What if she drinks? I don't want her to die next time. We could not move it with our muscles and I thought it would be a good thing to do. I tried to get help, but you took too long to get home. I went back and forth, back and forth." Zak's hands gestured in a tugging motion.

"Did you move the car part?" Sam asked. Mantha was impressed with the discussion, knowing whose ATV was a mangled, charred mess.

"Yes. It broke the part with POP! BANG. I moved it in two pieces." Zak was into the story. "I flew off when it popped. High into the air and landed on my head. I'm OK, I rolled. I got a hard head. The helmet flew off, though."

"Where did you get the gas, Zak?" Mantha asked trying to get further into the story.

"I used all the red cans. There was a little bit in each of them, and I put them right back where you said to, just like you taught me," Zak added.

"Where is the ATV now, Zak?" Sam redirected.

"It broke. It would not start after a loud pop and blue smoke. I knew I had to tell you and figure out how to fix it." Zak burst into tears. "I came back here, and you were all gone! So I fixed it up under the tarp like it was still there. I thought maybe Q could help." He looked at Mantha. "Or you, Mantha, but now it is not just broken, it is all melted and twisted. Now, it can never be fixed. I just borrowed it and was going to bring it right back. Put it back after I fixed the boneyard to be safer. I planned to replace the gas."

Zak gasped for air. His eyes darted around the garage and back down to his red shoes. Tears soaked his shirt.

A whirlwind of emotions coursed through Sam as he took a deep breath, knowing the importance of his next questions. He was grateful for his experience raising Shaun, as it helped him recognize the signs of confabulation in Zak's story. He understood that if Zak had merely borrowed the ATV without asking and returned it, it could be dealt with privately. He could counsel Zak on borrowing and ownership. Even if the ATV broke while Zak was trying to help, it could have been repaired. However, the fire that destroyed so much, including the melted ATV, involved more people and required a deeper understanding of Zak's actions. Sam needed to uncover the truth, as the stakes were higher than just a borrowed ATV.

"Do you think borrowing something without permission is the right thing to do?" Sam asked.

"I convinced myself it would be okay if I borrowed it. But now I know that wasn't true. This is a big mess, isn't it?" Zak admitted.

"Yes, it is a BIG mess," Sam agreed warmly.

"Can I ask you a question, Zak?" Mantha interjected kindly.

Zak nodded.

"Did you have any matches?"

"No, Ms. Mantha. I don't play with matches. Dad taught me that when I was little," Zak paused, then continued, "I did use a lighter from the container at the boneyard."

"When?" Mantha's voice escalated.

"About a week ago. I found it in the container with Missy's candles and a big clear soda bottle. She lights candles when she is alone. I lit some grass and then stomped it out. It caught fire so quickly that it scared me. I left the lighter in the container."

"And did you use the lighter again?" Mantha asked.

"No, I didn't want to start a big fire. I saw it was dangerous," Zak admitted.

"Did you start the fire in the boneyard?" Mantha pressed.

"Only the little one I stomped out. I didn't use the lighter again," Zak replied, folding his hands.

"I will ask you again: did you start the fire in the boneyard?" Mantha was more forceful.

"I started the fire in the boneyard a week ago. I stomped it and killed it. Did it come back to life and cause that BIG FIRE?" Zak gasped.

"Go home and get some sleep. I need to think more about this," Sam said, shooing him out the door.

"Wait!" Zak said. "Can I take the pile of clothes to my house? I promised Shay that Aunt Kate would wash them for her. They were on the line outside the trailer. Is taking them home borrowing them?"

"I've got clothes to wash in the morning. I'll do it." Sam was already lost in troubled thoughts. How could he be in the same place in his life for a third time?

—

"Sam, what's up? This is more than the four-wheeler," Mantha challenged him to answer. "Doc?"

"Doc," Sam spat as he rolled his eyes. "I'm going for a rag chew." Sam walked into his base station.

"What is a rag chew?" Mantha was sure details would eventually spill out. It was not tobacco. Sam didn't chew or smoke. He most certainly didn't chew on rags.

"Talkin' to my Ham boys," Sam's shoulders deflated.

—

Lindsay was independent and proud and used to responsibility and freedom. After sleeping at Margie's upstairs apartment above Dee's Cafe, Lindsay decided to move her family in. It was private, unshared housing centrally located and accessible for the kids to get to school. She was grateful her old car was at the cafe that night. It was unscathed.

Margie was delighted and offered free rent and meals for the first month of their stay. Neighbors left large tips for Lindsay and Q and a few envelopes with cash for Margie. The insurance settlement would take time. With the earth already frozen, it would be spring before they could excavate to build the new home.

Shay offered to help Margie in the cafe, doing whatever she could. She cleaned, polished, and straightened things out. Her family always gave what little they had to others, and being in a place of receiving was new and learning to receive gracefully was hard. Margie understood and embraced Lindsay and her family with dignity. Before moving to Riverdale, Margie had been on the receiving end of things.

—

It took Kate hours to create the spreadsheet. She sorted similar interests and formed seven teams. Just as she thought she was finished, more envelopes arrived from two other church communities that had learned she was the organizational point person. Three hours later, she finally emailed the complete contributor list to the volunteers, asking each team to appoint a committee chair and determine their next steps. It was crucial to Kate that the Larkin family was honored and their needs addressed without overwhelming them. It was getting late. Where was Zak?

Ben kissed her neck. "I love watching you. You're so good at this."

Kate bristled.

"I'll get us a glass of wine, and you can tell me all you've accomplished," Ben offered. He went to the kitchen to slice crisp apples, cut sausage and cheese, and find some crackers. He poured two glasses of red wine and returned with a lovely tray. "Tell me about your fundraising plan."

Kate moved to her recliner. "There are seven committee teams. Each committee plays a crucial role in ensuring comprehensive support for the Larkin family. Coordinating efforts between these committees will maximize fundraising outcomes and assist the Larkins as they rebuild their lives after the fire. Do you realize all three churches are working together on this project?"

"I like that. Tell me about your teams," Ben eyed Kate proudly. "It appears you are the point person." He raised his glass as a toast.

Kate smiled. "Doc Johnson volunteered to help me in the overall structure and finance. This is going to be a huge project." Kate sipped her wine, savoring the rich, deep flavor. "Mmmm...this is nice; what is it?"

"Cabernet sauvignon, 2004, my best for my best. It is from the rustic and unique soils of Sonoma's Knights Valley." Ben did not usually embellish nouns with details. Kate smiled at his attempt at sophistication. Then, in Ben's tone, he said, "Tell me about your teams."

Kate began, "Well, the Resource and Donation Team will focus on collecting physical donations like clothes, furniture, and household items, and coordinating their distribution. I'm also assigning them the task of seeking state and federal assistance. This committee has nine church ladies from all three churches, and they're very enthusiastic; they're already collecting." Kate continued, "Our pastor offered our community room as the initial drop-off site. I've requested that donors only give their best. We won't accept scraps, expired food, or non-working appliances. Additionally, we'll only accept clean and newer clothing. Local gift cards or money placed on store tabs for groceries and supplies are most appreciated."

"Wow, you've thought this through," Ben said, fascinated.

"I'm trying to get my head around this," Kate sighed. "It's vital to include Lindsay in building her new household. I need to make sure she trusts me to make requests for their current needs."

"Mantha seems to be friends with her. Maybe she could ask and get honest answers," Ben suggested.

Kate tilted her head. "Yes, that might work even better. Lindsay and I have never been close. I expect more donations than the family will need, so I plan to use the excess for a holiday craft, bake, and garage sale, with all proceeds going to the family. Each event will need its own team. Some people have volunteered to serve in multiple areas. That forms my first four teams."

"I'm impressed," Ben said, finally eliciting a sincere smile from Kate, a rare occurrence since Zak arrived. Kate savored an apple slice and sipped her wine.

"The fifth team is the Event Planning Team. They will organize benefit dinners, auctions, and community gatherings. There are many details for this team—coordinating logistics, venue, catering, entertainment, and promoting the events. The events must be spaced out, affordable, and fun for our community." She paused to sip. "This is so overwhelming. There are so many possibilities. We need the perfect person or pair of individuals to lead this."

"I bet the VFW would offer their pull tab revenue for a while," Ben suggested. "We always use that money to help others."

"Please ask them, would you?"

He smiled and nodded. "I hear five teams; tell me about the last two," Ben said with a playful, encouraging tone. It was one of the things that endeared him to her.

"OK, the Family Support Team will consist of the professionals in the community who can offer their services in emotional support, counseling resources, or help to navigate insurance claims and paperwork. Lindsay is independent, but there will be paperwork and filing, which needs coordination to avoid conflicts. I want to ease the strain on the family." Kate sipped as she thought. "Could you pour me another glass?"

Ben poured another full glass, hoping to ignite past passion. "Do you have a restoration team? Sign me up!"

"OK, thanks. So many of our area men were sleeping in today. They worked so hard last night. I heard they were able to save Doc's estate. He is grateful," Kate shared. You can get the word out to the first responder volunteers. We need help in that area."

"Happy to oblige." He felt a pang at the mention of Doc.

Kate looked at Ben lovingly. "The Building Team will probably contain most of the men in Riverdale. Our community has so many skills. The few men at church today were like racehorses at the starting gate, hoping to get the area cleared and fix things immediately. Insurance will be the only thing holding them back."

"If I counted right, that is the sixth team." Ben put cheese and sausage on a cracker. "What's your final plan of attack?"

Kate cleared her throat and took a long sip of wine. "Doc volunteered to head the Financial Team. He stated the importance of overseeing the financial aspects of fundraising, including setting financial goals, managing funds, creating budgets, and ensuring transparency in monetary transactions."

Ben glared as Kate exhaled loudly. "I added all the math teachers to that team, along with the civics teacher. I hope someone will research and apply for a disaster family support grant."

"Doc is a unique character," Ben hoped not to put a chill into the evening. "I wasn't here when he was in high school; what was he like then?"

"He was a football player; I was a cheerleader," said Kate, thankful to be easily objectified.

—

"Uncle Ben, Uncle Ben!" Zak burst through the back door; it shut silently, and then he charged over to swing around Ben, almost dumping the wine and accouterments. He grabbed a sausage and stuffed it into his mouth, then a cheese and cracker before he took a deep breath. "The Monogram Masters are going to fundraise for Q, Shay, and Lindsay. We're building a rocket at the station, and Mantha and Sam are helping us. Next spring, we will do a rocket launch and see how many rockets we can get to launch. We might get hundreds! There will be entry and entrance fees," Zak grinned wildly, his words speeding up as he spoke. "The money will go to the family to help build their house! We will challenge the school, and since it is before the holidays, everyone can ask for rockets for presents. It will be SO cool!" Zak spun around, arms in the air. Ben grabbed the tray and held on to his glass as a hand lunged for more sausage. Zak avoided all mention of the ATV. He did not want to be jailed.

Kate took a deep breath. "As the science teacher of astronomy and the point person for fundraising…" She paused, holding her glass tightly. "Yes! Let's do this. You can talk to Mr. Mason tomorrow."

"FIRE!" Shouted Zak, turning to run up the stairs for bed.

Kate jumped, looking horrified. "NOT funny."

"It means cool," Ben said casually.

——

Zak liked in-school suspension. He liked Mr. Mason and riding his bike to school. He arrived early enough to pick up all his assignments. His first homeroom study class remained the same. Q continued to help him. He was allowed lunch with Shay and Q away from the other students, who did not want to sit with the weirdos.

Being with Mr. Mason simplified his life. Since he never changed classes, he did not need to worry about getting to class. There was no late and only two on times. Zak relaxed. Monday and Tuesday were a breeze. ISS made school life so easy that he did not want to return to the chaos of his regular schedule. Zak missed art, but Mr. Mason asked him to draw notes. He missed gym but had the obstacle course whenever he needed it. Mr. Mason challenged him to the obstacle around the room everytime he got jiggly. The three Job and Action Jars sat on Mr. Mason's desk, a reminder to pay attention to all the directions before you start.

"Mr Mason, can I please use the obstacle course?" Zak asked politely.

"It's available anytime you need it." The friendly giant smiled, "My only requirement is be quiet."

Life was good. He loved the cleaning and detailing work at the garage.

——

"Hey, Zak, Mantha, and I are going to Dee's for a piece of pumpkin pie and coffee. Could you hold down the fort?" Sam asked. "AND I expect EVERYTHING to be where I left it. No funny business, you hear me?"

"Sure," Zak's heart leaped. Even after taking the 4-wheeler, they entrusted the station to him. He swept and serviced each customer, washing their windows and offering to take their trash. Penny barked as Zak entered the station after being neighborly to customers.

Crack. Crinkle. Crack. The Ham Shack was lighting up. "Mayday! Mayday! This is K9HAM, David, calling anyone on this frequency. We're in a dire situation here in Illinois. A massive ice storm has knocked out our power, and we need assistance. Over."

The radio crackled with static as David waited anxiously for a response. Zak knew Mayday meant help, emergency, and right now! He picked up the mike he was told not to touch. "This is Zak. I am not a Ham, but I am here. I hear you loud and clear. Are you OK? I am in Minnesota. Blue skies here."

Ham David: Thank you for responding. We're located in Springfield, Illinois. We've got a heavy ice storm here, and the roads are slick. There is flooding and strong winds, and we're cut off from the main road due to fallen trees. Cell towers are down, and cell phone communication is out. Our primary concern is a medical emergency. We have an elderly neighbor who requires urgent medical attention. Over.

"My Uncle is the Sheriff. He will know how to help you. Let me call him on the phone. Stay with me. I heard my uncle say that one time," reported Zak.

Ham David: Thank you, Zak. I will stand by.

Zak looked at the black rotary dial phone on Sam's desk. He had used cell phones and walkie-talkies but never tried one with a wheel on the top. It had numbers, but they were in a circle. This could be like clocks that were in circles. His wallet had Uncle Ben's cell phone. He put his finger in one of the holes and pressed. *Well, that didn't work.* He pulled. *That didn't work either. Could you twirl it?* He turned the dial clockwise to the first position, aligning the number '5' with the tiny metal finger that guided the dial back into place. Mechanical resistance came with every rotation. The number '0' required a complete turn counter-clockwise before Zak repeated the process for '7', '2', and '5'.

The phone worked like a combination lock as he tried his uncle's number. It was slower than a button and a tactile experience foreign to

Zak's digital world. When the final number clicked into place, Zak's heart raced. *Would this connect him to Uncle Ben? What awaited on the other end of the line?* His curiosity turned into excitement and impatience, unsure if the dialing process had worked.

An unexpected jingling erupted from the phone. The room came alive as the rotary phone sprang to life. There was a loud bell. He cautiously brought the strange earpiece to his ear.

"Sheriff Jordan, Hello? Can you hear me?" Came a faint voice. It was a crackly connection filled with distant echoes. Silence hung in the air as if both parties were simultaneously astonished by this improbable connection. "Who am I speaking to?"

"It's me, Uncle Ben, Zak! I am at the station, and there was a Mayday and an ice storm. David called, and an older person needs medical help in Illinois. I am all alone. Can you come to help them?"

"Whoa, Zak, slow down," Uncle Ben said. "Where is Sam?"

"Sam is eating pie, Uncle Ben," Zak seemed frantic.

Ham David's voice trembled: Our elderly neighbor's condition is deteriorating. Time is critical. We appreciate your assistance. David Over.

"Zak hit the mike and tell them I am on my way to work on coordinating help."

THUNK. Zak hit the mike. *'Oh my God, he hit the mike,'* Ben realized his precise instruction, "Zak, press the button on the side of the mike and hold it down to talk to David."

Zak pressed the button. "Zak here. My uncle is coming to the Ham Shack to help you. He is the sheriff. He knows everyone."

Uncle Ben arrived with sirens. Mantha and Sam left their pies on the table at Dee's Cafe and ran across the street. Ben hit the mike. "David, we're with you. This is Sheriff Jordan in Riverdale, Minnesota. I know this is challenging, but we'll do our best to assist remotely. I'll try to contact local emergency services in Illinois and see if they can send help your way. Sam is our base operator, and he is here now. I will have him try to reach out to any nearby hams who can assist on the ground. Over.

Ham Sam: David, Sheriff Jordan is already on the phone trying to make connections, and I'll do my best to contact hams in the region. We'll find someone who can get to your location. Can you give me GPS coordinates? David, keep your radio on and continue to update us on this medical condition. We'll coordinate help for you. Over.

Ham David's voice is shaky: She is having trouble breathing. Over.

"Zak, here's my cell phone. Dial 911 and get the dispatcher to send the Riverdale paramedics here to work remotely." Mantha handed Zak her cell phone.

Zak dialed 911, "We need an ambulance at Riley's garage." He hung up. The dispatcher was grateful for GPS tracking.

Mantha took the mike from Sheriff Ben. "Captain Mantha here. I am a military paramedic and will ask you to check her vitals. I will take this one step at a time. Zak has called 911."

Sam ran to his house where he had his other 'you never know when you will need it' station and quickly reached two Illinois Hams. 911 dispatch got local community support. Dispatch called Sheriff Ben advising they had first responders in Illinois arriving with chainsaws and an ambulance. They were cutting a path through branches and trees for the ambulance now.

The local Riverdale ambulance arrived, finding a mike instead of a body, and went to work with David virtually. Mantha watched John Mason spring into action. He was a volunteer EMT. Like many small towns or rural areas, Riverdale did not have full-time, paid staff. They relied on volunteers who dedicated their time and expertise to respond to emergencies, often balancing their EMT duties with other jobs. As a volunteer, John was on call to respond to various emergencies, including accidents, medical crises, fires, and natural disasters, including this one on the Ham Radio. He and his team members were the first responders, stabilizing patients and providing crucial care before transporting them to hospitals. Mantha noticed the pockmarks on his hand and arm, with a deep scar beginning at his wrist and going up vertically. Each person worked together to coordinate help for David and his neighbor amid the dangerous weather.

Uncle Ben proudly put his arm around Zak's shoulders, saying, "Thank you, Zak. You made this happen. You saved that woman's life."

——

"What happened?" Q strolled in.

"Zak just saved a person's life in Illinois by being quick on his feet and fast on the draw. Mantha and I were at Dee's—" began Sam as Q handed him two to-go boxes.

"Yes, eating pie," Q interjected; he rarely did this but could not contain himself. "I put what you didn't eat in containers and brought fresh coffee. Forgive me for interrupting. You may continue, please."

"The Ham Shack was alerted to a Mayday. Illinois has an ice storm, and power lines, cell towers, and trees are down and blocking the road. Zak got Sheriff Ben here using my old rotary landline."

Q looked at the old black phone. "Even I'm unsure how to make that work. Zak, how did you do it? I mean, work that phone?"

"I'll show you, watch." Zak dialed Uncle Ben's cell phone number. "Now, put this thing on your ear." Zak handed the earpiece handle to Q.

"BRRRIINNNG BRRRIIINNG Sheriff Ben Jordan, may I help you?"

"Wow, um, ah, this is Q. I just heard what Zak did, and he showed me how to use Sam's vintage phone. I am sorry to bother you, sheriff."

"No problem, Q," replied Sheriff Ben. "Thank you for being a good friend to Zak."

"Thank him for being a good friend to me," Q handed the phone to Zak.

"See you, Uncle Ben. I will be home after work. Bye."

"Bye."

"STOP, Uncle Ben. How do I hang this up?" Asked Zak.

"Put the earpiece in its holder," Ben instructed.

"FIRE!" Shouted Zak.

"STOP saying that!" Shouted Mantha.

"Mantha, the fins are dry. I could glue them tonight to make more progress on the rocket," Q pressed.

"Can I do the parachute?" Zak asked.

"Not yet, Zak." Mantha still firmly held the reins.

Shay arrived, and the chatter, banter, and laughter soon intensified. Mantha heard the slight squeal of the freezer door as it worked to glide open.

"Everything is one dollar. You want an ice cream sandwich?" Z reached in to get one for himself.

"Naw, get me a green freeze pop," Q nuzzled the head of the wiggly Penelope, who sat quickly in hopes of her special treat.

"I want the pink freeze pop," Shay reached for the tubed treat.

"Would you want any other color than pink?" Q challenged Shay.

Mantha rumbled loudly from under Sam's 1940 Ford. "Make sure you shut that door. Don't let my cold out!"

"I ain't gonna let your cold out, Mantha. It's a deep freeze, and Q says cold doesn't rise," Zak challenged.

"Three dollars, boys. Put the money in the till." Mantha instructed.

"What's a till? And where is it?" Zak's eyes scanned the garage.

"It's the drawer in the cash register where the money goes!" Mantha shouted when she did not hear anything open.

This was Zak's first time using the cash register alone. He typed in $1.00 and hit repeat two times to get $3.00, then pressed pay. Q handed Zak a five-dollar bill. Zak was stunned, not sure what to do.

"Zak, what is five minus three?" Q asked.

"Two."

"Perfect, give me two one-dollar bills, and put the five in the cash drawer on top of the other fives," Q coached.

"Mantha said to put the money in the till."

"The cash drawer and the till are the same thing, Zak." Q was not surprised.

"OK," Zak put the five dollars into the area designated for five dollar bills, then lifted the drawer to look underneath, finding a… why he kept seeing things he was not supposed to? He remained quiet.

"Mantha," shouted Shay, "we put five dollars and took back two dollars."

"Great," echoed Mantha, "See you tomorrow for rocket lessons."

Zak did not bid his boss his usual goodbye as his mind was racing once again with conflict and alarm.

–22–
UNCOVERING

John Mason stopped into Riley's to say hello and discuss with Mantha the possibility of working on his grandfather's 1970 Dodge Challenger. The Challenger was in good shape but needed detailing. The oversized garage doors were open, and he entered without them knowing he was there.

"I don't know, Sam. This just doesn't add up. I believe Zak's story is true once you sift through the details. Sometimes, his thoughts are like a tangled fishing line—you have to patiently pull the knots apart to make sense of it," Mantha shared.

"I know, Mantha. Zak reminds me so much of Shaun and Kevin in how his mind works. It's like I'm being led back to the same situation with divine orders: 'Sam, go through this again.' But another incident with the same ATV? I can't even believe the motor started! It shouldn't have without some work. Plus the dang thing always had electrical problems. Why now, with another fire?" Sam paused. "I know in my heart that Kevin didn't kill my friend Emmett. But who listens to an amputee who owns a garage? I'm not even sure Kevin ever walked the path between the old Johnson and new Johnson estates. I don't know why he would have gone up there."

"There were two paths," Mantha said. "Lindsay told me about another path made by the deer that ran parallel to the main ATV path."

Sam hit his forehead with his hand. "Of course there was. You have got to be kidding. That's why there were no tracks! It is how he got by with murdering Emmett and pinned it all on to Kevin. Two paths! Who else knew about them, Mantha?"

"Lindsay said only she, Mike, and Potts, the kid killed in the fire, knew about them. They used the narrow trail to get between each other's property without being seen," Mantha added.

"I hate to be eavesdropping, but," John was hesitant.

"Hi John, it's OK. You were special ops, right?" Sam asked.

"Yes," he confirmed guardedly.

"You have training and skills that Mantha and I lack. Could you help us unravel this situation before it escalates? I'm concerned Doc might try to blame the fire on Zak, and unfortunately, he may have some grounds to do so. We each understand Zak from different angles - you from an educator's perspective, John, Mantha as a leader, and myself as a father figure. Our varied experiences with Zak's behavior give us unique insights. Do you recall the incident when you had to transport Missy from the boneyard and couldn't bring the ambulance in through the central road?"

"Yeah. Good thing she was a lightweight," nodded John.

"Zak decided to move that old car part that blocked the way so if it happened again, you could save her. He took my old ATV and a chain. Then, believe it or not, he moved it."

"That old melted Polaris four-wheeler was yours?" John was surprised. "Does anyone else know that? It was the same one Grandpop bought me to play around on as a teen. I still have one, just like it, in the old garage. After the fire I even uncovered my brown tarp to make sure it was still there."

"Blue tarp here," Sam rubbed his beard. "Your grandfather and I bought them together to get a better deal. We thought it would keep you and Shaun out of trouble. Give both of you something to do."

"We rode the main trail many times together. Shaun and I spun out and played in that old field once crops were harvested. I know the machine well. It was the first thing I ever fixed. And I fixed both those machines a lot!" Smiled John.

"John, would you be willing to walk the main trail with me and find the deer trail if it is still there?" Mantha asked. "I would also like to return to the boneyard without the kids and get some pictures before the insurance investigator shows up."

John's eyebrows raised. "Can't refuse an offer like that. Let's roll."

—

"Lights out," Aunt Kate yelled from the bottom of the stairs. "Early tomorrow, be ready or else."

Zak laughed. Every night Aunt Kate was home, she said, 'lights out, be ready, or else.' This became an anchor in his routine. He knew his aunt's after that pattern—water running, toilet flushing, feet padding to room, door closing—time for him to press the lantern.

Zak never needed much sleep. Sleep is good, but sleep without rest made him feel worse. Sleep and rest were different. He drove his parents crazy with his lifetime 4 a.m. to 8 a.m. sleep cycle. He adjusted to a 2 a.m. to 6 a.m. sleep window in Riverdale. It was enough to keep him from Aunt Kate's 'or else' and Uncle Ben from getting so mad at him he'd make him sleep at the jail. Zak carefully prepared for bed. He made sure he prepared everything he needed to keep busy for the night between his sheets, under his mattress, and alongside the walls. Then he went to the bathroom. He turned off the lights in his room and waited until all was quiet. He practiced raps in his head to pass the time. He liked being able to hear in his head, that was a new development since he moved into Riverdale, before everything he thought had to be spoken so he could here it.

Hidden between the wall and the bed, Zak switched on Uncle Ben's LED lantern. His insatiable curiosity often led him to explore hidden corners and uncover secrets. In Riverdale, he tried to curb his impulse to sneak around, knowing Uncle Ben, the sheriff, kept a watchful eye on the town.

Tucked between the memory foam and his mattress lay a weathered journal from Uncle Ben's drawer. Zak felt a thrill as he opened the book marked "confidential" across its cover. Inside were handwritten notes from past sheriffs, chronicling decades of investigations. The names Benjamin, Lawrence, and Robert appeared throughout the pages. As Zak leafed through the journal, he absorbed new revelations about Riverdale's history and the events that shaped Harris County.

The steady glow of the LED lantern minimized distractions, allowing him to focus intently on each word. When he shifted, the light cast dancing shadows on the walls, enhancing the magical atmosphere of his clandestine reading. Wrapped snugly in blankets like a protective cocoon, Zak immersed himself in the mental movie unfolding before him. Tight swaddling calmed him and helped alleviate his prickled senses. He was determined to uncover every secret of Riverdale's mysterious past and perhaps even help solve some of the town's cold cases. The gentle ambiance brought each word to life, fueling Zak's imagination and his growing desire to seek justice for unsolved mysteries. One particular case caught his eye. It dated back to the years 2004-2007 and involved the murder of a prominent figure in Riverdale named Dr. Emmett Johnson, a respected chiropractor known for his generous contributions to the community.

The journal revealed a complex case from Riverdale's past. It detailed a well-loved community member who often helped neighbors with various ailments without charge. The case had been closed years ago, with a man named Kevin convicted and serving a life sentence in a high-security facility outside of town.

Sheriff Larry, who was in charge at the time, had noted that various leads and testimonies were disregarded, possibly due to pressure from influential community members. This revelation hinted at potential misconduct in the investigation process. Most intriguing was a red handwritten note at the bottom of the page, marked with two asterisks and an exclamation point: "There are whispers around town hinting at the possibility of a wrongful conviction. The most noteworthy proponents of that theory are Sam O'Riley, and, Margie and Quintel Jones or Q."

Zak recognized some of these names. Sam was familiar, and Margie owned Dee's Cafe where his friend Q worked. The mention of Quintel, possibly related to Margie, puzzled him. Could there be two people named Q? He made a mental note to ask his friend Q to help with some library research. Carefully, Zak softly shuffled his feet on a towel to return the journal to its hiding place and the lantern to the shelf.

He returned to the warmest place in his blankets, his mind jumped between what he had read and what he knew. *Was there a wrongful conviction?* He was determined to uncover more of Riverdale's secrets and if there was an injustice, he would right it.

—

John and Mantha hiked up to the boneyard, but instead of descending into it, they cut through the woods toward the old ATV trail that still ran between the old Johnson Estate and the new one. The trail filled with fallen leaved, was wide and easy. When they reached a slight bend, John stopped.

"What is it?" Whispered Mantha.

"This. This is the tree," John mumbled.

"What tree?" Mantha asked, a bit louder.

"I came home for the summer after my first year of college and volunteered at the Hanover Fire Department. When the Potts fire happened, I jumped at the chance to fight a massive blaze. A town can handle most fires on its own, but like the Larkin fire, it needed much more support. The Potts family ran the junkyard, where you could buy used car parts and pieces for other machinery. I was familiar with their layout because I often bought parts from Mr. Potts when tinkering with something," John recalled.

"What about this tree?" Mantha wondered aloud.

"I'll get to that," John said, pulling back his sleeve. "I was burned in that fire. I was young, dumb, and curious, like a crow drawn to shiny objects—I had to figure things out for myself. I had the fire hose when I noticed the large new vehicle battery alongside the school bus. I had no idea about thermal runaways. I didn't have the experience to foresee that in just seconds, there could be an explosion. I felt powerful with the big fire hose."

"1,800°F (1,000°C) in seconds, leading to fires or explosions." Mantha added. "Seems impossible, doesn't it?"

John looked at Mantha and recited: "No man is an island entire of itself; every man is a piece of the continent, a part of the main; if the sea wash away a clod, Europe is the less, as well as if a promontory were, as well as if a manor of thine own or of thine friend's were; any man's death diminishes me, because I am involved in mankind. And therefore send not to know for whom the bell tolls; it tolls for thee."

"'If a clod be washed away by the sea,' English metaphysical poet John Donne in the 16th century," Mantha added. "There go I."

"You know it?" John was surprised.

"I know lots of things," She raised her eyebrows. "What does this tree know?"

"It took a long time for me to heal. Burns hurt like hell. Later, I returned to what remained of the junkyard. Of course, there was no battery. The school bus exploded along with it. The area was already cleared and grated. I was from out of town, so except for the trail between the two properties, I was unfamiliar with Riverdale. I decided to walk the trail and stopped at this tree. The tree had been wounded, and I felt pain for it. I put my finger into the area where sap had flowed to heal itself, and I found a bullet and kept it. Afterward, I joined the military and have not thought about it since. This was the tree where you had to slow down your vehicle to get around. It was the only turn on the trail, and you had to brake and then gun it quickly. There was a shallow area on one side you had to avoid so you didn't tip over the ATV."

Mantha suggested, "Let's hop through the woods toward the boneyard and see if we can find the deer path. It still may be invisible without snow, depending on the overgrowth."

John reached to hold Mantha's hand.

She pocketed both hands in her jacket, "I can handle this myself, John." Two steps through the brush later, they discovered the parallel deer path and followed it toward the new Johnson estate. The path was remarkably more trampled and well-used than they had anticipated.

"Interesting," John reached down to touch the compressed leaves and noticed a broken branch. "Look, Mantha, someone has been using the deer trail to get to the containers very recently." John turned the flashlight on his smartphone to appraise the details and snapped a picture.

A large and ragged boulder provided the first step toward the containers and it looked like it was used as a jumping off point from whoever had been using the trail. As a gentleman, he reached out to share his hand as Mantha worked to step over the rugged rock. Mantha accepted his offer this time, "We need to return during the day. We need better light."

—

The day began early, and since his in-school suspension was complete, Zak walked through the crowded high school hallways pelted by a hailstorm of human activity. The cacophony of blended voices, footsteps, and laughter bombarded him from every direction. The noise amplified, magnified, and engulfed him in such a nonstop assault he could barely focus. He navigated the maze of sensory overload.

Moving between classes intensified with each hour creating a Jenga tower from his revolving schedule. He longed for the big windows of soft, natural light in Mr. Mason's room. The flicker of the overhead fluorescent lights pulsated with an unnatural glow piercing his eyes, causing visual fatigue. Zak rubbed his eyes. He passed the janitor's room on the way to 3rd hour; chemical smells hung in the air and made his nose itch. His mind fixated on the overpowering odor of disinfectant. He stopped at his locker to exchange textbooks. The echoing clangs surrounded him as slams and bangs reverberated in his eardrums. Each sound thumped against the walls of his head as the lockers echoed with a suffocating chorus of metal madness. A wave of anxiety crashed over Zak. The sounds, sights, and smells jumbled into a crescendo of discord.

He followed the smell of food and fell into step in the lunch line.

"Zak, are you OK?" Shay noticed the shut-down expression

"Just hungry, I guess," he filled a lunch tray with lasagna, bread, and a salad. He was grateful Aunt Kate had talked the lunch ladies into ordering Lactaid milk, stopping the digestive problems at home and school.

Zak made his way to a quiet corner of the cafeteria, seeking refuge among the familiar faces of Shay and Q. As he sat down, he noticed Mr. Mason at the end of the teacher's table, giving him an encouraging thumbs up. This brief moment of respite offered Zak a chance to recharge and gather his strength for the afternoon ahead.

Feeling drained, Zak remained silent. Q, understanding his friend's need for quiet, simply nodded in acknowledgment and returned to reading his book. The peaceful atmosphere of their small group provided a welcome contrast to the bustling hallways and classrooms that awaited them later.

Zak appreciated the unspoken support from his friends and teacher, allowing him to mentally prepare for the challenges of the rest of the school day. As he sat there, he felt his energy slowly returning, grateful for this pocket of calm in an otherwise hectic environment.

"Q, can we fly Big Bertha this weekend?" Shay asked. "She's pretty!"

Mr. Mason tried not to eavesdrop, but their mention of Big Bertha struck a childhood heartstring. He hadn't noticed rocketry being active. The Riverdale Rockets Rocketry project was shut down during Covid-19. Maybe someone was reviving it.

"I hope so, Shay," counseled Q. "We are still missing a launch pad and we have no engines. Maybe if I give Mantha some money, she can order them for us Online."

Zak ached for in-school suspension to escape the pressure of drowning in his regular schedule.

"I have reviewed the cost, and three engines will run us between ten and twenty dollars. Plus, we need a launch pad, wadding, and launch controller. It's over a hundred dollars, but I have tips." Q said.

Zak managed a weak smile. "Thank you, Q." The momentary respite faded as he realized he still had to face the rest of his classes. His exhaustion returned, weighing heavily on him.

In gym class, Zak's frustration got the better of him. He threw a ball with unexpected force, accidentally knocking down another student. The incident caused a commotion, resulting in Zak being sent to the principal's office for alleged violence.

As a consequence, Zak received two weeks of in-school suspension. While this might have been a punishment for some, Zak felt a sense of relief. The suspension meant he would be returning to Mr. Mason's classroom—a place he had come to see as a sanctuary. Mr. Mason, understanding Zak's situation, was more than willing to accommodate him during this time. Mason understood the act of throwing the ball too hard was an unintentional result of pent-up emotions rather than a deliberate action. He had seen it often in his military work and as an urban teacher.

—

John Mason dug through stacks of old boxes in his garage, searching for an old wooden ammo box with a Federal Cartridge label in bold navy letters across the top. His grandfather had given him the box on a cold, snowy Christmas morning when he was ten. Now, it was time to pass it on.

John had always been a spirited individual, showcasing his strength and stamina in athletics. His aptitude and dedication earned him a teaching degree in just three years. Driven by a desire for liberty and freedom, he enlisted in the military and pursued a career there. His grandfather had raised him well.

After boot camp, John never saw his grandfather again. He advanced to special operations and, upon returning to Hanover, found everything in its original place in his childhood home, covered with dust, spider webs, and mouse-chewed sheets. Two estates were left to him. Covid had been ruthless. In Riverdale, his grandfather's will, included the 1970 dark emerald green Dodge Challenger. The inheritance money allowed him to buy his big truck. He sold the family homes and spent a few years working in inner-city special education. When he saw the job posting in Riverdale, he applied, got the position, and bought a house in the small town where he had spent his free time as a youth with Grandpop.

—

Zak's elation subsided when he realized he would now need to explain this round of punishment. He had been so mad at his parents when he left for Uncle Ben's that he no longer cared what they thought. But his aunt and uncle? He cared now. Zak padded into Riley's with his head down and shoulders slumped.

Sam presided over the entrance, hunched like an ancient bird of prey settled on his perch. Intrigued by the unusual silence and sudden gloom in the office, Mantha decided to investigate further. She approached Sam and Zak with a concerned expression. "Alright, spill the beans! Something's going on here that I'm not aware of. Let's have an open and honest conversation about what's weighing you down and find a solution together."

"Violence," mumbled the hanging head.

"...Murder," whispered Sam, the bird of prey flashed a look at Zak.

"Ah hem," she cleared her throat. "I choose to start with…" she pointed her remaining right fingers, swinging them back and forth, back and forth, landing on Zak. "...Violence! You go first."

"In-school suspension for two weeks."

"Did you do it on purpose?" Sam asked. Mantha furrowed her brows, analyzing what could motivate someone to seek in-house suspension.

"I don't think so," said Zak blankly.

"My son, Shaun, loved in-school suspension. It was less chaotic than the regular schedule… he did everything he could to return. Just thinking…" Sam tapped his chin. Chimes rang as John Mason carried in an ammo box.

"Hi John, you planning to use the range? That is a mighty big and mighty old box you got there," Sam guffawed, released from Mantha's interrogation and thoughts of Shaun's struggles.

"I heard through the grapevine there was a reentry into the honorable pursuit of rocketry, and I thought you could use pieces and parts, provided the mice haven't been in this box."

Mantha, hearing the word rocketry, whipped around, just missing the box by an inch. "Do you like to surprise people?" She noticed the dark green Challenger with extra-large tires by the pump.

"Hoping to," John's smile was boy-like. "Here, it's yours now." He held out the old box.

"Open it, Mantha!" Exclaimed Zak. "It's a present!"

"Let's see." Sam recognized the box, remembering the young boy who received it. The young boy who loved rockets had grown into a mammoth of a man.

Mantha undid the latch. Her eyes softened as she looked inside. She felt youthful as she took out the launch controller, three launch pads, and a bag of wadding. There were some ancient engines, dried-up craft paint, and other odds and ends.

"Oh my goodness, oh my goodness, oh my goodness," Zak was beside himself, "Q will die and go to heaven when he sees this stuff! He was going to empty his tip money jar. This is a miracle! FIRE! ENGINES!"

Sam chuckled at the surprise. "This may be more than a miracle, Zak, it maybe a lifesaver."

Mantha rotated the launch pad, reminiscing the exhilaration of joyful launches and the sense of freedom she found flying rockets. Looking at John, she saw through her five-year-old eyes the ten-year-old mop-headed boy pressing the controls to launch.

John watched, admiring her, also immersed in memories. He remembered Sam, Grandpop, and the little girl now transformed into an incredible woman warrior. The thrill of rocket-chasing through fields and meadows, eagerly tracking their flight trajectory, and celebrating each successful recovery.

During those carefree moments, they felt invincible, unburdened by the pressures and setbacks of adulthood. Their faces lit up in vivid recollection of hours launching rockets, carefully inserting engines, and the excitement of counting down before ignition—year after year—launch after launch. They watched as their creations soared high, dotting the horizon with bursts of color and leaving behind a trail of dreams

"John, thank you."

John looked past Mantha's battle scars. "Let's reclaim fearless joy!"

"Mr. Mason! I'll be back in your class starting again tomorrow," Zak's words dispelled THAT poignant moment.

"Well, that didn't take long," Sam rolled his eyes.

—

Back in Mr. Mason's classroom for in-school suspension, Zak felt a sense of security wash over him. He knew Mr. Mason understood him better than most.

Earlier, Zak had asked Aunt Kate to write his astronomy assignment on an index card. While she prepared for her day, he walked the quiet hallways, meeting with each of his teachers. He handed them index cards, requesting, "Can you write down today's or the whole week's assignments on this, please?" He hoped this approach, inspired by Mantha's work idea, would be successful beyond Riley's.

Entering Mr. Mason's spacious room, Zak took in the carefully designed environment. Blinds, shades, and curtains covered the windows, while dimmer switches controlled every light fixture. The room's perimeter was lined with various seating options - bean bag chairs, office chairs, rugs, gym mats, and even pup tents. The obstacle course designed for stretching, crawling, swinging, and climbing created a unique atmosphere that catered to all learning styles.

Armed with his assignment cards, books, paper, and extra pencils, Zak felt ready to start his two-week stint. Except for lunch and bathroom breaks, he could remain in this comforting space. A smile of relief spread across his face as he spotted Mr. Mason reclining on the couch, reinforcing the welcoming atmosphere of his temporary sanctuary.

"Welcome back, my favorite troublemaker! I've been waiting for your glorious return. It was just a matter of time…um…three days in the chaos of high school halls and brawls." Two massive arms raised into the air.

Zak laughed. "Yeah, I can't stay away from this incredible space."

"Indeed!" Mr. Mason's voice was deep and full. "I've even added a personal touch with a "Welcome Back Zak" sign just for you."

Zak knew how to play this word party. "You know how to make me feel special."

"No, not special…" said the gorilla of a man. "Exceptional in ways you do not yet understand. Your growth is going well, and your safety is my top priority in this temporary haven."

Zak dropped his stack of books. "Who needs socializing when I have all these textbooks and walls to keep me company?"

"Plus, you have my delightful company," Mr. Mason winked. "You are the cherry on top of this disciplinary Sundae. I couldn't ask for a more captivating companion."

Zak blushed sheepishly. "You're good, Mr. Mason."

"Flattery will get you everywhere, my friend. Now, take two laps on the obstacle course to get started."

Zak stood still.

"NOW!" Shouted the mammoth. He dimmed the lights in the room and raised the shades, increasing the natural lighting.

Zak grabbed the zipline and hung upside down on the ladder. He scaled the climbing wall to the platform, dropped down the rope to play active hopscotch, and then commando crawled under a 20-foot underpass. He crossed the finish line. The teacher hit his stopwatch and grinned. "One more time, GO!"

Knowing he was being timed, Zak poured on the speed. Finish. Stopwatch. Big bear grin. "That's better. Let's focus on conquering the academic battlefield together, one detention at a time. Do you remember my three rules?"

"Fun, respect, try," said Zak.

"Show me your cards? Our mission begins NOW!"

Zak shared his cards with a newfound pride in himself. "Thank you, sir, Mr. Mason, sir."

—

Most of the professionals at Riverdale High were not churchgoers, but Kate was determined to involve them in the Larkin Fundraisers. She placed stickers with names, emails, phone numbers, and ideas to help the family on small envelopes, then distributed them into everyone's mail slots. The staff was deeply aware of the emotional devastation the family faced after losing all their personal belongings and sentimental items in the fire.

At the lunch table, the teachers were brimming with new ideas and suggestions on how to help. The art teacher proposed setting up a photo gallery of household items from which the family could choose, with all donors remaining anonymous. The math teacher offered to establish a bank account to allow donors to deposit funds, helping to alleviate stress during the initial stages of recovery. Kate handed him the envelope of money she had placed in the school safe, believing that a dedicated account could provide control, security, and accountability while allowing the community to support the family.

The civic teacher volunteered to investigate federal and state grants that could assist families after catastrophic losses. The collaborative effort among the teachers aimed to provide comprehensive support to the affected family, showcasing the community's solidarity and compassion.

"We must be transparent. Every dollar must be accounted for." Doc emphasized.

A math teacher shared, "The bank will give receipts on deposit. That process takes the responsibility off our hands and provides discretion for both the giver and receiver."

"Should we set up a crowd source Online?" Suggested another.

"Never did that before; neighbors here always have taken care of neighbors in past crises," countered the history teacher. "Twenty years ago, we lost the Porter Potts family. Horrific tragedy."

"You mean the junkyard explosion?" Questioned another. Mr. Mason remained silent. The word horrific did not do that event justice.

"Horrible tragedy," Doc remarked, a hint of smugness in his tone. He added rhetorically, "I wonder who did it?" His voice was flat, lacking any trace of genuine curiosity.

Mr. Mason didn't miss the disconnect between words and behavior. He took a big bite of his brownie. *The investigation stated the blaze was accidental, caused by a batch of methamphetamine that exploded because the cook was using a battery to extract chemicals. That battery was incinerated in the explosion that followed. The identity of the cook was never determined. Was it Mr. Potts or Porter? Was there someone else? The heat was so high it left mostly ashes.*

The teachers were excited to enlist the help of the parent organization and student council. The students voted to donate twenty percent of the proceeds from their winter holiday carnival. The rest was set aside for graduation and sports teams. The box in the office filled with clothes for Q and Shay. Funds rose in the family's set aside bank account.

—

When each bell rang for class, Zak played ninja. Things connected. The ninja course worked to support his mind and body. Mr. Mason understood and applied the concept of the eight healthy inputs necessary to receive one healthy output. Most teachers missed that. He was determined to succeed with Zak. He grabbed the stack of cards and loomed over Zak. "Let's organize these to make it easier. You can use the gym here, my young warrior. That gives us an extra hour to catch up. Tell me when you need a break if you get frustrated or overwhelmed."

"I can tell you that, and you won't get mad?" Zak was shocked. "Like when I say, 'make this make sense,' you won't yell at me?"

"I'll take it a step at a time and keep it simple," Mr. Mason paused to let his statement sink in. "I'll help you build on each thing. Then you'll know what to do!" His eyes were kind and he kept his statements and steps to less than 12 words. With a card in hand, he read, "I have three students with the same assignment: Zak, Simon, and Chelsea. We will do this as a group."

He read Zak's card. It said due in two weeks:
1. Find a quote from Ernest Hemingway.
2. Write a paragraph about Hemingway and how the quote you chose pertains to his life. Is the quote in one of his books?
3. Choose a book by Hemingway and write a book report.
   Be ready to give an oral presentation
4. Pick another author born between 1890 and 1900 and discover a new book.

"Wow, that sounds like a lot," John observed his students. All were bright with complex brain circuitry. He watched their eyes and bodily reactions as they processed the first card. He thought of the novels and novellas of Hemingway he had read. There was a robust library of censored and uncensored classics on his bookshelf.

"How can we do all that?" Chelsea was overwhelmed.

"I don't even remember number one," shrugged Simon.

"Who knows who Ernest Hemingway is?" Asked Mr. Mason.

"He's dead," said Zak.

"Yes, that is true and we can learn alot from dead people. Their legacy lives on. Ernest Hemingway earned the Italian Silver Medal of Valor He was wounded by mortar fire but managed to help Italian soldiers reach safety. He was the ambulance driver for the American Red Cross. Knowing more about the author gives you better understanding."

"He was brave," offered Chelsea.

"He survived two plane crashes in one day in Africa. His first plane hit a wire and his second plane caught fire, the media thought he died, but he didn't. He did, however, get to read his own obituary."

"Like social media, Dad says you can't believe what you read. They make stuff up and even create pictures that are not real," shared Simon.

"That is true, and it will be important for us to study how social media or miswritten journalism can fool us. Hemingway often wrote standing up. He emphasized the importance of simplicity and truth in writing. He famously said, "All you have to do is write one true sentence. Write the truest sentence that you know.""

"Q says facts are not always truth. Truth is truth." Zak shared.

"A valid point, Zak. We must dig deeper. So let's start backward," suggested Mr. Mason. "I think the first half of number four is pretty easy. We can search the computer and see what authors were born between 1890 and 1900. Who wants to drive?"

"I do!" Chelsea raised her hand.

"OK, what question would you ask the computer?" Asked teacher.

Chelsea froze, "I dunno," she whispered.

"Anyone else has an idea," Mr. Mason scanned the students.

"Put in those numbers and authors," said Simon.

"Yes, does anyone remember what I read from the card?"

"I heard we have to read a book by Hemmingwhere," offered Zak.

"He's already dead." Nodded Chelsea, keystroke ready.

"Let me reread only number 4" Mr. Mason offered as he knelt his colossal frame buffering the angst of education.

"1890!" Shouted Chelsea gleefully.

"1900!" Added Simon.

"So now, what do you do?" Asked Mr. Mason.

"I get it, Chelsea; put in 18, 90, and then a dash. It is up by the zero on top, then type 1 and 9 and two more zeros." Zak said slowly for Chelsea. "Now, type author."

"A U T H O R," Mr. Mason slowly spelled each letter as Chelsea pecked working hard to discover each key's placement. "Good job, great, awesome, way to go, yes! You did it!"

Zak continued. "And then, BORN!"

"B O R N," John's heart was tender toward these young people as he tried to discover what was missing in their years of struggling to learn. He realized that each puzzle piece found could provide a better adulthood.

"And hit the return button," Simon pointed. Chelsea hit the return button with her right hand after finding it in the middle of the keyboard.

"Nice job," Mr. Mason watched the computer spit out a list of classic authors, "Agatha Christie, J.R.R. Tolkien, C.S. Lewis, F. Scott Fitzgerald, and…" the teacher paused.

"Hem-ming-where!" Shouted Zak.

"I've heard he was friends in Paris with Pablo Picasso and F. Scott Fitzgerald," added Mr. Mason, knowing he was planting seeds.

—

The 6-foot by 6-foot bookshelf was filled to the brim, a thick warm rug lay on the floor, next to a sunscreen tent, oversized pillows, an old sofa, and a rainbow stack of bean bag chairs, "Grab a bean. Let's see what my 'I wonder shelf' holds that has Heming—" Mr. Mason sneezed loudly, "—WAY's name on it." Accentuating' WAY.'

Everyone laughed.

"Heming, who?" Said Mr. Mason.

"WAY!" The students called in response. Four more students rose from their desks, wanting to participate. Bean bags were thrown down and nestled into. John chose a thick blue storybook with Hemingway written in big gold letters on the spine. "What does the spine say?"

"HemingWAY!" Everyone said in unison, now laying in bean bags in all sorts of unusual body positions, each noted by Mr. Mason.

"Hmmm, Ernest loved fishing and hunting. How about that? Infact, I heard he set a fishing record in 1938 when he caught seven marlin in one day! Yes, yes. We can choose a shorter novella, 'Old Man and the Sea.'" Shared Mr. Mason, "A novella is less than thirty thousand words and yet we can find much to discuss. His ancient ideas may now be considered controversial enough to be buried."

"Dead." Said Zak.

"Things buried hold treasured and often an initial foundation for reflection on living we have yet to ponder while we discover," continued Mr. Mason.

"What's 'Old Man and the Sea' about?" Asked Zak.

"It is Hemingway's last work, written in 1952. It is one of my favorites and is regarded as one of his finest works. This story won the Pulitzer prize and the Nobel Prize in Literature. The Old Man and the Sea was made into a film. Will watch that on another day, today I want you to see the story in your mind. I will read it, and you will listen. Think about how much the world has changed. Also think about how people's daily lives and struggles of living remain the same."

"But what's the story about?" Zak wanted to know.

"I will read the story to you," repeated Mr. Mason, "Let your mind work like a movie screen. I want you to relax. Watch the story. Feel it. Unless you fall asleep—in which case..." he gestured to the obstacle course smiling.

"Can I run the obstacle course before you read?" Begged Zak.

"Me too," begged Chelsea, agreeing. "I want to be ready to hear."

Mr. Mason's voice boomed, "Line up! One, two, three go! Then back here on the double on your bean bag."

He had their cooperation and attention. His students were meeting their bodies' needs to focus and communicate constructively. He captivated all ten students by using his deep voice, varying tones, mixing sounds, and adding deep-throated hums. He knew how to engage these neurodiverse students, which delighted him. There was much to glean from this old story that could serve them well in a changing world.

-23-
LOVE IT
OR HATE IT

"Hi, Zak?" Mantha greeted him, "How was school?" From appearances, it seemed he had a good day, and asking would get a response, not a reaction. Mantha didn't mind his reactions. She knew a little energy explosion after sitting in a pressure cooker allowed the outlet Zak needed to begin to work.

Sam read aloud. "Ham Radio Technician License and Amateur Extra License. Looks like it's time for you to take charge of the Ham Shack, Captain. Your brain is healing well."

"What are those?" Asked Zak, hovering over Sam's shoulder.

Mantha greeted him. "Licenses to use the Ham Radios. Sam won't let me touch his radios until I am fully licensed. Done deal now! How was school?"

"I LOVE Mr. Mason! Okay, I don't REALLY love him, but he is like a REAL teacher. He gets me. I can put things together with him," Zak said excitedly.

"Tell me what you learned today." Sam wished his son, Shaun, had a Mr. Mason thirty years before.

"Mr. Mason read to us from Hemingway, but at first, I said Hemming-where, and no one even laughed. Then Mr. Mason sneezed so loud I thought it was an explosion. He laughed like a hyena and shouted WAY! I will never forget that name again. It was too funny!" Zak blurted out in a single exhale.

"Hemingway is a well-respected author," Mantha agreed.

"And OLD. Like, before I was born," said Zak point-blank, looking at Sam's poker face. "He's DEAD already."

"I'm mostly still alive." Sam teased playfully. "Which story are you reading?"

"I'm not reading, Mr. Mason is reading. I'm learning to listen by lying on a bean bag. It's a fishing story about old Santiago, who went fishing alone in the big ocean. I was worried about him because he had caught a huge fish called Marlin. Marlin didn't want to be caught, but more than that, he did not want to be eaten by the shark. That was intense. Mr. Mason hummed with scary, munching noises—like that music in movies when bad things happen. So then, Santiago brought back all that was left of Marlin and it was just…his fish bones. He had a kid my age who usually went fishing with him, and the kid brought him a cup of coffee. That was nice because Santiago was tired. There is a movie, too. Mr. Mason said we could watch it tomorrow BEFORE writing our report."

"That's a good summary, what did you learn in your heart from that story, Zak?" Asked Sam.

Zak looked at Sam carefully, "I learned that even when you are really old like you, Sam, you're never too old to put up a good fight. It took him 84 days without catching a single fish and the old man never gave up."

Sam laughed, "Do you remember any direct lines from the story?"

"I had to listen for a quote I liked. There is a little sentence in the book; you wanna hear it?"

"Absolutely, Zak," encouraged Mantha.

"I may not be as strong as I think, but I know many tricks and have resolution," Zak recited in an earnest voice.

"Good one to have in your pocket." Mantha gave a left thumbs up.

Zak pulled out a recipe card with the quote. "How did you know?"

Mantha raised her shoulders in a humble shrug. "Lucky guess."

"The book is titled, 'Old Man and the Sea'," Sam reflected. "I read that in Riverdale High School, too. Only when it was newly released then. It is considered one of Hemingway's best works. Last one he did, if I remember right."

"You went to Riverdale High School?" Zak was surprised. "That had to have been a century ago!"

"Well, not quite," Mantha laughed. "Three-quarters of a century almost. I graduated from Riverdale, too, and so did Uncle Ben, Aunt Kate, Lindsay, and even Doc. You'll find a lot of folk in this area who stayed here or returned."

"Did Mr. Mason go to Riverdale?" Zak asked.

"He was a Hanover Falcon, our rival school," Sam nodded to the north toward Hanover.

"Oh." Zak locked that information into his memory bank for his detective work on the murder case. *How could he ask questions without being found out? What could he tell Mantha, Sam, or Mr. Mason that wouldn't tip them off?* A spark lit. "Did you both live here before 2010?"

Sam chuckled, "Kid, except for my tour in Vietnam and a few vacations with my wife, I never left Riverdale since I was born here in 1940."

"When were you born, Mantha?" Zak asked, taking his cards out of his pocket to jot down information.

"1985," she answered. "And Mr. Mason was born in Hanover in 1980. He's five years older than I am."

"You are ALL OLD!" Zak exclaimed as Sam cleared his throat.

Mantha pressed her shoulders back with a rigid chin. "ENOUGH! Get to work!" She barked. "NOW!"

"FIRE!" Zak saluted and grabbed his stack of cards, which now numbered twenty. He wrote the numbers on his daily yellow index card number eight in code: M-85, MM-80, S-40. He would record the information onto his map of clues. He had $5.00 and planned on meeting Q at the library, where he hung out Monday through Thursday nights. "Sam, does the library have old local newspapers like the one with that big picture of Uncle Ben covered in soap suds?"

Sam grinned, "I am sure they have scans of many years of local papers. Do I have to say it, too? Get to work!"

Zak first card was card number eight, instructing him to take Penny for a walk and then brush her. Card eight was his favorite. He attached the leash. Sam looked surprised.

"The sign in the park says dogs must be leashed." Zak figured from Sam's look he expected an answer.

"Okay, but you never hold the leash," Sam observed.

"The sign only says dogs have to wear a leash. It doesn't say anything about holding it." Penny dragged her leash out the door as Zak nonchalantly walked alongside. Sam's hand rubbed his beard, pressing both lips together to suppress laughter. Shaun had done the same thing years ago with Sergeant Reg, his German Shepherd.

—

Sam stood in the doorway, watching their return. Penny's leash trailed behind her with Zak alongside. Penny curled up on her bed as Zak unlatched the leash.

"So folks, it's time I head to bed and listen to Old Man and the Sea, a new novel by…" Sam sounded like an old-time radio announcer.

"HEMINGWAY," exclaimed Zak.

"And from Bill Haley and His COMETS, out of Bethel Township, Pennsylvania, Released in 1956, the hit song, See You Later Alligator." Sam stood to sing the chorus and put a bit of movement into his step.

At the part he knew, Zak chimed in, "After While Crocodile."

With dance in his step, Sam left the garage singing as he walked to his home behind the garage to go to bed: "Can't you see you're in my way now? Don't you know you cramp my style?" Sam crooned his favorite lines.

"I didn't know that was a real song," Zak said as he completed five cards. He placed the completed cards in Mantha's 'Inspect what I Expect' box, hoping none would be returned for redo, except for number eight. "I'm done! See you later. I have to go early tonight. I can't hang around."

"See you tomorrow, Zak," Mantha called out.

—

She knew the voice.

"It's light enough out, Mantha." John Mason hung his coat on the rack, his hand unconsciously tracing the scar that ran up his forearm. He saw Mantha take notice. "I managed to shield my face, but my arm caught on fire in the Pott's explosion flames."

"It's remarkable what the human body can endure and still repair." Mantha acknowledged.

John winked. "I put my mojo on and marched into the military and then special ops. I faced my fear of fire by camouflaging it with grit. One cannot be as big and tough as me and have fear, right?"

"One can be as big and tough as you and still be human." Mantha wiped the grease from her hands.

"Do you want a ride up to the boneyard and take pictures? It's still light out and I want to take some pictures. Because of our experiences, you and I may find things others might not see," John suggested. "Ben said the investigator showed up today. Heard weather is blowing in."

Sam returned having forgot his thermos, "John, Mantha said you found a bullet impacted in that tree by the swerve in the trail years ago after the fire. You still have it?"

"Think so. It's probably in my old treasure box in the garage somewhere. You want me to look for it?"

"Be obliged if you would," nodded Sam.

"Mantha lights fading. We better leave." John opened his passenger door so she could climb in.

"Aren't you the gentleman?" Mantha tilted her head and smirked.

"Just a lady's man," John teased as he started the truck.

Sam raised his thermos, locked the front door, and armed the security in the back door on his second trip to home.

—

Once past the pumps, Zak sprinted the two blocks to the library, braving the bitter wind that nearly toppled him. The big red door almost blew open as he entered.

The librarian was not impressed. "Young man, I expect you to use care with MY doors," she scolded.

"Rules," mumbled Zak as he struggled to keep the door from slamming. "Is Q here?" he shouted over the shrieking wind.

"SH!" the librarian said, pointing to the back computer terminals. "SHhhhh!" she shushed him again, as if he hadn't heard the first time.

Zak tiptoed like a cartoon burglar and tapped Q's shoulder. Q, deep in research, startled.

"It's me," Zak whispered.

"What are you doing here?" Q asked, regaining his composure.

"I need your help looking for some old newspapers, and I brought $5.00 to print copies," replied Zak.

"Sure, tell me what details you need," Q said, eager for specifics.

"I need you to look up a murder in Riverdale, 2007," whispered Zak.

"A murder? Really?" Q was intrigued. "Yes, most libraries keep newspaper archives for a certain period. I'll check with the librarian about the cost, where to find the information, and how to print it out." Q left to find the librarian. Zak gazed at Q's screen, filled with small type and long words about rocketry he did not understand.

Q returned with a piece of paper. "The librarian has local news archives going back to 1880, including the first printing of Riverdale Press. We can find a lot here. What exactly are you looking for?"

Zak handed Q a note with '2007, Emmett Johnson, Murder' scrawled in his barely legible handwriting.

Q typed 'Emmett Johnson, obituary' into the search system. Within seconds, a headline appeared on the screen. Q read it softly: "Beloved Chiropractor 'Doc' Emmett Johnson Murdered."

In Loving Memory of Dr. Emmett Johnson of Riverdale Chiropractic.

With heavy hearts, we announce the passing of 'Doc' Emmett Johnson, a beloved chiropractor in our small town. Driven by a passion for healing and dedicated to the well-being of his patients, he touched the lives of many with his skilled hands and caring nature. He tragically left us on October 10, 2007.

Dr. Johnson was born on January 3, 1947, in Riverdale and was the son of Emit Ludwig Schulz Johnson and Helen Ann. From a young age, he was their only child, and he displayed an affinity for helping others and a keen interest in the intricate workings of the human body. After completing his education, he returned to establish his chiropractic practice, where he became an esteemed provider, practicing locally for over thirty years.

Through his expertise and exceptional care, Doc Johnson brought relief and comfort to countless individuals, guiding them toward a life free from pain and discomfort. His gentle demeanor and warm smile made each patient feel seen, heard, and truly valued. He had an uncanny ability to alleviate physical ailments, worries, and stresses.

Beyond his professional achievements, Dr. Johnson was known for his compassion and generosity. He regularly offered his services to those in need, regardless of their ability to pay. His commitment to giving back to his community extended beyond his clinic, as he actively participated in local charity events and mentored aspiring healthcare professionals.

Family was paramount to Doc, and he cherished his time with his loved ones. He is survived by his devoted spouse, Sally Ann, with whom he shared thirty-two beautiful years of marriage. He leaves one child, Michael, who was his pride and joy.

Doc enjoyed hunting, fishing, reading, and exploring the great outdoors. He had an adventurous spirit that led him to discover the beauty of nature, often going on wilderness fishing trips in Canada with local friends. His zest for life was contagious, inspiring many to live each day to the fullest.

A memorial in honor of Dr. Johnson will be held on October 12 from 4 to 8 pm at John Gleason Mortuary. Services will be held at the Lutheran Church of Peace, where a grateful community will gather to celebrate his life and commemorate his impact on so many. Lunch will be served. Pallbearers: Samuel O'Riley, Hans Hanson, Gunner Johnson, Sheriff Kelly, and Eddie Schulz. The family kindly requests donations to Riverdale Hospital Guild in Dr. Johnson's name, as he held this cause dear to his heart.

The legacy of Dr. Johnson will always be remembered by those who were fortunate enough to know him personally. His healing touch and compassionate nature made our town a better place to live. Everyone will deeply feel his absence. As we say goodbye to a remarkable chiropractor, friend, and family member, we honor his memory by showing kindness, empathy, and a commitment to helping others.

Rest in peace, dear Dr. Johnson. You have left an indelible mark and will be remembered with love, respect, and gratitude by all whose lives you touched.

There was a picture of Doc, Sally, and Michael, who looked much like a younger Doc Johnson, the principal at Riverdale High School.

"The principal can be difficult. It's best to stay out of his way," Q cautioned Zak when he noticed who was involved.

"I think Doc Johnson threatened me at Riley's," Zak whispered.

"What do you mean 'threatened you'?" Q asked, concerned.

Zak closed his eyes and lowered his voice to imitate Doc: "You're in big trouble, boy. You remind me of that creep Sam hired years ago! Good riddance, I could put you away, too." Zak shuddered. "I've never told anyone, but I wondered who this person was that reminded Doc of me. He sounded dangerous. Doc scared me."

"I try to avoid him myself," Q admitted. He printed two pages using Zak's quarter, leaving them with over four dollars for more printing. The librarian announced the library's imminent closing, prompting Q to suggest they continue their research another day.

"I think we should talk to Sam," Zak proposed. "He has surveillance cameras. He might even have recorded what happened."

Q advised caution: "This could be more complex than we realize. We must be careful and keep this investigation between us. Don't share this with Shay - I don't want her involved. Doc might not appreciate us looking into his affairs, and he could make things difficult for us. We need to focus on graduating, and I'll need scholarships for college."

"He's so mean," Zak said somberly.

"That seems true when he's not in public," Q agreed. "Remember, everyone is responsible for their actions and how they treat others. Be careful, Zak. Let's keep this between us for now."

———

John and Mantha walked along the charred containers, stopping at the Polaris ATV. "This is the model Grandpop bought to keep me focused on engines instead of girls. Moss camouflage and she turned on a dime unless you hit a rut! Then she'd throw you like a bronco."

Mantha pointed to the partially melted helmet on the ground, "Look, John. If Zak wore this, I don't think he strapped it on."

"Someone probably advised him to wear a helmet, but no one told him to fasten it securely," John sighed as he took pictures of the ATV and the damaged helmet, its straps fluttering in the strong wind. "Mantha, come have a look. Here are the tire tracks from the Polaris. It looks like Zak made about 10-12 runs back and forth between the trailer and the containers. Surprisingly, this thing was able to move that old car part. He must have been very determined."

"John, there's a different set of tire prints on top of his over here. If he was the last person down here, these tire prints would not be here." Mantha put her hand down for perspective.

John snapped more pictures. "I want to check one more thing before we lose light and the storm blows in. I want to see if there's a trail to the old blue container in the boneyard toward the deer path. And I want to see the direction it flows with trampling." SNAP–Snap–snap. John looked across the charred field where his fire crew stopped the flames from burning down the Johnson estate. They walked out into the field. A "whoosh" of air escaped John's lips as he recalled, "I have vivid memories of the night of the Potts' fire. I stood in this same place to battle that field fire twenty years ago. This field was the junkyard. The bus was hidden. Now I understand why…" he stomped his feet, "I was at this exact spot with the firehose when the battery exploded me into flames." He stood stunned by the full impact of the memory. "I was 20 years old." Mantha compassionately touched his shoulder understanding trauma responses.

"I pride myself on keeping my head even in the thick of chaos. At the Larkin fire, my mind raced, my heart pounded, and my breath vanished. I was struggling. It didn't show on the outside. But inside? I was embroiled in a battle to… persevere. The storm was within me." John turned away from her, remembering his persistence despite the grip of rekindled agony.

Mantha's arm released. He could see and recall it now, but the grip had loosened somewhat, leaving a subtle veil of distance between him and the searing memories.

Mantha reached out to touch his hand.

—

Southeastern Minnesota was blanketed in deep, drifting snow, creating a stark contrast against the clear blue sky. County snowplows worked tirelessly to clear access roads to farms and village streets for businesses. Riverdale took on a festive appearance with LED blue snowflakes adorning each streetlight, illuminating most days and giving the town an inviting glow. Shop windows and the giant spruce in Central Park were decorated with white lights and ornaments. Elementary school students contributed to the holiday spirit by hanging pine cones filled with peanut butter and birdseed, along with small suet cookies in the market square.

Thanksgiving passed without Zak seeing his parents, who were on a much-needed Caribbean cruise vacation. He often looked at their pictures in his scrapbook, remembering happier times when they weren't so stressed and angry with him. Zak found contentment in his life with his aunt and uncle. His initial two-week in-school suspension had been extended by another month, lasting into the new year. This extension came after he accidentally fell asleep in a quiet corner of the school library, missing two classes. The principal used this as an excuse to double his penalty. Zak resigned himself to the situation, thinking, "As long as I'm in Mr. Mason's class and maintain good grades, I can finish the year." He resolved to avoid further trouble and steer clear of the principal's office.

—

Uncle Ben was kept busy responding to accidents and near-misses caused by icy roads, as routine commutes and errands turned into unexpected spinouts and fender benders.

Aunt Kate found satisfaction in managing her fundraising committees. The craft, bake, and church basement sales were successful, helping the Larkins furnish their apartment and acquire necessary clothing and bedding. With winter setting in and house construction delayed, the family settled into their temporary home above Dee's Cafe.

In the cafe, Margie and Lindsay were hard at work creating holiday treats and dinner specials. Shay joined the kitchen staff, baking alongside them, while Q continued his serving duties. The young friends—Shay, Zak, and Q—decorated the cafe with handmade paper chains in festive red and green, complemented by intricate white paper snowflakes. Q added a finishing touch with lights around the windows and on two small evergreens placed in oak barrels by the door.

Margie praised their efforts, saying, "Monogram Masters, this is delightful." She then shared some exciting news: "My son, Quintel, is arriving from Alabama next week for the holidays. You'll meet your predecessor, Q."

Zak created a flier for the graduation rocket launch, challenging all students to participate in launching the senior class out, and the junior class into becoming seniors. Zak had paid Uncle Ben back for his school clothes and still money remaining to print the rocket launch announcements at the print shop. He dropped off a small stack at Hans Hardware, Dee's Cafe, Homestead Provisions, and the Laundromat. He posted five fliers on the school doors before classes—lunchroom, gym, Mrs. Jordan's classroom, the office, and the library.

He soon discovered that posting without permission earned him another month of in-school suspension from Doc. He laughed aloud at his good as he gained an extra two weeks. With this last mistake, Mr. Mason's class might last until Valentine's Day since winter vacations did not count. He was having fun learning and secretly hoped Doc would continue doling out punishment. School made little sense, but Mr. Mason did, and that felt good for a change!

———

Rocket deliveries began arriving at local stores and by mail to be wrapped for whatever holiday each family celebrated. Zak accidentally left his original flier in the copy machine and was surprised when the local paper published the article about the Riverdale High School challenge arranged by Doc Johnson. His flier was published alongside kudos to the principal for his innovation and kindness in reinstating the Graduation Challenger Rocket Launch on Friday, June 2, at the Riverdale High School Sports' field. Zak was just glad the message was getting out. Zak's idea, like most of his ideas in the past, was usurped by someone taking him out of the details. It did not make Sam and Mantha happy.

"Zak, I need to talk to you," stated Mantha. "How did you get press coverage on your rocket launch?"

"I dunno," Zak guessed.

"Maybe someone like Doc took another opportunity to co-opt others' good deeds to inflate his own ego," grumbled Sam.

"What did you say, Sam?" Zak asked.

"Nothing important. Get to work." Sam said.

"Job Card number eight!" Mantha shouted.

"Yes!" Zak jumped and spun, and grabbed the leash. Penny knew it was time to romp in the snow.

———

Shay made her rounds at the Memory Care Home, distributing evening snacks of fruit juice and cookies to the residents. She chatted and laughed as she went, saving her favorite resident for last. Shay often lingered with Ann, a sweet elderly woman with a remarkable past.

Ann, a former nurse, could vividly recall details of caring for local families, assisting with births, and comforting the dying. While her memories of the past remained vibrant, Ann struggled to recognize even her loved ones in the present.

Undeterred by Ann's confusion, Shay cherished their time together. She carefully documented Ann's stories in a journal, illustrating them with drawings. When Ann became disoriented, Shay would read these stories back to her, helping to anchor her memories. Hidden in a drawer by Ann's bed was a small book filled with these collected memories. Shay would lovingly read from it, allowing Ann to relive the lives she had touched during her nursing career. Ann's eyes would light up as she listened, sometimes adding new details to familiar stories.

Through these moments, Shay helped Ann reconnect with her past and the profound impact she had made on countless patients throughout her life. This evening, as Shay read a story about a young child the woman had cared for, frail hands reached out to touch Shay. Tears pooled in her eyes, and a faint smile appeared on her lips.

Ann recognized the story. "I cared for that child the night of Emmett's murder." She spoke. "I tried. I tried. I tried so hard to save him. He was my love, my best friend, my everything. He'd been shot through the heart…I couldn't…there was no way to save…he…I tried but….. He did not have a hand. MY HUSBAND…my glorious husband…even an ER nurse…I could not save Emmett."

"Ann," Shay gently held Ann's hand. "That must be so hard. You are a good nurse. You are a strong woman."

The woman's clouded eyes searched for a reassuring voice. "Yes, yes, I am. Aren't I?"

—

Zak and Penny walked to the containers through the deep snow. Penny bounded like a jackrabbit making a beeline for the Monogram Masters hangout at the end. The dog remembered the cookie. Zak trudged through following the dog. The ATV skeleton was drifted over. Snow never lies and he was surprised to see somebody had opened another container—this one was rust red.

He peaked inside. Beside the blanket was an LED lantern like Uncle Ben owned, three pillows, more blankets, and books on rockets. The combination seemed more like Q or Shay, but no trail had come from that direction. The trail had come from the woods. Penny and Zak followed the footsteps finding the narrow deer trail with boot prints cgoing to and from Missy's house. Zak returned to the rust red contain and shut the door..

"Well, that was quite some run," Mantha looked up from her desk at a snowy dog and rose cheek boy. "Even Penny is tuckered out." The dog was curled into a tight ball and already asleep. "Could we put twinkly lights in the windows and spiff this place up for the holidays?"

"Where is the card?" Zak responded, energized.

"Guess you have to make the card," Mantha handed him a black marker and index card.

"Huh? You do that!" Zak argued.

"Not anymore. I think it is time YOU begin to do it. Here are some extra cards. I am working on the Dodge Challenger in the back."

"Dodge Challenger? What year?" Zak was distracted from his task.

"1970, first edition," Mantha walked away.

"I want to see it!" Pleaded Zak.

"After I see your cards." Mantha shut the door.

"Whose car?" Asked Zak.

"Not telling until Mantha sees your cards," Sam sat in the office chair and tried not to smirk.

"Pssssst…Blankity Blank Blank," Zak lay on the floor to write what Mantha told him…what was it, spiff and lights? Lights, spiff, and Challenger?

Zak wrote:

1. Spiff

2. Lights

3. Challenger

"I'm done!" He shouted, waving the card like an entry ticket.

"Read me your card," Sam's eyes twinkled like Santa. Zak read the three words. "Has anyone ever told you about Mark Twain and his five w's? Get me some tape from that top drawer and six of your index cards."

Zak got up to fetch the tape and gave him six cards. Sam tore off a third of the cards to make six squares. Zak watched intently. "Give me your marker." Sam wrote on each card and then taped them together to create a solid box. "This is your thinking box. It will help you think outside of the box." He handed the box to Zak.

"It's like a die!" Said Zak, "Can I roll it?"

"That's what it is for, Zak. Roll the die and tell me what you think," Sam encouraged.

Zak rolled it. "It says WHERE."

"Okay, now read your three words starting with WHERE," Sam said.

"Where. Spiff." Zak thought for a moment and grinned. "Office! Spiff office." He scribbled the word office next to spiff.

"Roll it again, Zak," challenged Sam. The die rolled to WHO.

"Zak!" He looked at Sam, who nodded. "I get it! I get it. Thank you." The teen continued rolling the die, soon realizing WHO WHO WHO was not adequate, and he began turning the sides to read them all. "WHO, WHAT, WHERE, WHEN, WHY, and HOW." When he got to HOW, he said, "How is not a W word."

"You are right, but it is the most important. You have to figure that out yourself. How are you going to get it done?" Sam yawned back into his chair. Snoring sounds soon followed.

"I'm done!" He announced, having learned that if Mantha were under a car or on the ground, she would finish what she was doing before arriving. Sam continued to snore. Zak grabbed a broom to sweep.

Mantha arrived carrying holiday lights. "Trade your cards for lights."

Zak dropped the broom to the floor to take the lights.

Mantha examined his cards. "Impressive. How did you make this happen?" The snoring stopped, and eye slits above the white beard watched as lips curled into a grin.

"Sam made me a thinking tool," Zak handed her his die.

"I like it. Would you like to include me on the WHO card for lights, and then we will put them up together?" Mantha asked. "AND after that… YOU get a peek at the 1970 Emerald Green Dodge Challenger!"

Zak stool on the foot stool to add lights to inside Riley's and outside as Mr. Mason stopped at the far gas pump. "Hi, Mr. Mason. Can I fill your tank and wash your windows."

"I can handle that myself, Zak," the big man said stepping up to hold the lights to help Zak.

"Gee, thanks Mr. Mason. I was just too short!" Zak laughed.

"Your feet touch the ground. I think you're just right," Mr. Mason entered the garage. "Found it," John dropped an envelope into Sam's hand.

"Done, Mantha!" Shouted Zak.

"Come on back!" Replied Mantha.

Zak, was lost in admiration of the vintage muscle car. "Wow, I mean wow. I mean, who owns this? This is perfect. I mean, Docs 57 Chevy is cool, and Sam's 40 Ford is great, but THIS, this is super stupendous!"

"Stupendous!" Boomed the familiar voice. "And does it cause you astonishment in its amazing greatness?" Zak turned around, colliding with Mason's muscular torso. "Just checking if you know the definition of the word you use."

"Oh, Mr. Mason, sir," stammered Zak. "Do you see this car? It is like wow, I mean wow! And that is stupendous!"

"I came to check on my car and see how Mantha was doing." Mason's eyes twinkled.

"Where's your car?" Asked Zak. The giant pointed to the Challenger. "No way! Really? I mean, Really? FIRE!"

Mantha and Sam laughed. John jumped, pivoted, and scanned the garage near his car for a FIRE.

"It means cool." Mantha and Sam replied together.

—

The Ham Shack began to **crackly crinkle crack.**

"KØROK monitoring." Sam recognized the call sign. RocketMan was looking for a casual rag chew.

HamSam: "KØROK, this is KØZQR to initiate conversation."

RocketMan: "HamSam, ol' buddy, how are you?"

HamSam: "Doing well, RocketMan. Exciting news. Riverdale Rockets will launch again for 2024 graduation."

RocketMan:: "Good news indeed. Let me know if you need my help."

HamSam: "Will do. Heading to bed. 73."

RocketMan: "73."

Zak stood behind Sam. "Who's RocketMan?"

—24—
READY TO BURROW

am's workbench displayed a striking sight—a two-foot-tall model rocket in vibrant pink with prominent white fins. This was the Big Bertha, a classic design beloved by many rocket enthusiasts, dressed in fashionista styling. The Monogram Masters, shared ownership of their first rocketry project and were pleased with their creation, regardless of its unconventional color scheme. As the rocket awaited its inaugural flight, Mantha reminisced about her own experiences with the Big Bertha. She recalled launching her first one at age eight, a memory that sparked a decade-long passion for rocketry.

The Big Bertha, known for its simplicity and reliability, had been a popular choice for beginners and experienced rocketeers alike. Mantha turned to Sam and suggested, "Let's give this Big Bertha to Shay. It seems perfect for her. We can give the other rocket to Q. The one we set aside is more advanced—it flies higher and has a more complex assembly. What do you think we should give Zak?"

"The bigger the Bertha, the better," Sam rubbed his hands together. "We can build it together over the holidays. I say we build a SUPER Bertha. By the time it's complete, Q will have the skills to build whatever he wants himself."

"Sounds like a plan," agreed Mantha.

"Zak will still need a few more rockets to have a fleet," Sam said as he ordered the Super Big Bertha to be delivered on the last school day before winter break. "Zak will love this. It stands over 36 inches tall and reaches an altitude of over 1200 feet. This will give the two young men competition." Sam chuckled.

"It will be interesting," Mantha laughed. I think Zak has visions of hundreds of rockets in his fleet."

———

"Loser! Now you're in the class of the losers," the redheaded cheerleader in her cute outfit flicked her hair and slammed her locker. The noise reverberated down the hall.

Missy put her head down and looked away. Zak noticed her reaction as he entered Mr. Mason's room to run the obstacle course. He took another lap to shed the redhead's comment.

"Hey Zak! Not fair, my turn!" Simon complained.

Ten students gathered around the work table that held a heavy, old book on rocket science and a large, sealed white box. Mr. Mason, with his stopwatch, motioned each student to sit as they completed their laps. Zak sat.

"Heavy stuff." The teacher bench-pressed the old science book and began to read. "This is HIGH-level material, AND I know you can ALL understand this!" He started with propulsion's intricacies and watched flickers of lights go on in his eyes as boredom gave way to excitement and intrigue. He read carefully, repeated, paused, and discussed each part as he read.

"Who wants to see what is in my box?" Ten parade waves encouraged him. He opened it slowly with a myriad of fascinating facial expressions, rousing even further anticipation in his growing class of 'science students'. He peeled back the tape and tipped it over to peek in. "Ah, just as I thought. EXACTLY what I ordered for the holidays." His eyes sparkled with mischief as students craned their necks to look. Their eyes widened as he pulled out a rocket kit and then stood with a declaration.

"I do at this moment declare, by the POWER vested in me for the IN-SCHOOL suspension room, hereafter referred to as the Student SUCCESS Room, ALL students in this class accept the ROCKET CHALLENGE. The challenge YOU each accept is building a rocket for the GRADUATION rocket launch." He then pulled out ten more rockets, handing one to each student. "Holiday gifts for everyone! This is next year's class project." He pulled out another rocket. "I get one, too," he raised his high purposefully like a trophy. "We are all in this together." The room erupted in cheers.

Building their rockets sparked newfound enthusiasm to lift hope and confidence. "This is your opportunity to prove your potential to your peers and teachers. We WILL do this," Declared the colossal man. Zak noted he used the word 'we'; that was how Mr. Mason always rolled. "Let's discuss this, Simon. What do you think we can do?"

"Wow, just wow," Simon gaped. "I never got this nice of a present before."

"Our room is a rocket laboratory!" Zak shouted.

"The sky is not even the limit at THE STUDENT SUCCESS ROOM," proclaimed the magnificent Mr. Mason, raising his hands. "What else can we do? What else are we capable of doing?" His voice infused a fire for achievement in their hearts, inspiring their minds to this new vision of their potential.

"When can we start?" Zak looked down at the paper square on his lap under the table.

"Start what?" Challenged Mr. Mason.

"Building rockets!" Shouted the class.

"Do you accept the challenge?" His brown eyes met each face, one after the other, as he united them in the mission, inducing drive and passion within each student. "To do your best, learn everything you can, respect each other, and have fun."

"We WILL do it!" Promised the invigorated students.

Mr. Mason instructed. "First, we have much to learn. We will take this a step at a time, Rocketeers. Put your name on your rocket package—you will leave it in the classroom over the holiday break. You will NOT open them until YOU pass my science rocketry test. When we all have passed, we will begin building. We will all work together to help each other succeed." He handed each student two blank pieces of paper. "Here is paper so you can draw your notes." He opened the rocket science book to read aloud, noting that almost everyone was drawing pictures of the information as they listened.

—

Gentle snow fell as school let out for the two-week winter break. The delicate flakes shimmered and danced as they floated and twirled creating a whispery white scene. The forecast warned of an old-fashioned southern Minnesota blizzard, and all media channels communicated this. Warnings were issued for closed roads due to zero visibility expected by 2 am. There were also echoes of blizzard warnings, urging everyone to stay off the roads as plows, up to five deep, lined up and prepared to tackle the highways.

Blizzards were a neighborhood event that required everyone's readiness.

The townspeople were accustomed to heavy snowfalls, but this storm was expected to be one for the history books. Everyone prepared for the worst, ensuring they and their animals had enough supplies to endure the storm. Ropes were strung between buildings to maintain contact with animals and neighbors, and extra feed and water were replenished and safely stored. This demonstrated the community's resilience and preparedness, which was a source of pride for all.

People hurried to get last-minute supplies and dropped off gifts and goodies. Some enjoyed their final dinners out before staying indoors for days. They would reappear bundled up in wool knit scarves, giant parkas, and leather mittens while holding ice scrapers, brooms, or snow shovels that they had kept inside to clear their way out of their doorways after the snow closed them in. Snowplows were parked facing outward from driveways, and snowblowers were positioned behind garage doors. Slow cookers simmered with soups and stews to be served hot and steaming for famished, chilled-to-the-bone snow removers, snow angel makers, and snowball throwers.

—

As the first snowflakes descended, Trapper, clad in bright orange snow pants and parka, emerged to lead the Riverdale and Harris County emergency road crew. He gathered his team for a comprehensive briefing, assigning each driver a specific area of the town or outskirts for individual action. Together, they studied the town's layout, prioritizing which roads and areas required immediate attention. The task was formidable, but his team was up to the challenge. Each driver took one final test drive in their designated vehicle and area. Once finished, they rested and ate, remaining on standby for Trapper's mass alert text.

—

"Good evening. What brings you into our cozy cafe on such a snowy night," Q greeted a tall, handsome man laughing with a lovely short-haired woman. Their attire was too sophisticated for Riverdale. The gift bags each carried were refined. "May I hang up your coats?"

The woman was dressed in pressed navy slacks, a crisp white blouse, and a wool navy blazer, the precise color of navy pants. Above her right pocket was a US Navy wing lapel pin in what looked like solid gold. The gold matched her officer's cuff links.

"Table for two, please," smiled the man, dressed in pleated wool black trousers and a dark gray cashmere sweater over a Ralph Lauren white polo shirt. Patrons smiled at them as they arrived, they were obviously not strangers to Riverdale.

"Certainly, I have two perfect tables: one by the window or against the back wall, your preference," Q noticed her embroidered emblem.

"The window is perfect," the woman put her finger to her lips and pointed subtly to Trapper and his wife Annie in the booth. "I don't want to reveal my presence yet. Will you play along with me in this surprise?" She turned aside to reveal less of her face, hoping she hadn't been noticed by her parents.

"I am delighted to assist you with your strategy. Follow me," Q lit the table candles, carefully ensuring all the paper snowflakes were safe. "Can I get you something while you get settled?" He pulled out the chair for the woman, her back faced the booth.

"Two glasses of water, please," her smile was incredible smile with perfect white teeth. She mouthed 'stratagem' to her companion and asked Q, "Does Margie still have onion rings?"

"Most certainly, with her secret recipe for fluffy batter. They are lightly fried to golden crispness when you bite into them, but still tender on the inside for perfect texture contrast," answered the young waiter.

"Oh, Q, I can just taste them! It has been ages since I have been home," reminisced the mystery woman as she looked across the table to her companion.

"I do not believe I told you my name yet," pardoned the waiter. "I was getting to that. My name is Q, and I will be your waiter tonight."

"No, my name is Q." Corrected the gentleman.

"Then, sir, you must be Margie's son from Alabama. She was not sure when you would arrive," explained Q.

"Kissy and I ran into each other at the airport car rental and decided to come together. With the blizzard brewing, we are surprising both families before we get shut in." Whispered Kissy.

"They are talking about at least three feet of snow." Q added.

Kissy noticed her mother and father at the far booth. "Those are my parents," she said, tilting her head toward the booth. "I would like to order another plate of onion rings and two cups of hot chocolate with mini marshmallows for both tables." She put her finger to her lips to indicate quiet. "It was my favorite childhood order."

Q lit up as he delivered the water, rolled flatware, and menus. "A fine surprise. How may I continue to play a role in this ruse? I am at your service."

"Deliver the orders together, first to her parents, then leave the other order at our table. We will surprise Kissy's parents first. Then, as we are talking to her parents, run into the kitchen and tell my mom she needs to come out right away to deal with some bad onions," conspired Q, the elder, checking off the plan on his fingers.

"As indicated. I am happy to help," nodded Q. "Would you like to order your meal first?"

"Two cheeseburgers and sweet potato fries," Kissy noted her parents were eating cheeseburgers with fries and drinking water. The onion rings and cocoa could add a nice touch. Her father, Trapper, team leader in emergency orange, would be front line and on active status with the emergency road crew and would be relieved they had arrived before the storm.

———

Zak completed five job cards. Since he knew what was expected and how to do it, he could finish six cards if he chose the more manageable tasks. According to Mantha's rule, all the cards needed to be completed by the end of the week in any order Zak wanted. Job Card Eight was on a yellow index card and was a daily task, which was the dog's favorite.

Shay arrived with red eyes and wet cheeks, Penny instinctively followed her into the bathroom. The door shut. The door locked. Mantha observed and waited for the right time to approach. Shay emerged, face washed, big smile. Either she had kicked herself in the butt to get out of that funk, or Penny had licked her silly.

"Hi Shay. How are you doing?" Mantha gently asked. Shay stood by Pink Bertha, her chin resting on her hands, her elbows on the well-worn wood. Softly, Mantha coaxed, "Can you imagine her first lift-off?"

Shay smiled with soulful eyes. "Perhaps," sealing in whatever pain she held fast.

Q arrived beaming. Shay had seldom seen this expression on her brother. "I met Q, the other Q. The Q who belongs to Margie like I belong to Lindsey, I mean Mom! He was with Kissy."

Mantha whipped around to face Q, eyebrows lifted, "Goodness!"

Sam popped out of his chair, "Q and Kissy are back for the holidays?"

"They are at Dee's. Everyone is celebrating their arrival." Q's voice was unusually animated.

"Is Margie still cooking?" Asked Sam.

"I believe so. It was getting busy. Mom is helping," Q confirmed.

"Cheeseburgers on me!" Shouted Sam as he hunted for his coat.

"French fries for everyone, my treat," called out Mantha. "Let's go! I'll call John."

The large round table seating six fit the Riley crew perfectly and theyu slid the chairs slid closer to make room for John. A welcome with big bear hugs circulated the table as John joined them.

Margie hugged her beloved son, Quintel, who preferred to use his full name only in the courtroom and otherwise went by his nickname, Q.

Kissy was now Captain April Palmquist everywhere, but Riverdale. She and Q were warmly welcomed home! Having beloved adults home for the holidays was important in small towns across the Midwest.

Quintel and Margie sat next to Trapper, while Annie hugged Kissy in the large back booth. The elegant gift bags were opened, and two wooden boxes lay on the table, one olive wood and one made from African ofram wood. Each type of wood held a special family meaning. Margie wore a lovely Ghana hand-loomed Kente scarf and held two open airline tickets in awe.

"When do you think you will come south, Mama?" Quintel asked.

"February might be a nice time or early summer, Q," Margie looked lovingly at the tickets. "Never been to Birmingham, might have to include my best friend or…" She paused, "I could come visit you twice."

"Think about coming at the same time as Mom and Dad." Kissy offered as her mom peaked back into the box with glistening eyes. "Q can drive you to Sarasota to enjoy our Florida beaches."

The Monogram Masters jumped in to help at the cafe and their seats were quickly taken up by Ben and Kate. Shay flipped burgers while Lindsay oven-roasted seasoned fries. Zak carefully carried water or sodas. Q, Lindsay's Quint, named after Quintel, donned his apron and efficiently delivered cheeseburgers. The Monogram Masters ate burgers, fries, and sipped sodas set aside on the long counter as everyone enjoyed the spirited reunion before the coming storm.

—

Trapper checked the radar and sent his mass text the snow was accumulating. The intensity of the storm was three hours away.

Uncle Ben took charge. "Everyone home. Hunker down until this thing is over. Get every vehicle off the road!" He paused. "UNLESS you face an emergency, PLEASE stay home and stay out of our way! In an emergency, call 911 and tell us your route so we can help you quickly. We will keep the area to the hospital cleared as best we can."

Ben kissed Kate. "Katy baby, now go!"

Kate wrapped her arm around Zak. "Staying out of the way is the most important task so the plows and emergency vehicles can get through."

John raised his massive arm. "I'll head over to the hospital to standby for ambulance work. Which specific point would you like me to go to?"

"The hospital garage will be fine, John." Much of Trappers' team had gathered at Dee's Cafe.

"We'll support the plow station," Kissy and Annie volunteered.

"Mantha and I will keep the garage open for drivers. Fuel, beds, and hot coffee will be at Riley's," Sam offered.

"Warmth for drivers, hot drinks, food, and sandwiches to go throughout the storm," announced Margie, "I plan to stay at the cafe."

"We'll help Mom and Margie." said Q. "I stay here with Mama and Lindsay," said Q smiling at their similar thinking.

"I can help Mantha and Sam," offered Zak.

"No, Zak. You will go home and you can take care of Kate," corrected Uncle Ben.

"We can take shifts sleeping. Shay, you, Mom, and Margie take the first sleep shift. Sleep into the morning. The Q's will clean this place and have you covered." Q announced.

Elder Q gave a high five to his mini-me. "We've got this!"

Quintel shooed all the women away to the apartment to sleep, delegating younger Q to join him in the first shift as watchmen and provide support for the drivers. They cleaned the cafe and kept the soups and stews simmering. Dark roast filled the coffee machine, and a mountain of mixed sandwiches wrapped in plastic beckoned from the tray at the ready on the bar. The local grocer had delivered fresh fruit and granola bars. Drivers grabbed refreshments and headed back into the dark to their work. It remained a quiet night, which became two more nights.

—

The blizzard was forecast to bring three feet of blowing and drifting snow that ended up being four. The local plow station was strategically located in the heart of the town where a dedicated team of snowplow drivers anxiously waited. The crew knew they had a challenging task ahead; their duty was to clear the entire town's roads and perimeter to keep them passable for emergency vehicles housed in the adjacent buildings.

The town promptly shut down. It warmed Trapper's heart to have Kissy home for the holidays, but even more so at the plow station, supporting his team and keeping his wife company. He had missed his robust and courageous daughter, now a navy fighter pilot in line for her dream to become a Blue Angel. Having his home team at the station meant the mechanics had access to supplies at Hans Hardware, owned and run by his wife, Annie. Annie had set up a lead rope if it was needed. She had turned on the blue and white holiday lights in the display windows, and she had taken the olive box to the station to share in holiday celebration.

—

The snowplow drivers revved their engines and slowly began navigating the treacherous conditions. Despite the rapidly decreasing visibility and the relentless icy winds lashing against their windows, they pressed on, relying on their years of experience. The sound of metal scraping against pavement echoed through the quiet streets as the team, with unwavering dedication, relentlessly pushed forward.

Mantha strung her rope between the back station door and Sam's back porch to allow access to the house if needed. Sam pulled out a stack of old mattresses, pillows, and blankets from the props for shooting. He lined them up behind the jeep. He and Mantha planned to stay in the garage through the storm and keep the lights on, the gas pumps running, and the drive cleared. There were always motorists who had no business being out in the storm who tried to hobble in.

Mantha made more coffee, turned on the slow cooker, and made sandwiches. Sam left in the 40 Ford and returned fifteen minutes later with a 1952 Willys. His usually open jeep now sported an enclosed, with windows, cab, and plow. *What else didn't she know about Sam?*

Plow drivers encountered obstacles and difficulties and were grateful they had practiced their routes with and without their plows. Preparation was critical. This early practice allowed for out of the box thinking of detours, strategies, and alternative routes. They drove their test patterns with partners who were often family members, discussing approaches as each would handle a twelve-hour shift expected to last three days. During the first flurries, drivers responsible for their route added liquid and salt to areas that could cause the most trouble as the storm descended. They exercised particular care and caution in areas with gusting wind grateful that this storm arrived without freezing rain. They planned to avoid plowing shoulders until after the storm to prevent churning up blinding snow clouds.

Some roads were already impassable, blocked by towering snowdrifts. Others had abandoned vehicles buried underneath layers of snow, a stark reminder of the storm's impact on the community. The team, united in their efforts, coordinated over the radio, sharing information and strategizing the best action. Sam maintained the ham shack. Mantha was added as a dispatcher to the team. Riley's and Rodeo, despite their differences, joined forces to weather the storm. Tow truck drivers were stationed at Rodeo's Franchise to access highway and rural spaces, a testament to the community's support.

Trapper, led the charge. He meticulously carved a path through the blizzard, expertly maneuvering to clear the snow drifts. He was the guiding light for the team, a symbol of dependability amidst the chaos.

As the hours turned into days, the team labored tirelessly, working their 12-hour shifts and taking breaks at Riley Garage, Rodeo's station, or Dee's Cafe. Some could not yet get home and slept in Sam's garage. Mantha now understood why Sam had four extra mattresses on her cot. They were not just for travelers but for neighbors driving miles and miles with their iron down, not usually going over 30 mph. Drivers stated that visibility was so bad they relied on the fire numbers in the middle of the road, which marked the locations of farmsteads when other signs were buried under the drifts.

The storm raged on the second night, and the men and women drove relentlessly. Thankful for the miracles provided over their lifetimes, their community, and the people they loved, Annie and Kissy lit the central servant candle to light the first Hanukkah candle placed in the new menorah. The unusual timing of the holidays in 2024 shared many lights. Divers stopped for hot tea, coffee, or cocoa and took a few gold-wrapped chocolate gelt from the plow station. On the third day, as Annie and Kissy lit the next candle, while Margie and Q lit the Black central candle of Unity in a celebration with the Larkin family on the first night of Kwanzaa at Dee's Cafe. Weary workers grabbed quick cups of soup, coffee, fruit, and sandwiches tied with green, red, and black yarn. Dee's team happily shared details of this celebration that many had not understood. Riley Garage kept its white lights burning throughout the storm while multi-colored lights on the trimmed tree in the Riley office blinked a lighthouse style welcome.

—

Mantha and Sam took turns as drivers fueled and slept on floor mattresses. The hospital road remained open. Dee's Cafe lights remained on, as did Riley's and Rodeo's. Sam slept in his chair, finally waking to get coffee. "I love this time of year when Riverdale comes together to celebrate themes of light and freedom." Tree lights twinkles. "Light brings a sense of unity and peace to everyone."

Mantha gazed at the blinking multicolored tree lights in her front lobby, "I may not follow any specific spiritual beliefs, but I appreciate the beauty and significance of these celebrations. I like seeing people curious and coming together in the spirit of peace. The message of freedom and light transcends religious boundaries, doesn't it?"

"We can all carry different stories and still celebrate our common values." Shared Sam.

"True. So many people are helping each other. The lights remind me to reflect on the miracles I've had. I am alive in a new way." Mantha twirled a plastic icicle hanging on the tree.

"Well said, Mantha. Seeing people from different backgrounds and beliefs free to celebrate and share is heartwarming. It doesn't happen often that these three celebrations of light are this close together." Sam ate a frosted cookie.

"I guess you're right. Christmas, Hanukkah, and Kwanzaa all carry themes of light and freedom."

"They most certainly do." Sam explained, "Christmas symbolizes the light of Christ and freedom for eternal life. Hanukkah celebrates the miracle of triumph over darkness and freedom from oppression. Kwanzaa's lighted kinara represents unity, creativity, and faith. Its seven principles are suitable for everyone.

—

As the storm subsided, the exhausted drivers, their faces radiating with a sense of accomplishment, gathered at the snowplow station. Icicles clung to beards and eyelashes as they diligently cleared and de-iced the machines. They knew their work was far from over, with vast snow piles removed from the middle of the main street and parking lots still ahead. Taking a moment to refuel with hot coffee and hot dogs, they shared stories, inspiring each other with the headway they'd made against the blizzard.

Many shared harrowing stories of narrowly missed hidden vehicles, which were then towed to Riley's. A family had veered off the freeway as driving conditions became too hazardous. They'd gotten stuck in the middle of the county road as Trapper worked to clear it. "Inches. Just inches," he kept, recalling the near tragedy. Ben reported that three people were transported to the hotel, which was overflowing. Stories and tales were shared and would be repeated to inspire future generations. Fortunately, no one died, and there were no fires. Small-town volunteers often held multiple emergency positions, with many county workers also serving in volunteer roles. Trapper sent his team home for a well-earned rest. They took a break, secure in knowing they had made the roads safer for friends, family, and other travelers. Access was provided to first responders, and the path to the hospital and veterinarian was cleared. The remaining heavy snow wasn't going anywhere, but they were no longer in immediate danger. John reported that a baby had been born in the ambulance and that the mother and baby were doing fine at the hospital.

———

Once rested, Trapper and his colleagues would return to widen turn lanes and clear snow from spots without storage space. The dump trucks and loaders were ready to make room for the next storm. Some work would wait until the drivers caught up on sleep—many handled more than one type of emergency vehicle.

The sun's rays created iridescent sparkles and glimmers across the blanket of pure white. Branches hung heavily, laden with mounded curtains of snow. One by one, the citizens of Riverdale emerged from their homes, their snow blowers throwing powder high into the clear, quiet blue sky. Laughter and stories filled the air as neighbors lent each other a helping hand. The world resumed a new routine infused with a different tone. Winter had arrived in full splendor; after three days of hardship and hunkering down, it was time to celebrate, a testament to the community's resilience and the promise of brighter days ahead. Driverst remembered the lights shining from Dee's, the station, and Riley's, and it opened a conversation of different celebrations of light.

—

Before the storm, Q the younger had spent days rummaging through old murder news at the town's library. All his notes and materials were under his bed in a boot box in his room above the cafe. Q had calculated that Margie's Q was in Riverdale at the time of the murder of Emmett Johnson. He had copies of graduation pictures of Quintel, Michael, Kate, Lindsay, and Samantha twenty years ago. They had all graduated together. He knew from the resemblance Samantha was now Mantha. Kate was Ms. Jordan, Lindsay was his mom, and Quintel sat across from him. He thought he knew, but he was unsure of Michael.

Quintel, now an attorney in Alabama, noticed his quiet preoccupation. "You are deep in thought about something, Q? May I ask what it is?"

Younger Q contemplated trusting this stranger with the information he held in the strictest confidence.

Quintel watched Q's eyes lower as they moved with his thoughts. He listened for the sigh, hoping the young man would talk. It could be a long night without any discussion.

"Did you know Michael Johnson in your high school class?" Q, had a captive audience—Q the elder. Quintel was his age when all this happened, and they had plenty of hours alone.

Quintel tilted his head, "In what way?"

"I read in the library archives that his father died when he was my age. I wondered how that affected him?" Queried Q, "What happened to him?"

"I don't know what happened to him. I know he moved south with his mother, Sally. It was a sorrowful time in our little town. We both went different directions and on to college. I heard he might have been a medic for a while in the military, but that's all I know," replied Quintel.

"What was he like in high school?" Q pressed, "... after the tragedy?"

"He was our quarterback before a four-wheeler accident. His mother didn't want him to play football after his father died. I often felt slighted by him; he was the wolf always on the hunt, and often, I ended up being the comforting, understanding friend to girls he had offended in some way. He went through girlfriends like a change of clothes. They were merely decorations for his ego. He had the hots for your mom once, but she eventually got rid of him. Mantha didn't want a thing to do with him. Kate hung on his arm like his trophy. A lot of girls were taken with him for their reasons," Quintel paused. "He and I were quite different."

Younger Q listened intently, gaining names and attributes. Hesitant to pursue further questioning, he wondered how to switch the subject. "How do you know, Kissy? She was not in your class."

"Everyone knows everyone in a small town. You already know that. Kissy was a little girl when I graduated high school. I worked for her grandfather at Hans Hardware and spent time with her family. She was an incredible youngster who became an even more capable and dynamic woman," shared Quintel.

"She seems nice," Q's voice drifted, socially expended from the day. His whole being felt empty. He rested his head on his crossed forearms on the table and fell asleep.

—

The winter storm had transformed the landscape, creating a dynamic scene of snow-sculpted terrain. As the fierce winds howled, they reshaped the snow into ever-changing formations, carving out miniature canyons and mountains across the yard. The once-towering wood piles dwindled, their contents likely used to fuel fires against the biting cold.

Zak observed this winter ballet from the safety of his window, mesmerized by the swirling snow and the constant reshaping of the drifts. The billowing snow mirrored his own turbulent thoughts, as he grappled with the weight of his secrets. His mind, like the storm outside, was in constant motion, analyzing and reanalyzing the details of what he knew.

As night fell, the rhythmic rumble of snowplows punctuated the silence, their lights cutting through the darkness as they worked to clear the snow-choked roads. Zak found himself momentarily distracted by the idea of one day operating one of those powerful machines, imagining the satisfaction of carving paths through the snow-laden streets. However, Zak quickly refocused on his current situation. While the allure of driving a snowplow was tempting, he reminded himself that he had a more pressing mission at hand. The nature of this mission remained unclear, but it was evident that it occupied a significant portion of his thoughts, competing with the mesmerizing winter scene unfolding before him.

The aroma of Kate's spiced apple-cranberry cider wafted through the house as she called Zak to join her by the Christmas tree in the great room. The fireplace crackled with life, its dancing flames casting a warm, mesmerizing glow that filled the space with comfort and cheer. Zak had embraced the holiday spirit, helping Aunt Kate adorn the porch with festive garlands and twinkling lights. Uncle Ben had bestowed upon him the honor of crowning the tree with its star, a task Zak had executed with pride. Afterward, Ben had entrusted him with another responsibility: replenishing the wood butler to keep the fire well-fed.

As Zak descended the stairs, he felt a sense of contentment wash over him. The prospect of two weeks free from classes stretched before him, promising ample time for work, investigation, and camaraderie with the Monogram Masters. The recent blizzard had forced his parents to delay their holiday visit, with hopes of joining for the New Year's celebration instead. Zak found himself at peace with this turn of events, appreciating the cozy arrangement he shared with his aunt and uncle.

Settling into a comfortable spot near the tree, Zak wrapped his hands around the warm mug of cider. The tart sweetness of apples mingled with the spicy notes of cinnamon and cloves, creating a perfect complement to the festive atmosphere. As he sipped the comforting brew, Zak allowed himself to relax, savoring the moment and the promise of adventures to come.

As Zak finished his cider, he bid goodnight to Aunt Kate before heading upstairs to his room. The wind continued to howl outside, accompanied by the distant rumble of snowplows clearing the roads. Once in the privacy of his bedroom, Zak's relaxed demeanor shifted to one of focused determination. He retrieved his notepad and a journal marked "Confidential" from their hiding place. Illuminated by the soft glow of his lantern, Zak began to work, his mind racing with thoughts and theories.

He meticulously drew maps, complete with intricate diagrams and figures of people, each detail carefully considered and placed. Employing a technique he had learned from San, Zak used a cube labeled with the classic investigative questions: Who, What, Where, When, Why, and How. He dedicated a blank page to each question, jotting down his ideas and observations. Speaking softly to himself, he found that vocalizing his thoughts helped clarify his thinking process. As he worked, a sense of urgency crept over him. Despite the quiet of the night and the comfort of his surroundings, Zak couldn't shake the feeling that time was slipping away. His investigation, whatever its nature, seemed to carry a weight that pressed upon him, driving him to uncover answers before it was too late.

WHO - Who was involved and could have done the murder?

WHEN - When did it happen? He turned the cube…

WHERE - Where did it happen?

WHAT - What exactly happened? He turned the cube again.

WHY - Why did it happen? Zak hated the WHY questions. He attempted them anyway.

HOW - How did it happen?

Zak immersed himself in the old sheriff's notes, meticulously categorizing each fragment and sentence. His pages filled with words and sketches as he worked late into the night, eventually succumbing to exhaustion.

TAP TAP TAP.

Zak jolted awake, his heart pounding. Fearing Aunt Kate's unexpected entrance, he frantically surveyed his room, strewn with evidence of his late-night sleuthing. In a panic, he shoved the papers under his mattress and tiptoed across the room to stash away the journal and lantern. WHIRRR… RUMBLE… The lights flickered ominously as Zak froze in place.

TAP… TAP TAP…

He startled again, only to see yellow spinning lights accompanied by the harsh clang of metal on asphalt roaring past his window. Hastily, he tucked the journal into a drawer. Moments later, blue and red flashing lights pierced the darkness, a siren wailing in the distance. Glancing at his digital clock, Zak noted the time: 0400. With trembling hands, he switched off the lantern and carefully returned it to its hiding place.

TAP TAP TAP TAP.

Relief washed over Zak as he realized the source of the tapping—an old oak branch swaying in the wind, randomly striking his window pane. The immediate crisis averted, Zak's mind returned to the larger mystery at hand. Despite the late hour and his close call, the unsolved puzzle loomed large, demanding his attention and refusing to let him rest until he unraveled its secrets.

—

The snowplow team's collective effort paid off. On such nights, the whole system of highway workers and first responders knit tightly together, ready to overlap jurisdictions if needed. Ben hoped most people continued to stay home as the snowstorm transformed the landscape into a scene of daunting white windrows, towering over the center lane of the village, surpassing the height of the first story of local buildings. Parking spaces had become driving lanes, a temporary solution until the center windrow was cleared, a testament to the severity of the situation.

On his way home, Sheriff Ben noticed Zak's light on, a figure hunched over his desk. *'Why is Zak up at this hour?'* He mused, his concern for Zak was evident. Ben followed Trapper as he completed his final run to 'inspect what he expected' from his men running through the night.

Sheriff Ben kept a safe distance, his eyes on the plow's mirrors. The fewer people, the easier his job. Unexpected highway conditions with low visibility could move a plow truck into the nearest lane without any notice, especially if ice formed on the pavement underneath. Over the years, he had too often come upon a four-wheel drive vehicle that had been decimated after being crashed into by a plow that hit a snowdrift, moving at 20 mph. He kept a keen eye out for snowbound vehicles in the ditch or embedded in a snowbank on the side of the road. A running engine could block a tailpipe with the exhaust fumes to the outside, bringing the carbon monoxide inside the car. In a matter of minutes, the carbon monoxide could reach lethal levels.

Sheriff Ben, his deputies, and the entire first response team kept their eyes peeled for cars stranded or plowed over, often saying quick prayers for 'passenger calming and wisdom to turn off the engine.'

Dispatch had gotten a call from a stranded vehicle. Ben, with a few more men and a tow truck, was on the way to dig it out. 'Crunch-Scratch'. Another spin-out needed attending. *'Check with Zak later. What is he doing with my lantern light?'*

—25—
TEAM SPIRIT

Once the streets were clear, Riverdale came alive. Over the winter break, Kate remained busy with the Larkin fundraising efforts. She was determined to raise enough money to build them a house. While she worked with the event committee, Doc stole credit for the Rocket Launch event. He claimed he wanted it superbly done as it was 'his' idea.'

Zak slid down the banister and jumped off into the entry, landing on his bright red shoes and face-to-face with his high school principal, there IN HIS HOME! His day dimmed.

"I can't believe you let him get away with those shenanigans in your home, Kate," Doc scolded.

Zak grabbed a cold turkey leg from the fridge and took a swig of his lactose-free milk from the carton. He waggled the leg, took a bite, and gave Doc an 'I dare you' Cheshire cat grin. "Gotta go to work, Aunt Kate. Gonna grab a bite here and see you later."

The six ladies at the kitchen table drinking coffee and enjoying small delicate cakes gaped as Zak reached across them to scoop up a handful of the pretty delicate tea sandwiches and iced cookied Kake had made. He looked directly at Doc. "Thanks, Aunt Kate. These look great," he chirped, grabbing his coat and carefully shutting the door.

The door swung open, "I forgot. I finished all your cards. The wood is done. I shoveled the walk, and the porch, and the steps, and the path to the trash. I emptied the dishwasher and took out the trash. Back in a bit, Ka-Ka-Katydid." He winked and took another bite of the turkey leg. Then he disappeared while the coffee clutch women smiled approvingly at the large amount of work this energetic teen had accomplished, in addition to his amusing dramatics for Doc, who'd scolded his aunt. Touche.

———

Loud Christmas music filled the halls of the Memory Care Home. Aromas of balsam, fir, cinnamon, and apple lingered from doorway to doorway, changing with each room as different residents chose the fragrance they loved. Shay delivered the bedtime snacks to everyone except Ann. Staff had shared she was failing. Shay took a deep breath, steadied herself, and held out the apple juice and iced snowman cookie. "Ann, it is Shay. Would you like me to read to you today?" The woman stared blankly ahead. Shay touched her frail hand and tried again. "Would you like some juice? Ann, I brought you a cookie. I picked out the best one just for you. It is a snowman with blue buttons and a red scarf." The woman stared straight ahead. The presents delivered by a ranting man remained untouched.

Shay put the cookie to Ann's lips. "Would you like a little bite? Can I read to you?" There was no movement. Shay held her breath, then took out the memory book she was making. It was open to Ann's memories of her beloved husband. Shay began reading aloud, "Emmett, oh my dear dear Emmett. We had such fun. Such joy we brought each other. I look to the day to again rest in your arms, to kiss your lips…for you to wipe away my tears." Shay had read this passage so many times. Each time, Ann lit up as if seeing her Emmett. Ann did not move. Shay tried another passage. "Happy was our best dog. Happy tried to save him. I tried to save him. Oh, how I miss Happy." Somebody had printed a vertical message on the page in perfect capital letters. 'He's dead, and so is your damn dog.' Shay was stunned; she had not written that.

The journal she had penned with love, on Ann's behalf to help her embrace lost memories and smile, had been targeted with pure hatred.

Shay remembered the conversation she had overheard before the storm, and her stomach turned. She set the snowman and small juice on the table and gently kissed Ann on the forehead. Shay knew it wasn't allowed, but she wanted Ann to feel love, to know that she mattered and was important. Shay whispered, "Ann, you are a good person. I hope you get to find Emmett soon." Ann was still. Shay felt nausea rise from her gut. The area over her heart burned. The angry words she'd overheard ripped through her mind: "I took care of so many problems. You have no idea what I did to improve your life!" Something was dangerously wrong. The man. The rude message. The unopened presents. Ann's paralysis. It all felt so dark, so evil. The trauma was too much.

Shay ran out of the room, removed her apron, checked out her volunteer cards, and pulled on her boots and warm coat. She threw her shoes in her backpack and ran. Shay ran through the deep snow drifts, the pressure from the weight of the snow making each step harder. She ran up one side of the twelve-foot windrow and down the other—up and down—up and down—up and down. Finally, Shay bolted through Riley's garage door, followed by Penny, and into the bathroom, locked the door, sobbing.

Zak saw her arrive. "Shay, are you okay," he asked gently outside the door. "Can I come in?"

Shay unlocked the door and opened it to let Zak in. She shut it quickly and locked it again.

Mantha heard the door lock and put her ear on the door to listen.

Shay's head fell on Zak's shoulder, her body pulsating. "He was so mean to her! He was…cruel!! He—sucked out her glimmers like he wanted her to die."

"Who was mean, Shay?" Zak whispered gently worried for Shay.

"I don't know, I was scared to look. He, he, he said, 'you can't come home. You can't come because of the storm.' And she pleaded, 'Please, let me come home. Let me come home for Christmas.' And he said, 'I brought all your presents, and you can open them here. I have no time for this.' And she begged, 'Don't leave me, don't leave me, my Emmett darling.' And he said, 'Why do you care? He's dead. I took care of that issue long ago.' And there was a crack like a slap on wood. Then I heard his footsteps turn, and I was scared, so I ran to the bathroom until I knew he was gone. I was terrified and didn't know what to do. Now, she is a statue. Even our stories and the snowman cookies didn't make her eyes light up. It's like she's barely there in her body. She's… I don't know where she is!" Shay hiccuped between sobs and gulps, recalling the horrible scene, shaking and unable to breathe or hold her body still.

Zak held her carefully. He'd never held a girl. Most girls thought he was too weird. "That sounds mean evil, Shay. I bet he broke her heart."

"That mean man broke MY heart, too, Zak!" Her wailing grew louder, and she clutched Zak's shirt angrily.

Mantha knocked. "Hey, are you two okay in there?"

"I'm here with her, Mantha," Zak answered. "I can handle this." His voice was lower than usual. He felt the urge to protect flood up through his veins.

"I'll stand by if you need me." Mantha heard Zak's tone and recognized what it meant.

"That mean man took her life away. She only had old memories left. I was saving them for her. I fed her glimmers. She and I laughed and shared her long-agos. He wrecked our journal. He wrote on my pages, 'he's dead, and so is your damn dog.' Why would anyone hurt someone who has nothing left? Why wouldn't he let her go home? Make it make sense!" Her voice cracked with disbelief as she sobbed, aching over the sheer heartlessness she'd witnessed.

"Who did this, Shay?" Mantha's calm voice reached out from the other side of the door.

"I don't know, I only heard his voice," she stuttered as Zak gave her toilet paper to wipe her eyes and nose. Zak unlocked the door to let Mantha in.

Mantha knelt, putting her arm around the girl. "Shay, we can't stop all the bad in the world. We can only do our part with good. You did so much good with the journal you made. Do you know that love is the most potent weapon you have? Nothing can stop love, or kindness, or goodness. Shay, you are all of those things and more. You are patient and gentle, faithful to your friends, you bring peace to difficult situations, and you give me back my joy along with Zak," Mantha counseled. "You are a meliorist who believes in people and the good they can do to change the world. Evil may try to stop us through fear. But fear is not strong enough to win against kindness and goodness. Our kindness and goodness are too powerful. Shay, you keep you."

Sam got up from his chair to check what was happening, "Hey, when Q shows up, Mantha and I have a surprise." He tried to change whatever subject was so crushing.

Penny licked Shay's face. "Here's a towel to wash your face, Shay," Zak offered as the three emerged from the bathroom. John Mason and Q entered, surprised at Shay's disheveled appearance and puffy eyes.

———

Sam held two wrapped packages and PINK BERTHA. "Gather round," he gestured as he sat back into his chair. "John, will you take one of these packages from me?" John picked up the smaller box. "Well, that most certainly is a fine choice. Q: Would you step forward, and John, would you hand him the box?"

"Thank you," Q said, gently holding the box.

"Open it! Open it!" Shay was getting her glow back as she saw Q's anticipation.

"Go ahead," Mantha smiled, hoping to lighten the mood. Q carefully lifted off each piece of tape so as not to hurt the wrapping paper.

"I just love surprises!" Shay's sniffling passed as the excitement of the mystery brought her into the present.

Q's eyes widened. He pulled his lips over his teeth, breathing deeply through his nose. His eyes watered. He took another breath. "It's an Estes E2X Ascender Rocket kit with a projected maximum height of over 3000 feet when a booster is used. You have got to be kidding me." His face radiated.

"Zak, it is your turn," Sam handed him the bigger of the two boxes.

Zak held the box. He did not know what to do as he was unsure how to get the paper off without hurting whatever was inside, plus Shay could use diversion. "Shay, would you open it for me?"

"For real?"

"Yes," Zak watched her tear away the paper.

"Do you see what it is? It is a Super Bertha!" Shay cradled it in her arms and tenderly gave it to the wonderstruck Zak.

"Pro Series II Super Big Bertha, to be exact, Zak. It can fly up to 1200 feet. The Super Big Bertha is a classic design, originally released around 1990. You can launch a piece of rocketry history with this! I can't believe it. It is a Pro Series." Q was excited.

"Q, you are a walking encyclopedia," Mr. Mason was impressed.

"And then some, we've only scratched his surface," Sam responded.

"Shay, come here," Mantha held Pink Bertha. Shay stepped forward. "Shay, you have shown determination and creativity in helping to bring Pink Bertha alive. She belongs to you."

The boys cheered.

"Can I help them build the other rockets?" Shay asked.

"Of course, you can help us," Q and Zak agreed.

Shay gently rocked Bertha. "You are mine, girl. You are all mine."

———

Mr. Mason wanted to open the directions to one of the new rockets and dig in but held back, "What are the building plans, guys?"

"Can we start tomorrow?" Asked Q.

"How about tonight?" Zak jumped in.

"Now that is my kind of guy," Mr. Mason pointed at Zak while Mantha laughed.

"What are your work hours, Monogram Masters?" Asked Sam.

"I'm off tomorrow," said Q.

"Me too!" Shared Shay.

"I'll be here," Zak announced.

"Let's do teams," suggested John, breaking two toothpicks. "Zak and Q are the team captains." He marked two picks with a red marker and two unmarked wood. He hid them in his bear paw hand. "Who is the red team?"

Zak raised his hand. "Okay, Shay, pick first, but don't look." Shay drew a wooden stick.

"Your turn, Sam, don't look." Sam drew his stick.

"Mantha?" John hid one stick in his hand. "Open your hands."

"Red," said Mantha.

"Wood!" Sam reported.

"Red" Called Shay.

"Must be wood," said John. "We've got our teams. Zak, Mantha, and Shay are the Super Bertha Red Team. Q, Sam, and I are the E2X Ascender Rocket Wood Team. Let the games begin. I'll bring another folding table in the morning. What time?"

"10 a.m.?" suggested Mantha. "Give Sam and me some time for coffee alone with our dog."

"Yeah! Great!" Agreed the Monogram Masters.

"Can I keep Pink Bertha safe here?" Shay.

"Of course, you can," Sam replied as he stretched. "I'll see you tomorrow. Penny and I are going to bed. Good night." He departed out the back door and wound down the deep path Zak had carefully hand-shoveled until the old man showed him how to use the snowblower. The floodlight created a wonderland of glistening crystals. Sam shook his head. "Unbelievable. Penny, go take a run."

He watched as the dog bounded around a fantastic snow blown labyrinth of paths between the back of the garage and the rear of the house. Sam had wondered what had taken Zak so long, as he had used up the whole gas tank of the snowblower. Sam left the flood light on to get a look from the second floor of his home. He climbed the stairs and stepped out on the porch balcony. Penny's walking path was quite a creative piece of art. He might get Zak to walk it with a pedometer in the morning. He thought of Shaun. He thought of Kevin. He was grateful for his third chance with Zak.

"Thank you." He quietly looked up to the starlit heavens.

——

The contest at Riley's garage between the red and wood rocket-building teams was a tie, and three rockets stood proudly on Sam's workbench anticipating launches.

The wood team, consisting of Q, Sam, and John, would have completed their rocket days earlier if Q had not accepted Sam's added challenge of building two launch pads in the shop. Q was elated learning to use machines that whirred, spun, and drilled. Then John challenged Q to research and build an altitude tracker. The altitude tracker sent Q to the library to discover what he needed to understand and develop the mathematics involved. Two days later, he returned to the station holding his design.

"John!" Q called out. Everyone had ceased addressing the massive man as Mr. Mason in the station's privacy. "I have the altitude tracker."

Q held up his plastic green protractor from geometry and tied some fishing line to the washer Sam had given him earlier. "All I need is a good measuring tape and a stopwatch," he announced.

John reached into his pocket and held up his infamous stopwatch. "Stopwatch. Done deal. We can use this."

"What's your plan?" Inquired Sam, handing him a hundred-foot construction measuring tape wheel.

Q beamed, "I tried to figure out how to use the supplies I had on hand. I developed this cool method and believe I can track rocket altitude using a protractor, fishing line, and a washer. It may not be as accurate as the ones you can buy, but I believe it's a simple yet effective way to calculate the rocket's height."

"That sounds interesting, Q." Sam reached for the line and the washer. "So, this is why you needed that washer. Please explain to me how this method works."

"It is a simple mechanical approach. First, I attach a long piece of fishing line to the rocket. Then, I tie the washer to the other end of the line." Q paused. John put his hand to his chin.

"I see," said Sam, intrigued with his ingenuity. "But how does this setup help track the rocket's altitude?"

Q continued making eye contact with Sam. "Well, as the rocket launches into the sky, the fishing line will unwind from the protractor. We can calculate the rocket's height by measuring the angle the line makes with the protractor."

"Ah, I understand. But how do you calculate the altitude using this method?" This kid's mind was so far ahead of his school record status.

"Great question, John!" Q was excited. "So, before launching the rocket, I calibrate the protractor by setting it at a known angle, like 45 degrees. I mark that angle on the protractor. The fishing line unwinds, pulling the washer downward when the rocket goes up. I watch the protractor and observe the angle made by the fishing line."

"And how does the angle help determine the altitude?" John pressed, captivated by this young man's thought process.

"The angle is crucial. I can calculate the rocket's height or altitude using mathematics and basic trigonometry. I measure the length of the fishing line that unwound from the protractor and then use the trigonometric functions, specifically the tangent function, to find the rocket's vertical distance or altitude." Q raised his hands, palms up by his shoulders. "It's that simple."

John glanced at Sam, thinking that most people would need to study what Q had just said! "Why are you only in Algebra, Q? Your math skills are beyond those basics."

"That is a harder question and one without a simple answer. I believe my conversational and social skills are lacking, and unless you know me and I trust you, I do not speak my mind. I contribute solely based on my needs. Most people have no patience for the details that I think are necessary." Q looked away as he spoke, his shoulders drooped.

"What you figured out is quite ingenious! It's amazing how you found a way to calculate altitude with a plastic protractor and a bit of math." Sam said.

John added, "I've watched you tutor Zak for the first hour. You are quite the inventive teacher."

Q's lips curved into a timid smile, "Thank you. I love finding creative solutions like this. It will make tracking rocket altitude accessible. I can build problem-solving skills and understand explanations for mathematical concepts as I practice. My greatest joy is teaching someone else how to find solutions for themselves. I will never give up. If the student doesn't understand, it is the teacher's shortcoming, who hasn't yet found a way to reach the student's mind. Mr. Mason, you exemplify that responsibility using your plethora of teaching techniques."

"Calling me John here is okay, Q. I want you to go to the library to research Arduino Boards and Rocketry. I think you will find it very compelling."

Q looked at their unfinished rocket and the red team's progress.

"Don't worry, our rocket will be ready in time," John reassured.

Still bundled in his parka, Q pulled out his gloves. "All right, I'll be back!" He yelled as he ran out the door on a new space mission.

"He's a cut above the rest at Riverdale High," John shared with Sam, sipping his coffee. "His intellect is something else."

"He is, and we are blessed to see that intellect start to take off along with these rockets." Sam placed two bullet fragments by John next to another almost identical fragment. "What do you see?"

John picked up both bullets, rotating each. "40 caliber, same manufacturer, probably a handload."

"Exactly." Sam raised his eyebrow.

"Where did you get this one?" John asked.

"Had it in MY box."

-26-
WRONG IMPRESSIONS

oc lingered after the Rocket event coffee klatch ladies left for their respective homes. "I don't think there is anyone as qualified as you, Kate, to do this fundraiser with me." He said with the cunning of a master manipulator. "Could we have breakfast tomorrow at Dee's Cafe? The transcripts and earlier educational history regarding your nephew are back."

"Tell me," Kate replied, wondering what results the golden envelope with signed consent forms held.

"I believe it is better professionally if I review it carefully first." He reached out and pushed back her hair. "I will lay out the details so you can present them to Ben in a way that he will understand." Doc lifted her chin with his hand lovingly. He leaned in just as the door burst open.

It was Zak. "What are you doing here? Where are the ladies? Get out of Uncle Ben's house NOW!"

"Zak, it's not how it looks." Corrected Aunt Kate nervously. "We were just talking about you."

"Of course, YOU were!" Hollered Zak, stomping up the steps to his room as Doc slithered out the back door. He growled, threatening under his breath, "You'll be sorry." Guests always went out the front.

Zak was angrier than angry. He wanted to tear his room apart, throw everything around, and break something. He had a new pile of wood he had helped Uncle Ben split with the log splitter between holidays from trees hauled in after the storm. He ran outside without his coat or gloves. He stacked that heap of wood in his stocking feet, finishing the entire pile. Energy expended, he pulled off his wet, snowy socks with mini snowballs frozen onto the sock fabric and flung them across the kitchen, leaving them where they landed for Aunt Kate to pick up. He didn't care if she slipped in the melting puddle of wood, water, and mud.

He was about to run up the stairs when he heard sobbing. Aunt Kate sounded almost like Shay had earlier in the day. He put his fist up to knock and offer help as he had done for Shay but thought better of it and went upstairs to sleep, wishing he could cuddle Sam's dog, Penny.

Zak sat on his bed, bare feet dangling, his toes stinging from the cold. The tips of his toes were white, and the rest of his feet were bright red. The pain of potential frostbite kept him from making a mess of the entire room. Besides, it was Uncle Ben's room, which he shared. His uncle had done nothing to deserve this anger.

Zak paced back and forth, hoping Aunt Kate was sad because she finally got caught. "Aunt Kate badgered me for cheating when I was only looking for Q. But she did more than look! I saw her from the containers. It was a lot more than just looking! I saw her with the big gold envelope through the binoculars across the field. And this. THIS! This was more than looking." The pressure of his thoughts burst into desperate screams; "I hate you, Aunt Kate! I hate you!" Hurting and feeling the sting of helpless tears burn in his eyes, he wiped them futilely as they coursed down his cheeks, wrapped himself tightly in the cocoon of his blanket, and shut down into a hard sleep.

—

The smell of fried beef steaks and baked potatoes woke him. He heard Uncle Ben's laughter with Kate. They sounded happy. *'Oh, if he only knew,'* thought Zak, with a heavy chest and sick stomach. Zak pulled out the notebook he was keeping on the questionable murder. He opened up to WHO with names like Emmett, Sam, Margie, Michael, and Sally. Zak saw Trapper, the snow plow driver, listed with his wife, Annie, and daughter, Kissy. He saw the best friends of Kevin Abbott, the man imprisoned for murder. Those friends were Big Q and his sister, Tasha. Zak thought about Sally and her husband, Emmett. That was the same name as Ann's husband. Shay knows her from the nursing home! Maybe it was a popular name way back then. He would ask Q to sleuth it in the library for him. Maybe Q could get more information from the old records. They had taken a break from their secret investigation to build their rockets.

"Zak, dinner time!" Uncle Ben called from the bottom of the stairs.

The table never had a tablecloth and candles, but it did tonight! Ben poured two glasses of red wine, giving one to Kate. Zak's aunt placed a large green salad with pomegranate seeds on the table. She set down a bowl of sour cream and a red jello salad. Aunt Kate avoided making eye contact with Zak.

"Thank you, Uncle Ben. This looks amazing!" Zak reached for two fresh, steaming whole wheat rolls to slather with butter, again in a dish and not wrapped in paper.

"Thanks goes to Kate," Ben looked lovingly at his wife. "She did all of this: the planning, the shopping, the cooking, and the serving. I'm only doing the starving and the eating!" He put up his finger to stop Zak from biting the hot bun. "First, we say grace." With a wink, he put up his finger again. Ben clasped his hands and began. "Lord, In a world where so many are hungry, may we eat this food with humble hearts. May we share this time with the joyful presence of mind in a world where so many are lonely? Amen."

"Now can I say 'grace," Zak asked.

"Now you say, amen," corrected Uncle Ben.

"Whose a man?" Asked Zak.

Uncle Ben laughed as Kate ate silently. "'Amen' means 'it is true.' When we end our prayers with amen, we believe that God hears them and will answer them in His time. By saying 'amen,' we believe that everything we pray for, praise God for, and express joy or pain about will conform to God's will, not ours."

"So, do you believe in God?" Asked Zak, chewing his hot roll.

"Yes, do you?" Uncle Ben returned the question, reaching to scoop out some gelatin.

"I never saw God. I never talked to God. And God's never talked to me," Zak shrugged. "So, how do I know?"

"You know, by loving yourself and your neighbor," smiled Uncle Ben, raising his wine glass in a toast. "To know God is to love each other as we would love ourselves." He clinked Zak's milk glass to his and Kate's wine glass. She had not picked it up. "Don't like the wine, Kate?"

"Don't feel like drinking," she replied flatly. "How was your day, Ben?"

Zak loved listening to all of Uncle Ben's stories. There had been spin-outs and ditch dives. He'd had to put a couple of neighbors in jail to cool down their tempers and sober them up from a drunken fight. The local paper had nothing on the scoops from Uncle Ben; he never shared names, he always shared with love.

"Uncle Ben, can I ask you a question?" Kate took a long, slow, deep breath and filled a glass with water and ice, mentally preparing for what might come.

"When was the last murder in Riverdale?" Zak asked as Kate breathed a sigh of relief that the teen had digressed. Zak noticed her sigh but decided her news could wait. In the city and at his former schools, Zak had been repeatedly accused of misdeeds and mistakes and of causing trouble of one kind or another by being in the wrong spot at the wrong time. This once, he decided not to call her out in front of Ben. Instead, he would keep careful watch.

"As far as I know, we've only had two murders in Riverdale, and both involved the same family," Ben shared. "I have an old journal upstairs. Let me go up and get it. It's in the desk drawer in your room." Ben jogged up the stairs. Zak was thankful he had carefully put everything back right where it belonged. Ben quickly returned, holding the book that was marked Confidential.

"It says confidential. Can I look at it with you?"

Ben opened up about the murder of Emmett Johnson. "Do you remember when Doc Johnson died, Kate? I was away in college and then in the military. Weren't you a cheerleader when that happened? A little birdie told me you dated Michael."

"I'm having breakfast at Dee's Cafe tomorrow with him. Would you like to join us?" Kate flicked back her hair like the redhead had done in school. The gesture struck a wrong note with Zak, and it bothered him.

"Go ahead, I have reports to write during that time," dismissed Ben. "Fill me in with the details later. I heard on the grapevine that he's now in charge of the Rocket Committee for the Graduation Challenge and the Larkin fundraiser finances."

Zak tried not to spit his milk across the table. Uncle Ben snapped his head toward Zak. "Zak, are you alright?"

"Just …swallowed wrong," Zak mumbled, wiping his mouth on his sleeve. "Could I look at the book? I love to solve mysteries."

Kate's eyes widened, but Ben laughed, "No harm in that. Cases were closed years ago. If you find something you think is missing, let me know. It was before my time as Sheriff. Looks like some good bedtime reading."

"Wow, Uncle Ben, thank you," Zak gushed, accepting the Confidential notebook. "I will take GOOD care of this."

—

That night before, Shay drew pictures, wrote poems, and created origami animals. She longed to make up new happy stories with Ann about her beloved Emmett. She hoped her new creations would bring the woman back from the trauma that had locked her inside of herself.

Shay rose early, donning her winter attire before stepping out into the crisp Minnesota morning with her shoebox of paper treasure. The aftermath of the storm had transformed the landscape into a breathtaking winter wonderland. A pristine blanket of powdery snow covered every surface, creating an atmosphere of serene beauty and tranquility.

She walked by the Dale river taking her time to marvel at the snow-laden trees, their branches bowing under the weight of their white burden, resembling intricate ice sculptures. Fallen branches, now cloaked in snow, formed whimsical shapes that seemed to welcome her as she passed. The vast expanse of untouched white stretched as far as the eye could see, evoking a sense of purity and renewal.

The morning sun's rays danced across the snow-covered landscape, causing ice crystals to sparkle like countless diamonds. This ethereal display of light created a magical ambiance that filled Shay with wonder. "I am a flicker," she twirled, embracing the moment's joy. She fell backward into the snow making an angel.

With a heart full of plans and ideas, Shay bounded into the station, eager to transform Ann's loneliness into joy. She envisioned each thoughtful gift becoming a heartwarming story, reminding Ann of the enduring power of love and resilience. Shay's mission was clear: to reignite a spark of life within Ann, proving that even in the coldest of seasons, warmth and connection could flourish.

"Good morning, you're here early!" Mantha rubbed her eyes, holding her first mug of morning coffee.

"May I have more paper, Mantha? I used everything up at Dee's," Shay asked politely.

Mantha removed a ream from under the counter. "Will this do?" She offered generously.

"Oh, goodness!" Shay exclaimed. "Yes!" Her eyes wide with imagination. Super Bertha assembly table. Pink Bertha guarded Zak's rocket.

"What are you making?" Mantha watched Shay take rusted scissors, broken crayons, and short pencils from her old cargo pants pockets.

"Making glimmers for Ann. Maybe the lights went out inside her, but I can give her some of my shine. I will tape snowflakes all over her room! I am making animal and picture cards to put into our special book. Then, I will make up stories from what she tells me." Shay grinned.

"That's very sweet," Shay impressed Mantha because she took such joy in fixing things. "Could an old warrior help you make some glimmers for Ann?"

"You're not old," Shay scolded. "I think you're pretty."

Mantha stared forward in a hundred-yard stare, scanning the garage. "Mantha!" Shay clapped her hands as she had seen nurses do with patients in Memory Care. Mantha shook her head. Shay did not skip a beat. "I think you are beautiful, and so does John."

Mantha smiled her crooked smile. "You think so?"

"I know so!" The girl grabbed her scissors and started cutting out a snowflake. "Here, take my scissors and make some snowflakes."

"It's right-handed," said Mantha, softly as her voice caught in her throat. She looked down, feeling her face flush with nerves.

"So?" Challenged the girl, holding out the scissors. "My mom says where there's a will, there's a way. You can do it."

It took four crumpled snowflakes before a glimmer emerged with a full six-sided, ready-to-hang snowflake.

"Way to go, Mantha!" Shay raised her right hand for a high two-five.

—

Kate arrived for breakfast as Lindsay greeted Doc with a sullen nod and gave her a sly smile. "Hi Kate, what brings you in today?"

"Doc and I have some things to review before discussing the graduation rocket launch," smiled Kate. "Could we have that back booth?"

"Of course, you can since I don't see anyone sitting in it. Dontcha love that flier Zak made about the rocket project he came up with? We have three of them posted in our cafe. Got one in the front window," she pointed, "and entry." She turned while pointing again, almost swiping Doc on the nose. "Oh, and I put one up by the restrooms. Everyone is talking about it. Zak's idea is brilliant!" Lindsay chattered, not paying attention or looking for a response, as she escorted Doc and Kate to the back booth. She was one to chat but not converse. She knew Doc was an expert in deception.

The waitress spoke from years working at Dee's Cafe, beginning her tenth year in high school. She had more knowledge of the town than the newspaper, but her status did not provide her credibility. Lindsay played with her words, determined to make her point. She poked a piece of chewing gum into her mouth for good measure. "Zak's idea even made the paper. I LOVE THAT KID!" Lindsay put down two mugs of coffee.

Doc glared at her. Lindsay knew she held the Ace of Spades in her deck and would not let it go. "So many kids got rockets for presents this year and are building them with their families," Lindsay chattered. "Dontcha just love Zak's idea! Even overheard the cheerleaders talking about wanting rockets." Done. Seeds planted.

"That was my idea, Lindsay. I'm running the rocket event committee," Doc bragged. "I am glad to hear people talking about my project. Rockets are for boys. Missy got gas for her car."

"I'll take YOUR order, Kate." Doc glared at being cut off by a mere waitress. Lindsay shot him her Ace of Spades look, raising her eyebrows and lifting her chin with a slight smile, daring him to go on. "Do you want to go there? WE all have ghosts in our closets, Michael."

Lindsay left to place the order, noticing that Margie and Q, the elder, were watching the exchange from the doorway. Margie gave her a quiet high five. Quintel added a fist bump. They had all learned over the years to keep their eyes and ears open, but their mouths idle as tension built. It is what eventually made Q the elder a brilliant attorney, surprising the prosecutors with unexpected performances in court. He gained the trust of clients and witnesses before hearings, heard the truth, and knew when and how to wield its decisive power. He was grateful for his mother's teaching: her wisdom had served him well.

—

Doc leaned forward and pulled papers out from another gold envelope. "I believe Zak has a fetal alcohol spectrum disorder. It explains his behaviors and how he thinks."

"I don't remember David's wife drinking. How did you find that information?" Kate tried to remember when her sister-in-law was pregnant so long ago. "We all know there is no known safe amount of alcohol for a woman to drink during pregnancy or even while trying to get pregnant. It's all harmful—even wine and beer. But I have no recollection of her drinking during the pregnancy." *What was her sister-in-law thinking when she chose to drink while she was pregnant?*

Carrying a plate of two over-easy eggs, English muffin toast, and the coffee pot, Lindsay set down the plates and poured a warm-up of coffee into Kate's half-empty cup. "You want a warm-up too, Doc?" She set down his scramble. "Couldn't help overhearing…you know, as long as alcohol and romance go together, there is no 100% prevention. It's not the child's choice. I can't choose who I am because of what my Mama did, and neither can Margie. We live the best we can with the cards dealt. You drink when you're filled with another life––it can affect that person for a lifetime. Heard if its a girl it and those little ol' eggs are developing it can affect next generation too. We got it. I did that to Shay. No one, nowhere, is exempt. Didn't drink with Q, ASD often runs down father's genetic lines." Lindsay smacked her gum, turned, and went into the kitchen.

Nauseated, Kate ran to the bathroom.

———

Kate's dream, the wish she had wished and prayed year after year, was finally true. She had lived a marriage of monthly disappointments, so there was no reason to try a pregnancy test until now. She was always regular and was now she was over two months late. The test showed two red lines; she wished were for Covid-19 instead of a baby. Now she knew their infertility problem was his, not hers. Confirmed in the wrong way. She had to tell… she had to tell… Ben. She decided to wait until she thought this through well. Her life just took a sudden screeching left turn, leaving her breathless, unable to think beyond the moment. Her body held a life and a secret. This was real. This was all too real.

She returned and sat. "Doc, I am pregnant." She ran her finger through the peanut butter toast, bringing her finger to her lips, eyes on Doc. She remembered the weekend teachers' conference in the city— the elegant dinner, two bottles of wine, and his hotel room. She loved the excitement and desired things Ben was not interested in, like city plays, concerts, and white linen dining. Things Doc promised. The night had progressed and expressed itself. They had only planned to quietly discuss a complex Riverdale High School student named Zak who just happened to be living in her home.

Doc gently touched Kate's hand. "It will be okay." He migrated the unordered jalapeno and ghost peppers to the side of his plate. "You can get rid of it. Ben won't even know."

Dismissed. No conversation. Get rid of it? Get rid of it! All on you, Kate. All he wanted, he'd gotten already.

Doc paused, crooning an explicit direction: "I'll never tell, and neither will you. Eleven weeks ago, if I count right, was quite a night." His eyebrows raised, his eyes looked skyward and to the right as the words slithered out his mouth.

Kate was horrified. "Excuse me, I must go." Revulsion struck as shame overcame her. She pulled her coat off the hook and fled.

"What bee got into her bonnet?" Lindsay taunted. "Whatcha, didn't like the peppers? Margie's cooking is a little too spicy for you?" Doc's eyes narrowed to slits.

"I'll never tell, and neither will you." Lindsay leaned close to Doc's ear, mimicking his evil instruction. "But someday, my son will figure this all out." She chomped her gum and blew a full-size bubble, smacking it in front of his face for dramatic effect. Did Doc have any idea what she alluded to? She knew what was in the cards even if Doc appeared guilt-free in his arrogance. She rarely chewed gum.

—

Shay arrived at the Memory Care Center with her decorations and two rolls of tape from Mantha. Ann was propped up in a wheelchair with a safety belt to avoid falling out. She looked vacant, staring into nothing. Shay hoped Ann would wake up to life. She filled the baby blue wall with snowflakes. She taped a row of cards by Ann's bed. The teen added random pictures of the stories the woman had shared. Then, she went to volunteer in the kitchen, washed the dishes, and prepared night snacks. She set aside a white snowflake cookie with white grape juice for Ann. The community room was alive with grandchildren greeting grandparents, adult children returning family members from their holidays, and a game of checkers in play between a grandson and a grandpa. Holiday music filled the air as somebody pumped the foot pedals of the player piano. A festive time was underway!

"Ann, it's Shay. I came to read and bring your snack. I picked out the best snowflake cookie!"

She noticed Ann's face turn to her voice. "It snowed," Ann whispered in a shaky voice. "Do you see the snow?"

"Yes, it snowed," smiled Shay. "Would you like a cookie? I'll hold it."

"Yes, dear. You are so good to mc," Ann's head turned toward the girl's voice. "I can't see all the time now. What happened to my eyes?"

"I'm not sure, Ann. You received so many cards from people who love you," Shay encouraged. The night before Ann's blood pressure rose to over 260 systolic, and staff feared she would suffer a stroke. She did not, but she lost her vision. She had a Do Not Resuscitate or DNR on file. Everyone waited. She did not stroke, and she did not die.

"Yes, dear, read to me," said Ann softly. "Read me all my cards from my patients."

Shay read card after card. She used different voices. Ann laughed. "I remember that man. He is coming back to me. My Emmett is coming back to get me. He will, you know?"

"Who stole my battery? I need the truck to get to the hospital, and it has no battery." Ann was agitated.

"I'll find your battery, Ann," Shay assured her. "I'll go look for it now."

"Thank you, dear. You are so good to me."

—

Kate was struck with an overwhelming mix of emotions, caught in deception, she rocked between lust and love. On the one hand, she felt guilt and shame for betraying her loving husband, yet on the other hand, she could not deny the pull she felt toward Doc. *What made him so attractive to her?* Kate's intrigue with Doc was hot and passionate, a potent fantasy of resuming what had begun her senior year in high school. He was the opposite of Ben. Their relationship would break so many hearts, including hers.

She was married for eighteen years to Ben, a strong, kind, and loyal man. Together, they had built a solid life with early dreams of starting a family. Life had unfolded according to a different plan, leaving them childless until Zak entered their home as a fledgling adult. And now there was a baby on the way, signaled by the pink lines on her positive pregnancy test that came as a complete surprise in the bathroom of Dee's Cafe.

Doc's first reaction was to call their baby an 'it.' Ben would never call any baby an it. Ben had the privilege of supporting many babies born in Harris County through birth as a paramedic, and then as Sheriff, each one had sent him home ecstatic over the new tiny life. It was all he talked about for days. He was a sucker for puppies and kittens. She was not. But a baby? To give birth had been the hidden desire of her heart. She had longed to become pregnant and have a baby of her own all her adult life.

Finally, here she was, with the opportunity to carry a little person and experience all the feelings of pregnancy—yet all Doc wanted was to get rid of "it." Rid of the evidence of his activity with her, or rid of the evidence of her activity with him. Or rid of their togetherness. Rid of the outcome of their passion! A passion he had pursued as if he wanted her in the same way she had wanted him. If she terminated it—as Doc referred to their situation—would he still care for her, or would 'they' be over? Who were 'they' in reality? They were each married to other people?

It. The spell was abruptly broken, snapping her out of the trance. She faced the questions she feared, the answers she already knew. *What had emerged within her to disrupt her life so drastically? Had Doc's focus, pursuit, and affection been a lingering desire for seduction and conquest from his youth, left unsatisfied until now? Had a fantasy of romance entranced her, an urge of unexplored sexuality simmering since her adolescence when he'd treated her like a prize too precious to touch with their wildness?*

How could this have awakened amid her careful adult life of thoughtful, competent choices? If she continued involvement with Doc, she knew it would cost everything. She would have to give up Ben, a far better person. She realized she already knew he was the better person…so what was this poisonous lure towards a man who wanted to erase the evidence of life that connected them!? These pieces did not fit together. This was wrong on so many levels.

Doc charmed her into betraying values that had guided her whole adult life. Overwhelmed by her love for Ben, her head cleared as denial lifted, leaving guilt in the pit of her stomach. The guilt joined with the shame that once deceived her. She decided to tell Ben the truth, knowing it would shatter the life and security they had so carefully built together. Ben often said, "Two wrongs don't make it right, no matter how you slice it." Telling was the right thing to do, the only just thing in light of his character and the devotion that had nourished her throughout their stable marriage.

She knelt in the kitchen and prayed.

-27-
NEW GROWTH

The holidays closed with the celebration of the New Year. Kate was anguished; she fretted, struggling to break her news to Ben. Zak's parents had planned to come for the New Year weekend, but Kate declined, saying she had come down with the flu as she worked to summon her courage to tell her husband the truth. Meanwhile, Ben and now Zak, Ben's little protege, delivered soup, crackers, and ginger ale to her bedside, trying to help her feel better. Ben found a book on tape so they could snuggle and listen to it in bed. He chose a light action story instead of a murder mystery, as she seemed too distraught for more tension.

After days of feeling sorry for herself, angry at herself, and overwhelmed with the excitement of pregnancy and the early sensations of carrying a new life, Kate was finally ready. She steeled herself, steadied her voice, and said, "Ben, we need to talk. I need to tell you something. Something hard. I don't know how to say this, but know that I love you wholeheartedly. And I have done something dreadful." She clutched her pillow to keep her hands from trembling.

"You've got me worried. What is it?" Ben wrapped his arms around her, "Whatever it is, we'll face it together. You know I'm here for you."

"You remember when I visited the cities for the conference in October? Well, during that time... I, um... I had a brief…I had an encounter with someone else. It was the first time. The only time!" Kate whispered urgently, trying to brace herself for what will come next.

Ben let go of her, taken aback. He had known something felt off since the conference. Her behavior had been irritable, sniping, as if some resentment lay just under the skin of their connection, like a long sliver. The sharp end pierced the surface, stabbing him through the heart and creating a sense of gravity.

"I... I wasn't expecting this, Kate." His tone was leaden as if his world had cracked in two.

"There is more, Ben. I do not have the flu." Her eyes met his, pleading for mercy and a miracle amidst the pain between them now: "I am expecting."

"Are you saying what I think you're saying?" Ben concluded.

"Yes, I'm pregnant. I found out two days ago and can't ignore the truth. I'm carrying another man's child, and it tears me apart. You deserve to know and decide what's best for you."

Ben sat in stunned silence, his face etched with shock, pain, joy, and anger. The magnitude of this revelation hit him like a tidal wave, threatening to drown the love they once shared. He struggled to comprehend her disloyalty. His heart was torn between compassion and betrayal. Ben swallowed hard, "I appreciate your honesty. Wow, this infidelity... pregnancy... baby......A BABY...this.. is NOT easy to hear. It's shocking and painful...shock and surprise...we tried for years...and now...with someone else...I am crushed, but you know how much you, I, we—I've wanted us to have a child...but this... it's...whewwwww."

Ben was a battlefield warrior. As a county deputy, he had scraped body parts off the freeway. This was life, not death. Ben took another deep breath and held it until he could hold it no longer, "The most important thing right now is for us to communicate honestly. I guess I'm the one with the fertility issue. That's another blow."

"I know it's hard to comprehend, and I'm truly sorry. Holding my actions inside since last fall after my betrayal has been ripping me apart. I can't bear losing you, but... I will walk away and start over if that is your choice." Kate whispered, trying to brace herself for what will come next. Her chagrin and the pregnancy put her on the brink of vomiting. She held on, listening for his position. She loved him and respected him far too much to beg. They'd been best friends and lovers for over 20 years.

Ben sighed, "I need time to process all of this. Not sure how to react. But I also want you to understand the anger... the... confusion I have now that I know. It will take me some time to understand what's happened."

"It kills me to see the hurt in your eyes and know I'm the cause. I never wanted to hurt you, and I have been going over and over how I could betray what I hold most dear. I feel so stupid and sorry. Seeing our relationship tainted by my total lack of judgment tears me apart. Ben, I….I am so very sorry." Tears rolled down her cheeks as she fought for composure. Kate was sincere. Telling the truth was melting the iceberg of resentment she'd carried in her chest, hiding betrayal while picking at others around her. The burden of separation was lifting. She felt filled with remorse as it passed onto his shoulders, though he didn't deserve it.

"Betrayal is difficult to come to terms with, especially from you. I love you so deeply. My heart feels shattered…my trust is … it's broken, Kate… I can't say it any other way." Ben took another breath, "But…you know me. I believe love is resilient. It must be. We'll both have to work on healing if that's possible."

"I know that being sorry is only as good as my future actions. There is no real excuse. I'm so sorry for destroying your trust. I acted like a schoolgirl mad at a boyfriend because you brought Zak here. That is on me," Kate confessed. "All I can offer you now is total honesty, transparency, and my commitment to rebuilding what our relationship could be from here. I want to keep the baby."

"Of course, we're keeping the baby!" Ben startled in surprise. "We've faced challenges together before, and this one is no different. Our faith has overcome past obstacles and our faith will also guide us through this! I won't deny what I am feeling. But faith is my foundation. This is going to take some time for me to sort out. I love you, Kate, I always have. I've always wanted a baby with you, and if we could not make one together, I guess a baby is a baby."

"I love you, Ben. I am so sorry," Kate covered her face with her hands, breaking down and sobbing with relief. She was in awe as a new depth of love burst open her heart. What she had just witnessed washed through her like a cleansing river when there was not one reason for Ben to still be standing with her. This must be grace, she realized.

"The best amends now is how we both handle our future," confirmed Ben. "Who's the sperm donor?"

"Doc."

"I guess he and Missy will be half-siblings," Ben gulped, wishing he could retract what he said. Once out the snarky comment could not be stuffed back in. *How could he sleep after this unthinkable revelation his wife had just dropped on him?* His life had been moving just as he thought it would: career, wife, house. Ben had prayed for a child, and God had let him borrow Zak, *and now a baby.*

Ben would not let a innocent suffer. He was accepting of this. But now? *God was giving them a baby, except it was not his flesh and blood.* Ben tossed and turned. *"Dear God,"* Silent tears and words flowed in Ben's darkness. *"Give me the strength to deal with all of this. I know there must be a bigger purpose to this pain. In nature, nothing is wasted. Ever. Help me out here."*

Awkward clunking of shoes, bumps, and thunks stomped over his head in his den. "God, your ways are higher than my ways. I will take that as a yes," he sighed as his pregnant wife's arm draped over his chest.

—

In the days that followed, a cloud of uncertainty hung over their home. Discussions were tense as Ben wrestled with his faith and the betrayal that cut deeply into his soul. On the other side, the excitement of finally having a baby with the woman he loved, even if it was not his, was exhilerating.

The spell was broken, and Doc's trance of passion proved hollow in the face of Ben's sincerity, courage, and genuine love. Kate terminated all contact with Doc, committing to her marriage and unborn child. The disparity between the words and actions of these two men was unmistakable. She worked hard to knit back life through the shame and schism caused by the affair. Seduction and surcoming held a steep price. Her marriage was love that transcended limits through action. She and Ben put sincere effort, open communication, and a commitment to rebuilding trust. Together, they would work through infidelity and strengthen their marriage, recycling a potential marital catastrophe into a courageous, creative choice.

Kate delegated her committee work to the leaders. She ate lunch in her room and later chose to sit with John and the Monogram Masters at the loser table.

Ben researched information about ten-week-old fetal development on his smartphone. There were 3D pictures he could rotate with his index finger. The baby was the size of a strawberry and had passed from an embryo into a fetus. This meant all the major organs were already formed, including the brain, heart, lungs, arms, and legs. *'It's such a miracle already at this stage,'* He marveled.

Zak lay with his ear to the floor, listening to their conversations. He was glad Doc was out of the picture. He had grown to detest the man.

"Rebuilding trust will take time and effort from both of us. It won't be easy. I want to move forward. I need to see you are actively working towards healing and rebuilding a stronger foundation….I need the assurance that you're genuinely committed to our marriage and keeping our family secure. I want that other man out of our lives completely. You have to regain my trust," Ben's terms were clear, and his words firm. "I need to go sit on the porch." Ben returned thirty minutes later and sat in his recliner. The fire was smoldering orange embers. He did not stoke it.

Kate sat legs crossed, sitting sideways and facing Ben in her recliner. He noticed she had been silent. Tears ran down her face as she softly pledged, "I promise to do everything I can to regain your trust, Ben. I want nothing more than to repair the damage I've caused and to rebuild the love, respect, and confidence in each other we once shared." She paused and breathed deeply, holding back the air release, knowing she had more to say. "There's another piece I need to share. This involves our child and the future."

"What is it, Kate? You have promised transparency." *Mercy, what next?* He thought, his anxiety rising.

"I believe Zak was exposed to alcohol before he was born, and that's why he acts so differently and thinks the way he does. I think David's wife, Carly, drank before she knew she was pregnant." Kate took a large breath, looking into Ben's kind eyes with apprehension as her confession continued, "Like I did with you on all those fall nights with cheese, crackers, and sausages."

Ben's eyes widened connecting the dots. Ben finished her sentence, stunned, "And wine."

"Yes—and wine."

"Or as we made dinner together." Ben added. "How could we have known?" Remorse well up in his chest.

Neither knowingly endangered the baby. He shared in her regret, feelings, and responsibility.

—

Overhearing their conversation, Zak snuck into his room to get the Carribean Cruise scrapbook and count all the drinks in the pictures of the partying couples. Was THAT why he felt like an alien on Earth? He slowly turned the pages, counting the days. His mother drank heavily for ten days, consuming more than three or four drinks, including beer, wine, and cocktails with umbrellas! He was hidden in her belly! He counted back from his birthday and realized that their vacation was taken when he was the size of a gummy bear, only two months after conception old.

He couldn't wait! Zak took the scrapbook downstairs to show his aunt and uncle. He held the book, wanting to barge in and talk.

"Yes, Zak, what is it?" Uncle Ben turned to look at Zak.

"Sorry, Uncle Ben, but I was listening to you and Aunt Kate. Like eavesdropping, I was stair dropping and I've been listening to you both a lot. I know you're both hurting….I am excited about the baby. Aunt Kate is right. I counted the number of drinks in these pictures. It was more than thirty… or even forty drinks my mom drank in ten days. There was probably more," Zak blurted out.

Kate's emotions overwhelmed her as she put her hand to her mouth, realizing the implications, and feeling heartsick for her nephew. "Aunt Kate, it's okay. I like my life, and I can help with the baby," Zak reassured her. Kate's emotions were raw as she contrasted her cherished ideals about life and having babies with the messy reality she was living. Her life seemed so far from what she had imagined. While it didn't make sense, it also made total sense. Alcohol was a solvent! How could she assign shame or blame to Carly when she wore the same shoes? Her heart opened – to Zak, to herself, and with a rush of gratitude to Ben and their shared life. Newfound grief mingled with grace churned in her heart, leaving her at a total loss for words. She looked from Ben to Zak and back again, touching her hand to her belly, eyes brimming with tears. A strange sense of wonder arose as she considered what was unfolding in their family in this blessed mess.

"We've weathered our share of storms and been there for others. Looks like this will be a long and challenging journey for all of us. We may need more support from family and friends to navigate this one. I get the sense that Life is now going to take a strong team. Whew…!" Ben whooshed.

"I've got lived experience," Zak consoled them. "Sam says lived experience is the best. He told me I reminded him of his son, Shaun. I heard him and Mantha say Shaun had fetal alcohol syndrome, too, because Sam and his wife drank a lot back in the day. They didn't know any better. I wish I could have met Shaun. I bet he would have liked the Monogram Masters. I bet we would be friends with us!"

—

School resumed in full swing. Mr. Mason's Science and Technology Center, also known as in-school suspension was going full STEAM. With the study of rocketry came hands-on exercises with principles of physics, mathematics, chemistry, and materials science. The walls were adorned with diagrams, charts, and drawings by students of historic flights and ancient machinery. Their work was soon shared in the library window display.

Mr. Mason, the Science and Technology Center wizard, approached Zak before lunch. "Zak, I want to show you something to help your future. How would you like a powerful secret concept by Mason's four P's: Plan, Pain, Patience, and Prize? These can become your guiding principles to graduate," he emphasized. "The first step is to Plan. You must articulate your goals, such as graduating." He handed Zak an index card.

Zak wrote, '1. Plan - Graduate.'

Mr. Mason continued, "Number 2 is Pain. Life is a series of challenges, and setbacks are inevitable. My superhero is Christ, who empowers me to overcome these obstacles; He makes all things possible when I cannot do it alone."

Zak wrote on another card, '2. Pain - Challenges.

"Great!" Mr. Mason cleared his throat, then dove into step three. "Patience, is card three. That means you are going to need endurance, the keeping on of the keeping on. That takes investing your time and doing the hard work.

Zak wrote on the next card, '3. Patience - Hard work.

Mr. Mason smiled, his eyes sparkled. "Number 4 is the prize. The prize takes praise, not moping or negative talk. You must speak out good and possibilities. Be thankful in the little, see the tiny and be grateful. Suddenly, your prize will arrive with its rewards. Trust God's timing. Write down 'Graduate - Acts 16:25," instructed Mr. Mason.

Zak followed orders, '4. Prize - Graduate - Acts 16:25' and then asked "You mean act like you do, or am I supposed to ask a question? Help me understand this. Whats 16:25?"

"That's for you to find out," said Mr. Mason.

Zak pocketed his card and hurried to the lunchroom to share his newfound knowledge with Shay and Q. After getting his food. He proudly presented his new Plan to Graduate card to Shay. "Mr. Mason enlightened me with the four steps to graduate. Look at this. It's a secret, so I can't tell anyone, but I can show you. He told me I had to find this last thing out, Acts 16:25, but I don't have a clue."

"I can show you that Zak. I know what book it is in," said Q. "Did Mr. Mason mention a translation."

"English?"

"Zak, how do you get into Mr. Mason's class?" Shay hoped to join Mr. Mason's class, where learning seemed more straightforward and each student got to build a rocket.

"It's pretty easy. You start breaking the rules, fighting, and talking rudely to a teacher. Doc is so mad at me that I won't be leaving now until graduation," Zak grinned.

"What if I kicked him?" She said aloud before she knew what had happened. Shay was wide-eyed as the thought crossed her mind and popped out of her mouth.

"I don't think that is a very good idea, Shay," warned Zak. "Uh… Even I wouldn't try that."

—

Outside of school, Q handed his teacher a crisp Benjamin and asked John to order him an Arduino Uno 3 Ultimate Starter Kit to explore the world of electronics and programming. The price was less than $100 for the whole assembly, he expected taxes and shipping. *This was going to bve an excellent way to learn about components and build the altimeter tracker.*

Once the Arduino box arrived, except for school and work, no one saw Q for two weeks. "You won't believe what I have learned!" Q was practically crowing entering Riley's. "My first project was a traffic light system. I used LEDs, resistors, and a breadboard to create a miniature functioning traffic light. I programmed it to cycle through the different colors like a real traffic light. It may be the first traffic light in Riverdale."

Sam cackled in amusement. "That's cool! What other projects have you been working on?"

"Arduino is like Legos and an erector set on steroids. I made a digital thermometer. By connecting a temperature sensor to the Arduino, I could measure the current temperature and display it digitally. Learning about sensors, data acquisition, and how to program the Arduino to process and display the temperature readings has been very satisfying."

"Wow, I'm impressed!" Exclaimed John. "It sounds like you're diving into some complex stuff. Is there anything else you've created?"

Q's eyes lit up. "Yes, indeed! One of the most exciting projects I made was a Bluetooth-controlled car. I used motor drivers and Bluetooth modules to build a small car that can be controlled remotely using a smartphone or computer. It's entertaining to navigate it around and experiment with different controls. The librarian is not happy about my car running around under her bookshelves."

"Q, your ingenuity is awe-inspiring. What else have you been up to?" Pressed Sam, leaning into Q's astounding project reports.

"I am amazed at how much fun this is. I am learning about meteorology and how to collect and process data using the Arduino by building a weather station using various sensors. The station can measure humidity, temperature, and barometric pressure and display real-time weather information. I thought what I built could be useful to Riley's." Q was in his element. "I am ready to tackle the altitude tracker, but need more parts."

John opened his smartphone. "Tell me what you need. I'll order it right up."

"Really?"

John nodded. "Let me have your order."

"Arduino Uno Board, Barometric Pressure Sensor, Breadboard and jumper wires, LED display. The LED display will give me real-time altitude readouts. I need a good power source." Q listed by memory. "We've got the rockets."

John winked at Sam. "Should we order two?"

"Three would do fine," added Sam. "I'll chip in."

"Done deal," John clicked to place the order. "We need to start looking at colleges and scholarships for you, Q."

"I owe you big time, John," Q tried to interject.

"You owe us nothing. Your ingenuity and creative curiosity earned our support for your Phase 2. You're going to help build the future," Sam interrupted.

—

By the middle of April, the final snowfall of an additional twelve wet and icy inches landed like a lead blanket. Frustrated farmers wanted to till and plant. The ice on rivers and lakes had slowly thinned as the ground frost retreated. Maple syrup was bottled and made ready for market. The trees' first buds burst open, purple and yellow crocuses bloomed in Central Park, and daffodils sprung from the slowly warming ground. The townspeople of Riverdale were all saying ENOUGH, eagerly waiting on spring!

———

Three days a week, Shay volunteered and read to Ann. They talked of snowflakes, Happy the Dog, Emmett, and her son, Michael. Well, mostly Shay talked. Ann's eyes now spoke and her mouth added wee smiles and head nod. Then, one day, as she delivered evening snacks, Shay heard that horrible voice again. She stopped and listened, recognizing it as someone she was supposed to respect. He sounded evil. "He's dead. Will you shut up and accept he is dead? I took care of that! When are you going to realize I took care of that?"

This time, Shay stood her ground and marched straight into Ann's room. The man rushed out, facing away from her, but he had seen her and he knew who she was.

Holding a bunny cookie and pear juice, she forced herself to focus, *"He left. He's gone. I'll read to Ann."* Then she saw it all: the snowflakes on the blue wall lay on the floor, mixed with what shreds of her handmade cards. The story of Happy ripped outfrom the book's binding. Ann was a statue. She touched Ann's frail hand and kissed her forehead, knowing it was forbidden because Shay was not her family. "You are a good person, Ann. I love you." Shay comforted the elder, frozen with fear and trauma. She picked up the Happy story and put it back into their journal. She stacked the cards with the snowflakes on top. "I will be back soon," Shay reassured her. Then, putting her mouth near Ann's ear and touching her shoulder, she said with tenderness, "I'll see you later…"

Ann's mouth opened and closed, "Al, al..ga."

"Yes, Ann alligator. And I'm your crocodile." A strength snapped up her spine as she said it. Crocodile. That was it. No more of those cruel sneak attacks! Shay was fuming, ready to confront her nemesis! She felt like she became that crocodile.

Shay shot out of the Memory Care Center to confront the man. She refused to even think of his name—he did not deserve a name!

The next morning she sped away to school. She waited watching.

Waiting and then burst through his door like an army of one. She walked up to face him in the middle of the day. No one was looking when she kicked him as hard as she could in the shin. The coward yelped and jumped, holding his leg. "You insolent brat!" He shrieked with anger, "What do you think you are doing? I am YOUR PRINCIPAL!"

He might as well have said, "Draw!" She was furious. "I am NOT the brat. YOU!! YOU pulled down all Ann's snowflakes I made. YOU ripped our Happy story apart. YOU are evil and sneaky. YOU ARE A COWARD to be so cruel to an elderly woman! YOU HIDE, BUT I SEE YOU! WE ALL SEE WHO YOU ARE!!" Shay spun on her heel and went to Civics class.

It did not take long before she was called to the office to meet with the local police. Assaulting a teacher was a big deal. Besides his deputy, Sheriff Ben arrived on the scene.

Ben stifled his laughter reading the report, knowing both Shay and the victim. He recommended that Shay remain in school suspension for the rest of the year; *she was safe there.* He hoped Zak would get the whole story and bring it home. He couldn't wait to hear what had triggered the uncharacteristic detention of this otherwise sweet girl.

Her mom guffawed when Ben called her from the school to explain why her kind and helpful daughter was to serve detention in the in-school suspension classroom for the rest of the school year.

"About time he got something coming to him. It's best you handle it, Sheriff Ben, I'm not sure I'll do as well if I march into the school. Thanks for the low down. Though I don't believe in violence, and I'm proud of my daughter for taking a stand. I'm on Shay's side here. I'll talk with her. Tell the school I can't leave work. After all, I'm already one of THOSE mothers. Bye Sheriff." Lindsay hung up and doubled over with laughter.

Ben was not surprised at Lindsay's response. She stood up for her kids. He figured she'd wait to hear all sides before coming to a conclusion. So would he. Shay and Q were terrific kids.

"Good God, girl what's so funny," asked Margie.

Lindsay convulsed as she imagined her blithe teenage girl delivering a dose of justice to one of the most callous, conniving people the town had ever been taken in by. She knew as few others did. She gasped for air between belly laughs, "Justice may just roll down like thunder one day. Wouldn't that baste his banana!"

Margie watched and overheard the conversation. "What was that all about?"

"It was the sheriff."

"Really, girl, the Sheriff?" Her head was beautifully adorned with the new green, black, and red Kente head scarf that Quintel had given her from his trip to Ghana, which she now wore often.

Q arrived donning his apron, "I guess Shay kicked the principal in the shin." He stifled a chuckle. They took a minute to imagine this sweet girl giving a swift one to creepy Doc! The group shared smiles and nods.

"It's about time someone had the guts to take that man on," Margie grinned approvingly.

"I'll have to talk with her," Lindsay rolled her eyes, conflicted, not wanting her daughter to be a warrior for justice. She did life the best she could every day. She had never bought into superheroes. Yet, here was Shay challenging elder abuse. *Was her daughter supposed to let cruelty go unchallenged?* Lindsay did not want that either. She needed to find out what Shay had experienced.

"Well, you're her mama, so that's your job. Please do share THAT conversation," Margie wiped her hands on a clean cloth and went back to dinner prep, humming under her breath, "You can run on for a long time, run on for a long time…You can run on for a long time, but you can betcha God Almighty gonna shut you down…." The anthem by Sweet Honey in the Rock, about cruelty called to account, arose in her heart.

———

Ann Johnson died three days later. She went home to be with Emmett. The obituary read, "Beloved Sally Ann Johnson passed peacefully Thursday afternoon. She is survived by her son, Michael Johnson, the principal of Riverdale High School." The truth was exposed. Michael WAS DOC!

———

Q and Zak dug deeper into the history of the murder of Emmett, Doc's father. With the new public information of Michael being Doc Johnson and Shay's recount of both incidents at the Memory Center, pieces began to fall into place. Zak shared the map he had drawn of the murder with Q.

Kate's pregnancy progressed, and so did her connection with Ben. Their renewed commitment, fueled by forgiveness and courage to forge an unbreakable bond, became more robust and resilient than ever. They spent countless nights talking, supporting each other, and rebuilding their foundation, determined not to let their past define their future.

In a package addressed to Kate, she found two white linen tablecloths and various colored candles. There was a gift card from Ben. He signed up for the Internet, and they selected television programs that offered a broader menu of topics for mutual exploration. He gave his Friday night evenings to his deputies. He slept late on Saturday mornings, holding Kate and their future child. He did his best to create cosmopolitan in Riverdale, even if it wasn't the glitz of going out for fine dining or a hotel. Fridays, Zak stayed away until after dinner.

His two-sided job card from Ben read, 'Friday:

1. Hang out with Monogram Masters

2. When arrive home. Wash hands and dry on dish towel.

3. THEN fold linen tablecloth. Put it on the top shelf in the pantry

3. Do not light the candles

4. Eat!

5. Remember to put kitchen items back in their places.

6. Leave kitchen clean to surprise Aunt Kate in the morning.

Zak integrated into Ben and Kate's family. His funny way of looking at life and saying things that popped into his mind became endearing to Kate. She was curious about his thoughts and began understanding how his mind worked. If their new child was going to face living with prenatal alcohol exposure, she would do everything in her power to understand and find workarounds to help.

Kate figured Zak's unique take on the world was a suitable place to start. Ben was on board all the way. They contacted the national and state organizations for FASD to learn more. She took interest in Shay and Q, pleased with his new friends. The Monogram Master were sweet kids locally referred to as the weirdos. The more she knew them, the more she respected them. She saw capability, purpose, and compassion that could benefit any community.

Ben placed Zak's chore cards in the third letter-holder pocket on the kitchen wall. He taped an index card with ZAK in big red Ben-drawn letters. Kate was impressed at the quantity and quality of Zak's work.

———

Ben rounded the corner and touched Kate's belly, saying, "I would like to name our baby."

"Of course," Kate was curious about what Ben would say. Our baby, not 'it'. Not to get rid of 'it' when he had every right.

"If we have a boy, I like Yohan. It means 'God has shown mercy' or 'gift'. If we have a girl, I want her name to be Grace."

Kate's eyes welled up with joyful tears. Not only did her knight in shining armor think of beautiful names for their baby, but Ben also researched names that would be powerful symbols of the spiritual story of their family relationships.

"Thank you, God, for your forgiveness, mercy, and abundant love," she whispered.

-28-
PEACE WITH PIECES

Spring arrived, warming the earth. The mud dried into soil, and the fields were planted. Baby calves and lambs grew stronger as they browsed fresh grasses and bounded pastures. Baby chicks pecked for bugs, turning from fuzzy balls with beaks into feathered birds who came running when called. The hayfields were greening with the promise of an early harvest. The rocket field prairie was lush, showing no sign of the fall fire.

The demolition crew hauled the remains of the double-wide trailer away. The bulldozers graded the yard and prepared to dig a basement for the Larkin family's new home. Lindsay had embraced Zak as if he was one of her own. His aunt and uncle had taken him, yet he now felt like he belonged to three families, given how close he was to Mantha and Sam. He found it remarkable that no one was consistently mad at him except Doc, and Doc didn't count. Zak felt comfortable in Riverdale, where he was relaxed enough that his mind could wander and piece things together in his way. It felt good to have adults accept him and remind him that being different was okay. No matter how his parents had tried to mold him into what they called normal, it did not work. Now, he had friends of all ages who were true to their uniqueness. He found comfort in a supportive community that guided him through challenges, preventing him from getting into trouble.

The Monogram Masters carried buckets of soap and Riley's old car wash brushes to the boneyard and cleaned the soot off the containers. The fire had missed their storage area, which Q had placed closer to the woods. Using the random materials, they created a Mr. Mason-worthy obstacle course, complete with ladders connecting containers where the tops were too far apart for Shay to jump between, so she had full access to the fun.

After the fire chief's investigation had concluded, the demolition crew also removed the ATV and various burned hazards so the whole area was in better shape.

Lindsay motivated Zak to use images to aid memory and advised him to persist when tempted to quit or make excuses. Margie told him failure is just another opportunity to succeed. Mantha mentored him, helping him to recognize what triggered him and discover what helped as he worked through his fears and found ways to handle episodes. No one had ever understood how to help him cope with differences he didn't know how to describe. These women seemed to understand him inside out. They didn't even laugh when he used his Rocket Man toy like a puppet—to overcome social anxiety and carry on a conversation or solve a problem. Their support was palpable—he felt their kindness like a second skin, meaning he was no longer alone in the world.

Sam provided similar support, sharing ideas yet differently. Zak knew Uncle Ben loved him, and now that Aunt Kate was having a baby, she was full of questions no one had ever asked him. Kate made him consider who he was, his purpose, and how he could make a difference. It meant he mattered! But it was Mr. Mason who cinched it for Zak — Mr. Mason was the kind of man Zak longed to be. He was not only intelligent and funny, sharing everything he knew with anyone who wanted to learn, but he had all kinds of ways to reach people—so many that he was never dull! He put his whole Being into being there for the people he cared about. He wasn't pompous or full of himself, even though he was a massive man with impressive size, strength, and intelligence. He personified good judgment. Zak noticed he knew when to speak up and when to observe and put the facts together on his own. He didn't just do his job with everything he had; he did Life this way, with his whole body.

When Mantha realized Zak was considering enlisting to follow in these footsteps, she had him talk to the Army recruiter. Zak didn't just want to graduate high school. He was finding the confidence to go after his goals and wanted to give the compassion and dedication back to their community, which others had given him.

———

Shay loved cooking. Over the winter, she had watched and helped, learning about culinary science in practice, at the elbow of Margie and her mom at Dee's Cafe. Her list of recipes grew from simple Ramen and hot dogs to savory soups, stews, and meals. She was motivated, practicing the sequences of preparing and combining ingredients that turned some food into delicious and varied dishes.

—

The cafe was closed one Sunday when Zak entered by the kitchen's side door. The big mixer whirred, stirring a big bowl of dark brown batter all on its own. Zak smiled as the memory of Mickey Mouse and his enchanted brooms from the story The Sorcerer's Apprentice flashed to mind from when he lived with his parents in that other world of his childhood. Shay bounced into view, and they greeted each other.

"What are you making?" Zak asked Shay. She juggled an impressive scope of activities between Dee's, Riley's, school, and the Memory Care Center. He marveled at her ability to remember where to be when and how to get everything done correctly without index cards. Though she'd shared mnemonics, songs, dances, and other tactile and kinesthetic tips Lindsay had taught her for navigating daily life, to him, this was operating by her kind of magic.

"I am baking a chocolate birthday cake."

"Whose birthday?" Asked Q, looking up from the map Zak had drawn of owned properties surrounding Emmett's murder.

"It's a secret birthday," Shay smiled coyly, enjoying their curiosity. She poured the batter into two round floured pans and popped them into the oven, checking the temperature readings on the dented metal tool thermometer from the rack. She rinsed the bowl, dried it to dump in a boxed vanilla pudding mix, and added the milk. She handed Q a mixer blade to lick and gave the other to Zak with delight. The guys received them as if they were awards, holding them up and licking them with a flourish.

Shay had her flair, and Zak was pleased to be with her company. It wasn't like the tense crackling energy of the gangs he had been used by in the city, whose false smiles hid mean trickery. The Monogram Masters were a real team he could trust; they made fun and spread genuine goodness through happy surprises. Zak suddenly put it together. He was PROUD to be with Shay, and Q. Shay's warm positivity had charmed him since he'd caught the sight of her smile. Her gifts were just as crucial as Q's intellect. She was all heart, which was different from other cute girls he'd met. She wasn't just adorable. Shay was... Beautiful. He paused for a moment, letting out his breath. He hoped no one noticed.

Q peeked over her shoulder. "My little sister, are you creating a Boston Cream Pie?" Shay washed the beater blades in warm, sudsy water and clicked them back into place, grinning that her brother had guessed the recipe. She loved how insightful he was.

Lindsay sat at a table doing a crossword puzzle. Zak and Q joined her. "Mom, we need historical information," Q requested.

"Because I am older than you, do you think I might know something you don't?" Lindsay teased him with affection.

"Q knows everything," Zak supported his friend.

"Mom, you have told me that experience can also be a teacher. I learned from reading and reading books that we all learn by doing. We are intelligent in different ways. I remember seeing that there was a researcher at Harvard University who wrote about people having multiple intelligences. Howard Gardner. That's who it was," Q was halfway thinking aloud as he rooted out what information his mom might know.

As Q watched, Lindsay filled in one more word with her red pen, 'exigencies.'

"How do you know that word?" He asked.

"I know things you don't know I know," shared Lindsay. "I say it every day to my Father. 'Let all exigencies be extinguished.'"

"What does that mean?" Asked Zak.

Q was curious. "I thought Gramps was dead!"

"Some people say my life and my family's life is a hard road. But I have a purpose, Zak. We all have a purpose here. When I pray for all exigencies to be extinguished, I know I will face daily challenges and difficulties. There will be urgent demands and overwhelming stories shared by people in the cafe. They may not tell anyone their sorrow but me. So, I ask the Lord to extinguish these exigencies. I can be a listening ear, but that is all the relief I can give someone when life's burdens weigh them down besides giving the small comfort of a free coffee refill. I trust, once I ask, that God will handle the rest." As Lindsay shared, Q's respect for his mother grew. "Okay, ask me anything."

"Tell us about today's Doc Johnson, who is an impostor of his dad, Doc Emmett Johnson, because his real name is Michael Johnson. Michael was the son of Emmett, who was Sam's best friend." Zak supplied.

"Some information you're not ready for," Lindsay snapped as Zak and Q scrunched their faces behind her.

Q tried another tactic. "Mama, would you please look at Zak's map and tell us about it?"

"Please, Mama L," Zak begged Lindsay with his new pet name for her. It didn't feel right to call her Mom even though she told him he could.

"What's the red star sticker for?" Lindsay asked, peering at the paper while Shay put the pudding into the refrigerator.

"As far as we can tell, that is where Emmett Johnson's murder occurred. There is an old trail from here to here." Q indicated the area with his finger.

Lindsay began, "See the swerve in the big trail? Slide your sticker there. You see, there were two almost parallel trails. One went to the farm I grew up on; it was an old deer trail Mike, Potts, and I often used. No one else knew about it. It lies closer to the containers. We found it one winter. The main trail went to the junkyard where Mike and Potts often drove around on their 4-wheelers."

"The junkyard that blew up?" Zak's eyes squinted, and his brows furrowed as he.

"That's right," Lindsay confirmed. "It was right here, and now it is part of Doc Johnson's new estate. You'd never know that part was connected to the junkyard. The hill on his property is filled with what was left. Anyway, I was in bed, and the explosion shook our house. Woke me right up!" Lindsay recalled, "The Potts were a nice, odd family." She pulled her lips over her teeth and pressed her lips together in a thin line, pausing as she thought of what to say next. "I always felt sorry for Mrs. Potts and the children, Lord rest their souls. Mr. Potts... He…" There was another serious pause. "…left welts on little backs and black eyes with swollen lips. Mmmm Hmm. She paused to recall those sorry images. "Mama told me it was none of my business. She said, 'Treat them better than nice; be kind to the children and their safe place.' Sometimes I heard the whacks and wails when I walked the deer trail.'"

"I would have told someone." Sniffed Shay.

"One must be cautious. Sometimes, things can get worse when you tell," reminded mother with a wagging finger at her daughter.

Shay tilted her head, "But why?"

"Like when Shay kicked Doc Johnson in the shin, so now she's punished by being detained for the rest of the year?" Zak volunteered recent events, puzzled by what Lindsay meant by 'getting worse'.

"Kinda. It depends, though. Sometimes what seems so wrong and horrible provides …like Shay breaking a serious rule at school doing something wrong and finally landing in Mr. Mason's room to get the help she needs…what people called bad behavior brought about a blessing." She lovingly grinned at her daughter as Shay blended the shiny frosting. "Shay stood up to a bully."

Then she frowned, "However…people who are truly violent like Mr. Potts was back in the day, dangerous abusers like that… get more deadly when cornered. Things were different when I was a kid. Mama thought minding one's own business was best. But now we have shelters and people trained to help stop violence because it is more complicated than speaking up. Confronting is not always the best move. When people care, they plan for safety that won't put others at greater risk of more abuse."

The Monogram Masters said nothing aloud, but they glanced at one another. They all had the same thought, "Missy…!" Q pulled his shoulders back and focused on the map again.

"Sally and Michael lived here until he graduated." Q pointed to the property. "Then Sally sold the house."

Lindsay nodded.

"John Mason but grew up over in Hanover, then stayed with his grandpa here when he was home from college in the summertime," Q pointed to a house on Elm Street. "And his grandpa and Sam were buddies."

"There was a group of local men who were good friends––they liked shooting, fishing, building rockets, and flying airplanes. Mike's dad and John Mason's grandfather were part of that circle. They were always into something." Zak drew a bubble with a group of men, adding their names.

"So, you said the Potts house was next to your house. What happened to the house?" Asked Zak. Q and Shay thought she had always lived in Gramp's double-wide.

"Michael Johnson bulldozed it for his estate. We are blessed that grandfather left us our trailer, the boneyard, and that huge field for some extra income."

"Is that why you hate him?" Shay asked.

"Who?" Lindsay asked.

"Michael, er...Doc," said Zak.

"No, I do not hate him; I despise him!" She threw her head back, roaring as ferociously as a lioness. "His behavior is reproachable! People believe that when someone tells a lie long enough and loud enough. Worse, you, the liar, begin to believe it yourself."

Zak wrote notes on his map and drew on the deer trail. "Perfect placement." Lindsay approved.

Q wrote the names of the property owners, then Lindsay listed the names of all the children and their ages at the time of the murder and fire that followed.

"Did all these kids hang out like we do?" Zak asked.

"Yes, we played together in the woods when we were younger. Then…" She stopped abruptly. "I mean darn, I've got socks to darn." Suddenly, she sat up, scraped back the chair, and promptly left for their apartment.

Q caught the drift—conversation over. There was something more hidden that needed their attention.

—

Graduation was to be held on the Riverdale football field. Sam secured the clearances and worked with John to develop a launch plan. Zak worked building launch pads. They needed 25 if they did four launches or 50 if they did two. John taught him about prototyping and patterning for their manufacture while Sam set up the machines for Zak to duplicate each piece. The launch pads will be assembled in the new science and technology class.

Once Zak got the hang of each, his duplication was precise. The men crated all the launch pad parts. Zak counted and bagged up washers, bolts, and wing nuts. The total number of rockets entered by students was 105—five more than Zak had planned for.

"If everyone participates, we're going to need a different launch plan," challenged Sam. "How can we make this work, Zak?"

Zak drew a blank. Q walked up from behind to share the new electronic rocket launcher he had built. "What's the question?" Q was always interested in a good puzzle.

Sam cleared his throat, "We have 105 participants, each with a rocket. Zak has already cut the pieces to manufacture 25 rocket launchers.

What would be your launch plan?"

"Twenty-one rockets, five sequenced launches. It's like a 21-gun salute of goodbye to Riverdale High. There would be four left to usher in the new senior, junior, sophomore, and first-year classes, challenging them to the next year's rocket launch. It could become a tradition."

"How would you test this?" John queried, impressed with Q's quick thinking.

"I would simply use our three current rockets. We have enough people with the six of us to test this. Zak can use my launch deck for lift-off. Mantha, Sam, and Shay can each handle a rocket on a launch pad. John and I can test each of my altitude trackers." Q pointed to each launch location.

Sam looked at John, who looked at Mantha, who looked at Sam, who admitted with conviction, "Sounds like a good plan."

"Let's do this!" Shouted Zak.

"Next Saturday at ten o'clock, container field," ordered Mantha. "Weather permitting."

"FIRE!" Shouted Zak.

"No FIRE! Not ever again!" Q slammed his hand on the table with a loud crack! Mantha crossed her arms and nodded.

—

While the boys were at Riley's, Shay walked to the container to check the details, but to her surprise, everything was almost as if she had left it. The Rocket book lay beside the lantern, and the folded blankets were rumpled. She sat in solitude, wondering what it felt like to feel bad enough to want to run away. She loved her mom and her brother.

The door creaked, "Oh, it's YOU! What are YOU doing here?" It was Missy.

"No one knows we are both here. No one will judge you if we are friends here," Shay gently reassured. Sensing the sincerity in her voice, Missy took a hesitant step inside.

"Did you like the rocket book I left for you and the softer pillow?"

Missy smiled, nodding slightly.

"Do you want a rocket? I CAN get you one," Shay extended a generous offer.

"You're poor," spat the girl. "HOW can you do that? My dad won't even let me have one."

"I will let you have one, and I can help you build it," Shay selflessly offered. "But for now, I need to get home."

"See you 'round," Missy smiled dismissively.

"I'm not round," answered Shay.

"You are, Shay," Missy turned away from her. Shay left, running home to check on the pieces of the surprise cake.

—

Sheriff Ben stopped into the VFW, ordered a ginger ale, and sat next to fellow veterans John, Sam, and Mantha.

"Hey, Ben, how's your wife's pregnancy going?" Sam asked. Her rounded belly announced the news to the community, so everyone knew and was excited for the couple.

Ben was uncomfortable sharing his private thoughts. "It's been quite a journey, to be honest. As we get closer to the due date, I have mixed emotions. Excitement, of course, but also some fear about becoming the dad of a tiny person." He sipped his ginger ale.

"Ginger ale," Sam winked approvingly.

"Before we got the baby surprise, Kate and I often had red wine and appetizers to unwind after a busy day. We did not know about the baby for almost three months," Ben told Sam. "If she can't drink, I won't either."

"Shaun survived Deb's drinking and my fathering—quite the combo. Your child will do fine. I'm happy to help," Sam conveyed his support.

"You are doing a great job with Zak," Mantha complimented Ben. "He's come into his own. I'm happy to see that."

"Zak takes a team of people. It wasn't just me. It was all of you, plus Lindsay and her kids. The baby will be just us." Ben took another sip.

"It doesn't have to be," offered Mantha. Kids need aunts, uncles, and..." She winked at Sam. "They need grandpas."

Sam chuckled. "Seems like a hundred years ago, we had Shaun. What a little Dickens! That kid was full of it, like Zak. The dance of being a father and husband is knowing when to step in and step out without stepping on toes. What helped Deb and me was talking. Boy, was that hard! I say things once, then usually not again." He reminisced. "Seriously, if I told you I love you, I'm one of those guys. I DO. There is no need to talk or repeat it. Big mistake. Keep telling her you love her. Keep asking her how she's feeling, go to the doctor's appointments, and do not dare to leave that delivery room."

Ben shared, "Watching her deal with back pain, fatigue, and mood swings without being able to alleviate her discomfort is frustrating."

"You're responsible for all that," John laughed. "Takes two to Tango! How about—" John flashed a furtive glance at Mantha. He is attracted to her but subtly lets her know without making it a big deal. John flashed a furtive wink in Mantha's direction while the others chuckled at the Tango joke.

Ben swallowed hard, though no one noticed.

"Zak will do more around the house if you make him some new cards and show him what you need. He loves feeling appreciated and helpful. For Kate, I bet a gentle foot or back massage could give some relief," shared Mantha. "Just be there for her."

"It's challenging to find that physical connection right now," Ben chose his phrasing carefully.

"Things happen in life. If I ever have the blessing of children, they must be adopted." John shared. "For me, it's a long-lost peace."

Mantha suggested, "There are other ways to connect without putting any physical strain on your partner. The sexiest part of another human is the brain, guys... just sayin'. Intimacy is but a profound chemistry of thought, emotion, and spirit that resided in our skin suits," joked Mantha, quickly lifting one eyebrow at John.

"Ben, we're all in this together. I'm here if you ever need to bounce ideas off someone," Sam said sincerely. "I've ridden this pony on the rodeo circuit. If you are dealing with prenatal alcohol exposure, it's not as easy as a Merry-Go-Round, but you'll do fine. If Deb and I could pull out of our wreckage, put the train on the tracks, and keep it going, you and Kate will, too. You've got what it takes."

Ben looked around at his table of confidantes. They were giving him honest advice from their experiences willingly and readily: age, gender, occupation, income, ability/disability, none of it mattered. This was about being alive to each other, even when some things about living could not be set right again. He realized he needed these people in his life now more than ever. Would their baby story ever get told? He wondered in his heart of hearts. Perhaps, but right now, the power of support and friendship was what he needed. A gentle settling engulfed him. Ben suddenly felt peace in a way he'd not experienced in the pews where he worshiped. "Where two or three are gathered…" whispered the still small voice inside him. Looking around the table, he saw only the faces of the One.

—

Saturday arrived for the maiden voyage of the three rockets. Lindsay took the morning off to watch the Monogram Master's first team launch. The alfalfa under their feet was lush, and the deep blue sky was decorated with a few select cumulus clouds—a perfect backdrop for their debut launch.

Shay cradled Pink Bertha, carefully inspecting the rocket's fins to ensure they were securely attached, while Q reviewed the detailed launch instructions to ensure they were prepared.

"Guys, this is going to be epic! We'll get to watch Pink Bertha soaring high into the sky," Zak looked upwards and pointed aloft, bouncing on his toes, barely containing his enthusiasm.

With a grin, Shay chirped, "I know, right? Are you ready for this, Pink Bertha?" She asked her beloved rocket.

"I've been looking forward to this for months! I can't wait for the adrenaline rush when we press that launch button," Q declared.

Sam held up the instruction manual with both hands. "Well, let's make sure we follow these steps meticulously. Safety is our priority. We don't want rockets veering off course or something else going wrong."

The excitement in the air was palpable as they systematically assembled the rocket on a sturdy launchpad. Pink Bertha shimmered in the bright sun, reflecting their dreams of witnessing it majestically piercing the air and climbing into the brilliant blue.

With the rocket ready for liftoff, the three friends stepped back, anticipating the breathtaking sight they were about to witness.

"Wow, Pink Bertha looks so much taller than I thought she would be," breathed Shay, awe-struck. "Do you think she'll make it to that cloud up there?"

Zak chuckled, sharing in his friend's amazement. "I hope so! But no matter what, this will be unforgettable! You guys…for real… we're about to launch our rockets! Rockets WE MADE!"

Sam, double-checking the safety measures, nodded in agreement. "Okay now: according to the instructions, we just need to connect the ignition system, make sure the area is clear, and be ready for the countdown."

Taking their positions near the launch button, they shared one last round of ready glances filled with anticipation.

"Three... Two... One... LAUNCH!" They counted down, shouting in unison as they pressed the ignition button in perfect synchronization.

A roar filled the air as flames erupted beneath the rocket, propelling it upward. Their hearts raced, breathlessly following the trail of smoke as the rocket ascended higher and higher into the vast blue above the sky. The acrid smell of gunpowder filled the air.

"Whoa! It's... like...like... a shooting star!" Exclaimed Zak in sheer wonder, his eyes locked on the soaring rocket.

Shay clasped her hands together, her voice filled with awe. "Look how graceful she is as she climbs! I never imagined Pink Bertha would be so beautiful in flight!"

Q was wordless. He stood motionless, mouth ajar, hands outspread at his sides, until his head tilted upwards and followed Pink Bertha's trajectory with his chin pointing skyward. He was riveted to the rocket in complete hyper-focus.

When the rocket reached its pinnacle, a small parachute deployed perfectly, guiding it back to Earth. The three friends watched intently as their creation descended gently, drifting on the breeze.

Zak broke the silence, a satisfied smile spreading across his face. "That was amazing. We did it!" The brother and sister had the same impulse, joyfully embracing Zak triumphantly.

For the Monogram Masters, their first model rocket launch was a resounding achievement. They raced across into the field to gather their equipment.

The rocket launch's sizzle, fire, and reverberation echoed in Mantha's ears, triggering adrenaline and a flood of intense memories. Her eyes widened with alarm as she returned to the battlefield, reliving the chaos and danger she once had survived. In her flashback, the ground was shaking—she instinctively fell to the turf, rolling for cover, desperately seeking refuge from the recalled explosion that locked her in a physical reaction of utter terror.

John dropped the altitude tracker and threw his massive body over her as a shield to protect her from the perceived threat. "It's going to be okay, Mantha, I've got your back. It's John." He tented over her as the hiss of the rocket slowly dissipated, leaving behind an eerie silence.

Mantha's breathing trembled, and her heart raced in her chest. John lay next to her and held her tightly, whispering words of reassurance and comfort. "You're safe, Mantha. It's over. You're safe," he repeated like a mantra, gently stroking her back.

As the noise had been brief and discontinued, Mantha began to re-orient to her surroundings and took deep breaths to regain control of her trembling body. She looked up into John's determined eyes, gratitude and vulnerability mingling in her gaze as she whispered, "Thank you... Thank you for being here for me."

John smiled softly, his chiseled face expressing understanding and empathy. "We're veterans, Mantha. We take care of one another. We've been through hell and back, and in moments like these, we truly understand the importance of brotherhood and sisterhood."

Mantha rose slowly. Her trembling subsided, and she felt renewed strength and courage. She looked over [7] at Q. "How high did Pink Bertha go?" Sam smiled in recognition. He had lived through past momentary breakdowns. He understood trauma.

"450 feet," called out Q, cupping his mouth.

Together, they watched Shay gleefully running with intact Pink Bertha clasped in her arms. "She did it! She did it! She flew to the sky and came back!" Shay called out proudly. She was ecstatic. "Her recovery was perfect! Zak, your parachute saved her." [8] She promptly kissed her rocket.

"Let's shoot Super Bertha next, Zak," Mantha called out, blasting past protective reflexes by slowing her heart rate and breath, realizing the situation was safe, heart and breath regulating.

"Way to go, warrior," Sam encouraged, his face imprinted with wisdom and understanding.

John wrapped his muscled arms around Mantha in a bear hug. "Proud of your recovery, warrior."

Mantha raised her hand and squeezed the bear's paw. "Thanks for being my parachute," she whispered. She then commanded, in the loud voice of an Army captain, "EVERYONE to your positions."

John stepped next to Mantha, allowing her ample room to command. "Ready, Captain!" He reported, meeting her stern-set eyes.

"Standby, Master Chief Petty Officer of Naval Special Warfare Command," she ordered, smiling afterward.

How did she know? John mused, stirred by her precision with his credentials.

"Zak. PREPARE for the countdown of Super Bertha." The Monogram Masters took their positions near the launch button. They shared one last eager glance.

"Three... Two... One... LAUNCH!" They shouted in unison, pressing the button again in perfect synchronization.

Again, a roar filled the air as flames erupted beneath the second rocket, propelling it skyward. Mantha jumped. John put his arm around her shoulders as they watched Super Bertha soar. Mantha's heart pounded in her chest. "Yeah, just... the noise. It reminds me of … something."

John's knowing gaze penetrated deep into Mantha's soul. Then, Mantha met Sam's eyes, wordlessly confirming her truth. A mixture of gratitude and relief washed over her, appreciating their perceptive compassion as words weren't possible.

"Thank you," Mantha lip-synced to her comrades.

"No need for thanks," affirmed John.

"Sometimes, all it takes is a little company and a reminder that you're not alone," Sam said calmly.

"1800 feet! My turn!" Announced Q, handing John the altitude tracker.

"Your turn," agreed John.

Sam stood next to Mantha as the next rocket launch approached, giving John a thumbs up. Mantha braced herself. The comforting presence of Sam at her side reminded her that these were people who understood the remnants of battlefield scars.

They stood shoulder to shoulder, their eyes fixed on the rocket poised for liftoff. The countdown began, and anticipation built with each passing millisecond. As the engines roared to life, a fierce vibration echoed through Mantha's very bones.

But as the rocket soared, climbing higher toward the heavens, an unexpected transformation took hold within her. With each fiery burst, each resounding crackle that resonated through the air, Mantha felt the grip of the past weakening. She recognized in the hiss that the rockets' fire was a display of wonder and celebration, devoid of the later horrors, the weapons, that had forever altered her world. Then, as the last remnants of smoke dissipated into the vast expanse above, Mantha exhaled deeply, releasing the dormant tension that had plagued her for far too long.

Turning to Sam, she met his gaze with a genuine smile, a flame of hope slowly rekindling. "Grateful," she said in a steady voice filled with newfound strength.

Sam nodded, his expression full of pride in Mantha's victory. "You're welcome, my friend. Please know, there is a future beyond the battles of the past."

"2786 feet!" Bellowed John.

Q jumped to his feet with a "Whoop!" He ran into the field to collect his rocket, gently gliding down with its parachute.

"PACK 'EM UP!" Shouted Mantha, "back to the station to debrief."

The clouds had departed. Mantha found solace in knowing that her deepest scars might forever remain part of her, but they no longer needed to define or control her, though it would still take time and practice to live in her new, rearranged body and mind. She looked at John, feeling his presence beside her. Mantha and John walked together; their shared experience strengthened their bond. The rocket launches initially brought back memories of war, but their intuitive connection reminded them that they could overcome their past and find joy again. Mantha's spirits soared higher than the rockets, bringing tears of gratitude to her eyes. She was truly happy to be back home, where her future felt as boundless as the open sky above them, stretching out into an endless expanse of pure, limitless blue.

—29—
ABOUT FACE

loved puzzles, and national testing was the ultimate challenge. His tenth-grade PSAT was one of the highest the school had ever seen. It was put into his file with a note *'may need to be retested.'* The faculty believed the results must be a mistake for 'THAT STUDENT'.

When the opportunity for the ACT and SAT arrived, Q took both. He boarded the bus for the hour-long ride and sat in the front seat alone. College was not in his life's equation, so he didn't care about the results. He would do his best. He saved up most of the money, and Mom, who had barely graduated high school, covered the rest with her tips.

He brought extra sharp pencils—an entire box—and was allowed two. He had no calculator or other electronic device. He dressed in his best. Q checked in with the Proctor showed his ID and testing tickets, and proceeded to the enormous hall with individual desks to be monitored carefully. Test takers were encouraged to breathe and remain calm. Q chuckled to himself as test-taking itself calmed him.

He removed the first tests and scanned the document. He enjoyed the convoluted way the SAT disguised simple questions to untangle. The essay was a breeze. He was curious why the science component was omitted. He turned in the SAT to the Protor and requested the ACT. He filled in the ACT answers, which presented more of a Math challenge. His quick logic calculated even the most difficult. All in all, it was quite an entertaining day!

The ACT asked him about his career planning. He had none, so he imagined being a rocket scientist at SpaceX with a specialty in the StarShield project. It was more glamorous than being the afternoon waiter at Dee's Cafe. His racehorse of a mind learned from pure hunger for information that grades rarely measured.

Q's test scores revealed untapped passion, underscoring a talent that had not been recognized. His point total on the SAT was 1585/1600. He was disappointed. On the ACT, he scored a fine of 36. He did not drop a single point in English, Math, Reading, or Science. Sadly, he received only a 10/12 in the writing section, but he gained a final 150/152.

———

Shay stood beside Mr. Mason's desk, trying to work up courage. She bit her lip, shuffled her feet, and avoided eye contact. Her thoughts raced with sudden doubt. *What if he says No?* She felt vulnerable.

"Shay, what do you need?" Mr. Mason's kind brown eyes encouraged her confidence.

"I have a friend who is having a birthday and wished for a rocket, but…" she was determined to find the right words; she wanted to speak clearly. *I have to make him understand. Missy needs this. She's counting on me. We can't let her down now. Her dad is a monster. We can't let him win!* She struggled to think of what to say and then yelled. "Her dad said, 'Rockets are for boys.' That's not true. Rockets are for everyone.'"

"Yes, rockets are for everyone," agreed Mr. Mason. "May I ask who the student is?"

"No," Shay stated.

"Ahh, I see. I respect privacy." He sensed something big was at stake. *What noble mission did Shay have for this rocket?* "Shay, what do you want to ask me?"

"I'd like to give her a rocket for her birthday," said Shay. "Maybe she can fly with the Monogram Masters."

Mr. Mason's muscled arm brought his knuckle to his chin as he reasoned aloud, "Our class has built eighty-four rockets. You built four, plus you have Pink Bertha." He thought through the logistics of the number of graduating seniors. He had purchased nine packages of twelve rocket kits. There were more rockets to build. "If you use Pink Bertha for your launch at graduation, one would be available for another student."

"She's a junior like me." Hesitating, Shay shifted one foot and then the other.

"Pick one of your three classroom-completed rockets to give to this special person. I trust you, Shay." He was not surprised that Shay picked the one she named hot pink Baby Bertha.

John never dreamed this rocket project would take off in such a magnificent way. His first order of twelve rockets had morphed into a large box of Alpha, Viking, and Generic rockets that would attain 1000 to 1325 feet altitudes on a C6-7 engine. He had purchased 96 more as the rocketeers refined their skills. He got caught up in the excitement and was short on cash to buy the engines he needed to create the fleet launches—forty packs of three engines would run him over five hundred dollars.

—

The last month of school was filled with surprises. The school board recommended that the graduation speech be given by the student with the highest SAT or ACT score with a review of their PSATs if there was a tie. Typically, it had been the student achieving the highest grade point average from Freshman through Senior years.

Doc and the faculty were now in a quandary. The senior with the highest cumulative scores in every test was Q, and no one had heard him speak. In addition, his grade point average was under students whose steadfast effort yielded higher grades. The school board voted, and Q earned his place. The coveted speech would be given to Q. This would be interesting.

—

Sam's gun range remained quiet as everyone moved to the outdoor range with the warmer weather. Mantha and Sam continued to prepare for the First Responder weekly indoor shooting match. Sheriff Ben kept his tactical training private, he invited Mantha to join the team. John also joined them. He let Zak help with the setup and observe. The young man sat on a stool safely behind the shooters. He wore hearing and eye protection. Sometimes, Sam let him run the remote. Once the shooter was done and scored, and range cleared, Zak collected spent casings and hung new targets. He was not allowed to shoot, but that was okay.

—

"Mantha, this target has a hole. Did you practice recently?" Sam inquired.

"No, you and I agreed to only practice together," Mantha responded.

"Humph, I must have missed this target last month when I put them back into the box," Sam grumbled. Mantha unlocked and opened the till to check on her firearm. Interesting…she always placed its handle down, muzzle up for an easy left-hand grab. The Smith and Wesson M&P Pro, 9mm, was pointing in the opposite direction for a right-handed person. She checked the chamber and magazine. She was one bullet short. Her heart skipped a beat. Zak?

—

The school intercom blared, "Quint Larkin, come to the office immediately!" Q froze. It was May 1, thirty-one days until graduation.

Doc's arms were crossed over his chest. He looked stern and hissed with a steely chill, "You have been chosen to give the commencement address. I hope you can make this happen." End of conversation. He did not indicate what the school wanted him to talk about. That suited Q fine as the idea that leaped into his mind may not be approved.

Q had puzzled out most of the pieces of the murder of Michael Johnson's father and the junkyard explosion on the property next door. Zak had pulled together so many incredible random clues. He'd delivered them in snippets and bits, diligently building a blizzard of missing data in the trail of evidence. With Zak's map and a stack of documents he copied at the library, a grim truth emerged, along with an ominous sense of foreboding. Q's mind computed the data, and then recomputed.

No matter how the pieces were put together, it was simply impossible for the transient Kevin to have committed the murder. Logic indicated that someone else had intentionally set the fire. Then, there was the murder of Margie's daughter, Tasha, Quintel's sister. Elder Q had said a gangster was serving life but that he believed the person was also unfairly convicted. Chief was Quintel's childhood friend.

Zak and Q found the deer trail which led from Michael's old home to Doc's new estate. Currently only from the containers to Doc's new estate were well worn with Missy's human tracks adding to the trampling. The constellation of clues and events continued to point to one man. One. Free. Man. It was time to involve trusted adults.

Zak said to Q, "Are you working today?"

"I'm off today," answered Q. "I think it is time we tell your Uncle Ben what we know."

Doc skulked in the hallway in the corner by their lockers.

"Join me at Riley's. We can sit with Sam and Mantha to share what we've learned." Zak said. "Maybe John will be there, too."

"Good idea. Let's see what they think first," affirmed Q. "Then we can call your Uncle Ben."

The principal glared as he walked past the boys. "You will both be sorry with what you've unburied. You revived the dead." The sinister tone confirmed Doc Johnson overheard their conversation.

"I smell a rat," whispered Q.

"Maybe we should tell the janitor," answered Zak.

"Doc threatened us. This isn't good. We'd better get help." Q seemed scared. "We have to keep Shay out of this."

"Maybe we should tell the janitor," worried Zak. "About the rat."

———

Shay walked to the apartment with Pink Bertha's little sister, rocket. Her cake was ready and looked just like a professional Boston Cream Pie. She had decorated a large piece of art paper to use as wrapping. She created a card. She didn't want the boys involved in her adventure. She boxed the cake and packed everything else in a brown grocery bag. Then she walked to the container with a heart full of joy. She was going to make a difference. She just knew it!

The container was open. The warmth of spring heated the containers, and opening them allowed space to breathe. She peeked around the door with a soft knock and smiled. "Hi, Missy. Happy Birthday. I brought you a present and a birthday cake."

Missy was flabbergasted. "Oh—kaaay?"

Shay jumped into the container and took out the present. "This is for you, I made it."

Missy wondered what someone such as Shay could have made for her. Curious, she accepted the gift and peeled back the paper's layers. It was wrapped nicely and tied with a bundle of pink yarn colors in an incredibly artistic bow. Missy opened it tenderly. She recognized the rocket, its significance, the symbol, and the thoughtfulness behind this gift as a heavy layer of angst and depression melted away with tears beginning to spill. "This…this.. Is for me?"

Shay bounced on her knees in happiness. "Yes, of course, it is for you. I made it!"

"I've watched you fly rockets from my bedroom window. I dreamed of doing that, flying a rocket and chasing it into the field. This is mine?" Missy's hope and anticipation grew.

"Of course, it's yours," Shay assured her. "Do you see anyone else around that can have it? Just us two here." She pulled out the shiny, perfect Boston Cream Pie. "And this is to celebrate your birthday."

"Did you bring a knife and fork?" Missy eyed the beautiful pie.

Shay broke off a small piece with her hands and gave it to Missy. "Celebration means you don't have to use a knife and fork. If you like it, you can rip off a whole hunk!"

"Do you want some?" Missy suddenly remembered her manners.

"Well, it's yours," said Shay, "So I guess that is up to you."

Savoring the flavor, Missy glowed, "Shay, let's break the ice and get to know each other better."

"I didn't bring any ice, Missy," Shay apologized.

Missy giggled. "No, I just meant, we can…I want to…can we start over? I wasn't so friendly before. Then you do this kind of thing and… Shay, a rocket! And this birthday treat….this is really good." Her eyes softened. She sighed, looked down, then met Shay's gaze, smiling sincerely as she yanked off a gooey piece and handed it to Shay.

"Thank you, Missy," Shay's eyes sparkled. "It IS yummy."

Missy pulled her shoulders to her ears. Her face was covered in chocolate and vanilla pudding, "Thank YOU, Shay!"

Then, both girls burst into laughter, covered in chocolate goodness.

—

Q and Zak entered Riley's. "Hey, Zak!" It was the beginning of the strawberry season, and Mantha was ready for an afternoon break with Sam.

"We know," blurted out Q and Zak together. "Jinx!" They laughed with a high five as Mantha and Sam left together for their afternoon community camaraderie at Dee's Cafe.

"Guess the conversation will have to wait," Q hesitated. "What Doc said was creepy, Zak. His menacing words squelched the news I wanted to share, not just the uncovered data."

"They'll be back, and we have time. Let's get some of my job cards done and surprise them. Would you help me dump all the trash? I'll sweep and mop. Then we can all get out of here and go up to the containers for a game of ninja tag," bargained Zak.

"Sure, no problem," Q regrouped as he collected cans to carry out-back to the dumpster.

Zak glanced at the Riley Surveillance Monitor just as Q exited the back door. Someone ducked behind the dumpster and could no longer be seen. Curious, Zak climbed on the chair to get a closer look. That someone had a gun! That someone was... was... pointing the weapon at Q! He had to stop this! He knew where Mantha kept her firearm. He had seen it before. He even used it once at the range when Sam and Mantha had pie at Dee's. He had hit the target, but the gun scared him, so he'd put it back.

Zak ran to the cash register. If I call 911, it will take too long. There's no time!! Q might be shot dead. I have to protect him! Zak grabbed Mantha's weapon, raced out the front door, and then slowed, cautiously walked around the building on the opposite side of the dumpster.

The careful attention on the Sunday First Responder nights kicked in. This wasn't the movies. Zak shouted, "STOP!" In his most resounding voice. "PUT THE GUN DOWN! NOW!" He had heard the deputies in the scenarios say that in practice before they used their firearms. He stayed behind the concrete wall, gun lowered.

A shot rang out, exploding a piece of concrete off the side of the garage. Zak stayed behind the concrete. He quickly and quietly changed positions kneeling on one knee. *DO NOT PUT YOUR FINGER ON THE TRIGGER.* He recalled Ben's voice—*UNLESS you are going to shoot. DO NOT POINT ANY GUN AT ANYTHING YOU DO NOT WANT TO DESTROY. Choosing to shoot anyone or anything can destroy your life and the life of an innocent person.*

Zak stood and bellowed, "STOP! This is the police. STOP!" Then dropped to his knees. A shot hit the concrete where his voice had been.

The gunman mocked him. "You think you are so smart, Zak? You are an idiot!"

A piece of concrete block blew off where a bullet landed. Zak hoped Q was okay. He crouched low and pulled the trigger, aiming strategically for the chest area, flinched, and hit the shooter right below the kneecap. The man screamed and dropped his gun. Q threw the trash on him and ran. Without thinking, Zak ran up and grabbed the pistol. The screaming man lay on the ground.

"You'll be sorry, just like Kevin was sorry. You will never get away with this. You are too stupid," Doc was fuming! "No one will believe you, Zak. No one ever believes stupid."

Despite the groans and screams of pain behind him, Zak charged into the safety of the garage, holding both weapons. He put the firearms on the floor, locked both doors and collapsed.

Mantha and Sam heard three shots, two forty-four calibers and a nine. It might have been a 45, but the report was louder and more powerful than the final shot. It was an unusual sound typically heard in a deer rifle, but it sounded like a short barrel.

"Margie, call the police, NOW!" Mantha bolted upright.

"My kids are over there!" Wailed Lindsay as she started toward the cafe door. Mantha ran, with Sam following.

Margie held Lindsay back. "Stay here!"

—

Sheriff Ben and three deputies arrived, firearms at ready. They carefully circled the station and were surprised to find a furious man bleeding from the leg. Michael "Doc" Johnson was in agony: "Your kid shot me! I was minding my own business, and he shot me!" Doc had no gun.

"Call the ambulance!" Ben ordered as Mantha sliced through Doc's pants to assess the leg wound. Ben banged on the back door. "Zak, are you in there? Open the door NOW!"

Uncle Ben was serious. Q unlocked the door and ran to Sam's big chair, ducking behind it into a tight corner. Zak picked up the guns, pointing them to the floor. Zak faced Ben. His fingers were out of both triggers, barrels pointing down.

DROP would have been Sheriff Ben's initial order to anyone brandishing a firearm. But this was Zak. He paused. If the firearms were dropped, either or both could discharge. "Zak, turn and face the wall with the round clock. Keep your finger out of the triggers and keep the guns pointed down. Place them gently on the ground."

Zak took a shallow breath and turned slowly to face the clock. Ben hoped no one would enter the garage to interrupt his orders. "Very gently, put the guns on the ground. I want the barrels softly on the floor, pointed toward the clock wall."

"Yes, sir," Zak did precisely what he was told. Then he burst into tears. Q, curled up behind Sam's old chair, had his head covered under his arms into a ball. Uncle Ben wanted to wrap both boys in his arms, but he held his professional position. Ben holstered his weapon.

"He-he-he was going to shoot Q. He shot at me. He broke Sam's wall!" Stammered Zak, "I did what you do in training…not like the movies…I asked my head, c-c-could I hurt someone else if I shot? What would I break? What was behind it? You said never go bang, bang, bang. You said we will have no training scars in my county. I kept hearing your voice and Mantha's telling your team what to do."

"That's good thinking, Zak," Ben said calmly. "Sit on the ground right here." Ben could see that Zak's color was ashen, and his body trembled.

Zak sat cross-legged at a safe distance from the firearms. "I thought Q was safe if I held really still. You said if you have to shoot, don't kill unless you have to. I didn't have to, so I put my finger in the trigger and pointed at his middle. I think I hit his knee. I hit him, didn't I? He's still screaming," Zak was shaking. "I am so sorry. I didn't want Q to die. I didn't want to hurt someone, not even mean old Doc Johnson."

"He will be okay, Zak," Ben assured him. "The ambulance is on the way. They will transport him to the hospital."

"Zak, you need to be quiet and not say anything right now," interrupted Sam, thinking back to what happened to Kevin, who had now been in prison for almost twenty years.

"It's on the camera. That's how I saw him. He had a gun and was pointing it. Q was t-t-taking out the trash. It's on the camera!" Zak was babbling. "It's on the camera, like when he threatened to get rid of me."

"Zak, just SHUT UP, SHUT UP NOW!" Barked Sam, sounding very serious and scared.

John Mason arrived to attend to Doc and noted the automatic on the floor. "The 9mm is Mantha's. She painted her magazine follower with bright red nail polish. I never saw the other firearm before," he shook his head as he surveyed the guns from a distance.

"Zak, we need to go to the station to discuss this," directed Uncle Ben.

"No!" Shouted Zak. "That is the same gun that killed Doc Johnson before Michael Johnson graduated. He shot at me first. It was self-defense. Uncle Ben, you talked about that at the training; he shot at me t-two times. There were pieces of Sam's wall that fell off. I heard it! I smelled it."

There was no stopping Zak's mouth. "Michael lit the fire that hurt Mr. Mason's arm. It was the battery from his father's car. Why would the Potts' have that battery if it was NEW? The junkyard was filled with batteries." Zak paused to catch his breath. His heart pounded. He raced to purge his thoughts. "He and Porter used the secret deer trail between the houses. P-Porter and Mike were secretly best friends. Mike made Lindsay his girl in the woods instead of Kate or Amber. Kate never knew about Lindsay. Aunt Kate and Amber were Doc's high school decorations."

Zak gulped air. "Michael had a truck he drove to the cities to deliver what he had called the goods. I can prove it." Zak looked around wildly. "And-and-and THERE IS MORE! I think he killed Margie's daughter when he was delivering meth to the cities. This is bigger than me. This is bigger than me. He is a BAD, BAD, BAD man! And he would have killed Q and probably me too because I told Q what I knew, and Doc overheard us. He walked by us at school and said, "You will both be sorry with what you've unburied. You revived the dead.""

Zak's urgency to get it all out was bringing back the stress and turmoil of his life at his old school. He was hyperventilating. It was too much to grasp. He was jumping and flapping his hands by his head. "I, I, Okay I, I know how gangs work. I bet Kevin was just a mule like me because he wanted friends. I bet that's what they did to him."

"Zak, I will ask you to sit in Sam's metal chair. Q, you take his recliner. Do NOT move. Do you understand?" Ben's mind was racing with Zak's wild accusations, yet they were there with two guns on the floor. Ben's instinct kicked into high gear. Sam walked over and placed comforting hands on Zak's heaving shoulders.

"Okay, okay…," Zak was gasping and hiccuping. He felt empty of the heavy burden he had kept from Uncle Ben.

"I will keep them here," Sam reassured. "Ben, I think Zak is right. He has somehow put pieces together of Doc, the arson, and the other murder I was missing. Doc left Riverdale after the fire. For a small village like Riverdale to lose seven people to senseless deaths? It just did not make sense. I always believed Kevin was innocent. Let's rewind my tape and see what's going on." Sam moved over to the desk where the computer and recording mechanisms were kept.

Ben rewound the tape, watching blow by blow the exact scenario Zak had described. "I think Doc's got a skeleton in his closet," he growled.

"You better send the police to look in his closet, Uncle Ben," Zak offered as the Sheriff and Sam exchanged looks. The tape showed both shots. They heard Zak call out orders. They heard Doc's threat.

"There's more than one skeleton there," Sam whispered between tensed lips, lowering his chin and looking pointedly at Ben. "The kids were in danger. That man is unhinged, and he's clever."

Ben returned to questioning. "Zak," he spoke purposefully, pulling up a folding chair, "let's take this one question at a time. May I record this?"

"Please, Uncle Ben, I promise to tell you the whole truth and nothing but the truth," spilled Zak, tears of relief dripping off his face.

"I understand that you were facing an armed person who was shooting at you. Are you safe now?" Asked Uncle Ben.

"Yes, I am safe now. I had Mantha's firearm, and I only used it to help Q. Doc was going to shoot him!" Zak quivered.

"I see. Can you tell me more about what happened? Take it slow." Uncle Ben observed Zak closely.

"I saw Michael Johnson, Doc, with the gun coming from behind the dumpster pointing a gun at Q. He threatened us as we left school today, so I was afraid for Q's life. I went to get Mantha's gun. She locks it up, but I know how to get in," Zak recalled.

"I understand that you felt threatened and reacted with the intention of self-defense. However, it's essential to clarify a few things. Are you trained in the use of firearms?" Asked his uncle.

"No."

"Do you have a permit or legal authorization to carry and use a firearm?"

"I don't have formal training, and I don't have a permit," Zak replied sheepishly, shaking his head.

"Thank you for being honest. In situations like these, it's crucial to prioritize personal safety. However, it's important to note that using a firearm can be dangerous and requires proper training and legal authorization. Possessing and using a firearm without the necessary permits or legal authorization can have serious legal consequences." Ben informed his stunned nephew.

"I didn't know that. I just had to protect Q! There was no time!" Repeated Zak. "I didn't want to hurt anyone."

"We understand your intent, but it's always best to prioritize personal safety by seeking help from the authorities, such as calling the police, whenever you find yourself in a dangerous situation. It is their role to handle such incidents lawfully." Ben made sure Zak understood that his behavior was extremely serious.

"What if Q died?" Objected Zak. "What if you didn't come in time?" His anxiety for Q, without any weapon, being ambushed by an armed adult who had threatened harm, was all he could grasp.

"We will sort this out, Zak. I want to see Q and your notes plus and all that have uncovered that was not discovered in 2007," directed Uncle Ben. "I am grateful Q is alright. I am thankful Doc was only shot in the knee." He looked over at Sam. "I am extremely grateful for your surveillance system. I want everything you have about that old case, Sam. Everyone you remember who might know something. People who may not have seemed to matter to interview back then, we will interview now. I want to hit the ground running with this."

"Isn't that dangerous, Uncle Ben?" Questioned Zak. "I don't want you hurt. You shouldn't hit the ground running, I mean."

"It's a way of saying, Zak, I will look at ALL the details I can find, everything you have found, Q has discovered, or Shay knows. I will take all this information and run with it. It means I will speed up solving this puzzle," explained the Sheriff.

"Uncle Ben, there is one more journal. Shay has Sally Ann's journal. She took it from the garbage can at Memory Care when it was thrown away," Zak remembered. "You know, Mike's mother."

"Can you get that for me, too, Zak?"

"Yes." Zak gazed over at Q, still in a tight ball, hiding under an old garage blanket Sam had draped over him. He swallowed hard, glad Sheriff Ben and Sam were there to help, not angry. All he wanted was for his friend, Q, to be safe, and for the danger to be over.

-30-
GRADUATION LAUNCH

Sheriff Ben reopened the closed case of Emmett Johnson and the conviction of a life sentence for Kevin Abbott. Reopening the case required new evidence. Zak and Q provided enough new evidence, including legal errors that influenced the original outcome. What he knew was incredible. He called his brother David.

"David, I need a favor. I need a gladiator in the courtroom, and I don't know anyone better." His voice lightened. "Zak graduates in less than thirty days..."

———

It was the people who didn't matter that held the pieces of truth. It was two kids considered weirdos who became the catalyst for change—Zak volunteered all his drawings, maps, and notes to Uncle Ben. Q added his precise notes and notated historical documents.

———

Sam. The greasy garage owner, a crabby veteran and amputee, offered new tangible evidence—The two bullets Sam had matched the bullets that chipped his southwest concrete wall. Sam pulled out his old journal with all the details that were not admissible in court. He gave his journal to Ben. Ben read the journal, understanding Sam's anger and disbelief in Kevin's arrest, trial, and imprisonment. He ended the last page with an expletive. Reading Sam's writing regarding Kevin reminded him so much of Zak's perception of the world.

———

John. A person from a rival town knew things others did not—Ben listened carefully as John and Sam discussed Shaun's fatal accident. John Mason shared his memories of the fire, the battery, and finding the bullet in the tree that Sam's son Shaun had catapulted into. Having driven that trail with Shaun hundreds of times, he knew how well he drove. "Sam,

Shaun didn't make mistakes while driving; he was careful. I taught him how to handle that curve, and he did it the same way every single time. I've even seen him avoid wildlife even at that corner. We owned it. I don't think it was a rabbit. From how Shaun and Mike flew off that machine, I think a counterbalanced prank was being played that went wrong."

Sam's skin pricked, "Shaun was a lightweight. Mike was significantly heavier as a quarterback. YES. Yes, that is very possible."

"Like Zak, Shaun wore his helmet and let the straps flow behind him like banners. He impacted that tree hard without his helmet or a helmet that only partially worked. I realized that when Mantha and I were looking at the remains of the Larkin fire. When we found the deer trail."

"There's a deer trail?" Sam asked. "Where is it?"

"Runs the south side of the main trail. Zak put it correctly on his map. It would have been a safe spot to pull a trigger to shoot Emmett without anyone finding tracks or casings. I stepped over from the tree I found the bullet in years ago." John added. "I was thinking about the accident, the murder, and the fire."

Sam shook his head, "All four bullets are the same, John. The two are almost twenty years old and fired from the gun at Zak recently. Even with the same petal pattern, it's uncanny."

"The old school bus was used as a meth production lab, and there were plenty of batteries surrounding it. None were new except THAT BATTERY. Nothing was new in that junkyard; I was always looking for parts and pieces there as a teen. I knew most of the vehicles. That battery had no reason to be there." John shared.

"Emmett had just bought a new battery at Hans Hardware. I was with him when he ordered it special. Planned to add a plow to his truck the next winter." Sam added.

"I know more about accidents, fires, and explosives than I did back then." John recounted. "By the way, do you have any extra rocket engines? I need 108 to pull off the graduation finale."

Sam laughed, "Sounds like Zak's dream of a fleet launch is becoming a reality."

"IF I can afford all those engines." John laughed as Zak put another task card into his completed pile.

—

Shay, a nondescript teen not even alive at the time of the murders had gained access to information no one else had. Shay brought the ripped journal and shared her time with Ann. Ben paged through the old pages, dropping ripped snowflakes as he read. The last section of the journal was in Shay's handwriting, with pictures of the stories the two had shared. The beginning section had diary entries in Ann's script from 2007-2008—her angst about finding Doc and not being able to revive him, frustration at the truck not being able to start because the battery was stolen, worry over the sullenness of Michael, grief over the murder of her husband and poisoning of her dog, Happy. Sadness over the loss of life of the Pott family. The excitement of selling the property and moving away from Riverdale to start over. More worry over Mike.

—

Lindsay. Who wanted to interview an angry pregnant teenager? She was Mike's 'side girl' and his neighbor at the time. She told Sheriff Ben she had nothing she was willing to share, that to do so would indicate the paternity of Q, and she didn't need to rehash traumatic and painful memories from the past. Lindsay said, "Q is a great kid, and he never needs to know, and no one needs to tell him. What was done was done. I live my life in the present. I buried that memory, and I am not unpacking it. And if you ask me, would he? Did he? My answer is YES. End of conversation. I was the poor girl across the field to be used and abused down the trail." She paused, "I was not one of Mike's showcase girlfriends. Amber and Kate only saw his front side. They were just cheerleader trophies to hang on his arm. I was the one who saw him with his pants down."

—

Trapper. No one thought of interviewing Kevin's jailhouse roommates. Trapper had been arrested at that time for a DUI. It was his last.— Trapper, Harris County road emergency leader, declared the whole case against Kevin bogus; he roomed with him in jail. There was no way that kid was capable of an intentional murder. He laughed loudly when Ben mentioned it, saying, "No one ever asked me about this. If they had, I would have told them what I knew. I lived with him in a jail cell for weeks." I've been sober now for twenty years—never was arrested again. Without knowing Shaun and Kevin, Anny may have continued drinking with our brilliant girls. Kevin was like Shaun, prenatally exposed."

—

Margie and Quintel shared information that had never been allowed in court. It was in no records. They both believed Kevin was innocent. Quintel offered to take on the case as a pro bono attorney and work with David. As a mature, respected attorney, he had access to materials he'd had no idea about when he was only eighteen. He wanted more details of that murder, plus the loss of his little sister, Tasha. Tasha had run away to the cities to stay with her childhood friend, Lisa. Joining this case would allow him to dig deeper. Perhaps they were connected.

—

Kissy. Sam and Quintel recommended Ben talk to Commander April Palmquist (five-year-old Kissy). What on earth could a five-year-old remember? Ben was curious because Quintel said she was a very bright five-year-old at the time. And because she was a child, she may have overheard conversations while being ignored. Quintel remembered her telling him, "Five-year-olds know stuff. Someone talked real bad about Kevin." And he had always wondered but never asked again.

Ben called Kissy at the naval base. She clearly remembered a conversation between Porter Potts and Michael. According to Kissy, Michael admitted to killing his father. She had overheard the conversation while hiding behind the Hans Hardware ammo counter at Grandpop's, snuggling with Blue and Lovely Lady Lucy, her then-golden Labrador pup. Her mother had recently disciplined her for talking about a customer, and she was told to keep her lips shut about people. "The boys were laughing. Mike was mad that his dad had confronted him about dealing and doing drugs. Potts said he would take the blame. I think Emmett may have confronted his son, Mike, on the night he was shot. Mike had a pungent, smoky smell like Potts. Today, I know now that the smell was meth and weed."

"I've waited almost twenty years for justice. Kevin was my friend," she reflected. "He chewed all the green and blue gumballs so I could get the pinks and purples. I hope we can finally save Kevin. Tell Zak, thank you." Kissy seemed relieved.

—

The more Ben dug, the more solemn he became. This was more than unfair, and personally, if he did not know the people he interviewed well at this point in his life, he also may have overlooked them in a hot case. He continued to feed his attorney brother, David, information. Feeling the need for a bit of redemption, David took on the challenge pro bono. He was just the person with the right connections for the job. The deeper the brothers dug, the higher the iceberg rose into a mountain of truth.

"What about Lisa? The girl at the murder of Tasha Jones?" Asked David.

"Where do I find her?" Ben shirked.

"Social Media, try lower-hanging fruit." David laughed. "She was a Rule 25. Never know what they know!"

———

Lisa. Ben searched computer databases and social media to find Lisa Veritas, Kevin's girlfriend before Tasha. *Who would think these two murders, the fire and the accident, were connected? A beloved town chiropractor, a junk dealing meth producer, a not suitable for many young adults, and a runaway pregnant teen. There would be no reason anyone would interview the girl named Lisa, who was passed out cold in the park holding a newborn under her hoodie at the time of the murder. Weirder things can happen, and sometimes the truth is stranger than fiction.* By mixing her social media sites with his available databases and relative searches, he located her, "This is Sheriff Jordan from Riverdale. I am looking at the murder of Tasha Jones.

"Wow, that is a blast from the past," said the woman, "This is Lisa. Tasha was my best friend."

"Can you tell me what you remember?" Asked Ben.

"This isn't easy to talk about. Tasha was… killed while I was going to the bathroom in the bushes." Lisa spoke quietly, "When I returned, she was bleeding from the neck and covered in blood… Her head was almost severed. The last think she whispered was 'keep Oginga safe.' Then she died. Everything was happening so fast. Her and Kevin's baby was being born. The tiny baby was screaming and shivering. I put him inside my hoodie. I was an alcoholic at the time so I drank my whole liter of vodka, which was in my sleeve. I passed out and woke up in the hospital committed to Rule 25 for a year." Lisa sighed as if the weight of this secret had crushed her for years, and she could finally climb out from underneath it. She steadied her voice. "I am a much different person now, sheriff. I have eighteen years of sobriety. Alcohol took over my life the first week I tried it; it was like it was already living in me, and my body hungered for it."

"Who would have wanted to kill her?" Ben didn't need a time diversion, he continued. "Q said he believed you thought it was related to the murder in Riverdale."

"Yes, it is a longer story, but I will try to give you a short version. The Deliverer brought Meth to one of my roommates, nicknamed Chief, sometimes called Ghost. Ghost used Kevin as his mule. Supposedly, Kevin introduced the Deliverer to Ghost as a mover for the goods coming out of a town with River in the name. You said River, Riverdale? That may have been it. It has been so long. No one ever wanted to hear my side of the story before. I overheard the Deliverer, also called, hmm, can't quite remember his real name. The Deliverer talked hard and big. I remember him bragging about shooting his dad's hand off and then killing his old man. He said he was a cowboy shooter. I thought that was weird. Whenever he came with the goods, Tasha and I locked my bedroom door and added a kitchen knife in the casing. I never saw the guy's face."

Ben listened in silence as Lisa continued. "Chief blew a lot of smoke and talked big, but he would not have killed anyone. Chief liked Tasha. He was kind to dogs, kids, and babies. He didn't do the drugs he was into making money. He always respected Tasha and he liked Kevin. He was excited to see how the baby would look. Would the baby have Kevin's wild orange hair? Kevin made Chief laugh. Chief used Kevin as his watchman for deliveries. The police said it was Chief's knife that killed Tasha, and Chief's prints were all over it. They arrested him for killing Tasha and got sent to the pen. He already had a record."

Lisa took a breath. "Before Tasha and I walked to the park, I overheard Chief give his favorite knife to the Deliverer because he didn't have enough money for the goods." She paused again, "I think his real name was…Mike. Tasha knew things about Mike from that River place. It reminded me of a shopping mall, like dale, Riverdale. That's what you said, too. Right? I think that might have been it. Anyway, Tasha planned to challenge the Deliverer about Kevin. She told me she believed Kevin was set up. She was carrying Kevin's baby and wanted to marry him. That's everything I remember."

"This is all very helpful, Lisa," said the Sheriff. "Thank you. Here's my number if you think of anything else."

—

Click squelch click

RocketMan: Good evening. There are fine radio operators out there! KØROK RocketMan checking in. I was spinning the dial on my trusty rig, and it got me thinking...

Zak: Hi KØROK RocketMan. This is Zak.

RocketMan: Nice to meet you, Zak. Where is Sam?

Zak: Out. Can I ask you something?

RocketMan: Ok, go ahead.

Zak: Mr. Mason, his other name is John. My teacher needs 108 engines for the Riverdale Rockets Graduation Launch. Where can I get them? He's tapped out from buying all the rockets. He runs the In School Suspension class. Only he calls the In-School Student Success room. I'm in his class, and we make rockets for every Riverdale Rocket graduate. We've built 90 rockets! We don't have the engines, and they won't launch without them.

RocketMan: Whoa, that is some fleet.

"Zak, what are you doing using the Ham Shack, AGAIN? I TOLD YOU, you have to pass your first radio test…Give me that mike." Sam was not happy.

Zak pressed the mike, "Bye, RocketMan, Sam's not out now. 73

RocketMan: 73 Zak.

Sam took the mike.

———

If all of Ben's suspicions were correct, there would soon be an arrest and a new trial sooner than later. Twenty years was already way too long. Zak handed over every sketch and sticky note he had crumbled under his bed. Q's provided his chicken scratch and thought processes for David speaking with him by phone for over an hour on how he connected and why he connected all the pieces. The Monogram Masters hoped the adults could finally solve this wrong answer in Riverdale.

Ben's created a conference call with Attorneys David Jordan and Quintel Jones.

Thankfully, Doc was recovering from the bullet wound. He still believed Zak was the one going to jail.

———

The spring breeze announced the beginning warmth of a coming summer as Ben and Kate sat together on the porch swing. Ben's placed his hand on Kate's rounded belly feeling the flutter of the baby's kicks on his palm. "Honey, I've been thinking a lot lately. Living with Zak has made me consider how policing works when it comes to dealing with people who have FASD or other neurodivergent conditions. Being an officer of peace and living with Zak has helped me recognize how rules and laws can be misinterpreted and think of better ways to respond safely. There are pieces missing from our system that assumes everyone already understands right from wrong. Zak believes he is right but his mind sees things so differently." Ben gazed up at the budding trees. "In order to understand and not make a mistake, I need to get to the root of his thinking and work from there. For example, I looked on the Internet about Zak's crazy lying and discovered more about confabulation."

"You Googled 'crazy lying.'" Kate was surprised.

Ben smirked, "The phrase is a shorthand that the psychiatric field uses as they try to differentiate between planned, premeditated deception or reflexive, cornered babbling of mutually incompatible and implausible statements, like 'the dog ate my homework when you ask a student about it to 'I left it on the bus then I saw the dog eat it.'"

"Aye, aye, Professor Ben," Kate laughed. "Yes, it is called confabulation, and it happens from brain injuries like FASD, dementia, or trauma. What brought this on? Is everything OK?" Kate was curious.

"I believe some of my thinking might have been off-base. I want to make a change. I see things differently now, and it's not just Zak. Margie and Lindsay are important to our community, and sweet Shay. Then there is the reality of Sam's son, Shaun, and what happened to Kevin. They are all different people, all prenatally exposed—each individual has similarities and differences. I've realized that my previous methods may not have been the most effective when dealing with the people under appreciated in Riverdale."

"That's a big realization. What are you planning?" Kate asked.

"People like Zak are everywhere. I want to understand the challenges these individuals face and how I can better communicate and interact with them. The justice system is supposed to provide fairness for everyone. We need a training program for Harris County so that our first responders understand that some people may have comprehension differences even if they can talk. Or they can have trauma reactions, which affects how they react to a situation." Ben looked at Kate, "Zak is not the only person in this county with neurodiversity; I want to be prepared and have our community work hard to be fair for everyone."

"That sounds like a positive step. How do you think your colleagues will react to the idea?" Kate wondered.

Ben cleared his throat. "Change is never easy, but I believe it's necessary. I hope that by leading by example and providing practical training, we can create a more inclusive and understanding environment within our department. It's not just about doing our jobs but doing them in a way that respects the dignity and uniqueness of each citizen we encounter. When I dug into that old case, I realized even in Riverdale, there is a strong emphasis on hierarchical social structures. Certain people and jobs are viewed as inherently superior to others. Mine and yours are two of them. Even though Emmett and Sam were best friends, Sam owning the garage didn't rank with the chiropractic practice. A waitress, who knows everyone in this community is not ranked as high as a church pastor. Margie wasn't even interviewed. My profession and the justice system have a big effect on the lives of families. I don't want to make more mistakes."

"I get what you mean. I look at the school system and what Zak needed. Fairness. Opportunity to thrive. All students are promised this on paper, but the more I research and attend workshops on teaching neurodivergent students, the more I see it often does not work out in the real world. It seems there are ways to teach to help them learn better and discover—their talents and passions. How do they participate in our community? John Mason does an excellent job working with these kids. We are blessed to have him in our school and as a volunteer EMT and firefighter. Riverdale students who would typically drop out at sixteen are working hard to get into trouble and suspended so that they can learn. I always figured they were bad kids, and I never saw them as scared, overwhelmed, and frustrated in school. But that's before I embraced Zak."

"I've thought the same thing about people I've arrested," Ben closed his eyes. "You and I had the luxury of going to college. I was in the military. We've lived outside of Riverdale. And when we return for some doggone reason, we think we are better than those who stayed put."

"I never thought about that before, Ben. You are right." Kate was humbled. "It's all of us together. I want to see this change."

"I know I've ignored and discounted the skill and intelligence it takes in the practical roles of our community. The hard workers who keep Riverdale running. More than that, they lay a foundation to keep it healthy, yet medical persons, educators, and people like me get the glory."

"I want the best opportunity for our child and create an environment where students feel comfortable and supported—safe to learn. My teaching approach was not as accommodating as it could have been. Even my favorite teaching methods do not work for someone like Zak. Education should be accessible to everyone." Kate placed her hand upon Ben's, looking at him with sincerity.

"And the legal system should be just and fair," Ben added.

"What happens if our baby is like Zak?" Kate looked worried.

"Then we will figure this out, not just for our child, but for many. I will love this person." Ben patted Kate's rounding belly.

—

"Uncle Ben, can I ask you something?" Zak interrupted.

"Go ahead, Zak," Ben chuckled. Kate smiled, shaking her head.

"John needs over $500 for the rocket engines to launch the fleet. He already bought all the rockets. We can't just give everyone a rocket and not let them launch it. Sam had me make all the rocket launchers. I don't know what to do," Zak was exasperated.

"Zak, do you have the money?" Uncle Ben asked.

"I don't have THAT MUCH MONEY!" Zak exclaimed.

"Yes, you do. Your father sent me money to help care for you. Aunt Kate and I have been putting it into an account for your adult transition or future schooling. Would you like to use some of that money to buy the rocket engines?" Uncle Ben asked.

Zak's eyes popped. He had never thought of having more than five hundred dollars. "I have the money?"

"Yes, and if you want to use it for the engines, you can," said Uncle Ben. "We can go to the bank tomorrow. And I'll bet John or Sam would order the right engines for you."

—

The bank teller counted out five brand new hundred dollar bills and handed them to Zak in an envelope. Zak proudly rolled his bank envelope into his back pocket and walked to Riley's. Zak was part of himself and the community. Uncle Ben admired him. The young man walked tall, he no longer slouched.

"Sam, Sam! I need your help," Zak ran into the station, rounding the corner to the Ham Shack.

"Whoa, slow down, boy. Can't you see I am on a rag chew?" Sam was exasperated at being interrupted.

Zak sat down on the rolling stool. He sat on his hands. He spun the stool. He cleared his throat. His bum started going up and down as the stool spun wildly out the door, and he kerplunked to the floor, "Ouch!" He shouted.

Sam's headset didn't suppress Zak's 'ouch.' He ignored it. Mantha heard the hollering from under the hood of the Challenger. She caught the stool rolling out the door into the office. "What's going on?" Seeing Zak on the floor.

Sam turned to look at the commotion.

Sam: Hold on, RocketMan. It looks like Zak crashed off a stool in my Ham Shack. I have to check his status.

RocketMan: Will hold. I am waiting for an update. Greet Zak for me.

"Now what?" Sam grunted.

Zak pulled his now squashed rolled bank envelope from his pocket. "I got it. John needs 108 engines so everyone can launch their rocket... I got the money for all the engines. Are you talking to RocketMan? Can he get engines for the great rocket launch?"

"Slow down, boy." Sam stared at the no longer crisp Benjamins, his palm out. "I'll see what I can do."

Zak handed Sam the money and immediately ran out the door to tell Q his great news.

———

A large red motorcycle rode into Riley's with what looked like a too-old-to-drive driver with a cardboard box strapped to his passenger seat.

"FI - -!" shouted Zak. "I mean, Mantha, look at that bike. Look at that helmet. Do you know who this is? It's RocketMan! I know, I know, this is RocketMan! I saw this Harley-Davidson USA twin Pulse Jet engine Motorcycle on YouTube at the library." Zak ran out the door, "Can I fill your tank? Wash your mirrors? How 'bout I wipe off your boots? They look dirty."

A raucous laugh erupted as the heavily bearded man removed his helmet, "You must be Zak!"

Zak was on a roll, "Sam, Sam! I need help! It's RocketMan!" Zak turned and ran back into the garage to fetch Sam.

Mantha looked on from the doorway as the gentleman got off his bike and unlatched the box. Zak emerged from the doorway, almost pushing Mantha aside. She grabbed his collar, "Whoa, bucko!" Holding him fast.

Sam approached the rear as the man handed the box to Zak, "Hold that box carefully. It is very precious cargo."

"Are you RocketMan?" Zak asked.

"What do you think?" The man asked.

"Yes."

"Then the answer is yes," RocketMan reached out to bear hug Sam, noting Mantha letting go of Zak's collar. Before hugging him, he saluted. "Good morning, Captain, thank you for your service."

The box on the motorcycle contained a dozen packages of engines plus a wide selection of engines new to Q and Zak. It was apparent Sam and RocketMan went way back in friendship.

"Staying for graduation?" Sam asked.

"Wouldn't miss it for the world," answered RocketMan. "Just stopped by to go trout fishing in the Dale river, that is if you have any trout left."

—

The anticipated evening finally arrived—GRADUATION!

It was a beautiful evening with a clear blue sky as the summer equinox approached. The faculty sat on folding seats behind the podium. The principal's chair was empty, and it would remain so until a new high school principal was hired. Sheriff Ben had arrested and taken him to Harris County jail, placing him in the same solitary cell that Kevin had lived in twenty years ago.

—

Q smiled as he took his position, adjusted the microphone, and cleared his throat.

"Ladies and gentlemen," Q's voice was courteous yet personal.

"Today, we celebrate not only the end of our high school journey but also the beginning of countless opportunities and exciting adventures. As I stand before you, I want to share a perspective that might differ from what you are used to. I am a graduate with Level One Autism previously referred to as Asperger's, and my unique experiences have shaped how I view the world. Diversity affects more than just culture. It affects how we perceive the world we live in."

"I want you to look into the gloaming sky at twinkling stars. They will soon be visible constellations. Neurodiversity is like constellations you have not yet met. Without recognition, it feels like multiple bursts of light, but unless you are in the know, you cannot connect the dots to get the full picture."

"Consider for a moment the genuinely awe-inspiring endeavor of space exploration, the intriguing mission of the Challenger. Like the mighty rocket that soars toward the heavens, our high school years launch us into a journey of growth, discovery, and overcoming obstacles. Some of us may have felt like new astronauts, stepping out of our comfort zones, unsure of what awaited us. But we, like the Challenger, have triumphed over the gravitational pull that tried to hold us back, succeeding in reaching new heights."

"Throughout high school, we have faced challenges that have seemed impossible. However, with determination, resilience, and the unwavering support of our friends, families, and educators, we have proved that nothing is impossible. We are the crew of this magnificent spaceship, navigating uncharted territories filled with exams, assignments, extracurricular activities, and the ups and downs of adolescence. We have found a unique way to contribute to this mission, making our mark on the world."

"The greatest lesson I have learned throughout high school is that being different is not a limitation. It is a gift that allows people to see the world uniquely. My Asperger's has given me insight, determination, and a profound curiosity. It has taught me to approach challenges with a fearless mindset, embrace the unknown, and pursue my dreams."

"Just like the visionaries who propelled the Challenger beyond the sky, we, too, have the power to create change, launch ourselves into the unknown, and chase after our passions with relentless tenacity. Graduation serves as the ignition point, the blast-off from which we embark on the next phase of our lives. Let us strive to become explorers of extraordinary, innovative engineers and compassion."

"As we move forward, let us remember that our diplomas bear witness to our abilities, but they don't define the entirety of who we are. They are symbolic reminders of our growth and the potential that rests within us. We must not fear failure but embrace it as a necessary step towards our desired success. It may bruise us as we break down our emotional, mental, and physical barriers and explore what life offers. Like the

Challenger's crew, we must show resilience in the face of setbacks and believe in our ability to rise, adapt, and excel. It was from their brilliance and fortitude, even after the 1986 tragedy, that programs such as the space station emerged."

"To my fellow graduates, we are all united in our shared journey regardless of our paths. The friendships formed, the lessons learned, and the memories created will forever shape us. Let us not forget to express our gratitude to those who supported us along the way – teachers, mentors, friends, and families. Let us strive to be caretakers of connection to those who have been and will become our lifelines, the guiding stars illuminating our paths."

"We celebrate this pivotal moment. We are boundless, enigmatic, and capable of greatness. Embrace your uniqueness, celebrate your achievements, and prepare yourselves to explore the vast endlessness of the universe that awaits us."

Zak Jordan will come up and complete my speech. Q handed Zak five cards, "Go, my friend, you got this," he whispered. Zak flipped through the cards - Good evening, Challenges, Grateful, Launch, Graduating was all they said. He looked at his "Good evening" card. OK, here goes!

ZAK STEPPED OUT, his bright red shoes dancing.

Good evening, gather 'round, listen up close,

I'm here to drop some truths, not just prose.

Standing tall today, in cap and gown attire,

Triumphing through odds, my inner fire's entire.

My journey's not the norm, far from ordinary,

Life's lessons of perseverance and extraordinary.

Fetal Alcohol Spectrum Disorder has been my ride,

But I wear it proudly, with nothing to hide.

Embrace the difference. It's my strength. See...

You are not defining me but unlocking what's in me.

This community's warmth, patience, and love,

Lifted me high, guided from above.

Teachers, mentors, peers, and friends,

You held my hand, no matter the bends.

Rising beyond limits, FASD's constraints,

You believed in me and erased doubts and restraints.
Today, launching forth into our new phase,
Rockets soar high, our dreams we embrace.
Goals, hopes, and potential, sky high,
Let's lift each other, reaching for the sky.
Create a haven where all find their place,
Valued, supported, embraced in grace.
Extend a hand to those facing strife,
Seen and unseen battles, realities of life.
Let's erase the whispers, the feelings of shame,
Replace them with empathy. We are all not the same,
Together, we remove the stigma's hold
and create a world where acceptance unfolds.
Respect and love, Sheriff Ben's wise words,
Echoing truth, what our hearts have heard.
Graduating stands as diversity's decree,
Creativity, Patience, and Love are key.
Proud to be part of Riverdale, you see,
Diversity's power is what sets us free.
Shine like rockets, lighting up the night,
Our journey starts at this height.
So, my friends, let's spread our wings wide,
Into the universe, let our differences guide us.
We're just beginning, the future's bright,
Love your neighbor and yourself. That's just plain right.
Riverdale, I salute a community so grand,
Let's light up the sky with rockets in hand.
This, my graduation, speaks of love's might,
Diversity, understanding, shining so bright.

Zak spun around, pushing the microphone into the air, and Q took the microphone. "Thank you, Zak." The audience rose and clapped as Zak shared his speech. Q motioned for everyone to be seated quietly. He paused until peace resumed.

"As we strive for progress and innovation, we must recognize and value the unique abilities and perspectives that neurodivergent individuals bring. Their remarkable minds possess the capacity to think outside the box, challenge assumptions, and offer groundbreaking solutions to our society's complex problems. Their creative and unorthodox approaches can revolutionize the way we tackle challenges to unveil groundbreaking breakthroughs that have the potential to shape our future."

"Imagine a world where neurodivergent individuals have the tools and opportunities to utilize their potential fully. Their contribution could unlock previously closed doors and take humanity to unimaginable heights. We can pave the way for a brighter, more inclusive future by embracing our unique abilities."

"In conclusion, let us embark on a journey of exploration and appreciation, cherishing the hidden treasure in each of us. We must remember that we all see the same stars and sky, but depending on our culture, we see different constellations. Together, we can create a more inclusive, innovative, and prosperous society where no mind is left untapped, and the difference between a problem and the solution for coping with it is solved through compassion and creativity."

"Again, Thank you for allowing my friend Zak and I to share our thoughts today. May we all continue to push the boundaries, explore the unknown, and embrace the remarkable diversity within us all."

"Congratulations, fellow graduates. Let's Launch!"

———

John wrapped his arms around Mantha, who had leaned into his muscled frame. "I can't believe Zak had the money to buy every graduate an engine. That was so generous." The band played the first part of the USA national anthem. 'Oh, say can you see, by the dawn's early light, What so proudly we hailed, at the twilight's last gleaming,' The field was filled with measuring markers of small American flags. Sam sat on a folding chair, marking 'the line' for safety.

"Everyone, step back," commanded Shay. "Three - Two - One - Blast off!" The first 21 rockets were launched in perfect sequence. Q's invention worked brilliantly. Mantha nestled into John. Students ran, tossing their graduation caps to fetch the first rockets.

"Prepare the next launch," shouted Shay. The band played the following two lines. "Whose broad stripes and bright stars, through the perilous fight, O'er the ramparts we watched were so gallantly streaming."

"Everyone on the line, step back," commanded Missy, who smiled at Shay. "Three - Two - One - Blast off!" The second set of 21 rockets were launched in perfect sequence. The next group of students ran, tossing their graduation caps into the air to fetch their rockets. The Minnesota state, Federal, and POW flags blew in the very slight breeze. John felt Mantha relax, tilting her face up to him and smiling.

The band continued, "And the rocket's red glare, the bombs bursting in the air, gave proof through the night that our flag was still there."

"Everyone on the line, step back," commanded Simon, who soon stepped into a Riverdale Senior class position and tried his best to remain in Mr. Mason's class. "Three - Two - One - Blast off!" The third 21 rockets were launched in perfect sequence. As Mantha put her hand on her heart, John watched Zak as the students ran, tossing their graduation caps into the air to fetch their rockets. Each student would have adventures and calamities in their lives, and retrieving the pieces and successful flights were all part of the exploration. Life was never fair.

Oh, say does that star-spangled banner yet wave, O'er the land of the free and the home of the brave?

This time, two rows of rockets prepared to launch. A row of smaller rockets created by the Science and Technology class was gifted to each graduate. Twenty-one larger dynamic rockets stood steadfastly ready in the row safely behind the first row. Q. designed many. Some were designed by Zak and painted by Shay.

"Everyone on the line, step back," Commanded Missy, "Three - Two - One - Blast off!" The fourth of the 21 rockets launched in perfect sequence as the graduates remained at attention behind the safety line. "Everyone on the line, step back." Commanded Shay, "Three - Two - One - Blast off!" The fifth of the 21 rockets launched higher and higher, each in its way, with different engines and development.

Nicole, Missy's mother, stood tall in the crowd. Her head lifted and her shoulders square. It was as if a huge weight fell off. She clapped and cheered as her daughter launched the rockets.

Each rocketeer now commanded their rocket. "Everyone on the line, step back." Commanded Q in a magnificent and powerful voice, "Three - Two - One - Blast off!" Q's rockets shot into the heavens as Simon called out altitudes attained. "3,100 feet!" The crowd roared. John's massive arms lifted high with palms out, feeling the moment's gravity. Mantha's dark eyes sparkled, absorbing the long-awaited feelings that were missing as she first drove into Sam's station. She was home.

Nineteen rockets in glorious colors, sizes, and shapes lifted off one at a time. Mantha stepped away from John, her arms crossed over her chest. She savored each rocketeer's dedication to developing and creating this massive effort.

And Zak's Super Bertha was painted a glorious lime green and purple. The Monogram Master logo was emblazoned on its fuselage. Zak kept his ideas secret and used an advanced engine only the brave or the foolish would try. He called his rocket "The Challenger." He had made special modifications even Q had not seen.

Q handed off the altitude calculator to Simon. "Everyone on the line, step back." Commanded a robust Q, "Three - Two - One - Blast off!" As Simon called out, Zak's rocket shot into the heavens, altitudes attained. "3,450 feet!" Everyone cheered.

"I beat you, Q! I beat you!" Zak shouted. Mantha whooped and ran with Zak to grab The Challenger.

John heard the blast. He knew the sound of that engine. What was that kid thinking? That engine belonged in amateur rocketry. He hoped Super Bertha survived.

———

The final four rockets were launched to usher in the new classmates; Missy launched the Junior class into its new senior position. Shay launched the Sophomores into their junior year. Simon took care of the Freshmen moving ahead.

And then Zak, looking at the class of eighth graders watching the graduation, took hold of the microphone, "No matter how hard life gets. You must believe you can achieve. Each of you is here with a purpose. Find it. Do it. Be it! The sky is not even your limit!"

Q stepped forward with his sleek secret rocket, smiling at Zak. Something was up his sleeve as Zak handed the microphone to Mantha and shouted, "Everyone on the line, step back." He paused, "Three - Two - One - Blast off!" The slim, streamlined rocket rose into the sky until it disappeared.

"Your altitude tracker doesn't go high enough!" Simon shouted. High in the sky, a glimmer sparkled, and then a parachute as Q and Zak ran together to retrieve the final rocket.

———

Margie stood behind Sam's chair, eyes glistening, "Glory, Glory," she said.

Quintel, a grateful attorney, wrapped his arms around his Mama. "I did it, Mama. I did it! The truth is going to set Kevin free. We can finally let Tasha rest in peace. Why don't you come home with me? It's your time to rest, now."

"I still got me two tickets," Margie looked at Sam and Lindsay, "I think I will, Quintel. I would love to spend time with your family. Lindsay, here are my keys to your cafe. My time is up. Dee gave this to me, and now I give this to you. Sam, how 'bout using my other ticket."

Sam winked at Margie, "Then I might have to move to Alabama myself."

"Sounds like a good plan to me," said RocketMan.

———

Zak saw his Mom and Dad standing with Uncle Ben and Aunt Kate. He ran with Super Bertha, none-the-worse-for-wear from her exorbitant flight, to hug them, "Did you see it? Did you hear me? I did it! I graduated!"

His father's eyes were moist, "I'm proud of you, Zak."

"I love you," said his mother embracing Zak. David wrapped his arms around both of them in a family embrace.

———

"Ben," Kate tightly squeezed her husband's hand, "I think it is time. OUR baby is coming."

Two new lives began.

Baby Grace Ellen Jordan entered the world just as Kevin Abbott was released from the state prison. Kevin's son, Oginga, nicknamed Ginger-Snap or Snap, was now 18. His birthfather had spent all of those years in prison. Snap and his adoptive parents, LaMar who was Kevin's biological brother, and his wife, Tamara, escorted him finally back home.

Snap had Kevin's curly red hair.

Epilogue

hat is neurodiversity? It refers to the structural differences in the brain that lead to experiencing and processing the world differently from how others usually do. This is not a matter of choice but rather reflects atypical development. Is it a curse, a blessing, or something beyond those dualities—a unique wholeness?

Dr. Kenneth Lyons Jones, who coined the diagnosis of Fetal Alcohol Syndrome in his work alongside Dr. David Smith in 1973, recently stated on an episode of the podcast Living with FASD, "Alcohol is the number one teratogen in the Western world," teratogens being neurotoxic substances that cause congenital disabilities, which change a baby's development before birth. Dr. Jones went on to state, "The reason alcohol is so damaging, and so much more damaging than what we have thought about other illicit drugs, is because alcohol affects structural brain development." A physical reality is that when an object's structure is changed, its function also changes. Furthermore, once brain cells die, they are gone forever. Some congenital disabilities are apparent to parents and providers alike. Others, less so. Still others manifest over time as the dominoes begin to fall. Alcohol is a solvent.

Fire retardant chemicals in children's clothing, pesticide residues that harm bees and butterflies, and lead, as well as asbestos in schools and municipal buildings, were toxins that were easy to revile and eliminate from store shelves or industries that relied upon them. Companies had to seek safer alternatives because people are increasingly avoiding harmful toxins. Yet, society still embraces some toxins due to their special status.

Alcohol has historically been easy and inexpensive to produce, store, and sell. It has played a significant role in building alliances and economies. Alcohol is often consumed with food and during celebrations. It "has been associated with providing 'liquid courage,' sex appeal, and stress relief. Despite being a potent neurotoxin, alcohol has been viewed as a beneficial aspect of civilized culture rather than a potential harm to reproductive health and family well-being.

However, the possible negative impacts of alcohol on humanity may soon outweigh its perceived benefits. Throughout history, alcohol has sealed business deals and geopolitical alliances. Not being able to "hold one's liquor" was interpreted as a lack of strength of character in war or business negotiations.

The alcohol and advertising industries have promoted the idea that alcohol is beneficial despite its known drawbacks by shifting the blame onto individuals who use it. They suggest that it only harms people of "weak character," allowing the party to continue while ostracizing anyone who struggles with it. This tactic shapes public opinion and has been fueled by enticing marketing campaigns that portray alcohol as an instant route to relaxation, fun, camaraderie, or romance. However, these ads fail to showcase the harmful effects of alcohol on individuals and families. Embracing Zaks's story can help change public perception and encourage an honest re-evaluation of the impact of alcohol.

Because it is a solvent used to sterilize scientific environments against growing bacteria and other organisms, its job is to kill. We need it to do that in labs and medical settings. How? Alcohol dissolves lipids, the fat sheath protecting cell integrity, causing cell death. Ingested during men's and women's reproductive years, it causes changes to reproductive health. During pregnancy, alcohol exposure harms the protective barriers within a developing baby's body, killing many cells and forever changing others by way of epigenetic alteration, shaping the ways cells are replicated, not only within the rapidly growing baby but also in future generations. The cells outright destroyed are gone forever. Other exposures alter the way cells and organs function. Alcohol affects whatever happens to be developing throughout the whole body at the time of exposure. Gravely, this beloved toxin causes diffuse brain damage to babies in gestation and while breastfeeding, forever affecting the way that individuals interact with the world around them. This harm goes by an umbrella term, Fetal Alcohol Spectrum Disorder, or FASD. FASDs remain hidden because we cannot "see" the way someone's brain or body is working *unless we understand the symptoms* shown through their behavior. Human beings naturally have an internal frame of reference; we measure each other's ways of doing things based on how we do them. That is instinctual.

FASD has been with humanity as long as alcohol has and affects every stratum of society. Alcohol could care less about someone's skin color, nation of origin, language spoken, income, or vocation. It is a solvent that destroys lipids, changes brain development when ingested during pregnancy, and robs potential from people indiscriminately. Fetal Alcohol Spectrum Disorder (FASD) is one of those things the public thinks could only happen to "those people." The people with weak willpower or poor self-control. And they believe it could hardly occur to responsible, upstanding persons who contribute to society. But IT DOES! And it may become masked in misdiagnosis.

People who are neurodivergent, whose minds work differently than "typical," are routinely blamed, shamed, and punished for the effects of unidentified prenatal brain injuries that they had no role in bringing upon themselves. We find ourselves caught off guard when someone struggles with what we view as mundane. We may "other-ize" people by judging and rejecting them when what "they" do is at odds with what "we" do.

Sadly, the industry publicity has taught us, and their branding is clear that drinking is fun—it's legal—only people who aren't as fun as the rest of us have a problem. People want to pretend harm won't or can't happen to them. The reality is that 5% of people (USA) were affected by prenatal alcohol exposure pre-Covid, and the CDC now estimates current exposure rates is 14%.

Humans have a tipping point for personal involvement. When a problem is viewed as too big or complex for one to make a personal difference, we distance ourselves to avoid feeling helpless over what we can't control. The reality is that we are already touching the issue because alcohol is one neurotoxin we are in a relationship with simply by being members of the same human community. What if some of "those" people harmed by alcohol during gestation are "us," our neighbors, or children?!

As with other movements to introduce conversations about difficult things, Red Shoes Rock FASD Aware and The Embraced Project were envisioned to present education about FASD and other neurodivergence in such a way so that learning bypasses the age-old denial ingrained by industry propaganda and yet remains realistic and constructive about who we are, where we are and what is at stake as a human community. Current infertility rates and epigenetic changes point to the daunting problem of a modern environmental neurotoxin load now higher than we have been able to quantify in the past before massive decimations.

This book, Embracing Zak, is the first of several formats within The Embraced Project to be released, and its mission is to move the public's awareness of FASD as being something that happens to "others" to something that can happen to anybody when parents of childbearing age use alcohol. It is shockingly easy to look the other way when we believe we are immune to specific harm. As much as society preaches inclusion, we humans distance ourselves from what we don't understand—individuals with neurodiversity, especially a condition with the world's most popular drug, alcohol, in its name. Thanks to Jodee Kulp, we are brought back to reality by meeting a wonderful person named Zak and the group of people who reshape their lives and community towards a positive future for all.

Patricia Kasper, MA, MTh

> Patricia Kasper Training Services
>
> Neurobehavioral Coach and Professional Development Trainer
>
> Host of the podcast *Living with FASD: Candid Conversations with Patti Kasper*
>
> Author of *Sip by Sip: Candid Conversations with People Diagnosed as Adults with Fetal Alcohol Spectrum Disorders (FASD)*

Antonia Rathbun Lindsey, M.A., A.T.R., LMHC, BCPC, retired

> Author of *Parenting Your Porcupine, A Toolkit for Children with FASD, other Drug Effects, and Neurodiversity*

About the
Embraced Movement
Project

mbracing Zak tells the story of **Zak Jordan**, an 18-year-old student with undiagnosed Fetal Alcohol Spectrum Disorder (FASD). Zak has been expelled again due to classroom incidents, and his life is moving toward adult transition. The project concept, initiated by Joel Sheagren and The Embraced Movement, involved over a hundred interviews to create this composite character. Joel is the father of an adult who was diagnosed with FASD in 2016.

The Embraced Project aims to raise awareness of FASD in society through various utilization of initiatives in transmedia. The project will kick off with the release of the novel *"Embracing Zak."* Additionally, a script for a feature film with the same title is currently in development. The 90-minute feature-length documentary will incorporate Zak's story from birth through high school, along with educational materials and CEUs. The final component will be using technology to better inform and support society regarding this epidemic. FASD remains so far under the radar in society.

A bit of our history:

In 2017, Joel, an award-winning photographer and filmmaker, began seeking a deeper understanding of how this diagnosis affected his son. He used his professional skills as a filmmaker and interviewed experts, caregivers, and people with FASD worldwide. He continues to work on the documentary. In 2019, Jodee Kulp, a lived-experience FASD advocate and award-winning author, joined Joel as a consultant, volunteering to help move the project forward. Joel and Jodee worked through

COVID-19 to build the infrastructure for this exciting constellation of projects.

In 2022, Justen Overlander, another award-winning filmmaker, joined the team for the project development of a feature film. Joel, Justen, and Jodee worked to create Zak using insight from the planned documentary. Together, they gave Zak a fresh start by introducing him to a group of unsuspecting characters who learn to support him in a small Midwestern community. Joel developed Zak's passion for stars and rocketry, which takes a wrong turn in a classroom setting. Justen is proceeding with the development of *Embracing Zak a feature film.*

In 2023, Joel joined with Carl Young, another FASD advocate, parent, and trainer, to develop *a book for caregivers and parents written by fathers of persons with FASD.*

In 2023, Jodee wove the story tapestry of *Embracing Zak novel*, collaborating with Marcia Chambers, an educator of 32 years, and Patricia Kasper, pod-caster and social worker for children in care. Deb Evensen, another educator and FASD pioneer of 40 years, and Antonia Lindsey, an art therapist who counseled over 1,000 children with FASD. Together, they formed the Meliorists to work to collectively complete the legacy work of a lifetime of living, working, and advocating for persons with FASD.

Projects to be launched by the Meliorist Team in 2024 include:

- Antonia Rathburn Lindsay *Parenting Your Porcupine, A Toolkit for Children with FASD, other Drug Effects, and Neurodiversity* written to bridge knowledge between therapists and families.

- Deb Evensen *13 Moons* to support and help educators.

- Patricia Kasper *Sip by Sip: Candid Conversations with People Diagnosed as Adults with Fetal Alcohol Spectrum Disorders (FASD) 2nd Edition*

Why this type of investment?

Many individuals with FASD are drawn to the creative and caring aspects of life, such as nature, animals, music, and art. Through Zak's character, we explore his love for astronomy, a passion often considered abstract. We witness how recognition, support, and kindness can propel him towards remarkable success, despite the daily challenges he faces.

It's important to note that individuals with neurodivergence often defy society's stereotypes of disability, as they are warm, friendly, and lack visible signs commonly associated with disabilities.

The character Zak helps readers, listeners, and viewers understand the complexities of life with FASD and how living with these struggles within a community of concern can suddenly plummet into chaos beyond what is expected as "normal" for people of various ages. Through *Embracing Zak*, we learn that even with the ability to speak and communicate, social exchanges about simple information can get stuck when appropriate support is unavailable.

Disagreements and misunderstandings can deteriorate into disasters that entangle community members and are confusing because of hidden brain and metabolic injury. Too often, the trajectory of misperceptions begins in school and ends in street life, befriending and helping criminals, and dealing with the justice system's revolving door. Sadly, prison becomes a housing opportunity without interventions. Homelessness becomes a lifestyle without support. In the mental health arena, self-medication or over-medication abounds. In social services, child protection may become active. Even our health care and the medical system fail due to body variations that do not react to current treatments or medications.

Current statistics of school children qualifying for the diagnostic criteria of prenatal alcohol exposure during pregnancy is 1 in 20.* Yet, current research shows 1 in 7 women admit to using alcohol during pregnancy. This has led to worries about the potential rise in FASD cases, as FASD cannot be cured, reversed, or outgrown and can have devastating secondary effects. Alcohol, a social lubricant, lessens our inhibitions and increases our impulsivity; none of us are exempt from this possibility. With knowledge and understanding, there will be better outcomes.

Society must embrace individuals with disabilities and provide them with appropriate support throughout their lives. This support can come from family members, doctors, employers, the community, places of faith, and teachers who understand their disability and can assist them at every stage of life. Individuals need to realize that their disability is due to organic brain injury and metabolic changes. Behaviors are often symptoms of these factors, unintentional, and require healthy support.

Professionals who work with individuals affected by Fetal Alcohol Spectrum Disorder (FASD) need a thorough understanding of typical developmental trajectories. Healthcare, judicial, educators, employers, and community leaders have a stake in providing appropriate support.

Policymakers need to understand that women who drink during pregnancy are not a homogeneous group, and several risk factors influence the presentation of FASD. It is worth noting that binge drinking is a significant contributor to the development of FASD. However, any amount of alcohol consumption during pregnancy can also lead to severe and lifelong impairments. This has led to worries about the potential rise in FASD cases, as FASD cannot be cured, reversed, or outgrown and can have devastating secondary and later tertiary effects.

We may not have recognized it, but FASD has been around as long as alcohol has, and as long as alcohol changes inhibitions surrounding intimate relationships, everyone is at risk. Family planning looks good on paper, but individuals are often still surprised when carrying a new life. Earlier recognition of pregnancy and abstaining from alcohol provides better outcomes. Social, psychological, and biological factors all play a role in determining who will drink after a pregnancy is revealed and how it affects their child, and if a female child, how her eggs are affected for even the next generation.

The Embraced Movement Project Team hopes that by using our lived experience personal knowledge, our learned professions and education, and reaching out to listen to individuals, families, friends, caregivers, and professionals, we can Embrace Zak and embrace the Truth About FASD.

Resources:

- https://www.acf.hhs.gov/cb/report/prenatal-alcohol-drug-exposures-final-report, June 26, 2023. Download is available. US Children's Bureau
- https://www.apa.org/monitor/2022/07/news-fetal-alcohol-syndrome American Physiological Association

For readers who have enjoyed The Bootleg Brother's Series beginning with *The Whitest Wall** you will re-engage beloved characters in *Embracing Zak* twenty years later. which is the series conclusion. **The Whitest Wall** was a Foreword Finalist Multicultural, Mom's Choice Gold Young Adult and Adult Fiction (2008) USA Best Books - Young Adult Fiction (2012).

We hope you' enjoy our allegories.

The Whitest Wall - Book One
Tiger Butterfly - Book Two
Different Beat - Book Three

Embracing Zak

About the Author

Jodee Kulp has spent her life in Minnesota. Some pioneers not only pave the way for others to follow but also shape the landscape to show its existence. Jodee has authored and published more books about Fetal Alcohol Spectrum Disorders than any other parent advocate in our time. Her work has helped thousands of families and individuals living

Photography by Joel Sheagren

with FASDs and has also enhanced professionals' understanding to support parents and their children. Jodee's expertise and lived-experience are matched only by her creative insight in communicating complex information in a unique and entertaining manner.

Jodee is an illustrator, author, co-author, or contributor of many books and curricula that promote understanding and offer healthy and creative approaches to living with Fetal Alcohol Spectrum Disorders (FASD). She is an international and national speaker, trainer, and advocate, helping individuals, families and professionals address the emotional, mental, physical, and spiritual needs of individuals with this disability to enable healthy community living. Jodee and Karl are the parents of Liz Kulp (1986-2024), also an award-winning author.

Through Better Endings New Beginnings, a social initiative, Jodee's work sets the standard for creating a safe community environment for individuals with fetal alcohol brain injury. She is a co-founder of the International Red Shoes Rock, FASD Aware Alliance, the Expanding Mindz with Canines Program, Biblical Health Coach and a PraiseMoves certified fitness instructor. She offers hope for children, teens, and adults.